East End Boys

Also by David Brown:

For a Better Tomorrow
Russian Roulette

East End Boys

David Brown

AESOP Modern Fiction
Oxford

AESOP Modern Fiction
An imprint of AESOP Publications
Martin Noble Editorial / AESOP
28 Abberbury Road, Oxford OX4 4ES, UK
www.aesopbooks.com

First edition published by AESOP Publications
Copyright (c) 2013 David Brown

The right of David Brown to be identified as the author of this work has been asserted in accordance with sections 77 and 78 of the copyright designs and Patents Act 1988.

A catalogue record of this book is
available from the British Library.

First edition 2013

Condition of sale:
This book is sold subject to the condition that it shall not, by way of trade or otherwise, be lent, sold or hired out or otherwise circulated in any form of binding or cover other than that in which it is published and without a similar condition including this condition being imposed on the subsequent purchaser.

ISBN: 978-0-9572061-8-2

Printed and bound in Great Britain by
Lightning Source UK Ltd,
Chapter House, Pitfield, Kiln Farm,
Milton Keynes MK11 3LW

Contents

1	The Braun Brothers	7
2	Eva Goldberg's Story	27
3	The Goldbergs of Brick Lane	37
4	The O'Sullivan Brothers	50
5	Billy Reid's Story	62
6	The Deal	93
7	Another Life, Another Flight	103
8	The Countdown	114
9	The Le Feuvre Brothers	121
10	Wolfe Versus Dubois	135
11	The Return of a Nemesis	150
12	… To End All Wars	158
13	The Twenties	173
14	Entente Uncordial, 1933	185
15	'Dancing in the Dark'	207
16	'I'll Be Loving You Always'	221
17	'Let's Face the Music and Dance'	223

Dedication and thanks

*To my wife and children, family and friends
who encouraged me along the way.*

*This book would not have been written
without the inspiration of my Grandparents
who dared to escape the Pogroms in Poland
and with indomitable courage
travelled to an unknown land
to find Peace and Happiness.*

1 The Braun Brothers

Poland, May 1906

'ASHER, FOR THE UMPTEENTH TIME, we aren't being followed.' Two young men, unmistakably brothers, were walking side by side at dawn along a track which was wide enough to pass for a road.

Asher, the shorter and younger of the two, turned and walked slowly backwards, head tilted to one side, listening. He stopped for a second, staring intently back along the road, and then turned and caught up with his brother, pointing to the blooded shirt.

'Chayim, we have to quit. It's become too dangerous – you were lucky tonight.'

Chayim looked down at the shirt under his jacket. 'It isn't my blood, and luck doesn't come into it. Admittedly he was bigger than me, but size doesn't always matter. All I had to do was get to his flabby stomach.'

He smiled. 'I must have broken the big oafs' ribs. All I'm interested in is their money, anyway.' He pulled back his jacket, revealing the butt of a pistol. 'If they come after us ...'

The Braun brothers walked on, Chayim placing an arm around Asher's shoulders. 'One more fight – that's all we need.'

Asher looked anxiously at his brother. 'It could be one fight too many. I saw Kroshnev talking to some of his buddies. They looked ominously in your direction. I wouldn't trust that Russian as far as I could throw him.'

'What were the odds?' Chayim asked, ignoring the warning.

Asher shrugged off the arm around his shoulders. 'Chayim, Kroshnev is a dangerous man. For starters he's in the government and into all sorts of shady deals. Rumour has it that he was the instigator of the pogroms in 1903. You remember what happened then? Our grandparents murdered in cold blood. Kroshnev's brother is a Cossack officer—' he stepped in front of Chayim bringing him to a stop '—and he knows where we live. I'm sure something is going to happen, I just feel it.'

Chayim looked silently at his brother and was about to say something when Asher added, 'in answer to your question, thirty-to-

7

one, and before you ask, yes, I exchanged the money for diamonds and gold coins, but—'

Chayim waved an arm. 'Yes, we're going to take a loss they need to get one over on the Jew, but at those odds we can't grumble.'

It was Goran Kroshnev who offered to pay Chayim to fight after seeing how he was able to handle two men who attacked him and his brother. Goran hated Jews and would have killed Chayim in a second. But he saw a way of making money from the Jew.

'People will pay extra,' he told his brother Ivan that evening, 'to see the spectacle of a Jew being beaten up and maybe killed in a boxing ring. This Jew can fight, but against a trained fighter he won't last long.'

Goran was wrong: Chayim was a natural fighter with superb instincts in the ring. He was strong and fast and so far had won all his six fights.

The reason the brothers were in Krakow in the first place, even though it was forbidden for them to be there without a permit, was to find a way of earning money so they and the rest of the family could go to America. Chayim had seen people leave for the land of opportunity with very little money or none at all and was determined that he and the family would have money for their passage, and enough left over to start a business of some kind. Kroshnev's offer of paying him to fight appealed to him.

Since he was a young boy, he had always stood up for himself, being unafraid of the town's children who to their cost learned to stay away from him.

It was Asher who had come up with the idea of betting on his brother. The crowd hated Jews so much that they would bet heavily against Chayim, especially as Goran stacked the odds by bringing in bigger and heavier fighters. So far he had been lucky and managed not to get hurt, but he knew that one day his luck would run out. He looked thoughtfully down at the ground.

Just one more fight and we can leave, he thought.

The road bent slightly, straightening out to where a bridge crossed a stream. Side by side they crossed the bridge. Ahead of them was a *stadle*, a small village, and to their left a forest. They moved quickly into the forest, following the stream until hidden from view of the road. Asher stopped, turned left, walked a couple of paces forward and pushed apart a clump of bushes, pulling out a suitcase. Opening it, he turned to Chayim, taking a cloth bag from his pocket and giving it to his brother.

'It's the most we've ever taken.'

Chayim looked inside the bag and smiled. The diamonds and gold coins reflected in his tawny eyes from the light filtering through the foliage of the trees. Closing the bag, he walked a couple of paces to a tree where a faint tick mark had been scored on the bark. He moved a large rock to one side and dug into the soft earth pulling out a wooden box containing five other bags. He opened it and placed the bag beside them, closed the lid replacing the box into the hole, covering it once more with earth and the rock. Taking the pistol from his belt, he deposited it in a cavity between two branches of the tree. Finally he stepped back and stripped off his clothes, while Asher did the same. Hanging their clothes over a bush, they picked up two towels and soap from the suitcase, looked at each other, smiled again, and raced the few yards to leap into the cold, clear water of the stream.

Two hours later, refreshed from the swim, they donned clean clothes from the suitcase.

'Are you okay?' said Asher.

'I'm fine, a bit sore around the ribs. How's my face?'

Brown eyes lingered on his face. 'The right eyes a little red, and beginning to turn a blue, and you have a cut on your lip. Otherwise you're as ugly as ever.'

This was far from the truth. Chayim was a handsome six foot-one with thick, copper-coloured hair that framed his head. He was broad-shouldered; his shirt tight across his chest without an ounce of fat in sight, with even, white teeth and a killer smile. Like his brother, he was bearded. With a deft flick he sent a flat pebble skimming across the surface of the water. As for Asher, he was two inches shorter than his brother but with the same kind of build and similar hair; unlike Chayim he had kept the locks hanging down the side of his bearded face, and had inherited his mother's deep brown soulful eyes.

It was now daylight, the sky a leaden grey; the slight breeze carrying with it the scent of rain. They emerged from the forest; Chayim, carrying his now clean but wet shirt in his right hand, walked along the dusty road that sloped slightly downwards towards wooden houses that lay on both sides of the road; wooden fences surrounded them to keep in the chickens wandering around pecking at the ground, or a goat tethered to a rope just long enough to keep it away from the vegetable garden. Even at this hour people were awake, going about their business and calling to each other, while children laughed and shouted, playing happily together.

Chayim turned to his brother, a serious expression on his face. 'I know what you said about Kroshnev is right. I heard him talking to his brother and some other officers. They think we're stupid and can't speak their language; if he only knew.'

'What did you hear?'

'I should have told you earlier, and we could have—' He turned to look back towards the bridge as the ground under his feet began to tremble. A frown creased his forehead as the sound grew louder until it became a thunderous roar.

'They said tomorrow,' he whispered, disbelief on his face as parents ran into the street, faces showing fear. They snatched their children unceremoniously into their arms, yelling, 'Cossacks, Cossacks,' screaming their children's names as a troop of horsemen appeared over the brow of the slope, yelling and twirling swords above their heads. Their horses' eyes wide with excitement as they galloped ever closer, tails streaming out behind, muscles rippling, showing their graceful lines in full gallop, their riders whooping with delight, leaning over the side of their mounts.

Trembling with fear, people scattered trying to find safe hiding places, but they were soon found and slaughtered as one might butcher an animal. It was a horrific scene. Like savage beasts the Cossacks indiscriminately attacked the old, the women and the children, plundering the homes of their victims, and seizing possessions acquired through the hard work of many years.

With the shouts and obscenities ringing in their ears, Chayim and Asher moved towards their house, but by the time they had reached it, making sure the Cossacks didn't see them, they were too late.

For a minute they stood by the broken door, two pairs of eyes surveying the room. Pieces of furniture lay scattered around the floor, cupboard doors opened, their utensils missing. In panic they shouted, 'Papa! Mama! Saul! Mulka! Esther!' and rushed towards the back room where their sisters slept.

The door hung on one hinge as Chayim moved slowly into the room with Asher following behind, a sense of foreboding clutching his heart. A sob caught in his throat at the scene in front of him. They covered their dead sisters' half-naked bodies and moved apprehensively to the bedrooms.

At the sight of his father and brothers butchered bodies Chayim face was white with anger, lips tightly drawn together.

'He tried to protect them,' he whispered to Asher.

'Yes, he did, but where's Mama?'

Without a word they searched the house, but could not find her.

'Perhaps she escaped,' Asher suggested.

'Let's have a look outside – she may have crawled into the chicken coop.'

Asher moved slowly towards the coop, stopping in mid-stride, falling to the ground crying. Chayim, a pace behind, moved to one side, a yell of anguish escaping his lips on seeing their mother's blood-soaked body.

He knelt beside Asher, bent and kissed his mother's forehead, whispering, 'Rest in peace, Mama.'

A few minutes had passed but it seemed like an eternity. Chayim wiped away the tears.

'Come on, Asher.' He stood up, fists tightly clenched, eyes hard and set, as a rage he had never felt before threatened to engulf him.

Asher got to his feet and stepped back slightly on seeing Chayim grim face.

'What are you going to do?'

'What I would like to do is kill six Cossacks,' Chayim said, tight-lipped, 'but common sense tells me to run.'

Asher nodded. 'Let's go.'

Cautiously they worked their way through the town, still hearing the screams of those trying to escape the onslaught, and yells of triumph by the assailants as they cut short the scream.

'We need to get to the forest,' Asher said breathlessly.

Chayim didn't reply but just nodded. As they ran across the road Chayim came to a stop on hearing a woman scream for help. He looked back to see a Cossack, a big grin on his face, chasing the woman, standing in the stirrups leaning slightly forward, his horse galloping ever closer.

'Come on, Chayim,' Asher yelled.

Chayim glanced for a moment at his brother, turned, and ignoring his pleas, ran to intercept the rider, yelling, 'Go, Asher, I'll be there in a moment.'

But he was too late to help: the rider caught up with his prey, slashing down with the sabre. The woman dropped to the ground, her blood forming a puddle from the gaping wound in her back. Realising how futile his attempt to rescue the woman was, he stopped. The Cossack looked at him; Chayim turned quickly to cross the road, heading towards the forest. Knowing that he had foolishly put himself in danger, he looked back over his shoulder. The Cossack held back his mount as it fought the reins wanting to run, nostrils flaring and mouth flecked with foam around the bridle bit, white eyes wide and wild with excitement, its right leg pawing the ground.

Suddenly the horse leapt forward as its rider loosened the reins. Leaning over the right side of his mounts sweating muscular body; he spurred the animal forward, yelling at the top of his voice, sword pointing at the fleeing Chayim, ignoring the horse's saliva flecking his boots.

Knowing the horse would soon catch up with him, Chayim stopped and turned to face the charging duo. At the last moment he stepped to the right away from the sword, somehow he grabbed the reins and pulled down with all his strength. Until his dying day he could never explain how and why he did this. The horse's head came around, its body now off balance was beginning to fall. Chayim stepped away from the falling animal's flaying hoofs as its rider expertly leapt from his mount, rolling into a ball, losing his sabre as he hit the ground.

Seeing the sabre, Chayim picked it up and plunged it into the Cossack's chest. The horse got to its feet and ran back along the road.

There was a yell. Chayim looked up as two Cossacks galloped towards him. Knowing there was no way of reaching the forest in time; he knelt by the dead Cossack, took his pistol from its holster and faced the oncoming enemy. As he'd practised many times before, feet slightly apart, arms out straight, the pistol held steadily in his hands, he aimed and fired twice at the first rider, and then quickly at the second who was nearly upon him; he dropped to the ground and rolled away, quickly getting to his feet, fired twice and missed. The rider turned his mount to charge once again. Chayim fired, but there was just a click as the hammer came down on an empty chamber: he was out of bullets. Somehow Chayim dodged the charge and ran towards one of the dead Cossacks; picking up his sabre, he turned quickly to face the last of the duo who sat relaxed in the saddle, steam rising from his mounts body, white with its own sweat.

What's he doing? Chayim wondered, looking up at the rider, taking a step back as he recognised him. It was Goran Kroshnev's brother Ivan.

At the age of 23, Ivan Kroshnev was a dashing figure, his posture ramrod straight in the saddle. The ebony eyes that shone with humour could also turn into a ruthless, angry storm. Like many Cossack officers, he had a duelling scar on the right cheek, which in his case was attractive. Although an honourable man and in many ways nothing like his brother Goran, who was a schemer and would do anything to obtain what he wanted. Ivan hated killing defenceless people, but orders were orders. It stopped his men from getting bored and like his brother he hated Jews.

He was regimental boxing champion, and had watched with interest all of Chayim's fights, and although he wouldn't say it to his face, he was impressed by the Jew's bravery, wondering what the outcome might be if they fought. His horse tossed its head impatiently as its rider looked up to survey the village. By now the sound of looting and killing had dwindled. He dismounted and walked forward a few paces.

'I've watched you fight, you're pretty good, and yes, I know you can speak my language, unlike many of your kind.'

He took a cigarette case from the pocket of his tunic, flicked it open, and offered it to Chayim, who shook his head. The Cossack shrugged, extracted a cigarette and lit it, exhaling the smoke into the air, eyes still on the man in front of him.

'In actual fact, and to be truthful, you haven't really fought anyone worthwhile.'

Chayim looked at him in silence, wondering whether he might be stalling until some of his men arrived. He looked around, but they were still alone.

'Don't worry about my men. If I had wanted to kill you I would have already,' Ivan said arrogantly.

Chayim raised an eyebrow. 'I might have something to say about that.' Still wondering what this man was up to, he glanced towards the forest.

Ivan laughed. 'You can try it, but...' He inhaled on the cigarette, slowly exhaling the smoke through his nostrils, a thoughtful look on his face, studying the Jew in front of him. His small pointed moustache twitched as his lips moved in a slight smile.

I could fight him here and now, and then I'd know, he thought, taking two quick puffs of the cigarette dropping the butt onto the ground. *By rights I should just kill him* ... but he wanted to fight this Jew, just to prove to himself that he could beat him. It wasn't a practical idea, but ...

Chayim had had enough of his games. 'So, what do you have in mind – a duel?'

When have I ever been practical? Ivan thought. He took a step forward and then replied, 'Something like that.'

'Swords or do you prefer pistols?'

The Cossack laughed, 'Fists.'

'What?' Chayim stared at him in disbelief.

'A fight, man to man.'

'What's in it for me?'

'Your life,' was the clipped reply.

'What's in it for you?'

'Satisfaction; I've always wondered if I can beat you. I'm sure I can,' Ivan added with contempt.

'What's to stop you from killing me if I win?'

'The word of an officer and gentleman; don't get me wrong, I hate you Jews. But you, well, you're different from the normal peasant, submissive type of Jew. You speak our language although you pretend not to, and you show intelligence, and you are foolishly brave, which is also the way you fight, so…'

He slid the sword into its scabbard, unbuckled the belt, letting it drop to the ground, stripped off his tunic and pointed at the sword in Chayim's hand. 'If you're going to use it, now's the time.'

Chayim looked down at the sword, his mind racing, trying to decide what to do. He was intrigued by the challenge but didn't fully trust the Cossack. He shrugged his shoulders – what did he have to lose? Only his life – threw down the sword and stripped to the waist.

Ivan took off his shirt to reveal a slim, muscular body. Suddenly, five horsemen appeared, racing at a gallop towards them. Ivan turned to face the riders, holding up a hand. They reined to a halt in front of him looking at their leader, then contemptuously at the Jew.

'Dismount,' Ivan yelled in a commanding voice.

The five men looked at the officer, but obeyed the order, holding the reins of their mounts.

Ivan stood close to the men so that Chayim could not hear what he was saying. 'He's the Jew that won all the fights my brother promoted and—'

'I lost a month's wages through that bastard,' one of the men interrupted angrily.

'I intend to fight him.' The men were about to protest, but Ivan held up a hand. 'If I don't fight this Jew, I will always wonder which one of us is the better fighter, but I need to make a deal with him. He won't fight if he knows that, win or lose, he is going to die.'

'But, sir,' said a corporal, 'it's not right to let the Jew go if you lose. Anyway, why bother? Let's kill him now.'

'I cannot in all fairness fight this man, and if he wins kill him—' He held up a hand to stop them from interrupting him. 'If the Jew wins, give him a three-hour start, then you can go after him.' The men remained silent. 'I can order you to let him go here and now, and if it comes down to it I will, but I'd rather you agreed to my suggestion. This is a fight between two gladiators, and as they say, to the winner the spoils. If I win, I will have the satisfaction of knowing I'm the better fighter. If I lose—' He shrugged his shoulders.

The corporal thought Ivan was crazy, but kept the thought to himself. 'It isn't the right thing to do, sir, but putting it like that, and having seen you fight, the Jew will surely lose. I think I can speak for the others, that if it's that important to you, we will grant the Jew a three-hour start.'

Ivan turned to face Chayim. 'If you win this fight, my men have promised to give you a three-hour start. Will you agree to these terms?'

Chayim gave a wry smile, 'It seems I have no option.'

While Ivan was talking to his men, Chayim had been examining him. Kroshnev was two inches shorter. He knew the Cossack would not be doing this if he wasn't sure of his own abilities, but nevertheless Chayim was determined to beat the arrogance out of this Jew-hater. He moved across to his coat. Seeing the soldiers' hands move towards their weapons, he said, 'I need something from my pocket.' He reached in and pulled out a mould, placing it in his mouth as a guard. 'I'd like to keep my teeth.'

Asher had climbed a tree and, hidden by the foliage; saw a Cossack officer he recognised dismount and speak to Chayim, but he was too far away to hear what was being said. He wanted to dash out and help his brother, but knew it would be suicidal to do so, and Chayim would be very angry with him. A frown creased his forehead as five troopers raced towards the two men. They dismounted and the officer spoke to them for a minute, and then turned back to Chayim. It suddenly dawned on Asher that they were going to fight. He scrambled down the tree, making his way to where the suitcase and other items were hidden. Placing the money and jewellery into two money belts tied around his body, he picked up the suitcase and with the pistol in his right hand headed back to see if he could help Chayim in any way.

Once again he climbed the tree and parted the foliage, nearly falling off at the sight in front of him. The five Cossacks had been joined by the rest of the troop, who had formed a large circle with Chayim and the officer in the centre.

*

The village was silent except for the jingle of harnesses and the creaking of cartwheels under a mound of furniture, utensils, clothes and other looted items. A piano lay upended, its strings and hammers broken. Three goats were tied to the rear of one cart and chickens squawked in a crate on another. There was a yell from one of the troopers who pointed to where their officer and Chayim were about to fight. The column moved quickly in their direction.

'It seems we're going to have an audience,' Ivan said, turning away from his opponent to greet the men, who gazed with admiration at their commanding officer as they gathered around him. He explained the agreement with Chayim. It didn't go down too well but they consented to abide by his wishes.

The men dismounted, tethered their horse onto the carts, and formed a large circle with Ivan and Chayim in the centre.

Ivan grinned at Chayim. 'I'm going to show you, Jew-boy, what it's like coming up against a real fighter. I'm going to squash you like a bug. Even your own mother won't recognise you.'

'She's dead; murdered by your men, as were the rest of my family,' Chayim said in barely a whisper, his voice hard as steel.

'That's a few less Jews,' Ivan sneered, 'and you'll soon be joining them.' His voice trailed off on seeing the hatred on his opponent's face and eyes. Ivan executed a smart bow and then went into a fighter's stance, moving cautiously towards his opponent.

For a moment Chayim's heart beat a little faster; he swallowed nervously but a picture of his mother's slaughtered body flashed into his mind and he moved menacingly forward, blocking the first punch aimed at him as the ring of men cheered and jeered at him contemptuously. He swayed away from a left hand aimed at his head and then grunted with satisfaction as his counter-punch slammed against Ivan's jaw.

They had been fighting for over forty-five minutes. Both men were soaked with sweat, perspiration flowing like rivers down their faces. Chayim's arms were red from blocking the Cossack's punches. There were a few bruises on his face and torso, a cut under his right eye, and blood trickled from his lips where some of Ivan's punches had got through. He moved lightly around the ring of men, Ivan following him like a prowling tiger, face red, eyes puffy from the counter-punches; blood dribbled down his chin from a cut lip.

Chayim slipped between the Cossack's guard landing a punch to the stomach. There was a whoosh of air from his opponent, who tried to wrap his arms around Chayim so he could catch his breath, but clutched at thin air and another punch landed on his already battered face. Ivan shook his head to clear his vision as his opponent moved close to whisper in his ear, 'That's the problem with you people. You think you're better than us Jews and with your stupid hatred you can't see as far as your *shmock*.' Chayim landed a punch to the chin as he moved away.

Ivan was angry with himself: the Jew was beating him and he now realised how foolish and arrogant he had been in fighting the man. His face was sore and he could taste his own blood. What was more, he had to put with all the insults and comments from the upstart in front him. He let out a growl, launching himself at the Jew throwing a flurry of punches; some were blocked, but to his immense satisfaction one or two got through as they stood toe to toe, neither being prepared to give way. Then Ivan's head was jolted backward from two punches in quick succession, followed by another to the body, the Jew goading him once more.

'Perhaps you'd like five or six of your men to help you,' said Chayim.

Ivan lashed out angrily, grazing his opponent's chin, but in doing so left his chin unprotected. Chayim landed another counter-punch with such force that it lifted the Cossack off his feet, as he crumpled to the ground, mumbling, 'Jew bastard.' He tried unsuccessfully to get to his feet, but Chayim was already turning away and walking over to his clothes with the disgruntled faces of the Cossack troop gazing at him.

The corporal stepped forward to face Chayim. 'You have three hours, Jew, and then we are coming after you.'

Chayim didn't reply, just nodded, turning his back on the man to put on his clothes. He picked up the sabre he had dropped earlier and walked towards the circle of men who parted to let him through, their faces showing their hatred.

Asher nearly fell out of the tree when the Cossack dropped to the ground. Throughout the fight he only just managed to stop himself from yelling. Seeing his brother pick up the sabre and walk towards the silent, sullen ring of men, he held his breath, expecting them to pounce on Chayim and tear him to pieces, but they parted, letting him through.

Asher waited, still expecting the worse, but the men gently picked up their commander, laying him on one of the carts, then mounted their horses and rode away. As they disappeared over the bridge, Chayim entered the village as people, including Asher, slowly emerged from hiding. The street was strewn with broken furniture, torn clothes and bed linen; it almost seemed as though the Cossacks had ripped the heart out of the town with household crockery and utensils scattered across the road, food and their containers smashed and inedible, books and papers vandalised, precious paintings and personal keepsakes left to rot in the mud, and other items discarded and soiled just for the sheer pleasure of doing so. People moved slowly towards the blooded bodies lying on the ground; hands held to their mouths, stifling a scream, while others could not hold back their cries of anguish. Those more fortunate tried to comfort them, while others staggered around in a futile attempt to pick up and put back together the shattered pieces of their broken homes.

Chayim stopped in the middle of the road, slowly turning a full circle. Tears ran down his face as he witnessed the scene of mayhem, blooded fists clenched in anger by his side. This was a poor community and now many were left with nothing, not even food. He looked up at the sky, and like millions of Jews before him silently asked, *why?*

He was nearly bowled over as Asher threw his arms around him.

'You were fantastic,' said Asher. He moved slightly away, a serious look on his face. Why did they let you go? I thought they would tear you to pieces?'

'I thought that, but for some unknown reason Kroshnev wanted to show me how honourable he can be. He wanted to fight me, thought he could beat me, but knew I wouldn't fight if win or lose they would kill me. So he and his men agreed to give me a three-hour start, and then they'd come after me.'

'Well then, we can't stay here, Mama—'

Chayim placed an arm around his brother's shoulders and whispered, 'Let's go home, there are things we must do before we leave.'

Asher nodded, and the pair walked quickly home.

After preparing their family's bodies for burial, they packed a few clothes into knapsacks. From its hiding place under the floorboards they lifted out a large box. Inside were a variety of family heirlooms which they intended to take with them.

Finding a donkey wandering near the house they tethered it to a cart, carefully placing their family's bodies on it. Leading the donkey, they walked solemnly towards the cemetery where others were already gathered to bury their dead.

With just over an hour left before the Cossacks came looking for Chayim, the brothers received a blessing from the rabbi. Leaving a set of candlesticks to pay for a headstone, they asked the rabbi to distribute whatever was left in their home to those that needed it.

'Where are we going?' Asher asked.

'As far away from here as possible,' replied Chayim.

As they left their childhood home, Asher turned to look back. 'Will they keep their word after the way you beat up Kroshnev?'

Before Chayim could reply he added, 'It's not him I'm worried about; it's his brother Goran, he's a nasty piece of work and as a government official he has a lot of power and resources. We'll have to make a plan if we're going to avoid him.'

Chayim smiled. 'You worry too much.'

In his heart, though, he knew his brother was right and his mind raced, wondering what the best thing to do was.

*

They had been travelling for over an hour, with Asher looking over his shoulder from time to time. As he turned once more to walk backwards, head tilted to one side listening, Chayim pointed to a clump of bushes.

'Let's stop there, we need to come up with a plan, and I need a drink.'

Slipping the rucksack from his back, he extracted a bottle of water, drank from it and handed it to his brother.

'What do you have in mind?' said Asher.

'We need to leave the country.'

'I agree with you, but where?'

'Let's put ourselves in the Cossacks' minds. They know we can't stay in the country, especially with the Kroshnevs wanting revenge. They'll think we're heading for one of the Black or Baltic seaports. So, we have to do the unthinkable.'

'Which is?'

'Head in the opposite direction, and—'

'What, are you joking?'

'We'll head for the border, cross into Germany and make our way to Hamburg, where we will hopefully get a boat to—' his voice caught in his throat. They should have been making this journey with the rest of the family.

'We won't be able to travel by train; they'll be watching the stations,' Asher pointed out, 'and why Hamburg?' he added as he cut off his locks with a knife, looking up at the sky. 'Please forgive me, but they will grow again.'

Chayim stood up. 'You remember the letter from our cousin Abraham; he said there's an emigration city near the town of Veddel. We'll head there.' He lifted his rucksack on to his back. 'We have a very long walk ahead of us, so we'd better get started.'

*

Sometimes they hitched a ride in cart from a friendly farmer, but mostly they walked. Sleeping under bushes, occasionally in a barn, always leaving before the owner could discover them. They ate fruit, digging up potatoes and other vegetables along the way; now and again they caught a fish. Always vigilant, avoiding towns and cities, and hiding from men in uniform.

After trekking for nearly four weeks, Chayim and Asher reached the border town of Slubice. They sat munching an apple from behind a high hedge, undecided what to do, watching the line of people at the border gate moving slowly forward as soldiers checked their papers and belongings, now and again arresting people – sometimes just a single wretched individual, other times entire families – and taking them away.

With no travel documents giving them permission to move from one place to another, Chayim and Asher's only option was to try bribing the guards.

Chayim handed the pistol to Asher. Then taking one of their precious diamonds from a belt around his waist, and covering the sabre inside his coat, Chayim stepped out with Asher from their hiding place and walked towards the barrier and the long line of people waiting to cross the border.

They had been in the queue for over three hours and two places from the front when four men suddenly appeared from a hut by the barrier. There was a frightened murmur from the people behind. Chayim turned to see what was happening but Asher grabbed his arm and whispered, 'Kroshnev.'

Chayim's head whipped around, his eyes coming to rest on the Kroshnev brothers.

'How did they find us?' Asher whispered.

Chayim looked behind them: mounted Cossacks with sabres drawn were waiting on either side of the road, while two others pushed the line of people into a ditch. The Kroshnevs walked ominously towards them as the two men with them moved the people at the head of the line to one side, leaving Chayim and Asher standing alone.

Chayim opened his coat slightly to gain easy access to the sabre as he whispered to Asher, 'Make sure you can reach the pistol quickly and fire it.' He looked towards the barrier eyes squinting, about thirty yards, and then at the guards' hut, maybe two soldiers in there. He moved closer to Asher; 'If we have to fight, shoot anyone in your way and run as fast as you can towards the barrier.'

Asher nodded; face grim, as the Kroshnevs stopped in front of them, both with smirking grins on their faces.

'I suppose you're wondering how we found you,' Goran sneered. 'You Jews aren't as clever as you think,' Ivan joined in, a scar over his right eye clearly visible where the cut had been sown, and still black and blue.

Chayim stared straight back at the Cossack officer, unafraid, while Asher moved slightly away. Both the Braun brothers remained silent.

'We thought at first that you would take the shorter route to the Austro-Hungarian border, or Odessa,' said Goran, 'but when you didn't show up after ten days we knew this is where you'd try and cross. Unlike my brother I think it was pretty clever, but not clever enough.' He took a step forward. 'What I want from you two is your money and anything else of value you have on you.' He looked from Chayim to Asher, then back again, and was about to continue when Ivan moved beside him and intervened.

'You have two choices.' He placed a hand on the hilt of his sabre. 'Give us what Goran asked for and you can walk across the border. Refuse and we will kill you and take it anyway.'

Chayim stared defiantly at the brothers, and then looked at Asher, whose mouth was set in a straight, determined line, knowing they had only one option. He looked around. Ivan's men were busy holding back the people in front and behind them. He turned, trying to judge the distance to the barrier and freedom, and then, gripping the hilt of the sword with his right hand, and undid the buttons of his coat with the other.

Asher could not believe the audacity of the Kroshnev's demands and their obvious assumption of their superiority, which was evident on their sneering faces. He glanced quickly at Chayim whose face and eyes were set in that unwavering look he had when boxing. Asher placed his right hand inside the pocket of his coat gripping the butt of the pistol. He was angry at the way they were being ridiculed, not only now but in the past. A vision of his family's broken bodies came into his mind as he clicked off the safety catch, silently thanking his brother for teaching him how to fire it as he looked with hatred and loathing into Goran's eyes.

Ivan, on seeing the movements, thought they were going to give into their demands and turned to his brother laughing. 'I told you they would give in – they're Jews.'

Goran didn't answer, but took a step backwards on seeing the hatred in Asher's eyes. He glanced quickly at Chayim and in that moment fear clutched his heart. He was about to shout a warning as Asher in one fluid movement drew the pistol and fired. As Goran dropped to the ground, Asher ran for the barrier, shooting at the man who appeared in front of him. He leapt over the fallen body and dived over the barrier, quickly getting to his feet to see where his brother was.

As Asher drew the pistol, Chayim unsheathed the sabre and plunged it into the body of the unsuspecting Ivan, who dropped to his knees.

'That's for my family,' Chayim said, withdrawing the sabre, 'and this is for me.' He thrust the sabre into the Cossack's throat. A bloody froth escaped from his mouth; face no longer smiling, eyes glazing over, as he toppled sideways to the ground.

For a second Chayim looked down at the dead man, and then ran towards the barrier, but came to a halt as a corporal, a sinister smile on his face; sabre in his right hand, blocked his way. In a smoker's rasping voice he said, 'Your three hours are up.'

Chayim parried the thrust, knowing that he was no match against the corporal with a sabre. A shot rang out, and for a moment there was a look of surprise on the corporal's face before he slowly crumpled to the ground, face down blood spreading down his back. It was then that Chayim heard Asher shouting and waving the pistol in the air. 'Come on, Chayim.'

With a big grin on his face and bullets whipping up the ground behind him, he leapt the barrier and the firing stopped.

Chayim, breathing a little heavily, and Asher looked at each other, big grins on their faces that turned into relieved laughter, holding on to each other and dancing in a circle. Suddenly they stopped as the enormity of what they had done hit them. Tears filled Chayim's eyes and he was overwhelmed with a mixture of feelings: relief at their survival, sadness and grief for his dead family, and the adrenalin rush of excitement.

'You know we can never go back,' Asher said, 'but then who would want to?' He placed an arm around his brother's shoulders. 'Come, Chayim, let's take the first step to freedom.'

Wiping the tears from his eyes, Chayim nodded. Arms around each other's shoulders, they walked into the town of Frankfurt an der Oder on the German side of the border and to the railway station.

*

After a week of mourning with relatives in Berlin, Chayim and Asher arrived at Emigration Hall on Veddel Island, by the Elbe River, to register. Here, they received the humiliation of disinfection and were told that they would be in quarantine for fourteen days.

Emigration Hall could facilitate five thousand people with mass sleeping accommodation, including a canteen. It was built to stop the notorious lodging owners and emigration agencies in Bremen from defrauding emigrants of their small savings.

Fifteen days had passed since the brothers had arrived. They were in the canteen having lunch when someone called their names. They turned to see a man approaching their table: it was their friend Daniel Grizchinsky, looking completely distraught.

'I'm so glad I found you,' said the tailor.
'When did you get here?' asked Asher.
'Three days ago, I—'
'Why are you pleased to see us?' said Chayim.
'Goran Kroshnev is here, and looking for you.'
'You're mistaken,' said Asher. 'He's dead, I shot him.'

Grizchinsky shook his head. 'No, you wounded him, you shattered his left arm, and it had to be amputated.'

The shock of the tailor's news showed on the brothers' faces.
'How did I miss?' said Asher. 'He was that close ...' His voice trailed off.
'How did he recover so quickly?' Chayim asked.

'He wasn't fully recovered, but when the *Momzer* was well enough he order an attack on the village. They killed everyone they could find, I was lucky, if you can call it that. I was in the woods getting logs for the fire.' His voice caught in a sob and tears filled his eyes that looked past the brothers, remembering.

'Those animals killed my entire family. So, I decided to start anew and go to a country where I can live without being frightened, without pogroms. I wish I was as brave as you two, but I'm not.' He smiled grimly. 'If I were you, I'd get away from here as quickly as possible. Kroshnev has four very big men with him; most of the time they carry or push him in a wheelchair. Revenge is a very powerful thing. It consumes a man like Goran Kroshnev.' He held out a hand, which the brothers shook. 'Good luck, I hope we meet again.'

The brothers watched him as he walked away, dismay and bewilderment on their faces. Chayim couldn't believe it – just when they thought they were safe and free from people like Kroshnev.

He got to his feet. 'Come on, we have to get the first boat out of here.'

Two hours later, having spent one of their precious diamonds in a bribe, they boarded the ferry taking them to the steamship whose destination was not New York but London.

'We'll get a ship from England to America,' Chayim stated as he looked back to the dock. Four men, head and shoulders taller than everyone else, moved among the throng of people waiting to be ferried across. He grabbed Asher's arm.

'Kroshnev,' he muttered, but didn't point as the one-armed man looked towards the ferry.

Asher quickly turned his back, grabbing Chayim's sleeve for him to do the same. 'I'm sure he hasn't seen us, but he must have some very powerful friends to be able to get onto the dock so easily.'

'More like a lot of money,' said Chayim. 'We are well rid of that man.' A chill ran up his spine as the ferry pulled up alongside the steamship and they boarded.

In cramped, unsanitary conditions, the smell of unwashed bodies and vomit overpowering them, Chayim and Asher decided they would be better off on deck.

Two days into the voyage they encountered stormy weather, the bow of the ship dipping and rising. The screams of frightened passengers could be heard above the noise of the roaring waves that crashed over the deck where people cowered behind canvas shelters, which didn't stop them from getting a soaking. Three people were swept overboard. It seemed like the journey would never end, and then as suddenly as it had started, the storm clouds moved away, the sun appeared and the seas were calm.

The ship docked and after days of vibration and noise, the engines were silent. Tired, wet and hungry, the passengers craved a hot meal, bath and bed when they landed, but instead were met by an officer of HM Customs and a medical examiner who gave them a rudimentary medical inspection.

The newly arrived immigrants were also met by a representative of the Poor Jews Temporary Shelter. The temporary shelter, at 82 Leman Street in Aldgate, catered for single adult men for up to fourteen days. Women, children and families were housed in approved lodgings. Officials of the shelter were notified by telegram if there were any Jewish immigrants on board a vessel. This organisation was set up, like the Hall in Bremen, to combat those that preyed on vulnerable immigrants. Often these people were able to speak the immigrant's language; they hoodwinked their victim into staying in overpriced lodgings, or exchanging money for extortionate rates. Many of those guilty of the crimes against Jews were themselves Jews.

*

It was well past midnight before Chayim and Asher arrived with ten other men at Leman Street, where they were met with a mug of hot tea and sandwiches. After a shower they collapsed onto their beds and in an instant were asleep and, for the first time in their lives, safe.

Because of new laws brought in by the British Government regarding immigration, Asher and Chayim had to justify their right to settle in England by facing an Immigration Board at Great Tower Street in the City of London. This comprised a magistrate, a representative of the Home Office and a Jew.

Asher was the first to be interviewed, the brothers agreeing to tell them why they had immigrated to seek asylum in England. Asher came out of the room, a smile on his face, without saying a word to his brother, but instead pointing to the papers in his hand and winking.

Chayim, his heart beating, swallowed nervously as he entered the room and gave his name. He declined the seat, and stood hands behind his back as he looked at each man in turn.

The man on the right said in Yiddish, 'My name is Barry Cohen, the man in the centre is Mr Johnson, a representative of the government, and the other is a Mr McCloud, a magistrate.' Chayim nodded at the men as Mr Cohen continued, 'We have already spoken to your brother. Can you tell us in your own words why you are seeking asylum in England?'

'My village was attacked by Cossacks and every member of my family killed, except for my brother Asher. In our defence we killed a Cossack and—'

'By "we", you mean *you* killed the Cossack,' the magistrate said in English. Mr Cohen quickly translated.

Chayim took two paces forward, stared straight into the magistrate's eyes and said softly, 'What would you do if someone was trying to kill you—' he spread his hands '—say "Here I am."'

Mr Cohen translated again, but Mr McCloud was nodding before the translation, knowing instinctively what Chayim had said.

The room was silent for a moment. The three men leaned their heads together, conversing in a whisper. Finally Mr Johnson pointed to some papers in front of him, then at Mr Cohen, a slight smile on his face.

'Mr Cohen tells me that your second name is Zeeve. In English that means wolf. We feel that Braun should be pronounced the English way.' He coughed, a little embarrassed as Cohen translated. 'Your brother has agreed to change your surname to Brown. Will you be willing to change your name to Wolfe Brown?'

Heavily accented, the word strange on his tongue, Chayim said seriously, 'Wolfe Brown,' and then smiled as he repeated it – 'Wolfe Brown.' He liked the strength of the name. 'Yes I agree.'

Mr Johnson signed the paper in front of him, slipped it across the table to the others to sign, and then handed it to Wolfe Brown.

Over the next weeks the brothers rented a two-roomed furnished flat with a small kitchenette in Arbour Square, just off the Commercial Road. Asher got a job in a bank as a bookkeeper as he was good with figures. Wolfe found a job in a kosher butcher shop. As far as the brothers were concerned these were temporary jobs, having voted to stay in England for a while as they couldn't face another sea journey just yet. And it gave them a chance to learn to speak English and earn money to pay for a more comfortable journey to America.

2 Eva Golberg's Story

Belarus, May 1906

TWO PAIRS OF FRIGHTENED EYES looked at the wall separating them from the crazed people ransacking the house. The yells of abuse and obscenities from the mob outside in the street of the *Shtetle* filled the air in a crescendo of noise as once again Mogilev Gorodetz by the bridge was attacked by an anti-Semitic mob, inflamed by their priest's vehement speech from the pulpit, yelling for a pogrom against the Jews who, he raved, 'want to overthrow the Tsar'.

Eva Goldberg with her deep brown eyes that shone mischievously under long lashes, although scared, was not worried that their hiding place would be discovered. Her father built this hidden extension into the wall after his three sons and father were killed in the 1903 pogroms. If the girls thought they were about to be discovered, they could escape through a trapdoor that opened outside the house in the middle of some bushes, but throughout the pogroms of the last few years it had proved to be a safe haven.

Eva and her best friend Sarah Rosenfeldt were brushing each other's hair when they heard the shouts of the mob, and rushed to the hiding place. Eva hoped her grandparents were safe at the Shimonoseki's house, where her grandfather played dominoes every Sunday.

Day turned to night and at last there was silence outside, but the friends waited in case it was a trap.

An hour went by and then Eva said, 'I think it's safe to come out now.'

Sarah nodded, her auburn hair falling over hazel eyes that revealed her fear. Eva opened the door and peered out. The place was a shambles: broken windows, furniture and clothes lay scattered on the floor, cupboard doors ripped in rage from their hinges.

Slowly, holding hands, the two sixteen-year-old friends moved slowly into the street, the silence broken by low moans of the wounded and cries of grief from those cuddling dead loved ones. Women and young girls, trying to cover their nudity with torn clothes, stared unseeing, the horror of their ordeal on their faces.

They walked across the street to Sarah's house, the fence around the small trampled vegetable garden splintered. Sarah went through the opening, the front door lying on the ground. Eva trailed behind her friend who lit a candle, and then let out a scream. In the flickering light they saw the crushed and beaten bodies of her parents and two sisters.

Eva wanted to see how her grandparents were, but didn't want to leave Sarah on her own, but her friend, tears streaming down her face, said, 'Go and see how your grandparents are, I'll be okay.'

'Are you sure? I won't be long.' She patted Sarah's arm and ran to the Shimonosekis' house, stopping for a second before entering, taking a deep breath, and with trepidation walked inside. Her knuckles went into her mouth to stifle the scream; then she fell to her knees beside her dead grandmother, cradling her to her bosom, tears streaming down her face as she rocked backward and forward. After a few moments she looked around the room. Her grandfather and Mr Shimonoseki were in their chairs, heads and dominoes on the table. Laying her grandmother's head gently onto the floor, she got to her feet and moved into the kitchen. Her face formed a grim mask on seeing Mrs Shimonoseki's naked body on the floor. Covering the old lady's nakedness with her coat, she stood, fists clenched so tightly that she broke the skin, wishing she were a man and that she could avenge this atrocity.

*

Eva's parents with her sister Rachel had set off for England two months earlier. The entire family were supposed to go, but her grandmother caught a very bad chill and couldn't travel. Eva offered to stay, agreeing that once her grandmother was able to travel they would follow. They were due to leave in four days.

The next morning, having buried their dead, the friends stayed with neighbours, who themselves were in mourning.

Eva's sad face looked down at her plate as she toyed with her food. She looked up at Sarah and said, 'Let's go to England.'

Sarah was about to take a bite of fish on the end of her fork, now poised in mid-air.

'What?'

'I said—'

'I heard what you said,' she interrupted. 'You caught me by surprise.'

'Look,' Eva pointed the fork at her friend, 'we both have nothing to keep us here. My parents and Rachel are in England.' She took a letter from her pocket. 'They sent me their address. I'm sure they will let you stay with us.'

'Your sister is not going to like that.'

Eva shrugged her shoulders, her long dark brown hair rippling across her back. 'Is that a yes?'

Sarah put the fork down on her plate and smiled. 'When do we leave?'

'We have travel documents; you will have to be Leah Goldberg till we get to the port at Libau. We go in three days.' She spooned in a mouthful of food. 'Mm, this is tasty.'

For the last two days Eva and Sarah had put together a few belongings and heirlooms they wanted to take with them. Some roubles and other precious items their parents and grandparents had hidden were distributed in secret places in the clothes they were wearing.

They had been luckier than most, as their grandparents had at one time been partners in a bakery in the city, specialising in pastries. Since the Pale of Settlement forbade them to own property or work amongst non-Jews, Eva's grandparents brought their families here, secreting savings and some jewellery with them.

For two young Jewish girls this was a perilous journey, fraught with danger from corrupt officials, robbery, bribery and deception, but they were determined to leave, and hopefully find a safer place to live without fear of being killed.

*

The dawn greeted another day as the two friends, holding hands, stood on the bridge looking back at their place of birth, where, mixed with happiness and laughter, there was also sadness. They turned and, without looking back, began their journey to a better life.

As daylight became night, Eva looped her thumbs through the straps of the haversack on her back, looking at the farmhouse in front of them.

'What do you think, shall we take a chance and knock on the door?' she whispered.

Sarah shrugged. 'I'm not sure, but then,' she looked up at the darkening sky, 'I'm tired and it's getting colder by the minute.'

Taking her friend's hand, Eva pushed open the gate and side by side the girls walked up the path to stand for a moment at the front door. They looked at each other, and then Sarah nodded, took a deep breath and knocked on the door.

For a second there was silence, then footsteps approached and the door was flung open. A buxom woman with blonde hair tied in a bun looked at the young girls standing in front of her.

'What do you want?' Her tone was one of curiosity rather than anger.

'We're sorry to bother you at this late hour, but we have been travelling all day and are very tired,' Eva explained. 'Would it be possible for us to sleep,' she looked at a building to their left, 'in the barn?'

The woman smiled. 'Of course you can.'

'Thank you very much,' said Sarah, relieved.

The two girls started to walk away.

'I have some hot broth on the fire,' the woman called after them, 'would you like some?'

'Please!' they replied.

The woman opened the door wider and stepped aside, allowing them to enter. They waited for her to close the door and followed her into a cobblestone kitchen. Seated at a table in the middle of the room was a man, a girl and boy. All three looked up from their meal as they entered.

The woman beckoned for them to sit down, facing the boy and girl who Eva guessed were about eleven and nine. As she spooned the broth into the bowls, the woman said, 'Gregory, these young girls are going to sleep in the barn tonight. They've been travelling all day.'

The farmer's ruddy face broke into a smile; he gestured with work-worn hands at the seats to his right. 'Please, sit.'

'Thank you.'

The woman placed the food in front of them. It smelt delicious, and Eva suddenly realised how hungry she was as the woman refilled her husband's bowl.

Gregory looked at his wife as she sat down opposite him. 'Tanya, this is fantastic, you have excelled yourself.'

Sarah looked at Tanya. 'Madam, I agree with your husband. It's the best broth I've ever tasted.'

'Me too,' Sarah nodded.

Tanya blushed, her green eyes showing her pleasure.

Gregory turned to the friends. 'Where have you come from and where are you going?'

Eva looked at him, wondering what he would do or say when she told him. 'We are heading for the station at Belynici,' she said quietly, 'and from there ...' She hesitated.

'We are going to England,' said Sarah, her hand resting on her friend's arm as if to assure her that everything was going to be okay.

'That's a long way for two young girls to travel by themselves,' said Tanya.

'Yes, it is,' Eva agreed.

'Where are your parents?' Gregory asked.

'Mine are dead,' Sarah whispered, a tear forming at the corner of her eyes.

'Oh! You poor child,' Tanya leaned over, patting her arm.

'Mine are in England,' said Eva.

'What! Why did they leave you behind?'

Eva began to explain, and then stopped in mid-sentence. For a moment she looked silently around the table, and was about to carry on when Sarah said, 'Our grandparents, my parents and two sisters were killed four days ago.'

Gregory and Tanya stared in silence at them, disbelief on their faces.

'I'm so sorry,' he said solemnly, looking to his wife for help.

Tanya twisted the spoon in her bowl of broth. 'You don't have to sleep in the barn, we have a spare room, and you can sleep there.'

'I'm going to the mill in the morning. I can give you a ride as far as that,' said Gregory.

Eva and Sarah hugged them.

*

The next morning, sitting on the hay in the back of the cart as it moved away from the house, Eva and Sarah waved goodbye to the farmer's wife and their children.

They had been travelling for an hour when Gregory shouted, 'Cossacks, quickly, hide under the hay.'

Frantically, Eva and Sarah burrowed into the hay as the cart came to a stop.

'Where are you going?'

'To the mill, five miles further on,' they heard the farmer reply.

A Cossack moved his horse to the rear of the cart and drew his sabre, thrusting it into the hay. It cut Sarah along the hip but she didn't cry out, thrusting her hand into her mouth. Satisfied that the farmer wasn't hiding anyone, the Cossack joined his comrade and without another word they rode away.

Gregory watched them until they were hidden by trees and bushes lining the road. 'They've gone.'

Two heads popped up. 'I'm hurt,' Sarah whispered.

'Let's have a look,' Eva whispered back as the cart moved off.

The sabre had left a five-inch cut, which thankfully wasn't deep, along Sarah's thigh. Eva ripped a strip off Sarah's petticoat to stem the trickle of blood and then tied a strip from her own petticoat around Sarah's wound. Both checked the hay for blood, throwing out what little they could find.

At the mill they thanked Gregory, promising to write when they got to England.

*

The girls had been walking for three days. Each night they slept huddled together, the stars their ceiling. On two occasions they had to scramble behind hedgerows on hearing the thunder of hooves coming along the road, watching through leafy gaps as soldiers raced by.

It was mid-morning, and they could see Bilynici in the distance.

'Look,' Sarah pointed, 'a stream.' Laughing, the friends ran towards it, lying face down and cupping the cool clear water into their mouths.

'Ugh, I smell,' Eva remarked, and started to undress.

'What are you doing?'

'I told you, I smell.' She leaned towards her friend, sniffed, and giggled. 'So do you and I need to look at your wound?'

While one bathed the other kept watch. Eva took a look at Sarah's wound. Luckily the sabre had only broken the skin, and it was healing nicely. She cleaned and redressed it, asking, 'Does it hurt?'

'A little, more like a continuous ache.'

It was dusk by the time they arrived at Bilynici railway station. Holding hands, they went straight to the ticket office, purchasing tickets to the port of Libau, but before reaching their final destination they would have to change trains at Minsk and Kovno. The next train to Minsk left at six in the morning.

'It's too late to find a place to sleep,' said Eva. 'We might as well stay here overnight.'

Sarah looked around the station seeing other travellers settling down for the night. 'I agree, look, there's a bench over there.'

They settled down on the bench to be joined by a husband and wife who had just arrived and, like the two friends, didn't want to venture out into a strange town at night. What's more, they needed to save their money for the boat to America.

The friends were the first to board the train, settling into seats opposite each other by the window. Eva looked at the countryside speeding by with mixed feelings – excitement and apprehension, tinged with a little fear; she had never ventured further than the bridge of their *Shtetle*.

At Kovno they again had to wait till morning for the train to Libau. Sarah pointed to a ticket kiosk. 'We can buy our tickets to England from there instead of Libau, which I'm sure will be crowded.'

'Good idea.' Holding hands, they walked over to the agent. Not wanting to lose the tickets or have them stolen, the girls went into the ladies' toilet, hiding them in pockets inside their skirts.

*

Eva was asleep, head resting on her rucksack, arms wrapped around it. What woke her up was tugging at her rucksack. She opened her eyes to see two hands trying to wrestle it from under her. She gave a scream, startling the thief. Suddenly he was fending off Sarah who, hearing Eva scream, was instantly awake and, quick to see what was happening, leapt onto the thief's back. Eva got to her feet and kicked the man in the shin. He gave a yell when she kicked him again, while at the same time Sarah scratched his face. After a tussle, the thief managed to get Sarah of his back and ran away.

Two days later they arrived at the port of Libau, to be met by Jews owning boarding houses. Some were clean, others excessively dirty and did not provide bathing facilities.

Walking through Libau station they were accosted by a stout woman in a dark wig. 'Excuse me, ladies, are you looking for accommodation?'

Eva looked intently at her, noticing her clean hands and clothes. 'Yes, madam, we are.'

'I have a room available; do you know how long you will be staying?'

'Three nights.' said Sarah.

'I am a widow with five children,' she told them on the way to her boarding house. 'My husband died a year ago. I wanted to go to America, but he said we should buy a boarding house and we will make lots of money, which we did. The only problem,' she shook her fist at the sky. 'My husband was a bad gambler and all the money we made, he squandered.' She opened a gate, gesturing for them to enter. 'In six months, and with the sale of my property, I will be able to take my children to America.'

It wasn't until they were on the ship and heard stories about other boarding houses that they realised how lucky they had been to meet the widow.

*

By the time they were ready to leave Sarah's wound had healed. They said goodbye to the landlady and her children and made their way to the Winter Harbour to board the vessel taking them to London. At the gate they were met by two policemen.

'Papers please,' one said briskly.

Eva's heart missed a beat; she swallowed nervously and with shaking hand gave him the paper. Out of the corner of her eye she saw Sarah fumbling with her bag. The taller of the two policemen snapped his fingers impatiently. Eva placed her hands over Sarah's to calm her down, lowered her friend to kneel on the ground and helped her look for the papers, saying, 'We are very sorry to keep you waiting.'

Sarah finally found what she was looking for and handed the papers to the policemen who whispered together for a moment.

'I'm afraid these papers are not in order,' said the taller one.

Sarah and Eva stared at him in disbelief. 'But we're due to sail in three hours,' Sarah stuttered.

'Sorry, can't let you board, but—'

'Will this do?' Eva interrupted, taking some money from her pocket.

The policeman went to take it, but Eva closed her hand, a slight smile on her face. 'Once you have let us through,' she said sweetly, picking up her knapsack.

The policeman was about to say something when a crowd of people arrived. He nodded, handed back their papers, and in return received the bribe.

As they stepped foot on deck, the friends turned and silently hugged each other and began to cry tears of relief, jumping up and down in joy, as the tensions of the last few weeks were swept away.

Three hours later the ship shuddered as the engines came to life. Eva and Sarah went on deck, moving to the rail, arms around each other's shoulders as the ship moved away from the dock. There was no one to wave goodbye too as both girls thought sadly of those they had left behind, but amidst the sorrow there was also excitement and hope for a better future.

Eva reaches for the letter in her pocket.

'Are you sure about me staying with you?' Sarah said, looking at the letter.

Eva smiled. 'With you there they won't lock me in my room when someone comes to call on Rachel.'

Sarah smiled at her friend. 'Eva Goldberg, you are a devious ...' her smile changed to an expression of hurt. 'You want me to come with you so your parents ...' She couldn't keep a straight face any longer. 'Rachel isn't going to like that,' she laughed.

Eva's sister Rachel may have been much the prettier of the two sisters, but what Eva lacked in beauty she made up for in personality. She was a high spirited, mischievous girl, who loved to laugh, dance and sing, with an independent and even rebellious streak.

Protocol stated that the eldest daughter should marry first. Whenever a male caller came to see Rachel, his attention had often moved from the elder, quieter, sister to the bubbly Eva. Her parents had therefore decided that whenever a male caller came to see Rachel, Eva had to go to her room, and to ensure she wasn't tempted to come out, her mother locked the door.

'I suppose I'll have to save you from getting locked in your bedroom,' said Sarah, and both girls began to giggle, which soon turned into fits of uncontrollable laughter as they clung to each other to stop themselves falling onto the deck.

The vessel itself was registered under a Danish flag. The more people they could fit on board, the bigger the profit. The conditions were therefore horrific, with passengers herded together like cattle, little sanitation, no privacy and an appalling smell of unwashed bodies.

'Everything shakes,' Eva moaned. 'I'm not feeling well.'

'Do you feel seasick?' Sarah touched her friend's forehead.

'Not yet, I might be sick from the smell.'

Sarah lifted her arm. 'I stink.'

'Let's go on deck,' said Sarah. 'The fresh air will do us a world of good.'

Eva stood and the girls walked unsteadily towards the stairs and out on to the deck.

The ship dipped into the waves that sprayed over the bow, soaking the people lining the rail who were being sick. Others huddled together with blankets around them, drawing warmth from each other's bodies.

The two girls held each other as they gulped in the fresh sea air, Eva looking to her right and gripping Sarah tightly, a frightened look on her face.

'What's the matter?' said Sarah, following her friend's gaze. Then she saw him – a man with three long red lines down his right cheek. 'It's the man who tried to take your knapsack,' she whispered.

Eva nodded, brown eyes staring at the man who looked at them, turned and was lost in the crowd.

*

The following day the coast of England appeared, and for once the sea was calm. For Eva and Sarah it was a huge relief just to know that their journey was about to end.

At St Katherine's Dock, the anchor rattled down from its housing as sailors on the bow and stern threw ropes to men waiting to tie them to metal rings. The engines were silent and the five days of shaking and shuddering came to an end. A voice over a loudspeaker said, 'This is the Captain, please keep the gangplank clear. A medical team is coming aboard where they will examine you before you can disembark.'

Eight people, six with white coats, two in the uniform of the port authority, accompanied by two policemen walked on to the deck. One by one, the passengers were examined and every now and again one or two were put to one side.

Eva and Sara passed their examination and left the ship to be met by a member of the Jewish Welfare Organisation. Eva showed them her father's letter with his address. The lady smiled at them and called over a young boy.

'Stephen, take these ladies to 33 Musbury Street.' She turned to the girls, saying in Yiddish, 'Stephen has a cart. You can put your belongings on it, as it's a long walk.'

The first thing that struck Eva as she walked along the cobbled streets was the noise – not just one sound but a cacophony of different sounds – babies crying, the sound of horses and cartwheels on the cobbles, people shouting at each other, market sellers advertising their wares and the repeated tune of an old music hall song being played on a hurdy-gurdy.

Stephen stopped outside a terraced house and knocked on the door. Eva and Sarah stood slightly behind him as the door opened. There was a scream from her mother who rushed out to meet her daughter, hugging and kissing her, while at the same time calling, 'Solomon, Rachel,' tears streaming down her face.

3   The Goldbergs of Brick Lane

London, January 1907

IT WAS LATE FRIDAY MORNING and as usual there was a queue stretching outside the bakery. Thankfully it had stopped raining and the sun had appeared. Eva was helping her father take the bread and bagels from the oven, while her mother, Sarah and her sister Rachel served the customers.

In October 1906 Eva's father Solomon had opened a bakery with living accommodation above in Brick Lane. Since the opening, they had been so busy that Solomon had thought of taking on another baker, or a trainee, but Eva and Sarah talked him into teaching them, and it had worked very well.

Now Eva, her faced smudged with flour and perspiration, was taking the hot bagels into the shop. Her mother, Hadar, blew a wisp of hair from her eyes.

'We're running out of *cholla*.'

'Papa has just taken some out of the oven.' No sooner had Eva said it than he appeared with the bread.

The last customer had gone, and before closing Solomon handed the unsold bread and rolls to those that couldn't afford to buy them. This was called *Tzedakah*: those that had, giving to those that hadn't.

He closed the shop and while he took their takings to the bank, his wife prepared the Sabbath dinner. Once the girls had cleaned the shop and ovens they ran upstairs to help Hadar with the final touches before going to the Whitechapel baths in Goulston Street, and Solomon walked to Schevzik's Jewish baths in Brick Lane.

As usual on Shabbat morning the family walked the short distance to the Great Synagogue on the corner of Fournier Street. Inside the *schul* the girls looked down from the gallery at the men below. Rachel whispered to her sister, 'Isn't he handsome?'

Eva tried to see who her sister was looking at, 'Who?'

'Amos Hirschfield – he's so tall.'

Eva looked down at the gangly, bearded Amos; she tapped Sarah on the arm and leaned close to her ear. 'Rachel fancies Amos Hirschfield.'

Sarah's eyes widened. 'No.' she looked down, pulling quickly as Amos looked up at the gallery, but she needn't have worried, his eyes were on Rachel.

*

The following day, Hadar Goldberg sat facing the Widow Rosenblum, the matchmaker. She handed her a cup of tea, placing a plate of biscuits on the table beside her.

'My daughter Rachel is interested in Amos Hirschfield. Do you think this could be a good match?'

Yentas, as matchmakers were called, knew practically everyone in the community – it was their job to do so. The widow, a stout, happy, talkative woman, smiled. 'Amos is twenty-two, a nice boy, a little shy. The family have a drapery shop in Commercial Road. Amos works there. I think he and Rachel would be an ideal match.' She drank the tea, placing the cup on the table beside her and looked down at the biscuits. 'So, shall I make the arrangements?'

Hadar gave a slight nod of her head. 'Yes please.' She picked up the plate of biscuits. The widow's eyes followed them as she placed them in a bag, handing it to the matchmaker. 'Take this home with you.'

'Thank you,' The Yenta took the bag and got slowly to her feet. 'I will make the necessary arrangements, and I'll see you soon.'

'Guess what?' Rachel told Eva. 'Mama has spoken to the matchmaker and Amos is coming here tomorrow.'

'Really,' Eva whispered a slight glint in her eyes.

Rachel's eyes narrowed as she looked at her sister. 'Eva Goldberg,' she said, tight-lipped. 'I promise if you do anything to, to…' she pinched Eva's arm '… you'll wish you had never been born.'

There was an atmosphere of excitement, bustle and anticipation as the three girls prepared the dining room for their guest. Eva smiled as Rachel virtually skipped around the room singing. Amos Hirschfield was coming.

There was a knock at the front door and Solomon went to open it. Rachel rushed to the mirror, straightening her auburn hair; smoothed down the skirt of her dress, pinched her cheeks and joined her mother just as Amos entered the room with the matchmaker, who formally introduced Amos to them. Eva and Sarah brought in trays of tea, cakes and biscuits.

After some small talk to ease the young man's shyness, the parents left the room, leaving the widow as chaperon so the young couple could get to know each other.

An hour later there was a knock at the kitchen door. Solomon opened it to find Amos standing there.

'Please ...' he said nervously '... Mr Goldberg, can I have a word with you.'

Solomon nodded at the young man, who looked as if he were on his way to an execution, opened the door wider and stepped to one side, allowing him to enter. At the same time he motioned with his right hand for his wife, Eva and Sarah to leave. Solomon closed the door, a slight, knowing smile on his face, remembering the time he had asked Hadar's father for her hand in marriage. He was sure his future father-in-law could hear his knees knocking.

He turned to face the young man, but before he could say anything Amos blurted out quickly, 'I love Rachel and would like to marry her.'

Solomon took a cigarette case from his pocket offering it to the young man, 'Cigarette?'

'I don't smoke, sir.'

As he lit the cigarette, Solomon knew that this was a nice young man who would make his Rachel happy. 'Yes, Amos, you can marry my daughter.'

Amos grabbed his future father-in-law's hand, pumping it up and down. 'Thank you, thank you,' he said excitedly. He let go the hand, looking for the door and turned back. 'Thank you.'

Laughing at the young man's antics, Solomon walked to the door and opened it. Amos rushed past him to kneel by the seated Rachel, taking her hand and saying breathlessly, 'He said yes.'

Rachel smiled at her future husband and with tears in her eyes stood and moved quickly across the room, wrapping her arms around her father's neck. 'Thank you, Papa.'

A few days later, the families met to announce the engagement and make plans for the wedding.

*

London, July 1907

The friends were in the gallery of the Jewish Theatre in Commercial Street. Eva nudged Sarah, pointing to a man across the aisle. 'I'm going to marry him.'

Sarah didn't say anything for a second, just looked from Eva to him and then back to her friend.

'Eva Goldberg, you're a *meshugana*, how are you going to manage that?'

'I'll think of something,' she whispered, staring at the man as the lights dimmed and the show began.

When the curtain fell at the end of the show, Eva got to her feet, grabbed Sarah's hand, dragging her from the seat. 'Come on.'

Before Sarah could reply she pulled her along the aisle towards the stairs. If Sarah had looked at Eva she would have seen her eyes on the man she had pointed out earlier, but Sarah was too busy trying to avoid bumping into anyone. Just before they reached the stairs, Eva let go Sarah's hand, crashing into the man and dropping her bag, just as he dropped his hat.

'Oh, I'm sorry,' Eva said apologetically, kneeling on the carpet to retrieve the bag.

He bent down to help, at the same time trying to pick up his hat, but as Eva went to pick up the bag she purposely overbalanced and fell on top of him. It was like the stage antics of a music hall comic, arms and legs everywhere as he tried to get up and at the same time pick up his hat.

Eva burst into laughter as people leaving the theatre walked around them, some tut-tutting. Sarah smiled at her friend, who winked mischievously as she helped her up. Eva turned to the man as he picked himself up, saying as sweetly as she could, 'I'm so sorry.' They stood looking at each other, she with her heart beating from the excitement of what she had done. His tawny eyes looked sternly at her, but that lasted for only a second, and then he smiled back.

'Are you OK?' he asked quietly, concern in his voice.

'Yes, I think so,' Eva replied, straightening the skirt of her dress, adding as she looked into his eyes. 'My name is Eva Goldberg.'

'I'm Wolfe Brown,' he said in Yiddish. 'I've recently arrived from Russia, and I'm waiting for a ship to America.'

Sarah gasped as the usual formal introduction through a matchmaker was thrown out of the window.

As for Wolfe, although he still fully intended to go to America, in reality the poor man never stood a chance.

*

Later that evening, Wolfe was telling his brother about the girl he had met at the Jewish Theatre. 'She's nothing like any of the girls I have ever met before. She's lively and...' He was silent for a moment a thoughtful look on his face. '... It's as though she went out of her way to meet me.' He shook his head, 'No, I'm just imagining it.'

He poured himself a drink. 'I'm meeting her tomorrow night. She asked if I had a friend as she had to bring a chaperon. How about it, can you help me out here?'

Asher smiled. 'Why not, but knowing you and your taste in women, I'll have to wear glasses. Let's not get too involved, we're going to America.'

As soon as Asher set eyes on Sarah, all thoughts of America disappeared. Asher was immediately as smitten with Sarah as Wolfe was with Eva.

Eva may not have been very pretty by conventional standards of the time, but Wolfe could perceive that she had a unique, inward beauty and of course a fantastic personality. She made him laugh, holding his arm as they walked in the park getting to know each other. Eva was determined to keep Wolfe in England, but as, unknown to either of them Asher couldn't stop thinking about Sarah. There were already other forces at work that were affecting the brothers' decision to leave.

*

A month later, on a sunny August morning, the brothers were on their way as usual to meet Eva and Sarah: by now the four of them were seeing as much of each other as possible. They could hardly bear to be apart and within just a few weeks both couples had fallen in love, and bared their souls to each other, experienced the usual lovers' tiffs, broken up, got back together again, fallen out, started from scratch, and were, at last, really beginning to get to know each other. And even more important than the fact that they were in love, they had become friends – with the added spice and intoxication that, for each of them, that friendship was with the only person in the world that they wanted to spend the rest of their lives with.

Yet all the time, the prospect that their love and friendship was about to be torn apart by an ocean preyed on each of them, haunting them at night as they tossed and turned, unable to sleep, dreading their imminent separation.

'I need to talk to you about something, I—'

'That's funny. I wanted to talk to you.' Wolfe interrupted.

'What is it?'

'No, you go first.'

'Come on,' Asher smiled, 'elder-brother privilege.'

Wolfe stopped, took a cigarette packet from his pocket offered one to his brother. 'Don't be angry, but I can't go to America.'

Asher was about to reply, but Wolfe held up a hand to stop him. 'I'm in love with Eva and want to marry her. I know from what she's told me about her parents, she will not—'

'I was going to say the same thing,' said Asher.

'What, that you're in love with Eva.'

Asher took off his hat and hit his brother over the head. 'No, you idiot, I can't stop thinking about Sarah. I know from what she's told me that she'll never leave Eva. Let's meet the girls and then speak to Mr Goldberg.'

'What about America?'

'America, shmerica,' he waved a hand, 'Forget it.'

They met the friends on the corner of Whitechapel Road and New Road. Arm in arm they walked up Valance Road to Weavers Field. Wolfe steered Eva to an empty bench on the right, while Asher did the same with Sarah on the opposite side.

Wolfe gazed into Eva's brown eyes, wanting to kiss her, but instead took her hand, moving off the bench to kneel on one knee.

Eva wondered for a split second what was going on. Then her heart skipped a beat as he said, 'Eva Goldberg, in the short time I have known you, I have fallen in love with you.' She was unable to take her eyes off him.

For a moment she had wanted to look across at Sarah, but all thoughts were banished from her mind as she heard the words, 'Will you marry me? Naturally I will ask your father,' Wolfe was saying. 'Do you think—'

He couldn't say another word as Eva leapt on him, all propriety abandoned, arms around his neck, saying, 'Yes, yes,' between kisses.

She glanced over at Sarah who was laughing and crying at the same time. Eva stared at Wolfe, 'What's going on over there.'

'Oh! He's asking her to marry him.'

Eva grabbed Wolfe's hand, dragging him across the pathway.

'Let's go!' she cried, as Sarah turned to meet her, the friends laughing, kissing each other, and then, ignoring the startled looks of those in the park, kissing their future husbands.

At last there was silence between them and Wolfe was the first to break it.

'Eva, do you think it would be convenient for me to ask your father today?'

Asher turned to Sarah, sadness in his face and voice. 'I wish I could do the same with your parents, but sadly I can't, but I know that you look on Eva's parents as your own, so would you mind if I asked Mr Goldberg if I could marry you.'

Sarah gazed at Asher with love in her eyes, leaned over and kissed him on the lips. 'That is very thoughtful of you. I am sure that if my parents had met you they would have said I was a very lucky girl. Yes, Asher, please ask Mr Goldberg.'

The two young couples left the park to walk the short distance to Brick Lane. They were now quiet, but smiling, happy to be in each other's company.

When they reached the bakery, they hesitated for a moment, and then Eva opened the side door that led via a corridor to a stairway to the Goldbergs' first-floor residence above the shop, taking Wolfe's hand they entered the upstairs hallway side by side, with Sarah and Asher behind them. The girls left the boys in the hallway and entered the dining room.

Wolfe was nervous. The brothers had never met Mr and Mrs Goldberg.

'Is mine okay?' he asked Asher, as he straightened his brother's tie.

'Yes, you're fine,' Asher said, a nervous quiver in his voice, looking at the closed door. Both men jumped as the door suddenly opened and there stood Mr Goldberg.

Solomon smiled as he stepped to one side, 'Please, come in.'

As they entered the room, a woman whom they presumed to be Mrs Goldberg was seated in an armchair with the girls on either side of her. Solomon faced the two very nervous brothers. 'Can I offer you gentlemen a drink?'

Wolfe twirled his bowler hat in his hands. 'Tea for me, please, sir.'

Asher coughed to clear his throat, 'me too.'

Solomon looked at Eva and Sarah. 'You heard them, off you go. Mama and I will have one too.' Turning back to the boys, he gestured to some chairs. 'Please sit.'

'Thank you, sir,' Asher said, trying to smile, 'but before we do—' he looked at Wolfe, who nodded for him to carry on '—I would like your permission to marry Sarah.'

Solomon pursed his lips, turning his gaze on Wolfe.

'Sir, Mr Goldberg,' Wolfe nervously licked his lips, wanting to run, but his legs were now like jelly. And then suddenly, as in the boxing ring, he felt calm, and in a steady voice continued, 'I would like your blessing to marry Eva.'

Solomon was silent for a moment, looking from one to the other. Wolfe was clean-shaven, nicely dressed in a brown suit, starched white shirt and tie. His brother was bearded, in dark blue suit, white shirt and bow tie. Solomon wanted to know more about the brothers. It seemed that both Eva and Sarah had no need for a *yenta*, and the way they had spoken about these men, they were clearly in love.

Solomon picked up a cigarette packet on the table by his side, offering it to the boys, who nervously replied in unison, 'No thank you.'

'Before I say yes, or no, I would be remiss if I didn't ask – where are you from? Where are your parents? What do you do for a living?'

Wolfe looked at Asher, who gestured for him to do the speaking. 'We come from Poland. Our parents and sisters were killed during a pogrom in 1906.'

Asher took over. 'We were originally going to America, but we had to leave in a hurry after, let's say, a run in with some Cossacks, so we took the first boat out, which came to London, with the intention of going on to America at a later date.'

'Do you still intend to go to America?'

Wolfe smiled. 'No, not now, not since—' he looked embarrassingly down at the ground '—falling in love,' he added quietly.

Solomon looked at Asher.

'No, certainly not, I love Sarah too much to leave her.'

'I'm not going to ask about the Cossacks, we know only about them far too well.' He looked at his wife, then at the boys in front of him and got to his feet. 'Wolfe, you can marry Sarah.'

Wolfe sprung to his feet, 'What?'

Solomon laughed. 'Only joking; yes, you have my permission to marry Eva, and Asher can marry my adopted daughter Sarah. As we haven't received our tea yet, you might as well give the girls the news.' He pointed a finger at them, 'Don't forget your future in-laws' tea.' As the boys left the room he added, 'And the biscuits.'

*

A month later on 10 September 1907, Rachel and Amos married at the Great Synagogue. Eva and Sarah were bridesmaids at a wedding in which Solomon and Hadar Goldberg spared no expense.

The bride and groom honeymooned at the Grand Hotel in Bournemouth. Returning to live for a while at his parents' house in Jubilee Square.

Having lost Rachel, Solomon employed a young girl to help in the shop. Because of expansion in trade he searched for larger premises and, by a stroke of luck, found out that the property next door was for sale, so he bought it.

Solomon employed a builder to knock down the wall between the two buildings, enlarging the baking and shop areas, and at the same time have a bathroom fitted upstairs.

The builder completed the work on time and the refurbished bakery opened in November 1907. Solomon had employed another baker and two young girls to serve in the shop on Fridays and Sundays, leaving him to concentrate on his speciality, cakes and pastries. Eva and Sarah began the next phase of their tuition as Goldberg's bakery clientele encompassed half of the East End of London.

*

Sweat poured down his face as Wolfe bounced on the balls of his feet, slammed a right and a left into the punch-bag, pushing Asher, who was holding the bag backwards from the force of the double punch.

'Okay, change over,' Wolfe said a little breathlessly.

Asher smiled as they changed over, sending a flurry of punches into the bag.

'Stop pussyfooting around. Hit it,' his brother goaded him.

Asher gritted his teeth and, using the weight of his body, thumped a right hand into the bag with such force that it lifted Wolfe off his feet, landing him on his backside, a big grin on his face.

'That's more like it,' said Wolfe.

'If we're going to make a life in England,' Asher said as they showered, 'we need to decide whether you want to be a butcher for the rest of your life, and I a clerk, which to tell you the truth I don't want to do, it's boring, or—'

'No, I don't want to be a butcher either. The jobs are supposed to be temporary.' Wolfe looked intently at his brother. 'You've thought of something?'

Asher was silent for a moment. 'Yes, but let's not discuss it here. Wait till we get home.'

In their flat Asher pushed his dinner plate to one side and took a piece of paper and pencil from the pocket of his jacket that was hanging on the back of the chair. He looked across the table at Wolfe and said, 'There are four things people need.' He pointed the pencil at his brother.

'And they are?'

Asher glowered at Wolfe. 'I'm coming to that, if you'll let me.'

Wolfe stood picking up the dinner plates, moving across to the sink.

'Are you listening?'

Wolfe looked over his shoulder. 'I can wash up and listen at the same time, you can wipe. OK, continue.'

'People need food, drink, clothes, and accommodation.'

Handing Asher a plate, Wolfe asked, 'What do you have in mind?' He pointed a soapy finger at his brother. 'I can tell you now, I do not want to be a tailor or make clothes. Have you seen the sweatshops and the way the workers are treated?'

'No, I was—'

'Mr Goldberg makes a good living,' Wolfe interrupted, 'a very good living, may I add, but we know nothing about baking bread, and I am not going to ask him to teach me as I know he would have to say yes because of Eva.'

Asher whipped the tea towel playfully against his brother's buttocks. 'Will you let me finish?'

Wolfe smiled and flicked a hand for him to carry on. Ignoring the suds landing on his beard, Asher continued, 'Firstly we need somewhere to live when get married. Two families cannot live here.' He held up a hand to stop his brother from interrupting again. 'Working in the bank, I've seen the amount of money people made renting out property. What I propose we do is buy two properties. You and Eva live in one, and rent out the other rooms. Sarah and I do the same with the other. Once we have enough money we buy another and we rent that one out. What do you think?'

Taking out the plug, Wolfe watched the water drain away and cleaned the sink as he weighed up what Asher has said. Wiping his hands on a towel, he replied, 'It's a good idea, but there are two things I'd like to say if we do this. I don't want to use all of our money. We need something put aside in case of, let's say, emergencies. The second is: I don't want any properties to be in disrepair like this flat; we either do it ourselves, or employ someone to do it.' He returned to the table, leaned back in the chair, twisting and turning a box of matches between his fingers.

'I agree with that.' Asher slid onto the seat opposite and picked up a newspaper from the table, 'Okay, let's see what's for sale.'

That was at the end of 1907 and within a few months, Wolfe and Asher were able to put down deposits for mortgages on two houses, each renting out the unused rooms as Asher had suggested. By June 1908 they had earned enough to taken on mortgages for two more properties and thus in a remarkably short space of time had been able to acquire four houses between them. They and their fiancées enjoyed planning the décor and fittings and had made enough profit so far that year to buy another house.

London, August 1908

Eva looked at the clock and sighed. It was five in the morning and time was dragging ever so slowly. Far too excited to sleep, she pushed back the covers, got out of bed, walked across the room and opened the door just as Sarah appeared from the opposite bedroom. The girls silently looked at each other and side by side walked along the landing, down the stairs into the kitchen, and were surprise to see Mrs Goldberg sitting at the table, her hands wrapped round a mug of tea.

'Mama, what are you doing down here, it's—'

'Can't sleep,' she interrupted smiling at them. 'And you two?'

'Same.'

'I was the same on my wedding day,' Hadar said softly, a faraway look in her eyes. 'You should try and sleep a little; it's going to be a long day for the both of you.'

'Mama, we—'

'Can't, yes, I understand. Okay, have a cup of tea, and then go back upstairs. Lie on the bed and just close your eyes.'

An hour later, Eva and Sarah, their eyes closed, lay side by side on the bed. 'Mama is right,' Eva whispered to Sarah.

'Mmm?'

Someone was shaking them awake. 'Wakey, wakey, sleepy heads.'

The girls opened their eyes, immediately turning to look at the clock, leaping out of bed. 'Mama, it's eight o'clock.' There was panic in their voices. 'The hairdresser will be here soon and we haven't had a bath yet.'

Mrs Goldberg smiled. 'You have lots of time and the service isn't until two. I've run the bath. Eva, you take the first one. By the time you've finished, the hairdresser will be here, and then I'll run the bath for Sarah.'

Now dressed in their bridal gowns looking at themselves in the mirror Eva said, 'I feel like this is unreal.'

'I know what you mean,' said Sarah. 'I've had to pinch myself a couple of times in case it's a dream.'

'If it is—'

A knock at the door interrupted them.

'Come in,' they said, looking at each other giggling.

The door opened and Solomon Goldberg walked in, followed by his wife. For a moment they stood like statues, looking from one to the other. Finally Mrs Goldberg burst into tears as her husband walked towards the girls.

'I have never seen so much beauty in one room, you take my breath away. Every young man is going to be jealous of your husbands.' He took two slim boxes from his pocket, stopping in front of his daughter. 'Eva, I have never—' his voice caught with emotion '—in my life seen you as happy as you look today.' He kissed her on both cheeks, tears in his eyes and, handing her a box, and then stepped towards Sarah.

'I know your parents would have loved Asher as you do, and would be as proud as I am of all you have overcome.' He looked at his wife and then back to Sarah. 'We are honoured that you have chosen us to stand with you under the *chuppah*.' He took a step closer, kissed her on both cheeks and handed her the box, just as someone yelled, 'The cars are here.'

Both girls opened their boxes. Inside were identical gold necklaces, each bearing a gold Star of David.

'Thank you, Papa, it's beautiful,' Eva said, moving over to him and placing her arms around his neck.

Sarah, tears in her eyes joined her. 'Thank you, Papa, it's the loveliest present I have ever had.'

*

There was a low hubbub of voices, excitement and anticipation at the Stepney Green Synagogue.

The last few months had passed quickly, and at last the day was here. The girls wanted to get married on the same day and the boys thought it a great idea, as did the Goldberg's.

Now, as Wolfe stood with Asher as his best man under the *chuppah* (canopy), waiting nervously for Eva to appear, he thought of his parents and how happy they would have been today.

Suddenly the congregation got to their feet. Eva, a beaming smile on her face, stood for a moment at the open doors of the synagogue, feeling very nervous and shy, yet loving being the centre of attraction as the guests turned to look at her in the white silk wedding dress that flowed down to her ankles. The headdress and veil in stunning lace matched the lace around the neck of the dress, the hem of which brushed along the floor as she walked slowly down the narrow aisle, carrying a bouquet of lilies and stephanotis. Her face behind the veil glowing with happiness, brown eyes sparkled on seeing Wolfe, so handsome in his dinner suit; his eyes followed her. At last she was by his side. They looked at each other and he grasped her left hand as if to say, *I'm never going to let you go.*

As arranged with the rabbi, once he pronounced them husband and wife, they stepped to one side of the *chuppah* and Asher moved to where his brother had been standing, the three of them looking back to the doors of the synagogue as they opened.

Sarah stood for a second, smiling radiantly at the people on both sides of the aisle as she moved forward. Her lace wedding dress had a long train at the back that shimmered with sequins and beads and a pretty bonnet headdress with a short veil; her bouquet was the same as Eva's. She licked her lips nervously as she moved beside Asher, who whispered, 'You are beautiful.'

It was over, and as the newlyweds walked out of the synagogue, with beaming smiles on their faces. They stopped before entering the Rolls Royce wedding car and threw a kiss to the cheers of the crowd.

4   The O'Sullivan Brothers

London, March 1909

THE GOLDBERGS WERE OVERJOYED when in February their daughter Rachel gave them their first grandchild, a granddaughter, Naomi. And now Eva was three months pregnant. While she and Sarah knitted baby clothes, Wolfe was busy decorating the nursery. Eve and Wolfe were excited about the new arrival, shopping for prams, nappies and other baby things.

Wolfe was just about to finish papering the babies' room when Eva burst into the room, tears streaming down her face. Wolfe was surprised to see her: she and Sarah usually stayed at their parents' place once the shop was closed as the whole family met there every Sunday.

'What's the matter?'

'Papa was attacked and robbed just as he was closing up,' she said between sobs. 'We were upstairs helping Mama – preparing the dinner – when we heard shouting. By the time we arrived in the shop, Papa was lying on the floor, badly beaten.'

Wolfe's eyes turned hard. 'Is Papa okay?' he asked softly cuddling her to him.

'They took him in an ambulance to the London Hospital, told us to wait while they tended to him. Mama asked for you and Asher, so I left Sarah with her and came straight here.'

He kissed the top of her head. 'Wait downstairs, I'll get Asher.'

Arriving at the hospital, they found Sarah and Mrs Goldberg, looking distraught, sitting by the bed where Solomon lie eyes closed, white-faced and head bandaged, left arm and leg tied in a splint.

Wolfe knelt beside his mother-in-law, placing an arm around her and kissing her cheek. 'Mama, do you know who did this?' he whispered.

She shook her head, tears welling up in her eyes. 'I don't know.' She looked at Wolfe. 'Who would want to do this to him? He is a kind and gentle man.'

Asher walked back into the ward after speaking to the doctor and gestured with a movement of his head for Wolfe to join him.

Patting his mother-in-law's shoulder as he stood, Wolfe moved across the ward to his brother whose face showed his anger.

'I've spoken to the doctor,' said Asher. 'Whoever it was really beat him up. Papa has a broken arm, cracked ribs, concussion, and they broke his left leg so badly that they might have to amputate. They've drugged him to numb the pain. If I find out who did—'

'We will,' Wolfe interrupted, looking towards his father-in-law, 'and when we do,' he said with venom, 'they'll wish they had never been born.'

*

Three weeks had passed since the attack. Thankfully the doctors had managed to save the leg, but Solomon would have a limp and use a cane to walk. His arm was still in a splint but he could use the fingers. The scar on his forehead was a little red but had nearly healed. While he was in hospital, Eva and Sarah had taken over the running of the bakery. He had taught them well. Solomon had been flooded with get-well-soon letters, as well as gifts of food from customers.

Wolfe and Asher had not bothered him about the attack, but felt that it was now time he told them about it, so while the women were busy in the bakery they visited him.

The boys hugged their father-in-law. 'You look a lot better, Papa, how is the arm?' Asher asked.

'It's good, and I'm not in as much pain as I was.'

Wolf leaned close, saying quietly, 'Papa, do you know who did this to you?'

He nodded, but stayed silent.

'Papa, if you know who it is why won't you tell us?' Asher asked.

Solomon looked from one to the other. 'They could come back and hurt Mama and the girls.'

'I can assure you, Papa,' Wolfe said forcefully, 'they will never ever bother you or our family again.'

'What do you intend to do?'

The brothers could see that Solomon was frightened. Wolfe patted his hand. 'All we want to do is talk to them.'

'Talk – I can assure you, they are not the talking type. More ...' His voice trailed off. 'These are dangerous people – you could get badly hurt, and then what will happen to the family?'

'Let us be the judge of that,' Asher leaned closer. 'Papa, I'm begging you, tell us.'

Solomon let out a long sigh. 'Okay. A month before the attack, I'm just about to close and four men, big men, walked in. I asked them what they would like. At first they didn't answer. It was scary. Then one of them said in an Irish accent, 'We are here to offer you protection.'

'I asked him what he means by protection. One of the men picked up a cake and began eating it and the other two did the same. I asked them to pay for the cakes, but they say nothing, just smiled. The one doing the talking said, 'We can protect you from people stealing your cakes,' he looked at the till, 'or robbing you.'

'I tell him that I have left a country with men much scarier than him. I'm not going to pay for protection. I don't need it. Maybe I should have paid, but then what's to stop them demanding more and more money?'

Wolfe and Asher's wives were asleep when just after midnight the brothers met, and side by side walked purposefully towards the Irish area of Poplar.

Reaching the end of Crisp Street, just before East India Dock Road, they were confronted by four men, cloth caps lopsided on their curly-haired heads, open-necked shirts with braces and belts holding up their baggy trousers. One of the four stepped slightly ahead of the others.

'To be sure it's Jews. What are you doing walking around here at this time of night?'

Asher, his face a grim mask, gripped the handle of the pistol in his pocket, finger resting gently on the trigger as Wolfe replied harshly, 'We're looking for four men who attacked our father-in-law at his baker shop and stole his money.'

'Are you now?' The eyes narrowed. 'Do you know who these men are?'

'No,' Asher replied.

The men laughed, stopping when their spokesman waved a hand. They walked forward to stand face to face with the brothers. 'They say we're stupid,' said the spokesman, his voice mocking, 'But you have got to be the stupidest Jews I have ever come across. If you don't know who they are, how are you going to find them?'

As quick as a flash, surprising the man, Wolfe slammed a fist against his jaw. As he fell to the ground, Wolfe drew the sabre from the scabbard, holding the point at the man's throat. The others started to move forward, but were stopped by the menacing voice of Asher.

'I wouldn't if I were you.' They looked in his direction to see a pistol pointing at them.

'Well, that was easy,' Wolfe said, looking down at the man on the ground. 'You are going to tell us what we want to know.'

'You're crazy.'

Wolfe looked quickly at his brother then down at the Irishman. 'Did you hear that? He thinks I'm crazy!' As he said the word 'crazy', he flicked the blade and there was a yell from the man on the ground, who looked at the tear along his shirt: a trickle of blood oozing from it.

'Tell us what we want to know,' Asher demanded. 'Some of your people offered protection to our father-in-law and when he refused they came back and beat him up. Now—'

'We want to know what sort of cowards you Irish are,' Wolfe interrupted, 'that it takes four of you to beat up a defenceless old man.'

The Irishmen reacted instantly, fists clenched, bodies hunched forward as though about to pounce.

'I'm not an old man,' Asher smiled. 'Please keep coming, I do have six bullets, and without bragging, I'm a pretty good shot.'

'We asked you a question,' Wolfe moved forward. 'I am going to kill one of you if by the count of ten I don't get an answer.' He looked at them, then at the man at his feet. 'Get up and move over to your friends.'

As the man started to get to his feet, he lunged at Wolfe, who sidestepped him, slamming the hilt of the sword into his face, opening the skin. As the Irishman fell back to the ground, he stamped on his knee, the crack of bone and scream that followed breaking the silence of the night.

'Shut up or I'll shut you up for good.'

The man lay on his back quietly moaning, hatred in his eyes.

Asher began counting. 'One–two–three–four–five—'

'Okay, okay, I'll tell you,' said the spokesman, face white with pain.

'Don't, Jimmy,' yelled one of the men.

Jimmy hesitated for a second, looking up at Wolfe. 'What if we take you to them?' He gave a lopsided grin and sneered, 'We might be able to pay you back for this.' He pointed to his knee.

Asher waved the pistol at the men. 'Pick up your friend, and lead the way.'

'I need to get to a hospital,' said Jimmy.

'If you like, I can put you out of your misery,' Asher replied.

Carrying their injured colleague with the brothers trailing warily behind, the group came to a stop outside a detached house set slightly back from the road. A man with a rifle in his hands stepped out of the shadows, stopping them from going any further. Jimmy, who was the spokesman, jerked a thumb towards Wolfe and Asher.

'These Jew-boys want to see Billy.'

'Wait here.' The man turned and disappeared inside the house, returning five minutes later and beckoning them in with his hand. At the door to the house, the brothers were relieved of their weapons and the man with the rifle led them along a dimly lit hallway.

Wolfe glanced quickly through an open door to his left. Four men were playing cards; one looked round for a second then back at his hand. They stopped at a door on their right. The man knocked and a spy-hole opened.

'I have the Jews here.'

The door opened, the guard stepped to one side, allowing them to enter. Smoke floated up to the already blackened ceiling, forming a smoggy haze. The bare floorboards creaked as they followed the man towards a billiard table at the end of the room. To their right were a couple of roulette tables. One of the billiard players had just taken a shot, potting the red ball. He turned to look at them, straightened up and smiled, but not with the eyes. He held up the palm of his hand towards the wall as two men, who had been watching the game, walked slowly forward coming to a halt on seeing the hand movement.

'Do you play, Jew-boys?'

The brothers were silent until they stood within arm's length of the man called Billy. Wolfe looked into blue eyes that stared unflinchingly back. Billy's smile left his face, seeing the hatred in Wolfe's eyes.

'I asked you, Jew-boys, if you play. As you are in my house, have the courtesy to answer.'

'As a matter of fact, no,' Wolfe replied, 'but that's not why we are here.'

There was a strange silence in the room, the atmosphere electric, as if in a second the room would erupt like a volcano. Wolfe looked at the man who was a foot taller than him, back straight, feet slightly apart, balanced like a dancer. His red curly hair covered both ears and the starched open collar of his pale blue shirt, the sleeves rolled up to his forearms. The blue waistcoat fitted him perfectly, tapering down to his slim waist.

'So, why are you here?' he turned slightly, still looking at Wolfe as he picked up a packet of cigarettes, opened it offering the packet to the brothers, who took one.

'Thanks.' Wolfe lit a match and with a steady hand held out the flame. The Irishman looked up at him as he puffed the cigarette alight, exhaling the smoke through his nostrils, then moved to the end of the table, chalked the cue bent to take the shot, sliding the cue smoothly through the V of his left hand.

'You injured one of my men, he's my cousin.' He hit the white. It ran along the table, hitting the red ball and the other white.

Two men pushed away from the wall they were leaning on and moved towards Wolfe who briefly looked in their direction.

'If those two don't go back to their kennel, they'll end up with your cousin.'

One of the men took no notice of his boss and confronted Wolfe, who unexpectedly snatched the cue, held by Billy's opponent and smashed the thick end across his face. The Irishman's hands went to his bloody nose and Wolfe kicked him in the groin. Asher moved quickly with his back to his brothers as four men walked towards them.

'Get back,' Reid ordered harshly and without waiting to see if they had obeying him, turned to Wolfe. 'I'm sorry about that; we'll talk after my game.'

'No,' Asher said, body bent slightly. 'We talk now.'

The Irishman's face showed his anger at being spoken to this way, his clenched fists white around the cue. 'You're pushing it, Jew,' he said sternly.

Wolfe took Asher's arm and whispered, 'Thanks. Calm down and leave this to me.' He let go his brother's arm, turning to face the Irishman, his face hard, voice like steel. 'You,' he prodded a finger in the Irishman's direction, 'or some of your men, beat up our father-in-law and stole his money.' He moved menacingly forward. 'I'm in no mood to pussyfoot around with you, so this is why we are here. If it was you, then it's a fight between you and me. If we have made a mistake, I'm sorry and need your help to find the men that did it.'

Billy's face turned, hard eyes glaring at Wolfe, 'I do not beat up old defenceless men – maybe a thief at times, yes. Where did this happen?'

'It was the Jewish baker in Brick Lane.'

'What? No one I know would hurt him. He always gave what bread he has unsold at the end of the day to poor people, no matter who they are.' He slammed the cue across the table, breaking it as he yelled, 'Shamus!'

The door to the room opened and the man with the rifle ran in. 'Yes, boss?'

'Do you know anything about an attack by the Irish on the Jew baker in Brick Lane?'

Shamus didn't say anything for a second, looking away from his boss's gaze as he answered, 'No, Billy.'

In three strides Billy was in front of him, grabbing the front of his shirt lifting him off the ground. 'I know that look, Shamus; you know something. Were you involved?'

Shamus shook his head. 'No, Billy.'

'But you know who did it?'

Shamus nodded.

There was angry impatience in Billy's voice and on his face. 'Spit it out – who?'

'The O'Sullivan brothers,' was the muted reply.

Billy let go the shirt and Shamus dropped to the floor. He turned to Wolfe. 'They are nothing to do with me. I'm sorry about your father-in-law. If there is anything I can—'

'Yes, there is,' Wolfe interrupted, moving forward and holding out his hand. 'But first, I apologise. My name is Wolfe Brown.' He gestured towards his brother. 'Asher.'

The Irishman took the offered hand. 'Billy Reid.' He moved across to shake Asher's hand.

'We are sorry about the accusation, and barging in like this,' said Asher.

'I could have had you killed,' Billy snapped his fingers, 'just like that.'

A big grin broke across Wolfe's face. 'I don't think so. You're intrigued by two very angry Jews entering your domain, especially after—' he pointed to Asher and himself '—we were outnumbered and injured one of your men.'

'You're quite the philosopher. Did you mean what you said about a fight between us?'

'If that's what you want, but it will have to wait. Can you tell me where we can find these O'Sullivan brothers? Once we have dealt with them,' he went into a boxer's stance, 'then we can.'

Reid pursed his lips, eyes half-closed, 'Maybe.' He turned and walked over to a table with bottles of drink, saying over his shoulder, 'Drink.'

'I'm sorry, Billy, I don't want to be rude, but can we have that drink another time? We need to find these brothers and get back to our wives before they wake up.'

'You could wait till tomorrow,' said Billy.

'That wouldn't be a good idea,' Asher replied. 'The O'Sullivans could receive information that we are looking for them.'

Reid moved forward a couple of pace towards Asher.

'Are you insinuating that one of my men...?'

'Shamus knows about the attack. How is it that you didn't?' Asher said grimly.

Reid turned to Shamus. 'Why didn't you tell me? That man gave your mother bread when you never had a penny and you betrayed me and him.'

He stepped forward and grabbed the rifle from him, smashing the butt into Shamus's stomach. As he doubled over, Billy shifted the butt upward to the hapless Shamus's jaw and he collapsed to the ground.

His boss bent over him. 'You're lucky I don't kill you, I trusted you.' He straightened, angry eyes resting for a second on each of his men. 'The only way we can survive is to trust each other. You never bite the hand that feeds you. The Jew baker's kindness has been betrayed by Irishmen and it leaves a bitter taste in my mouth. We're thieves, and at times when need be, killers, but we never beat up a defenceless man.' He pointed to the man on the floor. 'If any of you feel that I am not worthy of being the boss, then step forward.'

The men were silent, some shuffling their feet in embarrassment.

Billy clapped his hands, 'Okay, that's settled.' He turned to the brothers who were looking down at Shamus. 'I've been wondering for a while about him, and until now couldn't put my finger on it, just a gut feeling.' He pulled a cigarette from the pack, offering it to the brothers who shook their heads. Billy lit the cigarette and blew out the smoke. 'Right, let's take you to the O'Sullivan brothers.'

'It's not your fight,' said Wolfe.

'We need to do this for ourselves,' Asher added.

'Okay, but we will be close by if you need us.'

'We appreciate that, Billy, but we won't need help.'

The Irishman laughed. 'You don't know the O'Sullivans.'

'They don't know us, but they soon will,' Wolfe said grimly.

'Okay, we'll show you where they are. You might need these.' He handed them back their weapons.

The brothers followed the Irishman along unfamiliar cobbled streets where people were still walking about. Whenever they crossed their paths, they moved back to allow Billy and the men through, always with a nod and a smile. Wolfe liked the Irishman. He had the respect of his men and, it seemed, the people. When this was over, he would like to know more about Billy Reid.

They came to a stop opposite a pub. The brothers moved to stand either side of him.

'That's where the O'Sullivan's are.' He looked at Wolfe. 'Your argument is with them, not the people with them. My men are going inside to persuade the others to leave and then you're on your own.' He pointed to four of the men who moved across the street and entered the pub. Within minutes people were exiting the building, Reid's men being the last to leave.

'Good luck,' Billy said. 'You're going to need it.'

*

The brothers walked across the road and entered the pub, coming to a stop just inside the door. There was a strong smell of beer, unwashed bodies, cigarette and pipe smoke that swirled around the room like fog. Four men sitting at the bar looked towards the door as they entered.

Wolfe stared at the men who were like clones of each other, unshaven with black wavy hair and small beady eyes. One of them slid off the stool, standing just less than six foot tall, broad-shouldered, barrel chest, his pale blue shirt open at the neck to reveal a hairy chest, the sleeves rolled up. He walked slowly towards Wolfe and Asher who had moved slightly apart.

The Irishman stopped in front of Wolfe. 'What are you Jew-boys doing here?' He waved a hand. 'Piss off, or—'

Wolfe slapped him once, very hard across the face. The man reeled back, stunned and silent. His brothers went to move off their seats.

'You'd better stay where you are,' Asher said icily, the pistol in his hand pointing at them.

The Irishman leapt the short distance towards Wolfe, his face red with anger, and didn't see the left fist that smashed into the side of his jaw and stopped him in his tracks. The next punch landed him on his back. The man on the floor tried to get to his feet but Wolfe kicked him in the face, breaking his nose.

One of the Irish brothers jumped off his stool, swearing and cursing. Wolfe smiled coldly, glancing at the one on the floor, and then turned his attention to his angry companion, who was no match for him. Wolfe easily dodged the blow aimed at his head, knocking the Irishman to the ground.

'Get back on to your stool,' said Asher as the Irishman got to his feet, pointing to the one on the floor holding his broken bleeding nose, 'and take him with you.'

There was hatred in the four men's eyes as they sat facing Asher and Wolfe who said coldly, 'I'm sure you want to know the reason we are here?' He stabbed a finger at them, 'You,' his voice like steel was deliberately slow and paced, 'beat up a defenceless man, our father-in-law, and stole his money.' He pointed to Asher and himself. 'We are his protection, and are not defenceless, unlike the kind, gentle and generous man you put in hospital.'

'Stand up, put your hands behind your head,' Asher ordered, waving the pistol at them as Wolfe moved quickly to the one with the broken nose who snarled at him, showing cigarette-stained teeth.

Wolfe opened the man's jacket, taking a pistol tucked into the waistband of his trousers, patted him down and found a knife tucked in his boot. One by one he searched the O'Sullivans, throwing a variety of weapons out into the street, and then stood beside Asher not taking his eyes off the Irishmen as he unbuckled the sabre belt from around his waist placing it on a table behind him, and then he took off his coat, folding it across the back of a chair and rolled up his sleeves. Asher handed him the pistol. The four men leaned forward as though they were about to rush them.

A grim smile crossed Wolfe's face, the pistol steady in his hand. 'Please do – I'd like nothing better than to snuff you out like a candle, but we—' he gestured to Asher who had taken off his jacket '—really don't want to do that.'

Asher moved slightly apart from Wolfe, who carried on speaking. 'Unlike the cowards you are, we are giving you a chance to fight us with these.' He waved his fists.

The Irishmen burst into laughter. 'Are you serious?' said Broken Nose with a sneer.

Asher's mouth was set in an angry line at their laughter, 'Deadly serious.'

'You have a gun.'

Wolfe moved to the door and threw the gun into the street, eyes still on the Irishmen. 'Now we don't.'

As one, the four men rushed Wolfe and Asher stepped back to the wall and met the onslaught. The months of work in the gym had paid off, and although some punches and kicks got through, the Irishmen came off worse. Two lay senseless on the floor. Broken Nose rushed Wolfe, and blood again streamed from his nose and mouth where two front teeth were missing. Wolfe met the rush with a flurry of calculated blows, dropping the man to the ground.

Asher moved quickly forward, planting a fist into the stomach of his opponent who dropped his guard, feeling the full force of Asher's fist on his chin flying backward onto the floor. Asher strode over to the man, stamped on his leg and broke it. 'This is for my father-in-law.' He stamped on the other leg and there was again the sound of breaking bone. The Irishman opened his mouth to scream, eyes wide with fear, as Asher dropped the full force of his body onto his ribs, his screams filled the room.

'Painful, isn't it,' said Asher.

Wolfe looked down at Broken Nose as a picture of Solomon lying in a hospital bed came into his mind and a rage engulfed him. He grabbed the front of the Irishman's shirt, lifting him onto his feet, slamming him against the wall. Letting go the shirt, he landed a rain of blows on the big Irishman's face and body, the ferocity of the attack breaking his jaw, cheekbone and ribs. As Broken Nose fell senseless to the floor, Wolfe, still in a blind rage, stamped on his knee and hand, breaking both. Someone pulled him away. He tried to resist as a soft voice said, 'That's enough – stop, before you kill the man.'

Gradually the rage within him died down and he looked at Billy Reid. 'Thanks.' He shook his head, saying in a whisper, 'I have never lost my temper like that before.'

Billy didn't reply as he looked at the O'Sullivans, then at Wolfe and Asher with respect in his eyes. Placing a hand on Wolfe's shoulder, he said, 'I won't be a moment.'

Billy walked towards Broken Nose kneeling beside him, and whispered in his ear, 'Patrick, you and your brothers leave the Jew-boys alone. If you see them walking towards you, cross the road. Do I make myself clear?'

Patrick gave a slight nod in reply, unable to speak through his broken jaw.

Billy patted him on the shoulder. 'Good, my men will take you to the hospital. You're lucky. If it had been up to me, I'd have killed you.'

Fear showed in Patrick O'Sullivan's eyes. Billy got to his feet and walked back to Wolfe. 'You had better come back to my place and clean up. You can't go home looking like that.'

Wolfe looked down at his shirt – it was covered in blood, not his, and then across at Asher, who smiled at him. 'Billy I appreciate the gesture, and we accept. You better be careful or your men will think you're going soft.'

Billy smiled, 'A Jew with a sense of humour – what next? By the way, have you ever heard of the rhyme, 'Who's Afraid of the Big Bad Wolf?'

'No, I haven't.'

'In your case, I think maybe 'Be Very Afraid of the Big Bad Wolf' would be more appropriate.'

One of his men handed Wolfe his sabre.

The night sky was fading and the moon gradually disappearing as Wolfe and Asher entered their houses, and without disturbing their wives, got into bed, both falling into exhausted sleep.

5   Billy Reid's Story

Billy Reid looked with loving eyes at his young daughter April, asleep in her cot, his thoughts on the Jewish brothers, especially Wolfe. It wasn't often that the twenty-seven-year-old took an instant liking to someone. He gave a slight nod; there was a confident air about the Jew, and he could certainly fight. It took guts – or was it brashness? – for the brothers to confront him the way they did. Placing a finger to his lips he gently touched his daughter's cheek, left the room and walked to the bedroom next door. For a moment he stood in the doorway looking at the empty double bed, and sadness swept over him. His wife Nancy had died giving birth to his daughter in April, hence her name.

Billy Reid was born on 17 October 1881 in Kilkenny, Ireland, the second eldest of six brothers and one sister. He left home when he was fifteen after knocking out his drunken father, who had been beating his ten-year-old sister Megan, and enlisted in the British Army. Billy, tall and well built, told the enlisting officer that he was nearly seventeen.

It was during his training that a Corporal Healy, nicknamed Bull, a huge man standing six foot three, shoulders as broad as barn doors, with tree trunks for legs and rocks for biceps, took an interest in Billy.

They were on the parade ground when Healy stood in front of Billy inspecting his turnout when he asked in his cockney accent, 'Private, do you box?'

'No, Corporal.'

Healy didn't say anything else, moving on to the next man.

That evening, Billy was resting on his bed when an unmistakable voice yelled, 'Reid, out here, on the double.'

Billy leapt from the bed and started to put on his uniform. 'Leave it,' Healy yelled.

Once outside, the corporal said softly, 'Follow me.' He turned and Billy, wondering what this was all about followed Healy, who came to a stop by some trees, turning to face Billy.

'Stand at ease.' He looked at Billy for a moment, and then in a low serious voice began talking. 'I think you can be a very good boxer, and—'

'I have never—' Billy began to interrupt.

'I know you have never boxed before, but have you ever been in a fight?'

In his mind's eye he saw himself knocking his father down as he answered, 'Yes.'

A smile broadened on Bull's face. 'There is something about you, Private Reid that makes me think you are going to be a good soldier and boxer.'

*

Two years after that meeting, Corporal Healy, now a sergeant, and the newly promoted Corporal Reid were friends and Billy the regiment's boxing champion.

Since joining the army Billy had written to his sister, but never received a reply. With two weeks leave before his regiment sailed for South Africa, he returned to Ireland to find out why Megan hadn't written back. On arriving home, he found the place deserted. A neighbour told him that his father had been killed in a drunken brawl and the children taken away. After three days of searching he found Megan in an orphanage. When she saw him Megan began to cry, her thin body shaking with her sobs. Without a word Billy picked her up in his arms and carried her to their old house. One week later they were in London.

Being a drill sergeant, Healy lived with his wife Margaret in married quarters. Mrs Healy offered to look after Megan while Billy and her husband were in South Africa. Megan would receive half his army pay, and was named next of kin. Bull was also happy with the arrangements, knowing that his wife would have company while he was away as they had no children.

With the influx of foreigners into South Africa, mostly from England, tension had escalated to a national level for control of the gold mining industry in the Transvaal by the British, which would mean loss of independence of the Transvaal for the Boers. Negotiations failed and in September 1899 the Boers sent an ultimatum to the British to leave within forty-eight hours.

Two days later, the ultimatum having proved ineffectual, the Second Boer War broke out, the Boers attacking British garrisons at Ladysmith, Mafeking and Kimberly and winning a series of tactical victories against the British offensive to relieve the besieged garrisons.

With the arrival of more troops in 1900, Billy and Bull amongst them, the garrisons were successfully defended and the British army moved on to capture the Transvaal and the Republic's capital,

Pretoria. During the battle, in which Bull was fatally wounded, Billy held him close, comforting him in his last minutes. Angry at the loss of his friend and mentor, Billy attacked the Boers with a ferocity bordering on madness: killing six men with a machine gun, and killing one with his fists, having to be dragged from the man by his comrades.

Billy was sitting on the ground, wondering what he was going to say to Bull's wife. As he picked up a stone to throw it, he noticed that it glittered in the sunlight. He looked closely at the stone, realising it was a diamond. He didn't move, feeling the ground around him and finding two more. On returning to his tent, he secreted them amongst his belongings.

*

Back in England in the August of 1903, Billy discovered that Margaret Healy had died of 'flu, and her quarters occupied by someone else. The money he had sent to Megan had not been collected for five months. Someone told him that his sister left a month before Mrs Healy died after an incident, but didn't know what it was about. She did say she saw Megan begging near Hyde Park.

The woman was right. After days searching around the park, he found Megan begging. She was also pregnant. She collapsed on the floor on seeing him. He bent, placing his hands on her shoulders.

'Please, Megan, get up.'

She shook her head, saying over and over, 'Oh! Billy, please forgive me.'

Eventually she was quiet; all cried out, and with her brother's help, got to her feet. He hailed a passing cab.

'Bridge Hotel,' he ordered, ignoring the cabbies knowing smile. As the cab set off Billy took Megan's hand, saying softly, 'What happened? Why did you leave? Who's the father?'

Megan shrunk into the corner of her seat, looking down at the floor. 'I was raped,' she whispered. 'I didn't want to bring any shame on Margaret, even though she insisted I stay.' She looked up, tears streaming down her face, 'Who would believe me against him?'

'Who is he?' Adding softly, 'You know Mrs Healy died?'

She stared at him, a look of disbelief on her face. 'How? When? Sergeant Healy must be devastated.'

'Bull was killed in Pretoria. Mrs Healy caught the 'flu just after you left, and died.'

She began to cry again. 'I should have stayed, I could have nursed her.'
'Megan, tell me who raped you.'
'I can't say.'
'Megan,' he looked her in the eyes, saying forcefully between clenched teeth, 'You must tell me, knowing he's got away with it, he will do it again. You must stop him.' He took her hand, making her look at him. 'Tell me.'
'Captain Jennings.'
Installing his sister in a room at the hotel and telling her to rest as he had to go out, Billy returned to barracks to change. Thirty minutes later, in dress uniform, medals on display, he marched to the rear of the officer's mess in search of the mess-sergeant.
'Afternoon, Fred, is Captain Jennings in the mess?'
'Aye, Billy, he's at the bar.'
'Thanks.' He moved past the sergeant and marched into the officers' mess, his eyes coming to rest on the captain seated at the bar, smoking a cigar. Without hesitation he marched smartly up to him, his face an angry mask of hatred.
The captain looked at Billy, surprise on his face. 'Sergeant, this is the officers mess, get out.'
Billy looked at the officers around the mess: some were still in their seats, others had got to their feet, including the colonel who was about to confront him.
'Gentlemen,' he pointed at Jennings. 'This officer raped my seventeen-year-old sister, and now she is pregnant.'
'He's crazy!' Jennings got to his feet, 'I never—'
'You're a liar and a coward,' he spat the words out like bullets.
'I told you—'
Billy interrupted again. 'Will you do the right thing as a supposed officer and gentleman? If not ...' Billy left the rest unsaid as he took a step forward.
'I'll have you arrested for—'
Jennings got no further as Billy punched him in the mouth. 'You're a liar!' He punched him on the nose. As blood poured from the officer's nose, he landed a punch to the groin. 'You won't be able to use that for a while—' He punched him again in the same area. Jennings doubled over and Billy upper-cut him. 'Or tell any lies.'
He didn't resist as the officers grabbed him, but bent and spat in Jennings's face. 'You're lucky I didn't kill you.'
At Billy's court martial, Megan told the court what Jennings had done to her. Although the court was sympathetic, Billy had assaulted

an officer and was dishonourably discharged without a custodial sentence. Jennings, meanwhile, was stripped of his commission.

*

On 6 January 1904, Megan gave birth to a little boy, giving him Corporal Healy's name, John.

After his discharge from the army, Billy rented a three-bedroom house in the Irish part of Poplar, while trying to figure out what to do next. All he had known was the army, and how to box. He and Bull had talked about opening a tavern and had saved a tidy sum from betting on the outcome of Billy's fights. With the death of Bull and of his wife, that money was now his. He didn't fancy opening a tavern on his own, and out of boredom he began playing cards.

In late September 1905 two things happened to change his life. He was in the pub sharing a table with a slim, bearded man with laughter lines at the corner of his eyes. Looking sadly down at the beer glass, for the umpteenth time the man let out a sigh, picked up the glass and took a long drink, then placed it back on the table.

Billy's curiosity got the better of him. 'You look like someone who has all the cares of the world on his shoulders. Perhaps you'd like to tell me about it.'

The man looked up.

'It might make you feel better sharing the problem.'

'Well, I'm a photographer.' He leaned forward, elbows on the table, hands cupped around the beer glass. 'I was taking some photos of the butcher, Mr Weiner, and his family outside his shop in Commercial Road. A horse was spooked by a dog and bolted. I just manage to get out of the way, but my camera was trampled on by the horse.' He took a long drink, nearly emptying the glass, looking sadly at Billy. 'I haven't enough money to buy another camera.'

Billy felt sorry for the man, pointing at his glass. 'Another?'

'Thanks.' The man handed his glass to Billy, moved quickly to the bar, returning minutes later to place the pint of beer in front of the man, then moved to his seat. 'Mr—'

'Brian Fairlop,' he held out his hand.

Billy took the slim-fingered hand, looking into Fairlop's light-blue eyes, 'Billy Reid,' and released the hand. 'I can lend you the money for a new camera.'

'What?' There was disbelief on Fairlop's face. 'You don't know me from—'

'You look like an honest man.'

'No, I cannot accept such generosity.'
'I want to lend you the money, so why can't you accept it?'
'I'm a total stranger to you. You don't know anything about me.'
Billy leaned back in the chair, took a cigarette packet from his pocket. 'Tell me about yourself.' He opened the packet and offered one to Fairlop.
'I'm twenty-two, unmarried, originally from Gillingham in Kent. From the very first time I saw a photograph, all I have ever wanted to do is to take photos. I've worked at all sorts of jobs to earn money to buy that camera. As soon as I bought it, I moved to London. I share a room with four other men in Waterman way, Wapping. Up till now I've made modest living selling pictures to the newspapers, wedding photos.' He rimmed the glass with a finger and shrugged his shoulders. 'That's about it.'
'Brian, it's your living, and something you enjoy, let me lend you the money.'
Fairlop shook his head, put out the cigarette in the full ashtray in the centre of the table and took a drink. 'The camera I need costs a £100, it's a Sanderson Field camera 15 by 12 inches with a Zeiss Prortar lens and ...' His voice trailed off. 'You have no idea what I'm talking about?'
Billy lifted the glass to his lips, looking over the rim at the man opposite and without drinking, moved the glass away from his mouth. 'Would you be happy if I lent you the money, and you pay me back a certain amount every week with, say, two per cent interest on the loan. Would you feel happier doing that?'
Fairlop's smile told Billy the answer. 'Thank you.' The smile left his face adding, 'It's a business loan.'
'Okay, I'll write out something which you can sign and will keep a check of your payments.' He wrote down his address. 'Be here tomorrow at seven o'clock. See you tomorrow.'
As he left the pub, Billy bumped into a young woman, knocking her onto the muddy street, spilling the contents of her bag. 'Oh I'm so sorry,' he said.
'Sorry! You, you blithering idiot, why don't you look where you're going?' She rose to her feet, looking down at her clothes. 'Ugh, look at my coat, you big oaf. She tried to brush it with her hand, not realising they were muddy and making things worse.
'Can I do anything to help?' he asked quietly.
She stared at him in disbelief, a curl of auburn hair falling over her right eye. 'Help, you moron? How are you going to help?'

He wanted to burst out laughing at the situation, but turned his head away for a second so she didn't see the smile and looked serious again as he turned to face her. 'Can I compensate you for the damage, perhaps …?'

His voice trailed off, struck by her beauty, the grey eyes showing their anger, her mouth, which he wanted to kiss, in a straight line, saying between clenched teeth pointing to the overturned basket, its contents covered by mud, 'That's my mother's and my dinner and groceries for the next two days, my coat and dress ruined, and all you want to do is give me money.'

She bent, scooped up the muddy groceries into the bag, and began to walk away, but quick as a flash, Billy was in front of her.

'Please let me help you – the least I can do is take you to dinner.'

She leaned towards him, her face close to his. 'Are you crazy? Look at me, how would I, in this state, be able to go to dinner?'

He leaned forward and was about to kiss her, but pulled away. 'I'm so sorry, my name is Billy Reid.'

For the first time since the incident she smiled, and it was as though the sun had appeared. 'Nancy Johnson.'

He bowed, looked up at her muddy hand and kissed the back of it, saying, 'It's a pleasure to meet you.' He looked quickly at her fingers. 'Miss Johnson, for the inconvenience I've caused, please let me take you home in a taxi.' He held his breath, waiting for the answer.

She looked down at her dress. He is so handsome, she thought, and that cheeky smile. Her heart skipped a beat as she looked at him. 'That will be nice, thank you.' She wagged a finger at him. 'But Mr Reid, you still owe me.'

A big grin appeared on his face as he took the bag and whistled for a cab, asking her, 'Where to?'

The cab pulled up beside them. '24 Sidney Street, please,' she told the cabbie.

Billy turned sideways in the seat. 'Miss Johnson, will you do me the honour of dining with me tonight?' Before she could reply he added, 'It's the least I can do for spoiling your dinner.'

'It was my mother's too.'

'She can come as well.' He could have bitten his tongue, thinking, I'm so impulsive, but the smile she gave him, the touch of her hand on his arm, sent tingles up his spine.

'Why, Mr Reid, that's a very generous offer, and on behalf of my mother, we accept.' She could see it was a spur of the moment thing, but for some unknown reason she wanted her mother to meet Mr Reid.

'Can we forgo the formalities of second names, please?'

'Yes, Billy, that will be fine.'

Billy asked the cab to wait as he escorted Nancy to the front door.

'Is eight o'clock okay?'

'That will be okay.'

He handed her the bag, 'See you at eight.' He tried not to skip back to the cab, turned before entering, but she had disappeared inside the house.

*

On the dot of eight, a bunch of flowers in his hand, Billy knocked on the door. He heard footsteps approaching; the door opened and once again he was taken aback by Nancy's beauty and knew he was in love.

'You are punctual, that's nice.' She stepped aside. 'Please come in.' He moved into the hall, waited for her to close the door before handing her the flowers.

'Thank you, they are beautiful.' She moved past him and he followed her into a room at the far end of a short hallway. Nancy moved to stand beside Billy as she introduced him.

'Mama, this is Mr Reid.'

Mrs Johnson's grey hair was tied in a bun; her eyes, the same colour as her daughter's, had a tired, pained look to them as she smiled and patted the chair with a gnarled arthritic hand next to hers. 'Please sit here.'

'But mother, we—'

'I'm sure we have a little time before we dine,' she interrupted, looking at Billy.

He smiled, knowing that Mrs Johnson wanted to know all about the man taking them to dinner.

'I'll put these in water.' Nancy turned, hoping her mother didn't embarrass her.

Billy looked at the paintings around the wall and on the mantle. Most were of ships; there was one of Nancy as a young girl; another of a sailor, his weather-beaten face smiling at something or someone beyond the artist. Billy took the seat next to Mrs Johnson, noticing that her clothes, although slightly threadbare, were clean.

'Can I offer you a drink? I must confess we haven't much for a man.'

'No thank you, Mrs Johnson, I'm fine.' He could see she was studying him, looking intently at his face then towards the door and back to him.

'You have made quite an impression on my daughter. She hasn't stopped talking about you all afternoon, and I can see by the expression on your face when you look at her that—' She stopped and patted his arm. 'Enough of that, tell me about Mr Reid.'

Billy didn't want to talk about himself, so he pointed at the painting of the sailor. 'Is that Mr Johnson?'

She looked at the picture, replying lovingly, 'Yes, that's my husband, Captain Theodore Johnson.' Tears filled her eyes; she dabbed at them with a hankie taken from inside the cuff of her sleeve. 'He was lost at sea three years ago when his ship went down with all hands in a storm.'

'Oh, I'm so sorry; I didn't mean to upset you.'

Nancy entered the room to see her mother looking at the portrait of her father; she walked over and hugged her. 'Please, Mama.'

Billy could hear the concern in her voice. 'I think it's time to leave,' he said, trying to change the mood.

Nancy looked at him. 'Thanks,' she mouthed silently.

The dinner was a complete success, with Billy telling funny stories from his time in the army, Mrs Johnson revealing funny things about Nancy growing up and about how she knew the minute she saw Captain Johnson that she loved him.

Billy looked intently at Nancy. 'So, you believe in love at first sight, Mrs Johnson?'

'Yes, Billy, I do, and my husband felt the same way.' She looked at her daughter and Billy, who were silent, just looking at each other, and nodded her head knowingly.

*

The next day Billy called on Nancy. 'She's not here at the moment,' her mother said. 'Come in, she won't be long; Nancy has gone to the doctor to get my medicine.'

He followed her along the hall, seeing as he did last night how hard it was for her to walk. She asked, 'Would you like a cup of tea?'

'That would be nice.'

He followed her into the kitchen, 'Sit,' she ordered pointing to the chairs around a wooden table set in the middle of the kitchen.

He sat down. She lit the stove and put on the kettle, taking two cups and saucers from the cupboard as he asked, 'Can I help?'

'No, Billy, I have to do this.'

She poured the tea, and he got up from the chair taking the tea over to the table.

She sat on the seat to his right, took a sip of tea, and then said, 'Billy, do you love my daughter?'

He looked at her for a moment, cup in mid-air, eyes sparkling. 'Yes, Mrs Johnson, I love her, I have from the moment we met.'

'Then marry her.'

'What?' He stared at her, surprise on his face at her comment.

'Marry her now.' She touched his hand. 'I can see that you love each other. My biggest worry is what will happen to her when I die.'

'That's not going to—'

'I have just a few months. I can see you are a decent man and I know she will be loved and cared for.'

'Does she know?'

'No, and you mustn't tell her.' He could hear the panic in her voice.

He shook his head. 'I won't, but do you think that's fair on Nancy?'

'Please, Billy.'

He took her hand. 'I promise.'

Her face lit up into a beaming smile.

'What if she says no? We have only known each other a day.'

'My husband went to my father two hours after we met at a friend's wedding, took him a glass of brandy; asked if he could speak to him on a matter of great importance. They went into the garden where he asked for my hand. My father took an instant liking to him and said yes. We were married a month later. I assure you, Nancy will say yes.'

Just then, they heard the front door open and footsteps along the hallway. Nancy entered the kitchen stopping in mid-stride on seeing Billy.

'Hallo, Billy'.

He was about to reply when Mrs Johnson asked, 'Did you get the medicine?'

'Yes Mama.' She handed her the bottle.

'Why don't you take Billy into the dining room? It's more comfortable than in the kitchen. I'll take my medicine and join you.'

Billy looked at Mrs Johnson. She gave him a head movement as if to say 'Go.' He turned and followed Nancy across the hall to the dining room. Billy closed the door behind them. She turned, surprise on her face. 'Why are you—?'

'I need to ask you something.' He gestured towards a chair. 'Please sit down.'

She frowned, wondering what this was all about. As she settled on the seat he took her hand and knelt, looking sincerely into her eyes. 'Nancy Johnson, I love you. I have from the very second I met you. I know that this is sudden,' he swallowed nervously. 'Will you do me the honour of marrying me?'

She was silent, eyes wide in astonishment. She was about to speak but he said quickly, 'I know I should have bought a ring, but – we can choose one together. Oh! I'm sure your mama would like to come to.'

'Yes, Billy I will marry you, but—'

The door opened and Mrs Johnson entered to see Billy on one knee and to hear her daughter say 'but'.

'What is 'but'?' she looked at her daughter, saying softly, 'Nancy there is no but, especially if you love this man.'

'What about you, Mama, who will look after you?'

Billy got to his feet, still holding Nancy's hand. 'Your Mama can live with us.'

'Is your house big enough?' Nancy asked.

'I'm sure we can manage,' he replied.

'Why not live here? You and Billy can have my bedroom. All you need is a double bed.'

'Mama,' Nancy said in a shocked voice.

'Well, that's settled.'

That afternoon the three of them set out to choose a ring. After that they went for a celebratory dinner and began planning the wedding. It had been such a busy and exciting day that Billy nearly forgot about Brian Fairlop. It was only when he glanced at the clock on the mantle that he remembered their appointment.

'I'm sorry, but I have to leave now, I have a meeting at seven.' He kissed his future mother-in-law on the cheek. 'I'll return tomorrow morning.'

At the door, he kissed Nancy for the first time. It took all his will power to leave her, but very soon they would be together forever.

On entering the house, Billy heard voices coming from the kitchen and opened the door to see a smiling Megan and Fairlop, who had a spoon poised in mid-air about to feed the baby sitting on Megan's lap.

'Sorry I'm late, but …' he hesitated. Would they laugh when he told them…? 'I'm getting married.'

There was a shocked silence for a second and then Megan plonked the baby in Fairlop's arms and leapt from her chair, asking question after question as she moved quickly across the kitchen.

'Who is she? Where did you meet her? Is she Irish? When are you getting married?' She wrapped her arms around his neck. 'That's wonderful.'

Billy gently took her arms from around his neck. 'I have some business with Mr Fairlop, and then I'll explain it to you.'

Megan looked at Fairlop, 'I'm sure, Brian won't mind waiting.'

'Megan's right, it can wait a while.'

'Okay, but I need a cup of tea first.'

'I'll make it while you tell us about your future bride, is she the one you—'

'Tea, woman, and let me tell you.'

He sat at the table opposite Fairlop and began with their first meeting ending. 'So that's it. You will be meeting Nancy and her mother tomorrow as they're coming here.'

'That's so romantic,' Megan sighed. 'It's like a fairy story.'

Billy stood up. 'Mr Fairlop, we can take our business into the dining room.'

'I know all about the loan, you might as well stay here,' Megan said as she cleared away the table. John was holding on to Fairlop's finger and slowly falling asleep.

Billy nodded in resignation, yielding to the bossiness of his sister. It suddenly dawned on him that there was a different air about her. He frowned, looking from one to the other, and his face changed from disbelief to amazement as a voice inside him said, No it can't happen twice in two days. Then he remembered asking Mrs Johnson, *Do you believe in love at first sight?*

There was a knowing smile on his face as he said, 'Let's get down to business.' He slid some papers across the table. 'Read the contract; if you are satisfied, sign it.'

Megan moved from the kitchen sink, wiping her hands on a towel to stand looking over Fairlop's right shoulder, reading the contract. She nodded, taking the sleeping John from him so he could sign on the dotted line.

'Thank you for this,' said Fairlop. 'You're a lifesaver.' He looked at Megan, then Billy. 'I need to talk to you about another matter, privately.'

Billy nodded. 'I'll show you out.'

Fairlop got to his feet and walked over to the sink. 'Thank you Megan, I hope we meet again soon.'

'Come round tomorrow, and you can show me your new camera.'

'I might do that.' He turned and followed Billy from the kitchen. By the front door he took Billy's hand. 'I really don't know how to thank you, but if you ever need a favour, all you have to do is ask.'

'You could have said that in the kitchen.'

'Would you mind if I came to call on Megan?'

'Of course I don't mind. Now go get your camera.'

*

Two weeks after the transaction with Fairlop he was having a quiet drink in the pub wondering what to do now he was getting married. The money he had saved while in the army from Bull and the diamonds wouldn't last very long. A woman was sitting on the chair opposite to him and, thinking that she was about to solicit him, he was about to get up and leave when she said, 'I hear you're a moneylender.'

'Who told you that?'

She brushed the question aside. 'What interest would you charge to lend me ten pounds?'

He was silent for a moment as he studied the woman. She was in her mid-twenties, in a straw hat with hair combed and no make-up except for a little rouge on her lips. 'I need to know why you need the loan.'

'My daughter is sick and needs medicine, and I would like to buy a sewing machine.'

'How do you intend to pay back the loan? Is your husband in employment?'

Her lip quivered. 'My husband died three months ago of pneumonia, and if I don't get the medicine soon, I think my—'

Billy placed a hand on her arm, 'Why the sewing machine?'

'I'm a good seamstress; I can make dresses and other garments to sell.'

'Can you make a wedding dress?'

'Show me a picture, or tell me what you want, and yes, I can. I promise you, Mr Reid, I'll pay back every penny.'

'I'm sure you will.' He wrote down his address. 'Come to my house at five o'clock.'

She took his hand and kissed it. 'Thank you, thank you very much.'

Within minutes of her leaving, another person approached him for a loan and by the time he left the pub ten people had secured promises of loans. He drew out the money from the bank, bought a ledger book, and returned home.

Over the next few months his loan business grew. Luckily for him, Nancy was good with figures, and she became his bookkeeper, and employed Megan to collect money from the women.

Having obtained her sewing machine, Mrs Flynn the seamstress was busy making Nancy's wedding dress. Her daughter was now well and helping her mother.

With all this and the wedding day coming ever closer, Billy became aware of another way of making money – a gaming house. With the docks close by, and sailors on leave wanting to let off steam and spend money, it could do well. He found a property in Dock Street and advertised for staff.

Mrs Johnson was very good at sizing up people, so that evening when visiting Nancy he asked her 'Would you like a job?'

'What? I'm not good with figures, or, much else.'

He smiled. 'You know people.' He leaned forward in the seat. 'I need honest people to work in the gaming house; two heads are better than one. Naturally I'll pay you.'

'There's no need for payment; it will be nice to feel useful again.'

On Saturday, 25 November 1905, Billy's gaming house opened and life was looking up for him. He married Nancy on New Year's Day, 1906, and Fairlop took the wedding photos. It was a small wedding with a dinner at the newly built Savoy Hotel where the newly-weds stayed the night.

Two months after the wedding, on 20 March Mrs Johnson, whom Billy affectionately called Mother, died. She must have known that it was going to happen as a few days before her death, she handed Nancy and Billy the deeds to the house, telling Billy that her husband had helped salvage a ship that was floundering after a storm. The money he made from that had paid for the house.

There were also happy times. In June Megan married Brian Fairlop, and in August Nancy told Billy she was pregnant, as was Megan.

*

By the start of 1907, Billy was looking forward to his first child and he could not have been any happier but in February things started to go wrong. Megan reported that three women to whom he had loaned money hadn't paid for over a month. He decided it was time to have a talk with them.

He woke up early to visit the debtors as Megan said they never answered the door, although she knew they were there. Billy looked at the pay-in book, making sure he was at the right address and knocked loudly on the front door three times. An upstairs window to his right opened, followed by others as a head poked out. 'Why the fuck are you knocking at this time of the morning? What do you want?'

'Are you Mr O'Malley?'

'No, he lives in that flat.' The man pointed to the window above him.

Billy knew the O'Malley's had heard him, so he yelled, 'O'Malley, open the door.'

There was no reply. Billy was getting angrier by the second and banging on the door again. The man he had spoken to a few moments earlier opened the door.

'He's on the third floor, door on your left; now can I get back to sleep?'

'Sorry.' Billy brushed past the man, climbing the stairs two at a time turning left onto the second landing and kicked the door. He could hear movement inside which angered him even more.

'Look, O'Malley,' he said through the closed door, 'you owe me money; if there's a problem and you can't pay, all you have to do is come and see me, but to ignore my sister and me is not the right thing to do. So, I'm going to count five: if you don't open the door by then, I'm coming in.'

He waited a second, giving O'Malley a chance to open the door then began counting. 'One, two, three, and four ...' the door half opened and a girl of about eight, a blanket wrapped around her body, said in barely a whisper. 'I'm sorry, sir but—'

'Where are your parents?'

The girl opened the door and pointed to a curtained-off part of the room. Billy took a step inside and gasped from the smell. Placing a handkerchief over his mouth and nose, he quickly walked across the room pulling back the curtain. Mrs O'Malley was dead. He stepped over to the window and opened it, letting in the fresh early morning air. He turned, looking around the room. The conditions were appalling. Condensation ran down the walls, even though it was like an icebox in there. In one corner was a bucket that was used for a toilet, which was nearly full. The girl huddled in a corner, shivering.

'Where's your father?'

'He died two weeks ago.'

'I thought you had brothers and sisters.'

'They're dead – I'm the only one left.' She began to cry, asking between sobs, 'Am I going to die, mister?'

Two strides and Billy knelt beside the little girl. 'Not if I can help it.' He took off his coat, wrapped it around the little girl and picked her up. 'What's your name?'

'Alice,' she replied, resting her head on his shoulder.

'Well, Alice, I'm going to take you to my house.' He stroked her cheek with a finger. 'I will make sure you don't die.'

Nancy was awake when he entered the house, he quickly explained the situation. While Nancy made Alice a bowl of soup, Billy heated up a large saucepan of water which he poured into the kitchen sink and for the umpteenth time promised himself that before the baby was born they would have a bathroom fitted in the house.

While Alice finished her soup, Billy called on Mrs Flynn about a dress for Alice. As it happened she had a couple that her daughter had grown out of. Armed with clothes for Alice, Billy returned home to find a clean Alice fast asleep in Nancy's arms.

'What are we going to do with her?' he asked his wife.

'She can stay here, but with the baby coming soon, it could be a little awkward.'

They were silent, both trying to think of a solution. Billy lit a cigarette pacing up and down the room a couple of times in thought, then stopped in front of Nancy.

'She can stay here. You will need help around the house. And when the baby comes she can help you then as well. It makes sense.'

Nancy smiled at her husband, then down at the girl in her arms. 'I insist she goes to school.'

As the weeks went by and Nancy grew bigger, Alice was a great help. The sadness at the loss of her family and the thought of death gradually disappeared. She loved going to school, and was always smiling and singing as she helped Nancy around the house. Billy kept the promise he had made himself and had a bathroom fitted just in time for the baby's arrival.

On the morning of 20 April, Nancy went into labour and the midwife was called. For twelve hours Billy waited, the ashtrays full as he smoked one after another. Alice made him something to eat, but it still lay on the table. At ten o'clock he heard a baby's cry and rushed to the door which was opened and the midwife came out carrying the baby.

'It's a little girl; would you like to hold her?'

He took the baby from her, looking at the screwed up face, and his heart filled with love. He stepped forward to enter the room, but the midwife blocked his way.

'I'd like to see my wife.' Alice appeared behind the midwife, tears streaming down her face.

'No, oh no, you're wrong,' Billy gasped. 'Let me in.'

The midwife placed a hand on his arm, seeing the shock and disbelief on his face, and he allowed her to steer him towards a chair.

'Your wife had a very difficult labour. After the baby was born, she haemorrhaged. We couldn't stop the bleeding. I'm so sorry. Give me five minutes, and then you can see her.'

Alice took the baby from his arms and he walked like a drunken man into the bedroom tears streaming down his face, he hugged Nancy to him the sobs of anguish racking his body.

*

For two weeks Billy was inconsolable. Flowers and letters of sympathy arrived daily, mostly from people he had loaned money to, and regular gamblers at his gaming house. Megan, although near to having her baby, took over the management of his business and the household duties, with help from her husband.

Billy watched Alice as she fed the baby, while at the same time Megan was trying to get him to listen to what she was saying. She held her back as she slowly got to her feet, and for a second looked down at him, and then slapped him hard on the face.

His hand flew to his cheek. 'What did you do that for?'

'Do you think Nancy would want you moping around here feeling sorry for yourself? No she wouldn't. You have a responsibility to your daughter, she has to be christened and named properly. Plans have to be made for Nancy's funeral. And if you haven't noticed, I'm about to have a baby, and then who's going to look after your businesses?' She turned. 'I'm going home, my back is killing me, my feet are swollen and I feel like an elephant.' She moved towards the door.

Billy stared at the door as it closed behind his sister. *She's right*, he thought, leaping to his feet heading for the door. Opening it, he walked quickly along the hall, catching Megan as she was about to put her coat on.

'Megan, I'm so sorry, you're right. Will you look after the baby and Alice for a couple of days till I find someone to take care of things in the house?'

She smiled. 'Of course, let's wait till Alice has fed and changed the baby, and you can send us home in a taxi.'

It took him two days to find a housekeeper who was also willing to look after a baby. She had been recommended to him by one of his clients.

Mrs Emily Burns was Irish and a widow. Her two sons had left home and immigrated to America. As soon as she arrived she went from room to room, the last being the kitchen.

'Do I receive a weekly allowance for buying food, clothes and—'

'Mrs Burns, you are now in charge of this house,' Billy replied. 'When you have decided what and how much you need, let me know. I'll return in a two hours with the children.'

Mrs Burns was a wonderful cook and very good with the children. Gradually Billy picked up the pieces of his life. He was amazed at the number of people who paid their respects by attending Nancy's funeral. A week later he did two things: christened his daughter, naming her April, and with Alice's permission adopted her. On 10 May, Megan had another boy, naming him William.

*

Through his gaming house and loans, Billy was slowly becoming a wealthy man, and still had one of the diamonds secreted away for a rainy day. Walking around the streets of East London collecting money from his borrowers, he couldn't fail to notice the poor: men out of work, sitting forlorn and helpless; children in bare feet, undernourished, their bones showing through ragged clothes; mothers begging, holding babies, pinching their bottoms to make them cry, hoping a sympathetic passer-by would give them money to put food on the table.

Each area had its own ethnic identity – English, Irish, Jewish, French – and for the first time Billy saw the furtive side of these areas as he explored places he had never been before.

It wasn't just the sights in these areas, but also the different smells that hung in the air, from Aldgate to West India docks, Surrey docks to Rotherhithe, ships from all corners of the globe unloading their cargos into warehouses: tea, tobacco, spices, oils, honey, and sugar. Strange languages heard in pubs that smelt of beer and stale pipe tobacco. Best of all was after it had rained, when the air was fresh and clean. There were also the sounds – of mothers yelling to their children, buskers selling their wares, a hurdy-gurdy playing an old music hall song – the dirty faces of chimney sweeps and rag and bone men, and children playing hopscotch on the pavement, all adding to the atmosphere and sounds of East London.

One evening the smell of baked bread made Billy stop opposite a Jewish baker's shop in Brick Lane. The baker and his family were distributing unsold bread and rolls to the poor.

It was a cold October afternoon, a week before his twenty-sixth birthday when, on his way to the bank after another day of collecting payments on the loans, when he was viciously attacked. It happened so quickly that he had no idea who his attackers were. One moment he was walking along the street the next he was laying on the pavement and someone seemed to be standing over him.

'Are you okay?' a man asked, kneeling by his side, his face a blur.

'I think so – did you see who did this to me?'

'No.' If Billy could have seen his face he would have realised he was lying.

'Please help me up.'

The man helped him to his feet, holding on to him as Billy's legs buckled. He shook his head to clear his vision, taking deep breaths to take away the nausea until he could stand on his own.

'Thanks.' He felt like he'd been run over by a herd of elephants. There wasn't a place on his body that didn't hurt.

'Would you like to go to the hospital? You don't look too good; your forehead will need stitching up.'

Billy touched his forehead – it was wet; he looked at his fingers, red with blood, and it was then that he noticed he was bare-footed and cold. They had stolen his coat, wallet and takings of the day, the keys to his home including a fob watch, a present from his mother-in-law, and his wedding ring. He clenched his fist in anger, jaw set, saying quietly between clenched teeth, 'Whoever you are, I will find you, and when I do …' He left the rest unsaid as he looked at the man, and for the first time noticed his ragged appearance. 'What's your name?'

'Frank Mullen.'

'Can you do me a favour, Frank?' He hesitated for a second, observing the man for the first time. Mullen was about five foot ten, broad-shouldered, as bald as a coot, his face pale and drawn from hunger. Billy touched his arm. 'Please take me to the hospital, then go to 24 Sidney Street and see my housekeeper, Mrs Burns. Tell her what's happened, and that I need a change of clothes. Bring the clothes to the hospital. I'll pay you for your time.'

Frank helped Billy to the hospital, leaving him in the capable hands of the doctor before going to collect his clothes.

After stitching his forehead, the doctor said, 'Mr Reid, I'd like you to stay overnight, just to make sure you're okay. It's a pretty bad wound. Your ribs are not broken but you're going to be sore for a few days.'

Billy took his clothes from Frank and began to dress, still livid about the attack and the stolen jewellery which had meant so much to him. 'Thanks, Doc, but I'm going home.'

'Please, Mr Reid, stay – you could have a concussion.'

'Thanks, Doc, but I'm leaving,' he repeated emphatically.

The doctor sighed. 'Okay, if you're that adamant, but, I—'

'Yes, I know.' He patted the doctor on the shoulder. 'I could do with something for the pain.'

'Sure, I won't be a moment.'

A few minutes later, the doctor handed him a small bottle of painkillers. 'Take three a day.'

Billy and Frank left the hospital. He was still a little woozy, but with Frank's help made it home where Mrs Burns ordered him to bed. He gave a little smile at her bossiness and, painfully climbing the stairs, stopped and leant over the banisters, 'Give Frank something to eat and two shillings for his help. And Frank, come back tomorrow, I have a job for you.'

He crawled into bed, his only thought: revenge.

*

Three days after the attack, his brother-in-law came to see him. Billy could see he was nervous about something, but doesn't say anything for a while as Brian made small talk about the children.

'William is going to be a big—'

'Brian what's the problem? You're waffling – just spit it out. What's happened?'

'The club was robbed last night.'

'I thought Fred changed the locks.'

'He did.'

'So, how did they get in?'

'It was just after three in the morning. Fred was there with a couple of the men who were tidying up while he counted the night's take. They were armed – shot one of the men in the leg.'

'Were they Irish?'

'No, Fred said they were English.'

'Anyone know who they are?'

'No, but they cut the initial J on Fred's arm.'

Billy swung his legs out of bed and slowly got to his feet. 'Is he okay?'

'Yes – what do you think you're doing? Mrs Burns—'

'I'm getting fucking dressed,' he replied angrily.

'Billy, you still need a few more days rest.'

'Don't you think it funny that I'm beaten and robbed, and then a few days later my club is too?' He was white with anger, seriously wanting to hurt someone.

Brian had never seen his brother-in-law so enraged.

'Help me put on my shirt.'

'See you're in—'

'Fuck it, Brian, just help me.' Brian shrugged and helped him dress.

Brian walked down the stairs in front of Billy as he slowly and painfully descended. Mrs Burns, hands on hips, face red from cooking, yelled, although she was only feet away from him, 'Mr Reid, get back to bed.'

Billy gave a white-faced smile trying not to show the pain. 'I need some fresh air, Mrs Burns.'

'Come in the kitchen,' she ordered quietly. 'I'll make you a cuppa.'

'Is Frank here?'

'Yes, he's playing with April.'

While drinking his tea, Frank entered the kitchen and walked over to the table to stand silently in front of Billy, who looked up at him.

Billy frowned. 'Something's worrying you, Frank? What is it? Is there something you want to tell me?'

'I'm sorry, Billy, I lied to you. I do know who beat you up. They aren't from East London. They come into the East End from time to time, rob a few shops that are about to close. They always beat up the owner, and their boss raped any women that happened to be there. Three weeks ago he raped a French girl in Fournier Street, leaving the letter J on her breast. They call themselves the J Gang. No one knows who they are as their faces are always covered. I'm so sorry.'

Billy didn't say anything for a second, his mind working overtime. He picked up the cup, downed the tea in one gulp, and got to his feet, ignoring the pain and patting Frank on the shoulder. 'Come on we have work to do.'

'You can't go out in the state you are in at the moment,' said Mrs Burns.

'I won't be long, I promise, and Frank's with me.'

Billy and Frank went to the pub, moving to a corner seat. While Frank went to get the drinks, Billy's eyes wandered slowly around the bar area. Frank placed a beer in front of Billy, who took a sip, eyes wandering around the room over the rim of the glass. Settling the glass on the mat, he said, 'Tell me about yourself, where are you from in Ireland?'

'Becerra in County Mayo. I left when my Mum died. I intended going to America, but like an idiot I caught the wrong ship. At first I couldn't find any regular work, doing odd jobs here and there. Eventually I got job on the docks, but to keep it you had to give a small donation to the manager, who was an arrogant bastard.'

He stopped talking, a faraway look in his eyes and his face softened. 'I got married.' There was a tear at the corner of his eye as he continued, 'She was run over by a dray cart. She suffered for ten days, pleading with me to put her out of her misery, but I couldn't.' He looked at Billy. 'How could I kill someone I loved?' He wiped his eyes. 'Anyway, after the funeral I went back to work, but my heart wasn't in it, plus I couldn't stand you-know-who. So one day I hit him. Since then I haven't been able to get a job.'

'Well, you have one now. I need a manager.'

'For what?'

Billy took a wallet from his pocket, looked around to make sure they were unobserved and peeled off some notes, handing them to Frank. 'I want you to find me some tough Irishmen, and I mean tough.'

'How many?'

'Six or eight; you know where my gaming house is?'

Frank nodded.

'Bring them there at eight o'clock tonight.' He took another sip of beer, stood and walked slowly and painfully out of the pub.

*

That evening, eight men filed into Billy's office, forming a line in front of him. He studied each man as they waited silently for him to speak. He lit a cigarette, blew a smoke ring into the air and said, 'My name is Billy Reid. A few weeks ago I was beaten and robbed and certain pieces of jewellery, precious to me, were taken, plus some cash. A few days after that, this gaming house was raided by a group calling themselves the J Gang. I know by information I received that they are English. Their leader raped defenceless women – that in itself is disgusting.'

He pointed to Frank. 'My manager has chosen you because you are supposed to be tough.' He took a puff of the cigarette pointing a finger at them. 'I need men who are not afraid of a fight, even if it means using weapons.'

He looked down, putting the cigarette out in the full ashtray on the desk, then up at the men. 'I demand loyalty, not only to me, but each other.' He stepped towards them, blue eyes moving along the line saying softly, 'If you ever betray me, my family, your friends and their families,' his voice turned to steel, 'I will kill you.' There was a long pause. 'If you don't think you can handle that, walk out now.'

No one moved. He nodded and walked round his desk, lowering himself onto the chair, sliding a piece of paper across the table holding out a pen. 'Please write your name and address. If you have nowhere to stay, tell me.'

Two of the men had nowhere to stay. 'Go to the Bridge Hotel, tell them I sent you. Gentlemen, I want you to meet me at the clothes shop in Commercial Road tomorrow morning at ten o'clock. Goodnight.'

The men filed out of the room. 'Frank, please stay here.'

The door closed behind the last man. 'Sit down.' Billy pointed to a chair in front of his desk and opened a drawer, extracting a bottle of whisky and two glasses. As he filled the glasses, handing one to Frank he asked, 'Do you know the men you've chosen?'

'Six of them, yes; they worked on the docks with me. Shamus and Sean were recommended.'

'Okay, keep an eye on them.' He took a sip of his drink, 'Are you okay with this? It could get nasty.'

Frank smiled. 'Don't worry about me boss, I need a bit of excitement in my life right now.'

The following day, after taking the men to buy new clothes, Billy went to see Mrs Flynn, the seamstress. 'You're a day early;' she said, 'but I can still give you the money.'

'That's not why I'm here.' He sat in a chair watching her for a moment, saying in a matter-of-fact voice, 'Do you know any Irish in the police?'

She looked up, 'What's going on, Mr Reid?'

'Nothing, I just need some information that a policeman might be able to give me. I only trust the Irish.'

'Mr O'Brien, he lived at 5 Tarling Street. I just made two dresses for his daughters.'

He stood, walked the few paces over to her, and kissed her forehead. 'Thanks, you don't have to pay me this week.'

Still in a little bit if discomfort from the beating, he slowly made his way to the O'Brien's.

Luckily for him, the policeman was off-duty. Billy held out his hand, introducing himself. 'I'm sorry to bother you, Mr O'Brien. My name is Billy Reid; could you please give me a few moments of your time?'

The policeman was tall and slim, hair straight with a right-hand parting, the ends of his moustache waxed to a point. The studded collar of the blue uniform shirt was missing, the top button undone. 'Can this wait for another time, Mr Reid; I'm on duty in an hour.'

'I have just one question.'

'That is?'

'Do you know anything about the J Gang?'

'That's police business,' O'Brien said sternly.

'I was beaten and certain items dear to me were stolen. Then a few days later my gambling house was robbed, my manager shot. So,' he smiled grimly, 'I wonder if you can help me with any clues as to who they are.'

'I heard about the incident, and as you probably know there have been others, including serious crimes.'

'You mean the rapes?'

The policeman nodded.

Billy handed him his card. 'This is my address. If you hear anything please contact me.'

'As I said, Mr Reid, it's police business.'

Billy held out his hand; as O'Brien shook it and Billy looked into his eyes. 'We Irish have to stick together.' He let go the hand. 'Good day to you, Constable O'Brien.' He turned and didn't look back. If he had, he would have seen O'Brien looking at him thoughtfully rubbing his chin.

*

Two days after his meeting with O'Brien, the policeman, attired in civilian clothes, called at the gambling house and was shown into Billy's office by Frank.

The two men shook hands. 'Would you like a drink?'

'A whisky will do nicely, thank you.'

Billy nodded at Frank, who left, returning minutes later with a bottle of whisky and two glasses. As Billy poured the drinks, O'Brien said, 'I have some information about—' He looked at Frank.

'You can speak freely; he is one of my managers.'

'As you know, no one knows what they look like, but, yesterday they robbed a house in Camden owned by a Lord Fotheringay and raped his housekeeper. The man who raped her told her to give a message to the earl. 'Tell him I owe him for ruining my life.' She said he spoke like a gentleman and smelt of cigars.'

Billy sat bolt upright in his chair, as if a thunderbolt had struck him, stopping himself from saying the name as O'Brien leaned forward in his seat, eyes like slits. 'You know who it is?'

Billy was silent, looking at nothing in particular, and then looked at the policeman and smiled. 'I cannot say anything that might incriminate me.'

O'Brien took a drink, emptying the glass, and then held it out to Billy. 'Can I please have a refill?' He grinned and tapped a finger to the side of his nose.

Billy laughed, picked up the bottle and poured a large one, then nodded at Frank who left the room. Ten minutes later, there was a knock at the door.

'Come in,' Billy ordered. The door opened and one of the dealers entered.

'Sorry to bother you, sir, but there is something that needs your attention.'

Billy looked at the policeman. 'I'm sorry, but—'

'I understand, thank you for the drink.' As O'Brien reached the door, Frank handed him a bag. 'A little thank you for your time.'

Taking the bag from him, the policeman opened it to see two bottles of whisky. He closed the bag with a smile on his face. 'Any time,' he said and walked out.

As soon as the door closed, Frank gathered up the men and headed for Billy's office, knocking on the door, entering when his boss said, 'Come in.'

The men followed Frank into the room to see a grim-faced Billy cleaning a pistol. They silently watched as he loaded the weapon and slid it into a shoulder holster, looked at the men, placing his hands on the table and getting to his feet.

'I know who the leader of the J Gang is. His name is George Jennings.' He lit a cigarette, the smoke drifting from his nostrils. 'He left his calling card on the housekeeper of Lord Fotheringay. Luckily for him, the earl was out of town.'

'Lucky. Why?' Frank asked.

'Jennings was a captain in the army. He raped my sister and she testified against him. He was stripped of his rank and dishonourably discharged, as was I for hitting him. Lord Fotheringay was the man in charge of his court martial, and scathing in his remarks when passing sentence. I'm sure; if Jennings had found him at home he would have killed him. What surprised me is why he didn't kill me.'

He moved away from the desk towards a padlocked cupboard in the corner of the room, at the same time taking a key from his pocket. Before unlocking it he turned to face the men with angry eyes, fist clenched and venom in his voice. 'I, we, have to send a message to the J Gang and those like them, that coming into our house has its consequences. If you haven't got the stomach for this, you can freely go. I know some of you have families and I will understand.'

Not one man moved as Frank said, 'Boss, we know this man and his gang are loathsome. I'm sure that I speak for every man here.' The men nodded their heads. 'To rape a woman is, is ...' he tried to find the right word '... abhorrent. These men and those like them need to be taught a lesson, and we are with you, no matter what it takes.'

Billy was touched by their loyalty. He nodded and turned back to the cupboard, unlocking it and opening the double doors to reveal rows of rifles, pistols and knives. He swept an arm towards it. 'Gentlemen, take your pick.'

*

It had taken Billy a week, and crossing a few palms with silver, to find Jennings's address: 12 Duncan Terrace, in Islington, was a quiet, leafy area with Georgian terraced houses. It was three in the morning as Billy and Frank stood in the shadows, watching the house after reconnoitring the area. Billy tapped Frank on the shoulder and beckoned with his head for them to leave.

On the way back to the gaming house Billy said, 'Tomorrow—' he looked at his watch '—sorry, later today, take two men back to that place. I need you to make a note of how many people are in the house during the day and evening, and what time they go to bed. If you see Jennings go out, he's about six foot tall, slim, bony featured, always immaculately dressed; leave one man at the house and follow him.'

Two days later, Frank and the two men who had been watching Jennings's house were in Billy's office. Frank was doing the talking. 'There wasn't a lot of activity till the evening. Jennings with another man and two girls went to the George pub in Upper Street.'

'Fancy girls, nicely dressed and—' Derek made a shape with his hands.

'They sat in a cubby,' Frank continued. 'After an hour the girls left and six men who were at the bar joined Jennings. At no time did they draw attention to themselves; I believe they are regulars there. They didn't drink much. Jennings did most of the talking. Just before closing time they began to leave. We quickly went outside to see where they might go.'

Frank lit a cigarette offering them to the others. After lighting up he took a piece of paper from his pocket, placing it on the desk in front of Billy. 'The six men went off together. Derek and I followed them, and George,' he pointed at the other man, 'tailed Jennings and the other chap.'

Billy refilled their glasses with whisky. Frank nodded his thanks as he picked up the glass, took a sip pointing at the paper. 'The six men entered a house in—' he looked at his writing, '—10 Bewdley Street. We thought they might go out again, but they didn't. After hanging around for an hour we assumed they had gone to bed, had a good look around the area, and then went back to Duncan Terrace.'

'The two girls,' George added, 'are in permanent residence there.'

'Thanks,' said Billy. 'I'll see you tomorrow, well done.'

As the door closed behind them, Billy spread a map out on the table, lit a cigarette rolled his head back exhaling the smoke his face like stone.

*

The streets were silent and in darkness as a lorry entered Bewdley Street, turned off its lights and engine, rolling slowly to a stop. Billy who was the driver, with Frank beside him, got out of the vehicle. Billy looked up and down the street, turning his head to one side listening for any sound. Satisfied, he gave the thumbs up to Frank who moved to the rear of the vehicle and whispered, 'All clear.'

The eight men silently got down from the lorry, moving quietly to the house at 10 Bewdley Street. George picked the lock, looked at Billy and nodded. As they had practised for the last two days, the men entered the house, moving quietly into each room, but they were all empty. Slowly and soundlessly the group moved up the stairs to the first-floor landing to find three closed doors. As rehearsed, they split, with two men at each door. Billy pointed to the stairs leading to the second floor. Frank moved halfway up the stairs to see how many rooms there were. He turned back, looked at Billy showing two fingers.

Billy tapped George on the shoulder, motioning with his head for him to go up. The men looked at Billy, who showed five fingers, then climbed the stairs to the next landing, counting silently. On the fourth floor he stood by one of the doors, with Frank and George by the other. At the count of five there was a crash as each door was flung open. Billy entered the room, gun pointing at the man and woman naked on the bed. The woman stifled a scream as he pointed the gun at her.

'I wouldn't do that.' He waved the gun. 'Get up, put your hands on your head and face the wall.'

Frank came into the room, gagged the man and woman and tied their hands behind their back.

'Make your way downstairs,' Billy ordered, adding, 'don't try anything funny.'

They put the men and women in different rooms, giving the women robes to cover their nudity.

Billy pointed to the man nearest to him. 'Bring him into the kitchen.'

Two men grabbed him, he struggled, but a punch in the stomach soon stopped that and they followed Billy who pointed to a chair. 'Tie him to it,' he said harshly.

The men stepped away from the chair. Billy slapped the prisoner hard across the face, leaned over him, face red with anger.

'You and your friends beat me up, and stole something that is dear to me.' The prisoner's eyes widen in fear at the iciness in Billy's voice. 'But you have also done the vilest thing a man can do – help another rape a woman, and for that you have to pay.'

The prisoner babbled into his gag, shaking his head, but Billy slapped him again and then looked across to where Frank was standing by a stove, a knife over a flame. 'Is it ready?'

'Yes.' Frank moved away from the stove, handing the knife to Billy. The prisoner's eyes widened with fear and he urinated on the floor.

'I am not going to kill you, but for what you have done, you will wear the mark of Cain on your face. If I ever see you again, I will kill you. Hold him down.'

The prisoner was unable to move or scream as Billy burnt the letter R onto his forehead, and then cut off the trigger finger of his right hand. They did the same to the other five men.

One by one, the prisoners were carried out to the van and dumped like sacks in the back while Billy entered the room where the girls sat huddled together.

'We are very sorry that you were caught up in this,' he said softly. 'We are leaving now; please, for your own safety, don't leave this house tonight.'

Placing placards around the gang's necks, with the words J GANG MEMBER, Billy and his men hog tied them outside Islington Police Station and moved on to Duncan Terrace.

Once again George picked the lock and they entered the house. Billy waited in the dining room as the men found Jennings and the other man whom Billy recognised as Lieutenant Smyth. He was jailed and drummed out of the army while in South Africa for beating a black man to death.

Billy pointed at Smyth. 'Bring him.' He walked out of the room and into the lounge, moving the furniture against the wall, and drawing the curtains.

Billy stripped off his coat, placing it neatly across a settee, then looked at Smyth standing between two of his men.

'I know that you like beating people up, especially if they cannot defend themselves. You—' he stepped angrily over to the ex-officer '—can try and beat me up.'

Smyth tried to say something through the gag. Billy ripped it from his mouth and slapped him hard across the face, his fingers leaving red marks on the prisoner's cheek, saying between clenched teeth, 'I'm going to give you a chance to walk out of here.'

'Give me a chance?' Smyth questioned, glancing at the men either side of him.

'You can fight me. If you beat me, you are free to go; but if I win…' He left the rest unsaid.

'You're a joke, Sergeant Reid. What's to stop your men from killing me if I win?'

'I can assure you that will only happen if you try and escape.'

Smyth laughed. 'Escape, when I can beat you to a pulp and enjoy it?' He looked down at his nudity. 'But you do have an advantage already.'

'Yes, you don't look a pretty sight.' Billy nodded towards the ex-officer's penis, 'Especially with one so small. George, bring him some clothes.' To his satisfaction he could see that he had angered Smyth.

Putting on a pair of trousers, Smyth sneered, 'Are you sure about this, Sergeant? You know how to box, but you don't know how to fight.' He slipped a shirt over his head. 'I wanted to kill you when we saw it was you, but Jennings said no, we could do that another time and also have some fun with–' he held up his right hand showing Billy's wedding ring on his finger '–your wife.'

Billy saw red and uncharacteristically rushed Smyth. He was jolted back by a sledgehammer punch to the face, tasting blood.

His opponent laughed. 'You haven't got what it takes.' He landed two blows in quick succession on Billy's chin and right eye. 'You haven't enough brains; you care too much, no killer instinct.'

Billy shook his head to clear his vision and just in time blocked the next punch. Smyth was wrong, as he was going to find out. Billy instinctively put his guard up.

'Come on, Reid, Bull isn't here to wipe your bum,' the ex-officers sneered. He had what was coming to—'

He didn't finish as Billy landed a punch to his mouth. 'Is that all you've got? You punch like a woman.' He landed a punch to the side of Billy's head, but received two back in exchange. Smyth was silent.

'Never had someone hit you back, sir,' Billy said with contempt. 'I'm going to teach you a lesson you will never forget.'

Smyth's right-hand punch was blocked and a flurry of punches jerked his face back. He spat out broken teeth and rushed Billy, who sidestepped, landing a blow to his opponent's kidneys. Smyth turned quickly face red with anger, blood trickling from his mouth. He moved forward to be met by blows to the body and face.

'Anything else you want to say?' Billy landed a left and right to the ex-officer's face. Blood poured from the nose, eyes slightly glazed, he tried to hit Billy, but the arm was knocked away.

'This is for Bull.' He landed a punch to the jaw, hearing the crack as it broke.

'This is for defiling my ring.' He grabbed Smyth's arm between his hands and snapped it like a twig. Smyth screamed in pain, falling to the ground. Billy stared down at him and stamped down on his groin.

'You know what that's for.' He looked up and pointed to two of his men. 'Hold him down.' He picked up a knife from the table and cut the letter **R** on Smyth's forehead and then sliced off his trigger finger and the one with his wedding ring on it, whispering in Smyth's ear, 'I have the killer instinct, which you will find out, if I ever see you again.'

The man was silent, unable to speak through his broken jaw, but the expression of submission in his eyes told Billy all he wanted to know.

He got to his feet. 'George, take him where we dumped the others.'

'Yes, boss. What about Jennings?'

'I had better go and see our illustrious prisoner. You carry on.' Billy entered the dining room.

Jennings, now wearing a pair of pants, was tied to a chair. He smiled at Billy. 'Hallo, Sergeant, how's your sister and my son. I keep meaning to pay them a visit, especially your sister, but I have been pretty busy.'

Billy stopped in front of him. He wasn't going to get into a verbal match with Jennings.

'What's the matter, Reid? You thick-skulled ignorant Irishman; nothing to—'

Billy slammed a fist into his mouth, breaking the front teeth.

Jennings spat them out and smiled, blood running down his chin. 'Untie me, be a man.'

Billy smacked him across the face. 'You are going to know what it feels like to be helpless and used as a punch-bag.' He landed four punches to Jennings face, and then gestured for the men to take over. Frank ripped a leg from a chair, slamming it against Jennings's knees, ignoring the man's screams and breaking both kneecaps.

Billy moved in front of Jennings a knife in his right hand. 'I believe this is the end for you, and I wanted to be the last thing you see as you died.' He thrust the knife into Jennings, holding on to the hilt looking into the dying man's eyes as they slowly glazed over.

They placed Jennings body outside the police station, still tied to the chair with a placard around his neck: **LEADER OF THE J-GANG**.

The press had a field day with the headlines about the J Gang, with pictures taken by Billy's brother-in-law of the gang in front of the police station after an anonymous tip-off. A young boy had woken Brian, handing him a note telling him to go immediately to Islington police station with his camera.

The police never charged anyone for Jennings's death. His men were imprisoned for life. Smyth died in mysterious circumstances while awaiting trial. There was a rumour that he was going to tell them about his assailant.

Later all sorts of people, ignorant of what Billy and his men had done, tried to muscle in on his success. Opium dealers, prostitutes, card sharps, conmen – all realised, too late, that you didn't mess with Billy Reid.

6   The Deal

London, April 1909

A MONTH HAD GONE BY since the incident with the O'Sullivans. Wolfe and Asher were in the gym doing their usual routine with a punch-bag, when a rotund man in a check suit walked over and stood a few feet away, his back to the training ring an unlit cigar hung from the corner of his mouth. He watched them for some time and it was getting on Wolfe's nerves. He slammed a right hand into the bag and then turned to face the man, saying harshly, 'You've been standing there for some time, and it seemed to me that you want to speak to us about something, so spit it out.'

Taking the cigar from his mouth, the man smiled his cheeks and chin wobbling like jelly. 'My name is Fred Small.'

The brothers couldn't help smiling at the name.

'I'm promoting some fights tomorrow night; one of my fighters has guts ache, and I wondered if you'd like to take his place. Naturally, I'll pay you–' he waddled forward a couple of paces '–five pounds for the fight and another five if you win.'

Wolfe looked at Asher, who shrugged his shoulders as if to say, your decision. He gestured for Asher to hold the bag and started punching it while he thought over the promoter's proposition. They could do with an influx of money, and he wouldn't mind having a fight – just sparring around was at times boring and he needed a bit of excitement, that adrenalin rush at the start of a fight. The thing was Eva – what would she say? Mind you; she never said anything after seeing the bruises on his face the morning after the fight with the O'Sullivans. He stopped punching to look at the promoter. 'Okay, I'll fight.'

The following morning Wolfe said to Eva, 'I won't be home this evening as Asher and I have some business to attend to.' In the morning she'd know where he'd been, knowing nothing got passed her.

After a light snack he and Asher took the bus to the fight venue.

Wolfe's fight was the third bout on the programme. While he prepared himself and changed, Asher left to put on some bets, returning thirty minutes later.

'What odds did we get?'

Asher smiled, 'Fifty to one.' Helping his brother on with his gloves he asked, 'Are you sure about this? You don't know who you'll be fighting, and it's the first time since—'

'Asher, stop worrying,' Wolfe interrupted, punching his fists together and shadow boxing the wall.

Mr Small strolled into the dressing room, a fawn Crombie overcoat over his shoulders, cigar in his mouth. 'You're on, Jew-boy.' It was spoken in a sneering tone which angered Wolfe; he took a step forward, but Asher moved quickly in front of him. The promoter's mouth moved in a sort of smile. He turned and walked out.

'Okay, let's go,' Asher said.

Wolfe nodded. The brothers walked side by side towards the hall, the noise of the crowd becoming louder and louder. Wolfe swallowed nervously as they pushed through the double doors to a crescendo of sound. In Poland there had been no boxing ring, just a circle of people, but that didn't faze Wolfe as he and Asher had sparred in the one at the gym. He entered the ring, and for the first time saw his opponent sitting calmly on the stool, and knew why he was called the Streatham Bear. His body was covered in hair except for his head which was shaven. Wolfe studied the man, who stared unblinkingly at him until the referee called them into the centre of the ring and said, 'I want a fair fight, shake hands.'

'You're going down, Jew-boy,' Bear turned, throwing punches in the air as he walked back to his corner.

The bell went. In a flash, Bear was across the ring, landing two quick punches to Wolfe's face, but he was able to block the next and counter-punched. Bear swayed away, landing another on Wolfe, who moved across the ring to gather his senses, but again the speed of his opponent took him off guard, lifting his hands to protect his head. Bear landed two punches to the stomach, and then moved into a clinch.

'How do you like that, Jew-boy? Why don't you go back to where you came from?' Bear turned him round, hiding the rabbit punch from the referee.

It was the first time since arriving in England that Wolfe had met anti-Semitism. The bell rang to end the round and he returned to his stool.

'What are you playing at?' Asher demanded, taking the gum shield from his brother's mouth with his left hand and giving him a drink with the other. 'He's killing you out there. Look at him, he's laughing at you.'

Wolfe looked across the ring at his opponent and suddenly knew how he could beat him. The bell went and he stood as Asher placed the gum shield in his mouth; Bear raced across the ring, but Wolfe sidestepped him and Bear crashed into the ropes, turning quickly face red with anger, to be met with a left jab and a right to the jaw from Wolfe. Bear tried to grab Wolfe, but he moved away, just staying slightly out of reach. Bear rushed in again, punching thin air; Wolfe landed two quick punches and glided away. The bell went.

'That's better,' Asher said as he held the stool for Wolfe to sit down. 'He's running out of steam, take a look.'

Wolf peered around his brother. Asher was right. The bell went and he got to his feet, but there was no quick rush from Bear this time. Wolfe moved around the ring, allowing Bear to do the attacking, blocking punches on his arms. Bear was wheezing and the power had gone from his punches. This time as his opponent moved in, Wolf blocked the punch landing a right to Bear's stomach. His head came forward from the power of the blow, which was followed by an uppercut. Bear was out for the count before his body hit the canvas. The place was in uproar at this unexpected result.

*

While Wolfe took a shower, Asher collected their winnings. Wolfe was putting on his coat when Mr Small entered the dressing room.

'Here's your money,' he said, handing over ten pounds. 'I have another fight for you, if you want it?'

'When?'

'Three weeks.'

'Who is he?' Asher asked.

'Tougher than the Bear – he's won all twenty of his fights, eight knockouts.'

'His name, idiot,' Wolfe said harshly, still remembering Small's anti-Semitic use of the term 'Jew-boy'.

'Fred the Hammer Floyd,' was the reply, a smile flickered across Small's face.

'What's funny?' Wolfe took a step forward, and once again Asher moved in front of him, pointing a finger at the fat promoter. 'You're pushing your luck. I suggest you leave very quickly.'

'Will you fight Floyd?' Small asked as he opened the door to leave.

'Where does he train? And yes, I'll fight him for ten pounds, another ten if I win.'

'Ten pounds,' Small laughed, 'if you win. He comes from Newcastle and trained there. He will, as always when he fights in London, arrive on the Monday before the fight and stay with his manager at a cousin's house somewhere in Hoxton.' He waddled out of the room. 'Good luck.' They could hear his laughter until he left the building.

'Are you mad?' Asher looked at his brother.

'No.'

'He's out to get you because of who you are.'

Wolfe placed an arm around Asher's shoulders. 'Tell me, Asher, what's new? Anyway, you're going to help me explain this to Eva.' He pointed to his cut lip and the bruise under his right eyes.

Asher laughed. 'You can do that yourself, and also explain the bruises on your arms and body.'

With an admonished look on his face and voice and slight smile, Wolfe said, 'I thought you were on my side. Anyway, how much did we make?'

'You'll never believe it.'

'Try me.'

'Eighty pounds,' he said excitedly.

'What?'

'I said—'

'That's okay, I heard you. That calls for a taxi home.'

Eva was sitting at the table in the kitchen, a cup of tea between her hands when he entered, with Asher in tow. She quickly got to her feet, a worried frown on her forehead on seeing the bruise under his eye, which was getting a darker blue by the second, and the cut and swollen lip. He winced as she touched the lip.

'You've been fighting again, who was it this time?'

'This time – what do you mean?'

She didn't answer but looked at Asher. 'Are you here for support?'

Before he could reply, she said, 'Go home to Sarah.' She turned her gaze on her husband, hands on hips. 'Wolfe Brown, explain yourself? Asher, are you still here?' Without a word, Asher turned and quickly left the room.

Wolfe stared down at his wife, a slight smile on his face. She looked so beautiful when she's angry.

'Well, I'm waiting.'

'I told you about my fights in Poland.' She nodded. 'I, we, was in the gym the other day, and this man – do you know there are anti-Semites here?'

She sighed. 'Are you that naïve; there are Jew-haters all over the world. What about this man?'

'As I said, we were in the gym, he told us that one of the boxers due to fight had been taken ill, and would I box in his place? The fee was five pounds and another five if I won.'

'Did you?'

'Yes. Asher put on some bets. We made eighty pounds, and—'

'Do we need the money that badly?'

'No, not really, but with the baby coming I thought—'

'Sit there.' She ordered pointing to a chair by the table. 'Let's have a look at the eye and lip, and that's a silly excuse, and you know it.'

He sat as ordered. As she gently tended to his wounds she said quietly, 'I don't like you fighting. It was different with the men who beat up Papa.'

'How did you—'

'I'm your wife. You and Asher didn't get the bruises on your faces from bumping into the door.'

'But this time—'

'You wanted to fight.'

'I was a little bored and needed a bit of excitement.'

'Fighting is exciting? What, beating each other up?'

'It's not like that.' He took her hand from his lip. 'It's a contest between two men,' he said enthusiastically. 'Like a duel between two knights. The blood pumping through your veins and the yelling of the crowd – it's a feeling I can't describe. But the other thing is the anti-Semitic abuse. I didn't like it in Poland, it made me angry, and by beating my opponent – who everyone's sure would beat me – I shut them up.'

'Does this mean you're going to fight again?'

He took her hands in his and looked into her eyes. 'Eva, I promise to stop fighting before the baby arrives. I have another fight in three weeks.'

She was silent for a moment, and then kissed him gently on the lips. 'Just promise me that you won't get hurt.'

He laughed, and then held his lip. 'Ouch.'

*

The fight with Floyd didn't last long: Wolfe knocked him out in the third round.

Once again, the promoter Mr Small offered him another fight to take place in three weeks. Wolfe agreed to fight.

During that week he had offers from men who wanted to manage him. He told them all politely that he already had a manager – his brother.

The bruises from his last fight had all but disappeared as he entered the ring and noticed Billy Reid sitting in the front row. He nodded at the Irishman, who nodded back.

His opponent, a German, Clause Gother, was two inches taller than Wolfe, with a shaven head and muscular body. Wolfe watched him in training at a gym in Hoxton. It was not going to be easy to beat him, but he noticed whenever the German jabbed with the left hand, he dropped the right.

As the referee gave them his instructions, Gother whispered, 'I'm going to break your jaw, Jew-boy.' He returned to his corner, making the sign to Wolfe of a long nose.

The bell went and the two men met in the middle of the ring. As predicted, Gother jabbed with the left, exposing his chin, finding himself on the canvas with Wolfe's first punch. He sprang quickly to his feet, shaking his head. Wolfe threw a jab which was blocked by his opponent, who once again threw out a left. In a flash Wolfe landed a vicious right to the exposed chin, followed by a left as Gother's hands dropped to his side, falling like a sack of potatoes onto the canvas.

The crowd was in uproar at the quickness of the knockout. Smelling salts were put up against the Germans' nose; he suddenly leapt to his feet, looking for Wolfe, but he had left the ring.

*

The following morning, Asher found Wolfe in the kitchen looking thoughtfully into the half-filled cup of tea between his hands.

'What's the matter with you? Anyone would have thought you had lost yesterday.'

'We need to earn more money.' He gulped down the rest of the tea.

'Doing what? We don't have a trade as such, and I for one don't fancy working in a bank for the rest of my life, and I'm pretty sure you don't want to be a butcher.'

'I don't want to sit around all day, do a few repairs to a house and collect the rent once a week. And before you say it – no, I do not want to box for a living either.'

'We could learn to be bakers. I'm sure Eva's father would jump at the chance to teach us.' He dropped on to a chair opposite his brother.

'I know you have no intention of being a baker either, so, what do you have in mind?'

Taking a cigarette from a packet, he tapped the end on the table. 'The bag of jewellery we brought with us – is it any good?'

'What do you mean by good?'

'Is it worth anything?'

'Are you crazy, it's worth a fortune, but we said—'

'I know what we said.' Wolfe leaned forward. 'We could open a jewellery shop.'

'We know nothing about jewellery.'

Wolfe stood, dragging the chair behind him as he moved round the table to sit close to his brother. 'We could learn.'

'You're crazy.'

'Look, Asher, we were lucky. We had, in comparison to many emigrants, a lot of money when we came here, and yes we have invested it in the houses.' He touched Asher's arm, stopping him from interrupting him. 'But we need more. In a few months we are going to be parents. If we stay at home with our wives and the children, as much as we love them, it will get on our nerves.'

Asher looked at his brother, mind racing. Wolfe had always had this drive to do better. He took the cigarette from Wolfe's hand and lit it, blowing the smoke into the air. He was right, they needed another outlet, but—

There was a knock at the door and Wolfe leapt to his feet. 'I'll get it.'

There were muffled voices then footsteps along the hall. Wolfe walked into the kitchen to be followed by a man and a woman whom Asher recognised as their tenants, Mr and Mrs Shaffer.

Wolfe pointed to two chairs. 'Please sit down, would you like a cup of tea?'

'No thanks,' Mr Shaffer said, twisting his hat nervously between his hands. He looked at his wife, who nodded, and then at the brothers in turn, saying quickly, 'Can you lend us some money, please?'

There was surprise on the brother's faces. 'What did you say?' Wolfe asked, adding quickly, 'Never mind, I heard you.'

'Why are you asking us? We aren't moneylenders,' said Asher.

'Yes, we know that, but—'

'Why do you need the money?' Wolfe broke in.

'My wife is a wonderful cook, I am a butcher, and without bragging, make the best *viennas* and *worscht* you have ever tasted.'

'What's that got to…?'

'We would like to open a kosher restaurant,' Mrs Shaffer leaned forward in the chair, 'but we don't have the money.' Before the brothers could say anything, she added quickly, 'There's a shop for sale with living accommodation above, opposite the Ravioli Theatre. We thought that you might want to invest in another property.'

Surprised, the brothers looked from husband to wife and then at each other. Wolfe gave a slight nod to Asher and was the first to speak.

'It's not a bad idea, especially a restaurant opposite a theatre.' He moved towards the door. 'So I think we should go and look at this property before someone else had the same idea.'

The brothers liked what they saw, and the potential of the restaurant, but it was going to take a lot of money for fixtures and fittings, plus a specialised kosher kitchen. The flat upstairs was adequate for the Shaffer's and their two children, but would the investment be worth it?

Asher licked the tip of the pencil and began making notes and drawings as he wandered around the property. Slipping the pen and paper into his jacket pocket, he said, 'Right, let's go back to our place and discuss—'

'May I suggest,' Mrs Shaffer interrupted, 'that you and your wives come to dinner tonight and discuss everything then.' She smiled. 'It would give you an opportunity to taste my cooking.'

Asher looked again at Wolfe, both knowing it would be rude to refuse the offer.

'We accept,' said Asher.

'Is eight o'clock okay?' she asked.

'That will be fine,' Asher smiled, leading the way to the front door saying something to the estate agent, who nodded without saying a word in reply.

*

At eight, Mr Shaffer welcomed them in with a smile and a 'good evening', taking their coats.

'Where are the children?' Wolfe asked.

'They're staying overnight with my brother,' Mr Shaffer replied, leading them into the dining room where the table was set for six.

As they ate the three-course meal of chicken soup with *lockshen* and dumplings, followed by sliced chicken, baked potatoes and a variety of vegetables, the conversation was about Eva's pregnancy.

Mrs Shaffer's account of her own – especially her husband's role – brought laughter.

As she placed the desserts on the table – Apple Strudel, and peach *kuchen* – her husband handed Asher a piece of paper.

'These are the figures for furbishing the restaurant and kitchen.'

Asher looked at the figures in front of him, raised an eyebrow and handed the sheet to Wolfe, who pinched his bottom lip with thumb and forefinger in concentration as Mrs Shaffer placed a piece of both pies on plates, handing them around the table. She then handed Wolfe and Asher a card.

'This is the proposed menu.' She moved back to her seat. 'Naturally as time goes by and we become established, we will extend the menu.'

Wolfe handed his to Eva, Asher to Sarah.

The dinner over, Mr Shaffer offered the brothers a brandy and their wives a sherry. This was the signal for business to begin. After nearly an hour of talking figures and potential profit, Asher leaned back in the seat.

'It will not be a business proposition for Wolfe and me to buy the property and let it out to you. He fiddled with a placemat as the Shaffers' faces dropped. 'But, we can go into partnership.'

'We haven't the money to form an equal partnership,' Mr Shaffer pointed out.

'To be honest Mr Shaffer, we—'

'Hymie.'

Asher smiled. 'Hymie, we can see there's money to be made in your idea. Naturally we need some sort of collateral. Unfortunately you don't have the cash, otherwise you wouldn't have approached us; and you don't own anything.' He took a pack of cigarettes from the pocket of his jacket. 'Do you mind?'

'No, of course not,' the Shaffer's replied.

Asher offered the pack around, the women declining. He lit a cigarette, as Wolfe continued from where his brother left off.

'What we are proposing is that you pay us a weekly or monthly sum, the amount of which we will agree upon, until you have paid your half of the partnership at an interest rate of one and half per cent. You won't be paying rent as that flat is part of the partnership, which means that if at any time you decide to move, the flat can be let out, bringing in more revenue.' He paused taking a drag of the cigarette. 'That's our proposition.'

'Does that mean the partnership will be fifty–fifty once we have paid our half?'

Wolfe nodded.

'I know you are putting up the money,' said Hymie, 'but we are putting in all the work. I don't want to be rude, but I think that once we have paid our half of the partnership it should be seventy–thirty to us.'

'If that's what you feel, then how about you paying us back seventy per cent of the layout?'

Husband and wife looked at each other and then back to the brothers. Mr Shaffer took a pencil from his waistcoat pocket and scribbled some figures on his napkin. He looked up for a second, eyes narrowed in concentration, then scribbled some more, replaced the pencil back in his pocket and looked at his guests, right elbow on the table as he stroked his bearded chin.

'It will take us four years to pay back the seventy per cent, plus the interest. If you are willing to wait that long, you have a deal.'

Wolfe looked at his brother who nodded his agreement. 'That's settled then,' Wolfe said. 'We will have a lawyer draw up a legal document. Once it's signed, we buy the shop.'

Mr Shaffer stood and shook the brothers' hands. 'You won't regret this.'

'If this evening's meal is anything to go by, I'm sure they won't,' Eva said.

7 Another Life, Another Fight

September 1909

WOLFE WAS IN THE KITCHEN when Eva screamed his name. His heart skipped a beat, wondering what had happened as he ran from the kitchen into the hall. His right foot was on the first stair as Eva stood at the top of the stairs, looking down at the floor.

'My waters have just broken – you'd better get the midwife. I think we're having a baby.'

For six hours he paced outside the bedroom, down the stairs, in and out of the front room, the ashtray was full of cigarette butts. Asher and Sarah were shooed out of the bedroom by Eva's mother and sister, who were assisting the midwife. Suddenly, there was the sound of a baby crying. Wolfe rushed up the stairs two at a time, reaching the landing as his mother-in-law emerged from the bedroom, carrying the baby. She looked at him, tears in her eyes.

'It's a boy.'

'How's Eva?' he asked.

'She's fine – you can see her in a few minutes. Would you like to hold your son?'

He nodded, carefully taking the baby from her, looking down at him with tears of joy in his eyes. 'He's so small.'

'Don't worry, he'll soon grow.'

The midwife came out of the bedroom. 'You can go in. Would you like me to take your son?'

Wolfe nodded, handing him over to her and entering the bedroom. Eva looked exhausted. He knelt by the bed and stroked her damp hair, leaning across to gently kiss her lips.

'Thank you,' he said tenderly.

'Have you got it?' she whispered.

He took a small box from his pocket and opened it. Sitting on a bed of cotton wool was a small gold Star of David, safety pin and red ribbon. The ribbon was to ward off evil spirits.

'It's perfect, our son will love it.' She gave a tired smile. 'He is so beautiful, and he has your eyes.'

'Can you tell this early?'

She gave a slight nod, and then closed her eyes, falling into an exhausted sleep. Wolfe kissed her forehead and on tiptoe left the room.

'Have you decided on a name?' Asher asked.

'Jacob.'

'Papa's name, that's nice.'

Five days later, Asher sat in the armchair, holding his nephew Jacob, a look of tenderness and happiness on his face mixed with a kind of wistfulness. 'I wish Mama and Papa were here.'

Wolfe knelt by his brother, placing an arm around his shoulders. 'Can you imagine what Mama would be like now?'

Asher smiled. 'She would be cleaning the place while Papa spoke to the Rabbi about the circumcision.' There was a pause and then he added pensively. 'I must tell you, Wolfe, I envy you. Sarah and I have been trying all these months, but we're beginning to think there might be a problem ... either with her or with me.'

At first Wolfe didn't know what to say. He and Eva had begun to wonder whether Asher and Sarah had possibly decided not to have children, or perhaps to delay it, but now he knew the truth, his heart went out to both of them.

'There is always another option, you know ...' he said tentatively.

'You mean adoption?'

'Yes.'

Asher smiled. 'We have discussed it, and I must admit, although we always imagined we'd have children of our own, and had our heart set on it, over the last couple of months we have started to consider the possibility.'

'Do you know anyone ...?'

'You mean do we know anyone who might have a child they don't want?' Asher sighed despondently. 'Can you imagine such a thing, Wolfe?'

'There are sometimes reasons why it could happen ... Let me talk to Eva, she may be able to suggest something – if Sarah, doesn't mind of course.'

Asher chuckled. 'I somehow imagine they've already discussed the matter, don't you!'

Wolfe grinned. 'Yes of course, you're right.'

Asher kissed his nephew's forehead. The baby's mouth twitched in a lopsided smile.

'Did you see that?' said Wolfe.' He smiled.'

'No, it's wind,' Asher said laughing and sniffed, 'and something else. Now I know he's your son.'

New Year's Eve, 1909

The party was in full swing at Shaffer's restaurant, which had been transformed with streamers and balloons around the walls and ceiling. A six-piece band and singer were on a small stage at one end; the tables, after the meal, formed a square around the floor where couples wearing party hats were dancing.

Wolfe's eyes were on Eva, a smile on her face, as she and Sarah chatted to some women. It had been a fantastic year. He was a father, the restaurant had been a great success, they were financially sound and the future looked bright.

Regarding Asher and Sarah's childlessness; it so happened that Eva's sister Rachel was friendly with a Jewish woman called Rifka who was unmarried and pregnant and had somehow managed to hide this from her parents. Rifka had gone to Rachel for help, and Rachel in turned had approached Sarah. After an intense discussion that continued into the early hours of the morning, followed by animated talks with their family – Solomon and Hadar as well as Wolfe and Eva – Asher and Sarah had made their decision.

On a late afternoon in early October, a few weeks after the birth of the child, Rifka had visited them. The handover had been tearful and poignant for all of them, but Sarah assured Rifka that she would always be welcome to see her son who was named Abraham.

'You're so kind,' Rifka had said, 'but I think maybe it would be better for all of us if I stayed away.' Asher and Sarah understood.

Now, on New Year's Eve, with their first child nearly three months old, a miracle occurred: just a few days after Christmas and Chanukah, Sarah said something to her husband that he had never expected to hear.

'Asher, I think I'm pregnant.'

He stared at her, unable to believe his ears.

'Sorry, repeat that?'

'You'll have to buy another cot – we're going to have a baby!'

Wolfe chuckled to himself as he remembered the look on Asher's face when he told him the news. Truly, miracles could happen. He adored family life with Eva and Jacob and knew he was blessed in every way and should be happy and content, but the truth was, he was still restless, looking for some other enterprise. His thoughts were interrupted by a smiling Mr Shaffer, standing in front of the band.

'Ladies and gentlemen, please form a circle around the floor as we count down to end this year and bring in a New Year.'

Wolfe grabbed Eva's hand. As a Hasidic Jew in Poland and parts of London, he would not be doing this as the men would be separate from the women. It wasn't long after their arrival in London that the brothers realised how archaic it was in this day and age, especially after all he, Asher, and their wives had been through to escape the pogroms. He looked at Asher, who had not grown back his locks, and then to their wives who had not followed the old tradition of cutting off their hair once married. It didn't mean they had rejected their religious beliefs, or stopped going to the synagogue, but it gave them the freedom to express themselves. Anyway, Eva told him before they were married that she would never shave off her hair.

Everyone holds hands in a circle around the room as Mr Shaffer called out, 'Ten, nine ...' until with a resounding 'Happy New Year' echoing around the hall along with the popping of champagne corks, the band began to play 'Auld Lang Syne'. Wolfe and Eva kissed, and as they pulled away, she said, 'I'm pregnant.'

With the noise of the music and singing, he didn't hear her. 'What did you say?'

'We are having a baby.'

Joy and wonder appeared on his face as he picked Eva up and twirled her around – and Asher and Sarah, stood beside them, roared with laughter and joined in.

'We're having a baby, we're having a baby.'

It seemed that 1910 was off to a very good start.

Because of the success of the restaurant, other people had approached the brothers for a loan, or to become partners in a business venture. After being conned a few times because of their naivety, they had learnt to be cautious and made sure the person was genuine before undertaking any new venture.

One venture they did not hesitate to embark upon was a jewellery shop on the corner of Brick Lane and Chicksand Street. The premises had become vacant and Mr Kinsky approached them into becoming a partner. They knew nothing about jewellery, so they did the same deal they had with the Shaffer's. The brothers decided not to show their jewellery to Mr Kinsky just yet: it was there for emergencies. In the middle of all this, tragedy struck: Eva had a miscarriage. Wolfe was beside himself with anxiety for her, but he needn't have worried. That night as they lay in bed she said softly, 'It is fate, it wasn't to be. I promise there will be other children.'

Three days after the miscarriage she was cleaning the house, cooking, singing, and playing with Jacob as if nothing had happened.

The brothers invested money in another house and expanded the restaurant and its kitchen by buying the property next door.

But although free of financial worries and rejoicing in his son Jacob, Wolfe was still restless. He was sufficiently self-aware to know what the problem was, but dared not say it out loud as he landed a right into the punch-bag, nearly knocking Asher off his feet.

'Hey, what's with the attitude?' But Asher knew his brother better than anyone. 'Stop!' he yelled, just as Wolfe was about to land another punch on to the bag.

Wolfe ignored the yell, moving away from the bag shadow boxing and muttering angrily, 'What's the matter?'

'You.'

'Me? What have I done?'

'I know you better than anyone; you have to get this out of your system.'

'I don't—'

'You need another fight. Just tell her. Or is the big, muscular, brave, Wolfe Brown too frightened to face his little wife.'

'I'm not—' Wolfe smiled. 'Yes, you're right, but how do I tell her?'

'I'm sure she will understand.'

Wolfe raised an eyebrow. 'I don't think so; I promised that when Jacob was born I wouldn't fight again. I know what it is: she's scared I'll get hurt.'

'That's a normal reaction.' Asher moved over to his brother placing a hand on his shoulder. 'If you don't say anything it will eat you up and make you bitter, but you know that better than me.' He could see the disconsolate look on his brother's face. 'Let's get showered and changed. I'll give you an hour to tell Eva and—'

'Can't you come with me?'

'You need to do this on your own. In an hour I'll bring Sarah and Abraham to your house.'

'You're right – let's get this over and done with while I'm feeling brave.'

Asher laughed. 'Oh the scorn of a good woman frightens the toughest of men.'

*

Wolfe could hear Eva in the kitchen singing a lullaby. Taking a deep breath he pushed open the door. She stopped singing as he entered, giving him a welcoming smile. He walked over to her, bent to kiss her on the forehead and then took Jacob from her, looking down at his sleeping son and his heart swelled with love.

'Lay him down, and I'll make you a cup of tea. Would you like something to eat?'

'Thanks – a sandwich will do nicely.' He turned, kissed Jacob's cheek before placing him gently into the pram, covering him up.

He moved across the kitchen, wrapping his arms around Eva's waist as she placed the sandwich on a plate then turned to face him, her eyes looking into his and frowned. 'Okay, what's happened?'

'Nothing has happened.' He kissed her cheek, picked up the plate and mug of tea and sat down at the table.

Eva moved to the chair opposite, her hands wrapped around the cup, silently staring at him. 'Talk to me. Something's bothering you, why don't you tell me what it is?'

He took a sip of his tea, wondering how to tell her. If he didn't say something now, Asher would. 'I want to fight again.'

'What?'

'I want to—'

She held up a hand, stopping him from saying anything else. 'You promised me that once Jacob was born you wouldn't fight again.'

He stood and was quickly kneeling by her side, taking her hands looking into her eyes. 'I need some excitement, no that's not ... I didn't mean it the way it sounded. It's hard to explain why, but I need another fight. I know I promised. I won't if you say no.'

'How many fights do you need, and what would happen to us if you're injured?'

'I only need one now and again, just to get it out of my system.' He gave a wry smile. 'I promise not to get hurt.'

She sighed. He had been restless for the last couple of months. Usually he or Asher would come up with a new idea to invest their money, and that would take all his attention, but lately ... Eva stroked a lock of hair from his forehead.

'Okay, if it will give me back my smiling, happy-go-lucky husband, I will agree. But if you get injured I'll knock you out myself.'

He leaned forward. 'I love you, Eva Brown,' he said just before their lips met.

Minutes later, Sarah, Asher and Abraham arrived. Asher could immediately see the change in his brother. 'You told her.'

'Yes.'

'What did she say?' Just then Eva, Sarah and the children walked into the room.

'She said yes,' said Eva. 'As long as it stops him moping around and not getting beat up.'

*

The following day in the gym, Wolfe approached the promoter Fred Small as he watched two boxers sparring in the ring. 'Good morning, Mr Small.'

'What do you want?' he asked offhandedly.

'I was wondering if you needed another fighter for one of your bouts.'

Small looked him up and down and smiled. 'For you, I might—'

'Just tell me when and where.'

'After your last fight I'll have to find someone a little tougher.' He narrowed his eyes as if in thought. A sly grin crept over his face. 'I think I have just the man.'

Wolfe loathed Small. If he knew another promoter he would go to them, but he didn't. Between tight and angry lips he said, 'Who? And when?'

'Blackie Torres, in six weeks,' the usual place.'

'What's the purse?'

'If you beat him, which I doubt, fifty pounds. If you lose, which you will, twenty pounds.'

'Where might I find this, Torres?'

'Why?'

'I'd like to see who I'm up against.'

Small burst into laughter his belly moving like jelly in a bowl. 'What's so funny?'

'You.' He turned back to look at the men sparring in the ring. 'Once you've seen your opponent, you'll run a mile. I haven't been able to find him an opponent for over a year and it's costing me a fortune to keep him.'

'Don't worry, I won't run.'

'You'll find him at Tilbury Docks; just ask anyone where Blackie trains.'

'Thanks.' Wolfe turned and walked back to Asher, to the sound of Small's laughter.

*

The next morning Asher and Wolfe took the train to Tilbury. Asher asked one of the Dockers where they could find Blackie. The man pointed to a warehouse.

'You'll find him in there.'

The docks were busy, with scores of men unloading and loading ships. They entered the warehouse to the noise of shouting and rumbling wheels on concrete from barrows piled high with goods. They approached a man with a board, who seemed to be in charge.

'Excuse me, sir, can you tell us where we can find Blackie Torres?' Asher asked.

Seeing the smartly dressed brothers, the docker looked curiously at them at them. 'What do you want with Blackie?'

'We know the person he's going to fight in a couple of weeks, and we just want to see what he's up against.'

'You mean to tell me you have never seen Blackie fight? And someone has offered to fight him? Has this person got a death wish?'

'No, I don't think so.'

'This time of the morning you'll find him at the working men's club. He works out in the hall at the back of the building.' He pointed. 'Go out of here, turn right and right again at the end of the road. The club is on your left.'

'Thank you,' Asher said.

As the brothers turned and walked away, the man yelled after them, 'I must see this fight. Who's Blackie fighting?'

Without turning, Asher shouted back, 'Wolfe Brown.'

'I've never heard of him.'

'You will,' Wolfe said, but the man could not see the smile on his face.

They entered the Club, and immediately there was silence. The members' eyes followed the two strangers as they walked towards a door marked 'gym', opened it and entered. Inside, about twenty men were exercising, using weights, skipping; two were using a punch-bag while another punched rhythmically at a speedball. They moved towards the boxing ring in the centre of the gym.

His black muscles rippled under a skin that shone like ebony; rivulets of sweat slid down the bald head tucked behind boxing gloves; black-cat-like eyes were intent on the training mitts that moved left and right, up and down, in the hands of an older Blackie.

The brothers watched the boxer move across the ring, landing lefts and rights.

'He must be at least six feet two and as strong as an ox,' Asher whispered. 'Are you sure about this?'

Wolfe's eyes followed the man, watching every movement as he whispered back. 'Positive.'

Blackie finished his workout in the ring, and then took up a skipping rope. Wolfe didn't say a word, eyes concentrating on his future opponent as Blackie's father approached them.

'Can I help you, gentlemen?'

Wolfe didn't reply as he squatted down, head moving slightly from side to side. He straightened up, a smile on his face, 'No thank you, we're leaving.' He took Asher's arm, leading him out of the gym.

On the train back, Asher asked, 'Are you still going to fight him?'

'Why do you ask that?'

'Well, first of all he is at least two inches taller than you, has a stomach that looks like rolled logs, and biceps like rocks.'

Wolfe burst into laughter. 'My dear brother, you walk around with your eyes closed. Muscle isn't everything. It's also a person's state of mind.' He looked out of the window, saying quietly, 'Blackie lived off people being scared of his size, and straight away they had lost.'

'You promised Eva you wouldn't—'

'Yes, I know.' He turned back to his brother, 'And it won't happen this time, but I need your help, and I need to go and see Billy Reid.'

'What do you need Billy for? And how can I help?'

'While I go and see Billy, you buy a bicycle.'

Wolfe knocked at the gambling house door. A grill slid open: recognising him, the man inside opened the door. There was a quiet hubbub of sound as he entered the gambling house and was met by the manager, Frank. 'I'd like to see Billy if he's not too busy.'

'I'm sure he'll be pleased to see you, won't be a moment.'

While Frank went to see if Billy was available, Wolfe wandered round the room, amazed at the amount of money being gambled.

'Fancy your chances?' Billy asked a smile on his face.

'I only gamble on certainties.' They shook hands.

'I haven't seen you for a while, where have you been?'

'Fatherhood keeps me busy, and a couple of financial ventures. You know what happens – you mean to get in touch with someone and then get side-tracked.'

Billy laughed. 'I know what you mean. Boy or girl?'

'Boy, Jacob. If I remember, you have a daughter.'

'April, she just turned three, light of my life. Anyway, I'm sure you didn't come here to talk about children.'

'I need your help.'

'Come into the office, it's quieter and more private.'

As they entered the office Billy walked over to the drinks cabinet. 'Can I offer you a drink?'

'Whatever you are having will do fine.'

'Not in training?'

'Not yet; that's what I want to talk to you about.'

Billy handed Wolfe the drink, gestured to a chair and walked to the desk, taking a sip of whisky before sitting down. 'Okay, I'm listening.'

'I'm fighting Blackie Torres in two weeks' time and—'

'I know, and I think you're crazy. Do you know what he did to his last opponent?'

'No, and to tell you the truth—'

'He broke the guy's jaw, his nose and three ribs.'

'I presume you've seen him fight?'

'Yes, and—'

'Great.' Wolfe leaned forward in his chair placing his near-empty glass on the desk. 'Have you noticed how he tucked his chin behind his gloves?'

Billy nodded.

'And the way he moved around the ring?'

Billy frowned, trying to visualise Blackie in the ring, and shook his head. 'To tell you the truth, no, I haven't.'

'Well, he's flat-footed, and the reason he hides his chin – it's his weak spot. He doesn't have to move around the ring, he lets his opponent come to him, blocking their punches and then hits back hard with a counter-punch.'

Billy slammed his hand onto the desk. 'By all that's holy, you're right.' He narrowed his eyes, looking at Wolfe as if to say *where do I come into this?* He took a cigarette from a pack lying on the table, offered it to Wolfe, who shook his head. Billy lit the cigarette, blowing smoke into the air. 'Okay, what do you want from me?'

'I need a sparring partner.'

'What, why me, I haven't—'

'Yes, you have,' Wolfe interrupted, smiling. Billy stubbed out the half-smoked cigarette as Wolfe pulled his chair closer to the table. 'You were not an army boxing champion for nothing. I've been lucky so far with what natural skills I have, but now I need other skills that only you can teach me, and if my plan works we can make a lot of money.'

'Okay, I'm listening.'

'Blackie isn't fast across the ring, relying on his opponents to come to him, which they do. He is so powerful and accurate with his punching that when he lands one on his opponent, that's the end. He only has to come forward a couple of paces to finish the fight. My plan is to make him miss, use up his energy and back up a couple of paces so he has to chase me.'

Wolfe pointed to Billy. 'I need to spar with someone who has quick hands – that's you. And learn to counter-punch just as quickly as Blackie so that when he exposed his chin, which he does for a fraction of a second, I can beat him to it. There's another way to his chin, that's an uppercut, but to do that I have to be able to move in fast while avoiding his punches. That's where Asher and maybe a couple of your guys can help. Asher is buying a bike so I can build stamina.'

'Where does making a lot of money come into this?'

'Because of his reputation, everyone will be backing Blackie, but I'm going to beat him.'

Billy smiled. 'I'm getting to like you more and more.' He looked at the glass of whisky on the table and let out a sigh. 'One last drink, and then we are in training.'

He picked up the glass, clinked it against Wolfe's, and both men downed their drink in one gulp.

8   The Countdown

THE NOISE AROUND THE RING was deafening as Wolfe stood in his corner, waiting for the announcer to finish. He glanced down at Billy sitting in the front row. The Irishman gave a slight bow and winked. Over the last few weeks in which Billy had helped Wolfe prepare for the fight they had become close friends. Wolfe's body that leaned against the ropes was lean and muscular – he was ready and prepared for a hard fight. Wolfe looked across the ring at Blackie, who snarled, pointing a gloved fist at him. As usual when the referee was giving his instructions, Blackie tried to intimidate him: 'I'm going to beat you to a pulp, white boy.'

At least it was different from 'Jew-boy'.

The bell rang and Wolfe leapt across the ring landing a flurry of punches before Blackie had a chance to move. Taken by surprise, Blackie stepped back and threw a counter-punch, which missed as Wolfe swayed to one side, landing a hard right into the side of his opponent's body, and danced away. Blackie moved forward a couple of paces and stopped, chin tucked into his shoulder, eyes staring coldly at Wolfe, mouth set in a smiling snarl.

Wolfe gave an inward smile as he advanced slowly towards his opponent. Blackie threw a left, but Wolfe swayed away; Blackie grunted on receiving a right to the side of the ribs for his trouble. Wolfe was in front of him again, Blackie threw a left and right, then another left, but the punches were blocked. Wolfe danced slightly away from him, allowing the man to advance a couple of strides, then moved quickly away, avoiding the blows thrown at him, once again forcing Blackie to advance as he backed away. The bell rang to end the first round. Blackie had landed just three punches, all blocked on the arms of his opponent.

This pattern went on for the next four rounds. As the bell sounded to end the round, Blackie was puffing, and his punches were losing their power. Asher placed the gum shield into his brother's mouth as he got to his feet. Wolfe glanced at Billy, who mouthed, 'Now.' He nodded in agreement. This time when the bell went, Wolfe didn't rush across the ring as he had done in the last four rounds but waited for his opponent to advance to him.

The crowd was getting restless, wanting to see blood, preferably Wolfe's. Blackie threw a punch at Wolfe, who went into a huddle to whisper in Blackie's ear, 'You hit like a woman.' As he pulled away, Blackie let out a yell of anger, throwing a punch that missed and moved flat-footed across the ring like a raging bull. Wolfe back-peddled as his opponent threw lefts and rights, all missing their target as Wolfe moved away, or swayed to the right or left, throwing counter-punches which angered his opponent even more. As Wolfe had planned, he was forcing Blackie to follow him around the ring, whose punches were hitting only air. The bell went to end the round and Blackie walked slowly back to his stool, breathing heavily.

Asher fanned the towel in front of Wolfe as Billy yelled through cupped hands, 'It is time – go for it.' His new-found friend looked down at him and winked. The bell went and Wolfe was across the ring; he landed two punches and moved away saying, 'Come on, Blackie.' Blackie snarled in reply, nearly losing his gum shield as he trudged across the ring after him, blowing heavily through his mouth. His hands dropped slightly, and in a flash Wolfe landed a left to the face and a right to the jaw. Blackie rocked on his feet as the crowd yelled for him to fight back; he tried to fend off a flurry of left and rights, back-pedalling to the ropes, then his arms dropped wearily to his sides as Wolfe landed a left and right to the jaw, ending with an uppercut. As in a slow motion movie, Blackie swayed for a second then crumbled to the floor and to the silence of the crowd was counted out.

*

Wolfe was just getting out of the shower when Billy and Asher entered the dressing room smiling and were about to close the door when Mr Small walked in, looking subdued.

'Here's your money,' he said angrily, jowls wobbling as he added, 'You cost me a lot of money, Jew-boy.'

Billy moved towards him but Wolfe stepped in front of him. 'How much is a lot of money?'

'Three hundred pounds, I will not forget that,' the promoter said between clenched teeth. Dropping the money he owed Wolfe for the fight on the floor, he turned quickly and left.

'I think he doesn't like you very much,' Billy said.

'I couldn't care less.' He looked at Asher, 'How much?'

'Between the three of us, thanks to Billy taking bets in his gambling house, and Mr Small telling everyone that you wouldn't last two rounds, we made a fortune.'

'How much is a fortune?'

Billy touched Asher's arm, 'A thousand pounds.'

'What? That is a fortune.'

'Thanks to you,' said Billy.

As the three men left the hall, Frank and two of Billy's men tagged on behind them. Wolfe jerked his thumb backward as he asked, 'Why the bodyguards?'

'There are a lot of angry people who lost a lot of money because of you. In a couple of days it will be forgotten, but I'm not taking any chances tonight.'

Wolfe placed an arm around Billy's shoulders. 'Thanks, you're clever for an Irishman. Seriously, come over to my place for dinner tomorrow evening, I have a proposition for you.'

'Sounds intriguing – what time?'

'Shall we say seven o'clock?'

'Okay, I'll see you tomorrow.'

*

Eva and Sarah were waiting for them as they entered the house. Eva was immediately in front of her husband, looking for any damage to his face, but all he had was a bruise under his right eye, which by morning would be black. His arms were a different story. They were bruised and red from the blocked punches, and, if he was honest, quite painful.

Eva could see at once a different husband from weeks ago. She stood on tiptoe, placing her arms around his neck. 'You let him hit you,' then kissed him.

'That's about the only punch he did land on Wolfe,' Asher said.

'I've invited Billy for dinner tomorrow night at seven, if that's okay with you. Asher and I have a business proposition for him.'

'That's fine. I like your Irishman even though I haven't met him.' She gently touched the bruise on his face. 'It's the least I can do as he helped you keep your good looks.'

'That's not fair. I'm the one that did the fighting.'

'You should have been there,' Asher said excitedly. 'The crowd were silent as the referee counted Blackie out.'

Eva took an instant liking to Billy. In spite of her Belarusian accented English spiced with the odd Yiddisher word on the one hand, and Billy's thick Irish brogue on the other, but by the end of the meal Eva knew most of Billy's life story and he hers. He tried to coax her into telling him about Wolfe but she only knew a few snippets. When

Wolfe left the room for a few moments she said, 'Speak to Asher, he will tell you about his brother.'

The meal over, the men retired to the lounge. Wolfe poured three glasses of whisky and then offered his brother and Billy a cigar. Once the cigars were alight and all three sitting comfortably, Wolfe said, 'We should use the money we won, take out one hundred pounds each and invest the rest.'

Billy pointed the cigar at Wolfe. 'Invest in what?'

'Build a plush gambling house, with—'

'I have a gambling house,' Billy broke in.

'Yes, you do, but it's drab,' Wolfe pointed out.

'We are talking about catering for the big gamblers from the West End,' Asher added.

'A relaxing atmosphere with fine decor,' Wolfe took over from his brother. 'Give the big gambler special treatment, like transport to and from the Club if needed. Have pretty girls serving drinks, no hanky panky! Hire the best croupiers. Make it a place where the gentry will want to spend their money.'

'Have you a place in mind?' Billy asked.

'Yes,' Asher placed his cigar in an ashtray. 'It's a large four-storey house on Queen Victoria Street near Blackfriars. I've put a holding deposit on it, but we have to make up our minds by the end of next week.' He put a hand in his jacket pocket, pulling out a bunch of keys and looked at Billy. 'Are you free tomorrow morning?'

'As it happens, I am.'

Wolfe raised his glass. 'To us,' he toasted.

'I haven't agreed to anything yet.'

'You will, Billy, you will,' Wolfe smiled.

*

The following morning the trio walked through open, ornate wrought-iron gates, along a curved shingled driveway. On plinths either side of the six steps leading to the front door were stone carved rampant lions. From the bunch of keys in his hand, Asher unlocked the door leading to a long hallway whose black and white tiled floor had small diamond-shaped inserts in the corners. The high ceiling, pastel walls and chandeliers along the length of the hallway all showed off its opulence. They moved to the door on their left, entering a red floral carpeted room with two bay windows facing the street and another two to the side of the property, all with heavy drapes pulled back.

French doors at the far end of the room led to the rear garden with oak, plane and apples trees dotted here and there.

They moved out of the room to the one opposite which was identical except for a fireplace against the right-hand wall. The trio exited the room and walked to the end of the hallway up a wide, curving staircase, their shoes echoing on the stairs as they ascended to the landing and another hallway with three bedrooms, all empty of carpet or curtains. At the end of the hall was a toilet and bathroom. The stairs continued upwards to another landing where they found two more bedrooms and a toilet with washbasin.

Finally they descended to the basement where there was a kitchen. Outside the kitchen, four stairs led to the rear garden and a small plot for growing herbs. There was also a wine cellar, naturally empty.

'Well, what do you think?' Asher asked.

'It has great potential,' said Wolfe.

Billy made a circle with his sword stick on the ground. 'Good location, but it will need a lot of hard work and money.'

'We have the money,' Wolfe pointed out as he moved down the hall, pointing to the two rooms. 'These can be the card rooms, and the room opposite the roulette room. We can fit three or four roulette tables in there.'

'What about the rooms upstairs?' asked Asher.

'They can be ...' Wolfe smiled. 'Let's change the downstairs. The room at the rear can be a dining room. We can offer snacks to the gambler—'

'Punter,' Billy corrected him.

'Okay, punter, and drinks from the wine cellar.'

'If the ...' Asher looked at Billy, '... *punter* is a big gambler we can offer a complimentary drink, coffee if he or she wants.'

'Good idea,' Billy nodded in approval, adding, 'What about the two bedrooms on the next floor?' There was silence between them for a minute as they thought about it.

'They can stay as bedrooms,' Billy said. 'We—'

Wolfe waved a finger backward and forward, 'No hanky panky.'

Billy burst into laughter.

'What's so funny?' Wolfe asked.

'It's the way you said it. No, I was thinking that it could be accommodation for the manager; we are going to need one. And for any of the croupiers that don't have a place to stay.'

'Whoever said the Irish are dumb never met you,' Asher pointed out.

'So, Billy, what do you think?' Wolfe asked.

'It looks great. How much do they want for this place?'
'Two thousand,' said Asher.
'Can we beat them down?'
'We have dealt with this agent before. I am sure we can get a deal for cash,' Wolfe pointed out.
'Even if he doesn't, we will still buy it,' Billy said, holding out his hand. 'Put it there, partners,' He shook the brother's hands.
As they descended the front steps, Wolfe said, 'We are going to need a decorator.'
'I know just the person,' Billy said. 'Let's meet back here tomorrow with the agent to sign the papers and the contract of our partnership.'
'Good idea,' said the brothers in unison.

October 1910

There was an air of excitement and apprehension as the three partners and their manager Frank, attired in dress suits, greeted their guests with glasses of champagne. The opening night was by invitation only. The guests included MPs, titled gentry, local councillors and many others, among them a number of heavy gamblers.

There was a relaxed air and low hubbub of voices, the click of gaming chips, and the croupier's cultured, clipped 'Ladies and Gentlemen, place your bets' and, as the ball span around the roulette wheel, 'No more bets.'

Wolfe was smiling at their guests' reactions as they entered the house and wandered around, feeling at home with the ambiance of the place. The partners had changed their minds in regard to the rooms on the first floor. The two bedrooms on the left had been knocked into one room with tables and chairs, where gamblers could, if they want, have a drink and refreshments.

The room opposite was the manager's office with a safe at one end. The bathroom and toilet were now ladies' and gents' toilets. The top floor was Frank the manager's living accommodation.

Eva slid an arm through Wolfe's as she whispered, 'This is ... magnificent, it's so ... luxurious.' Her eyes showed her love for him. 'You look very handsome in your dinner suit, but I prefer you ...' She left the rest unsaid.

'Eva Brown, have you been drinking?' He tried to sound shocked, but instead burst into laughter.

'I hope our son is behaving himself,' Eva said.

'I'm sure he is.' Wolfe crossed his fingers behind his back: it was the first time they had used a nanny as the entire family were attending the party.

December 1910

The first New Year's Eve party at the Victoria was in full swing. The only criteria for admittance for the guests were they should wear fancy dress. By now the gambling house had become the premier venue for West End gentry to meet up in the East End and enjoy the Victoria's atmosphere, opulence and ambiance. The food with the hired chef was a great success, enabling hard line gamblers to stay all day; if slightly drunk they could be taken home in hansom cabs. Taxi drivers formed a queue every night as most of the fares were very lucrative.

In the garden was a marquee with a running buffet, dance floor and band. As the year wound down the three partners with their families mingled with the guests.

With five minutes to go, the gambling stopped and the waiters handed out glasses of champagne. Finally at 11.59 Billy moved to the stage, looked at the timepiece in his hand and in a loud, clear voice began to count down the seconds. As he yelled 'Happy New Year,' balloons dropped from the ceiling and outside there was a firework display. Billy's daughter April, perched on his shoulders, joined the crowds' 'oohs and ahs'.

In a dark corner, towards the back of the marquee, half hidden in shadow, a slim man with a pencil-thin moustache, dressed from head to toe in black, sat apart from the rest of the guests, desultorily drinking his champagne. Uninvited, he had managed to slip into the party along with a bunch of noisy revellers. He scowled, ignoring the festivities, instead concentrating his piercing gaze on Wolfe and Asher. Finally, he put his half-empty glass on the table and walked out of the Victoria Club into the darkness of the New Year.

9 The Le Feuvre Brothers

October 1911

WOLFE RAISED HIS ONE-MONTH-OLD DAUGHTER in his arms, his heart fit to burst as she held onto his little finger. 'I promise you, my little Chandel, you can always hold on to me.' He tenderly kissed Eva. 'We are so blessed.'

He smiled, remembering the present he had given Eva at Chandel's birth: he had taken a small box from his pocket and opened it. Sitting on a bed of cotton wool was a small gold Star of David and safety pin with a red ribbon, which would be pinned to the baby's vest.

'I'm sure our little girl will love it,' Eva had said, 'but, Wolfe, two is enough.'

He kissed her forehead and said, 'Thank you.'

It had been quite a year for babies. In August of the previous year, just a few days before Sarah had given birth to Adam – her second child but the first to be born from her womb – Eva had had a miscarriage. It had devastated both her and Wolfe, and over the next few weeks and months, Wolfe had been particularly tender and affectionate to her, only too aware of their loss. In January 1911, Eva had fallen pregnant again and throughout the term, Wolfe had fussed around her like a mother hen, anxious that nothing would endanger Eva or their unborn child. Then in May, Rachel, Eva's sister, gave birth to her second daughter, Ruth; in July, Billy's sister Megan had Nancy, naming her after Billy's wife. Finally, in September, to their joy, Chandel was delivered to Eva without a hitch, a beautiful baby girl.

On most weekends the families met alternatively at each other's homes, or took a picnic to Victoria Park. These were always happy occasions. Megan's husband Brian always took photos, especially of the children. Everyone was trying to match Billy up with a woman, who was usually invited to the Sunday get together and was often as embarrassed as Billy at both the arrangement and the result.

It was Eva's parents' turn to host the Sunday and Hadar had invited Esther Poznanski, a neighbour from her *Shtetle* at Mogilev Gordetz. She and her four-year-old son Yaakov had been in London for six months, but met by chance when Esther came into the bakery to buy bread.

As people began to arrive, Esther and Yaakov were introduced to them. Billy was immediately smitten, and Esther couldn't speak as their eyes met. It was an instant chemistry – magical, unexpected and miraculous.

As they ate, Esther related her story. 'My husband was killed at Veddel Island while we waited for a ship to bring us to England. Four men, one of them with one arm, tried to rob us. My husband fought them off, but not before the man with one arm shot him.'

Wolfe and Asher immediately looked at each other, both knowing that the man with one arm must be Goran Kroshnev, but they remained silent, not wishing to upset Esther by telling her.

Nobody noticed at first, but gradually as the year came to an end, it became apparent that Billy and Esther were becoming more than just friends. She was now part of the family Sunday get together. It was Eva who noticed it first. The way they looked at each other, smiling and touching hands whenever they passed, thinking that no one had noticed. Eva spoke to Sarah about it. At the end of the following Sunday's get together, Sarah agreed with her friend: something was going on between Billy and Esther.

They decided to tell Eva's mother. She smiled when they told her, saying, 'Yes I know.'

'But Mama, he is a Protestant and she is a Jewess,' Eva said in a shocked voice.

'In a sense, I feel that way too, but love knows no boundaries.' Hadar looked from her daughter to her adopted daughter. 'Would you have married your husbands if you didn't love them? You don't have to answer that – I know the answer.' She pointed a finger at Eva. 'Why didn't you shave your hair off when you got married like your sister?'

'Because I ...' Eva hesitated. 'The old world shuns modern music and dancing with the man you love, all those things. We love and adore our husbands, but does that mean we have to forgo our religious beliefs?'

'Who said Esther and Billy are doing that? I know they cannot help the way they feel about each other.'

'Why, has Esther spoken to you about it?' Sarah asked.

'Do you confide in your best friend?'

'We do,' they replied in unison.

Hadar smiled. 'Well, there's your answer. It is not our place to judge. Just be happy for them, that after such trauma and tragedy they have both found happiness.'

'You are a wise woman, Mama,' Eva said.

'No, just older,' was the smiled reply.

And for the first time in many years, Billy was smiling again.

*

They were in the middle of the ring sparing. 'You punch like a sissy. You're not holding back on me, are you?' Wolfe asked.

Billy smiled. 'I promised Eva I wouldn't hurt you, ouch, that hurt.'

'You deserve that for holding back.' Wolfe landed another punch, this time to the stomach. 'What's the matter with you? You're a million miles away?'

'I love Esther, and I—'

Wolfe stood still hands, dropping by his side. 'We all know that, and she loves you. So what's the–' Billy landed a punch on Wolfe's mouth. 'Hey! That's cheating.'

'Sorry, but I couldn't resist.'

'Okay, let's call it a day.' They jumped down from the ring, collecting Frank and Asher who were using the weights. Entering the dressing room Wolfe placed an arm around Billy's shoulder. 'So what's the problem?'

'I'm not Jewish.'

'We know that, so what's the problem?'

'We can't marry. If we do, the Jewish community, especially her rabbi, will disown her, and so will my church, although I must admit I don't go, and haven't been for many years, to my housekeeper's horror.'

'So why marry?'

'What?'

'Do you have to get married? I know living together will be frowned upon, but what choice do you both have? The only other way is for you to become a Jew, and I don't think the Irish community would like that. On the other hand, you could always decide not to see each other any more.'

'I can't do that, and you are not helping. I thought you would come up with something we haven't thought of.'

'Okay, I'll tell you what, we are meeting at your place this weekend. So why not talk it over with both families.'

'You sure they won't mind?'

'I'm sorry, Billy but that's all I can think off, apart from what I have just said.'

As they walked from the dressing room, a man wearing a dark-blue double-breasted suit entered the gym, dwarfed by two men who were unmistakably twins, and by their size appeared to be bodyguards. The trio came to a halt in front of Wolfe and Billy, who went to walk round them, but the twins blocked their way. Frank moved towards them, but Billy waved a hand behind his back and Frank moved into the shadows.

The slim man gave a slight smile, brushed his forefinger across a pencil-thin moustache, bowed slightly, looked at Wolfe and with a strong French throaty accent said, 'My name is Henri Le Feuvre. You are the fighter that beat Blackie, *no*?'

Amused by the Frenchman's accent, Wolfe said, 'Yes.'

'*Ah bon*, I would like to meet your manager to arrange a fight with my fighter, Jacques Dubois.'

'I don't have a—'

'I'm his manager,' Billy interrupted.

Le Feuvre smiled, showing even, white teeth. 'Can we make arrangements for a match between our fighters?'

'Well, *monsieur*, I'm afraid –' he gestured towards Wolfe '– my fighter had hung up his gloves.'

'What, that's not right. He has to fight Dubois.'

'He doesn't have to do anything.' Billy was gradually losing patience with the arrogance of the Frenchman who stepped towards Wolfe.

'I will give you five hundred pounds if you beat my fighter.'

'And if I lose?'

'Which you will, you get nothing.'

Wolfe stared at Le Feuvre as if he were mad. 'As my manager said, I have retired.'

'*Mon dieu*, you are a coward!' the Frenchman sneered.

Wolfe moved towards him, anger on his face, but the men on either side moved in front of Le Feuvre, the bulge under their jackets unmistakable.

'I don't think that even you, *monsieur*, are stupid enough to start something here.'

'It isn't me who is the coward, but you who hide behind these two. If I agree to this fight, where do you intend it take place?'

'We have a hall attached to our church in Spitalfields, which can accommodate three hundred people.'

'That's a lot of people in one hall,' said Billy.

The Frenchman smiled. 'We have a large congregation.'

'It seems this fight is very important to you, especially if you're putting up a purse of five hundred pounds?'

'Only to the winner,' La Feuvre pointed out.

Wolfe was intrigued by the offer – plus he would like to wipe the smirk off the Frenchman's face. He was still in pretty good shape; all he would need was a couple of months' training. He turned to Billy and whispered, 'Have you ever heard of this Dubois?'

'No,' was the whispered reply.

Wolfe turned away from the Frenchman and his bodyguards, leaning across to Asher.

'What do you think? I'm intrigued by the offer.'

'If I say no, you will still do what you want. I can see you want to, so what's holding you back?'

'Eva,' he replied with a slight smile.

'It's never stopped you before.'

Wolfe gave a slight nod and turned back to face Le Feuvre. 'If you feel so sure your fighter will win, I'll fight him, but the winner to receive two thousand pounds.' He thought the Frenchman would back down at such high stakes, but he was wrong.

A big smile creased the Frenchman's face, 'I agree. When would you like the fight to take place?'

'Two months.'

Le Feuvre nodded. 'Agreed, will Tuesday, 22nd May be convenient?'

'That's fine. Where is this hall?'

'It's at Christ Church in Spitalfields.' The trio turned and walked away.

'Where does your fighter train? And how will I get in touch with you if I need to?'

Without turning, Le Feuvre said, '25 Brushfield Street and you don't need to know where my fighter trains. You'll see him on the 22nd.' He waved with the back of his hand and walked out of the gym.

As he disappeared, Billy grabbed Wolfe's arm, spinning him round to face him, pointing at his forehead. 'Are you an idiot?'

'Yes, he is a *shmendrek*, a *meshugena*,'* said Asher.

'He was sneering at me, and I thought that he would back down when I said £2,000.'

---

* A fool, an idiot.

'He was goading you, and you bit.' Billy wagged a finger at Wolfe. 'Could you not see that he is a *gonif* and *shtaker*?'

'Our honorary Jew was right. As you have never seen this Dubois, how do you know you can beat him?' Asher asked.

'Did it not enter your head that from the way he spoke, his man must be a very good fighter? I thought you were clever, I've changed my mind.' Billy headed for the exit.

'Where are you going?' asked Wolfe.

'I have a beautiful woman waiting for me, who I am—'

'I need your help,' Wolfe pleaded.

'You should have thought of that before agreeing to the fight. Anyway, how can I help?'

'The same help you gave me with the Blackie fight.'

'And if I say no.'

A big grin on his face, Wolfe said, 'I know you won't.'

'Asher, I hope you still have that bike?' He wagged a finger at Wolfe. 'You are going to wish you never asked for my help.'

'I'll take that chance.' He walked up to Billy and gave him a hug.

'Get off me, you big oaf.'

Smiling, Wolfe moved slightly away, saying quietly, 'Can you help me find out where the Frenchie trains?'

'I'll let you know on Sunday. We can start training on Monday.'

'Thanks.'

After a shower they parted. Wolfe was apprehensive. Eva had just told him she was pregnant again: she was angry about the pregnancy as it was hard to cope at times with two young children.

He needn't have worried. All she said was, 'Don't get hurt. Otherwise I will hurt you more than your opponent.' He cuddled her to him, arching his back against her belly.

At that moment Sarah, who was also pregnant again and expecting a month after her friend, wagged a finger at her brother-in-law. 'Isn't it enough that you have two children to look after and one on the way that you agree to this stupidity? Your wife needs you and you want to fight. What happens if you get badly hurt?'

'Calm down,' he said. 'Eva said its okay.'

'Of course she will say that – she loves you.'

There was no answer to that. 'Would you like a cup of tea?' he asked.

'No thanks, I've left Asher with the children.' She gave him a withering look and kissed her friend. 'Eva, say no for once.'

Eva looked down at her belly and said jokingly, 'A bit late for that.'

'You always see the bright side. See you in the morning.'

*

The Sunday get together was in full swing as Billy, his arm around Esther's waist, clinked the glass in front of him a couple of times to get everyone's attention, which he did. He looked lovingly at the woman by his side. She squeezed the hand around her waist. He turned to glance around the room saying, 'We – Esther and I – need your help and advice. It isn't a secret.' He smiled. 'Well, I don't think it is; that we have been—'

'We are in love,' Esther interjected.

Billy took his hand from around her waist, taking hers in his, and held it to his lips. 'I couldn't have put it better myself. In normal circumstances that wouldn't be a problem, but Esther is a Jew and I'm a Protestant.'

'We have a variety of choices,' Esther joined in. 'Stay as we are, or—'

'One of us changes. We –' he looked into Esther's eyes '– want to be together. Ideally we would like to get married. So, there it is. We don't want to antagonise our religions, the rabbi or priest. But most of all,' he swept an arm around the room, 'our families and friends.'

'What happens if you have children?' Megan, Billy's sister asked.

'We have spoken about this at great length,' Esther replied, 'and we will show them both religions and when they come of age they will choose. We will not sway them one way or the other.'

'Billy, if it meant losing Esther, would you contemplate becoming a Jew?' Solomon, Eva's father, asked.

'To tell you the truth, Mr Goldberg, I have thought about it, as I am not a practising Protestant – to my housekeeper's dismay – and I don't know how my family and friends would feel about it, but …' He shrugged his shoulders.

Before anyone could ask Esther the same question she said, 'I am in the same boat as Billy. This is why we are asking for your advice.'

'You don't have to make a decision about it today. Please, think about it. Come to us at any time if you need to ask us any questions.'

'What we don't want to do,' Esther uttered, 'is for any of you to shun us without speaking out.'

'To tell you the truth,' Wolfe said, 'we can see you love each other, and I see no reason for us to deny you happiness. Personally, I'm happy that after the tragedies you have both been through in the past, you are happy. Anyway, I'm hungry, let's eat.'

That evening as they lay in bed, Wolfe asked, 'What do you think Esher and Billy should do?'

'What is your decision on it?'

He smiled. 'You answer a question with a question. That's just like a woman.'

'I'm sure, knowing you, that you have already made up your mind, so, tell me.'

'It was meant to be,' he turned to face her. 'The Lord works in mysterious ways. Think about it. Asher and I were supposed to go to America, but through certain circumstances we boarded a boat for England.'

He smiled and stroked a wisp of hair away from her forehead. 'And because of that I met you.' He sat up. 'The next thing in this round of fate is your father being attacked, and through that I met Billy, who I love like a brother.' He bent to kiss her forehead.

'We then become partners and he helped with my last fight. Then fate stepped in again. Esther happened to go into the bakery which her neighbour from back in the old country owned and is invited to our Sunday get together where she and Billy meet. Eva, it's meant to be. They love each other; you can see it on their faces. In this instant, believe it or not, religion doesn't come into it.'

He looked up at the ceiling. 'I believe that if Hashem had not wanted it to happen, it wouldn't have. I want them to get married, and the sooner the better for them and everyone else.'

Eva wrapped her arms around her husband, pulling him down to kiss his lips, then pulled slightly away, saying, 'My feelings exactly.'

That was the unanimous decision of both families and friends at the next Sunday gathering which happened to be at Sarah and Asher's home. It was decided that the wedding would take place two weeks after Wolfe's fight with Dubois.

*

In the meantime Billy intensified Wolfe's training with speed and weight work, using different sparring partners, some fast lightweights for speed and heavyweights that punched hard. Three weeks into training Billy pulled Wolfe aside.

'Dubois is a French champion. He lives and trains in a small place just outside Paris. He's due to arrive here next week and will be staying at Le Feuvres' house at 21 Brushfield Street.'

'How do you know this?'

'Frank and a couple of the boys went to reconnoitre the area. Monsieur Le Feuvre and his brother own a brothel at number 25.'

Wolfe laughed 'I cannot imagine what Frank and the boys were doing to get this information.'

'From what the girl said to Frank, the Le Feuvre brothers are not to be trusted.'

'What? Did Frank tell her why we need the—'

'Don't panic,' Billy interrupted. 'You should know Frank by now.'

A sheepish look on his face, Wolfe said, 'I'm sorry, you're right.'

'Come on, we'll go for a run, and thanks for your support with Esther.'

'You two are meant to be together. Everyone can see that.'

Billy smiled. 'Save your breath – you're going to need it.'

*

Billy stood behind Wolfe who had a bar with 160 pounds across his shoulders. Asher counted rep squats, and Billy urged him on.

'Come on, this is the last set. Give it all you have.'

Wolfe blinked the sweat from his eyes that ran from every pore in his body. His legs felt like jelly as he stared at the wall in front of him, the weight across his shoulders heavier by the second as he pushed up from the squat position with Asher counting '... fifteen, sixteen ...' Wolfe gulped in air then continued with Asher encouraging him, 'Come on, just one more.'

Wolfe gritted his teeth and slowly straightened up as his brother said, 'Well done – twenty.' With Billy's help he placed the bar on the rack just as a voice said, 'Monsieur Wolfe.'

Wolfe, Billy and Asher turned as one to see Le Feuvre in a grey suit, a red rose in the buttonhole of the lapel, a cane with a silver top in his right hand, the identical twin bodyguards by his side. He clicked his heels, mouth forming a slight smile, but his eyes were not smiling as he took a card from his jacket pocket and handed it to Wolfe.

'I am Gérard Le Feuvre – yes, Henri is my twin brother.' He stepped closer to the three men, looked Wolfe in the eyes, saying quietly in a matter-of-fact voice, 'I want you to throw the fight.'

Wolfe was silent, stunned by the audacity of the man. Billy stepped forward, fists clenched, to be confronted by the twins. Frank, who was training on the other side of the gym, put the weights down and walked towards his boss, saying something to two men behind him, but Billy, seeing him out of the corner of his eyes moving towards them, shook his head. He didn't want Le Feuvre or his bodyguards knowing Frank, not just yet. Frank stopped in mid-stride, turned away, saying something to the two men and they moved back into the shadows.

White-faced and tight-lipped, Wolfe said, 'Go away, little man, before I do something to you I might regret.'

One of the twins moved forward, and was suddenly doubled over holding his testicles as Wolfe, without warning, kicked him there. His brother's hand moved inside his jacket, but Le Feuvre placed a hand on his arm. 'That was a foolish thing to do, *monsieur*.'

'No, Frenchie,' said Billy. 'What you ordered him to do was foolish. By the way, does your brother know about this?'

Gérard ignored the question. 'You will regret your decision.'

Billy's eyes narrowed. 'Is that a threat?'

The Frenchman shrugged his shoulders. 'If you think it is, monsieur.' Le Feuvre mouth twitched in anger: this was not what he expected, and he was not used to anyone ignoring his requests. Without another word he turned and walked angrily and haughtily out of the gym. As he disappeared Billy waved Frank over.

'Find two men that didn't go to Brushfield Street the other day. I want to find out more about the Le Feuvre brothers. Do not go yourself.'

'Yes boss, I understand.'

'I'm going to have a shower,' Billy said.

'I'll join you; I need to get the smell of that Frenchie out of my nostrils,' said Wolfe through clenched teeth.

'He was very threatening,' said Asher.

'We can be just as threatening,' Billy retorted as he entered the shower.

The three men left the gym walking stride for stride along the street with Billy between the two brothers. He suddenly stopped; the brothers carried on a few paces before coming to a halt, turning to look back at Billy.

'What's the matter?' Wolfe asked.

'I wonder if Henri Le Feuvre knows about his brother's proposition.'

'We could pay him a visit and find out,' said Asher.

'Good idea, we'll get a cab.'

The taxi drove away. Two men stood either side of the front door of 25 Brushfield Street, one hand inside their jacket pockets, looking down at the trio who waited for a moment before climbing the five steps leading to the front door, coming to halt in front of the men. 'We would like to see, Henri Le Feuvre,' Billy said quietly.

'And you are …?'

'Tell him the Irishman.'
One of them pointed at the brothers, 'And them?'
'You don't have to know their names.'
One of them moved menacingly forward.
'I wouldn't do that if I were you,' Wolfe said coldly between tight lips.
The man stopped, looked at his companion, saying something in French and then turned to face the three fiends as the other man entered the house. 'He has gone to tell Monsieur Le Feuvre that you are here and want to see him.'
The second man returned and beckoned them to follow him. They entered the house, trailing behind the guard along a maroon-carpeted hall. He stopped at a door on the right and knocked. On hearing, 'Enter,' the guard opened the door, holding it so the three men could enter the room, and then left, closing the door behind him.
A red Persian carpet covered three-quarters of the grey mottled tiled floor. Pulled back maroon drapes with a fleur-de-lys design were drawn back from three wide windows with an arched design that looked over a garden stretching the length of the two adjoining houses. The furniture was of eighteenth-century French design. To the left of the door, covering the length of the wall and floor to ceiling were bookcases, their shelves full. To their right, getting up from a leather-bound chair behind a mahogany desk was Henri Le Feuvre. He walked around the desk, a smile on his face, but the eyes were cold and questioning. 'Welcome, *messieurs*, to my humble abode. May I offer you a drink?'
'No thanks,' Billy said, not taking the outstretched hand as the Frenchman stood in front of them, trying to keep the smile on his face at their refusal to have a drink with him and gestured to a settee and armchairs by the windows. 'Please sit.'
'This is not a social call,' Wolfe said angrily.
The Frenchman was taken aback by Wolfe's open hostility and moved back towards the desk. Opening a silver cigarette box, picked it up, offering it to them, but the trio shook their heads. He shrugged his shoulders, turned away extracting a cigarette from the box, placing it in a long holder and lit it, letting the smoke trickle from his mouth as he moved back behind the desk. He dropped on to the chair no longer smiling looking from one to the other, 'So, why are you here?'
Wolfe moved angrily forward, but Billy pulled him back, whispering, 'Let me handle this.'

Wolfe looked at his friend, his anger gradually subsiding at the calmness of Billy's voice as he took a couple of steps towards the desk.

'Your brother came to see us today with a ... proposition – no, more like a demand. We want to know if you are in on this demand as well.'

A perplexed look appeared on the Frenchman's face. 'What are you talking about? Why should my brother visit you? We are in agreement about Dubois fighting, but anything else I know nothing about.' Le Feuvre gestured with his hand, clearly puzzled.

'He told me to throw the fight,' said Wolfe.

Le Feuvre leapt to his feet. 'What?' He shook his head, walked with long strides to the door, flinging it open. Saying something to the man by the door, and then walked back, slamming the door behind him to stand in front of Billy and the brothers.

'I may be many things,' he said behind tight lips, 'but to ask someone to do such a despicable thing ...' Lost for words, he turned to walk over to the drinks cabinet and without offering, picked up a cut-glass decanter, pouring the liquid into a matching glass and taking a long drink.

The door opened and in walked Gérard, smiling. Glancing at the trio as he walked aloofly towards his brother, but stopped in mid-stride as Henri erupted in an angry tirade in French to which Gérard replied just as angrily. Henri stepped forward and without warning slapped his brother hard on both cheeks. Gérard reeled back, one hand holding his right cheek as his brother continued spitting out words like a machine gun, with Billy and the brothers looking on, not understanding a word that either of them was saying.

Gérard turned to the trio, hatred in his eyes as he shook his head, saying, '*Non, non.*' Henri's face was red with rage; he picked up a bottle by its neck and was about to strike his brother who raised a protecting arm to his head.

'Stop,' yelled Billy, moving quickly across the room to grab Henri's arm, taking the bottle from him placing it back on the cabinet, and then dragging Henri across the room, forcing him down onto the settee, turning to Wolfe. 'Bring that piece of crap over here. If he resists, knock him out.'

Not taking any chances, Wolfe searched Gérard, finding a small derringer in his pocket, and unceremoniously pulled him towards an armchair, pushing him down onto the seat. 'Stay there.'

Billy stood between the French brothers. 'Unfortunately we don't speak French, so can you,' he pointed to Henri. 'Tell me what was said?'

'Firstly,' Henri said, 'I had nothing to do with asking Monsieur Brown to throw the fight. I am very angry with my brother. If it were one of my men that did that, I would have killed him.'

'So why did he—'

'Debts I know nothing about. He is—' he waved an arm, looking for the English word '—heroin addict, spends all his time in Chinatown out of his mind, playing Ma-Jong. Naturally he thinks he is a good player.'

'I am,' said Gérard.

'Pff, *mon dieu*, are you that naive. You owe then a fortune.' Henri pointed at Wolfe. 'Did you think about the dishonour you are asking of him, and the dishonour to Dubois?' He stood and walked over to his brother, kneeling beside him. Gently touching his face, saying softly, 'This is not who you are. Yes, we are not entirely good men, but when it comes to a fight between gladiators ...' He left the rest hanging in the air. 'I think it is time we did something about your addiction.'

He kissed his brother on each cheek and got to his feet. Walking quickly over to the door, he said something to the man outside, leaving the door open, and walked back to stand in front of Billy and the brothers.

'I am sorry about this. If there is anything I can do to make amends for my brother's stupidity, don't hesitate to ask.'

'There is one thing,' said Wolfe.

'And that is?'

'I think the loser of the fight should receive some money. As you have put up a two thousand pounds to stage this fight, which is an awful lot of money, I think the winner should receive three-quarters of the purse and the loser a quarter.' He smiled. 'I would hate to think of Dubois going back to France with nothing.'

'If you are so sure you are going to win, would you like to make a small wager on it?'

'What do you have in mind?' asked Billy.

'Shall we say, a hundred pounds?'

'And the odds?' said Asher.

'Odds?' The Frenchman stroked his moustache. Just then, the twin bodyguards walked into the room. The one with the sore testicles gave Wolfe a withering look as he passed. Henri spoke to them in French, pointing to his brother. As they helped him to his feet, Gérard looked at Wolfe and in barely a whisper said, 'My brother is right; I am sorry, monsieur, for the way I have acted towards you. Please forgive me?'

'If it helps you, yes, okay, I forgive you.'

Gérard nodded, and with the twins dwarfing him, left the room, the door closing behind him.

Henri walked back to the drinks cabinet. 'Can I offer you a drink?'

'We are in training,' said Wolfe, 'but thank you for the offer.' He turned to go.

'The wager?'

'Let's say, evens,' Billy suggested.

The Frenchman smiled and held out his hand, which this time Billy took.

La Feuvre looked questioningly at the brothers, who smiled and shook his hand, saying in unison, 'Hundred pounds.'

It was a week before the fight. Billy, Wolfe and Asher had secretly managed to get into the gallery, looking down at the boxing ring where Dubois was sparring.

The Frenchman was about two inches shorter than Wolfe, broad-shouldered, with muscular chest and arms, a slim waist, tree trunks for legs and fast on his feet.

'He doesn't punch very hard,' Wolfe whispered to Billy.

'I've noticed that.'

'I don't understand how he can have six knockouts.' He looked at Billy. 'Do you think they know we're here, he's acting like a *klutz*?'

Asher looked around and behind to see if they had been discovered, but they were alone.

'I wouldn't put it past Le Feuvre,' Billy replied. 'I think he can be a devious bastard.'

Wolfe's eyes followed the boxer across the ring, a frown creased his brow. He shook his head and then said, 'Let's go,' and took one last look at Dubois, thinking, *whatever happens, I'll be ready for any surprises.*

10 Wolfe Versus Dubois

IN THE WEEKS AFTER THEIR MEETING with Henri Le Feuvre, Billy had gathered a lot of information about him. The private detective he hired without telling the Brown brothers didn't come cheap, but it was worth it.

In France the Le Feuvre brothers were thieves, specialising in fine art and jewellery, but they were also big gamblers who did not like losing. This statement caught Billy's interest. He sat thoughtfully back in his chair, slowly rimming the glass of brandy in front of him. After a few moments he carried on reading.

Henri had lost a lot of money in a private chemin-de-fer game to a well-known politician who he thought was cheating and killed him. The police arrested Henri and with four other criminals, including the twin bodyguards, were being transported to prison when his brother Gérard rescued him with two of their cousins, killing two policemen and the driver, and went into hiding.

With the French police scouring Paris for them, the brothers, their cousins, the twins and two others decided to rob a bank and escape to England. They robbed the Bank Lyonaisse and fled the country to East London and the French quarter of Spitalfields. They bought – well, let's say the occupants of the three houses in Brushfield Street were given an option, to sell, or – Billy's jaw tightened, fists clenched in anger as he read on. The owner of number 25 refused to sell. He was dead and hardly recognisable when they found him in Bunhill Fields. His widow and children, now without a husband and father, sold the house to the Le Feuvres. Soon after obtaining the houses they opened the brothel.

Most of the girls were poor immigrants who needed a roof over their heads. Henri and Gérard befriended these girls, giving them a nice time and seducing them. A month into the relationship, while having a meal in a restaurant, Le Feuvre would not be his usual bubbly self. The girl, believing they were in love, would ask what was troubling him. Naturally it would be money worries. While Le Feuvre left the table to go to the toilet, a man would come along and sit down. The girl would naturally ask him to leave. Of course he wouldn't. It was then that Le Feuvre returned, looking very upset on seeing the man who would threaten Le Feuvre, demanding the money he owed him.

Before she knew it, the girl would say she would do anything to help her lover – who she believed was going to marry her – to pay back his debts. The man got her to sign for the IOU. Too late, she realised her mistake and the French brothers owned her. If she tried to leave, she was beaten, or to prevent others from trying to escape, she would be used as an example and killed.

Billy leant back in the chair, thoughtfully looking up at the ceiling. He suddenly leapt to his feet, ran to the door yelling, 'Frank!'

Frank nearly collided with his boss, gun in his hand as he ran into the office, quickly looking around, a puzzled to find it empty.

'You okay, boss?'

Billy felt a little sheepish. 'Sorry, Frank, I didn't think it sounded that bad.'

'That's okay, boss.' He replaced the gun into its shoulder holster. 'It must be important for you to yell like that.'

'Yes, it is. I want you to send two men round to the Browns. Tell them I need to see them immediately.'

He paced up and down the room. 'Make sure they bring their wives and children and pack clothes for a week, maybe more. Send some men to Spitalfields who the Le Feuvres have never seen before, here, or at the brothel. I want to know if Gérard Le Feuvre is back at the house; make sure the enquiry is discrete. I don't want them knowing we,' he waved a hand in the air, looking for the word, 'are checking up on them.'

'Yes, boss.' Frank went to leave the room.

'Make sure the men are armed.'

'What?' Apart from Frank, Billy didn't nowadays allow the men to be armed.

'I'll explain later.'

When Frank had gone, Billy left the club and hailed a taxi, returning an hour later to the office and making a couple of phone calls. He had just replaced the receiver when Wolfe entered, the others trailing behind.

'What's going on?' he asked.

'I'll tell you in a moment,' Billy turned to Eva and Sarah. 'I'm sorry about this, but I need you and the children to go away for a week or two. I cannot explain why, yet, but please trust me. Esther, Yaakov, Mrs Burns, April and Alice are going with you. I have arranged accommodation for you at a hotel in Westcliffe.' He pointed to the two men who had brought them there. 'These two men are going with you.'

Eva went to say something, but Billy held up a hand stopping her, saying in a quiet but earnest voice, 'Please Eva, do as I ask. I assure you, that as soon as I can, I'll explain it to you, but for now, speed is of the essence.'

'Okay, Billy,' Eva said, but as soon as you can, I – we – need to know why the urgency.' She turned, and with Sarah looking strangely at Billy as she passed, they left the room.

Billy was about to explain to Wolfe and Asher what was happening, when Esther, Mrs Burns, April and Alice entered. Billy gave his daughter a hug and a kiss, taking Esther's hand moved across to the other side of the room. 'Please don't ask me why now,' he said. 'I need you to do this for me.'

'Are you in some sort trouble?'

'No – Esther I love you very much. Please forgive me if I don't tell you right now, but when I do, you will understand.'

She kissed his hands. 'I trust you, my life.'

Just then Frank entered. 'Everything's ready, boss.'

'Thanks. You and the others can give us a hand with the luggage.' Picking up a case, he headed for the door.

Outside, standing at the kerbside, was a bus. The men said their goodbyes to their women and children. Looking anxiously around, Billy told them to get aboard. The men waved goodbye as the bus pulled away. They watched it until it disappeared from view. Before following the others who had entered the Club, Billy looked up and down the road, and then followed them. Wolfe, Asher and Frank were waiting in the hallway for him.

'Follow me, and I'll tell you what it's all about. Frank, ask the men to come into the office.'

Billy settled into the chair behind the desk. Wolfe and Asher took an armchair facing Billy. Frank and six of Billy's men entered the room.

Billy, absentmindedly took a cigarette from the box in front of him, but didn't light it as he said, 'You are all wondering what's going on?' He looked down at the unlit cigarette between his fingers.

'As you know,' he pointed to the men, 'Wolfe here is fighting the Frenchman, Dubois. Certain things have happened that made me think that this fight is—' he waved the cigarette in the air '—going to be rigged in some way in the Frenchman's favour.' He stood to walk around the desk, perching himself on the edge. 'I did a little digging, well to be truthful someone did it for me and found out that the Le Feuvres will stop at nothing to win, or gain what they want. It was

Wolfe's remark while we watched Dubois sparring that got me thinking.'

He stood and paced slowly up and down the room, head down, as he continued. 'Let's take the last fight Dubois fought. In the third round he knocked the man out.'

'What? That's impossible, 'Wolfe interrupted, adding, 'Unless he knew we were—'

'No.' Billy held up a hand stopping his friend from continuing. 'His opponent was drugged.' He took a telegram from his pocket and waved it. 'This is a reply from the trainer of the last man Dubois fought. He says he couldn't prove it, but it was either in the drink at the ringside or maybe the meal at the hotel. It seemed that even though the Le Feuvres don't live in France, they have contacts there, and Dubois is their cousin. The trainer told me the agreement was, the loser gets nothing. They also bet very heavily on their cousin to win at odds of twenty to one, and made a fortune.'

He stopped pacing. 'The fighter before that threw the fight after they kidnapped his family.' He poured some water into a glass. The room turned silent at what Billy had revealed.

'Is that why you sent our families away?' Asher asked.

'Yes.'

Wolfe got to his feet, anger on his face and in his voice. 'The bastards, I'm still going to fight him, we just have to prevent, Henri's plan. If what you say is true about the Frenchmen, then I'm sure they know the Goldberg's are my in-laws, and Megan you're—'

Billy turned quickly to Frank, interrupting Wolfe. 'Go to Megan's house, tell her that she and Brian must take the children to the hotel, she will know which one. Make sure they aren't followed, and then come back here.'

Without a word, Frank was out the door and on his way. Billy looked at Wolfe. 'We have to find some men to guard your in-laws.'

'They have to be Jewish,' Wolfe pointed out.

'Well then, we'd better get cracking,' said Billy, moving behind the desk. Opening the drawer he took out a pistol, placing it in a shoulder holster under his jacket.

With Billy's help, they found six Jewish men. Three had been forced into the Russian army and escaped. The other three were young, seventeen years of age, with no jobs and, at this moment in time, no future.

While Wolfe and Asher explained the situation to their in-laws, Billy armed the new Jewish recruits and set up a twenty-four-hour guard rota inside the bakery. Within a couple of days, Mr Goldberg had his guards making bagels.

The man sent to reconnoitre the Le Fuevres returned, whispering something to Billy about Gérard.

Billy nodded. 'Thanks, get a drink, pick up a rifle and make sure we have no unwanted guests.'

When the man left, Wolfe asked, 'What's this about Gérard?'

'He's in a drugs clinic,' said Asher.

Billy shook his head. 'No he isn't, and the drug thing is a lie to put us off the scent. Yes, Henri was truly angry with him as he hadn't yet found out where we live, so he couldn't kidnap anyone, and there is no way of him blackmailing you to throw the fight. Our good friend Gérard has returned home as we speak.'

'There is just under a week till the fight, what do you have in mind?' Wolfe asked, and then gave a wry grin. 'I can see you have a plan.'

Billy smiled back. 'You've been reading my mind.'

'Excuse me,' Asher butted in, 'but this is no laughing matter.'

'I agree,' Billy said, turning to look at Frank. 'You are to stay with me at all times.' He pointed to two other men. 'You are to stay with Wolfe and Asher wherever they go.' He gave a slight smile,' I hope you three are fit, as training continues tomorrow morning.'

'They can't come into the synagogue on the Sabbath,' Wolfe pointed out.

'Then I'm afraid, you and Asher will have to give it a miss this week. I'm sure you will be forgiven. And another thing: no one- and I mean no one—' he pointed at Wolfe and Asher '—and that includes your parents-in-law – must know where our families are.' He walked over to the other four men. 'Split into twos, I want a twenty-four-hour guard on this place. Anyone that looks suspicious, or you haven't seen before, does not enter unless I say so. Is that clear?'

'Yes boss,' they answered in unison.

'Where are we staying?' Wolfe asked.

'A lady I helped some time ago is going to put us up. We will still train at the Repton Club,' Billy replied.

'They know we train there – shouldn't we train somewhere else?' said Asher.

'The place is always crowded. I'm sure they'll not start anything there.'

'Sorry, you're right, it makes sense.'

*

With four days to go till the fight, Billy intensified Wolfe's speed and stamina but, although they haven't said anything to each other, both were worried.

Since the retribution he had handed out to the Jennings gang, Billy and his men had kept a low profile. With Esther now in his life he didn't need this confrontation with the Le Feuvres, but in his heart he knew that once the fight with Dubois was over, win or lose, the Le Feuvres would always be a threat to him, the Brown brothers and their families. He was not the sort of person that liked to be looking over his shoulder.

Wolfe landed a punch to his chin, catching him by surprise. He took off his head guard.

'Let's take a breather.'

Wolfe was also worried by the same thoughts as Billy. He never thought he would meet anyone like the Le Feuvres in London. They were the kind of people like his nemesis, Goran Kroshnev. He knew the Frenchmen would always be a threat to him, Asher, Billy and their families and he had to talk to Billy and Asher about it. He moved across the ring to face his friend. 'Billy, we have to talk.'

Billy nodded, taking off his gloves. 'I know what you are going to say and I agree – we need to discuss the situation.'

They returned to Mrs Flynn's, the seamstress's house. The three friends and their bodyguards sat round a table eating a meal their hostess had made.

Wolfe was the first to break the silence. 'We have, I think reached a situation, which in all honesty I never thought would happen in this country where it's kill or be killed. We have to take the initiative because as I see it at the moment, the French brothers hold the trump cards.'

'Why do you say that?' said Asher.

Wolfe leaned forward, elbows on the table, and was about to reply but Billy interjected, 'Wolfe is right. It's not their families that are in hiding, or have a twenty-four hour guard protecting them.'

Asher remained silent, realising for the first time how dangerous these Frenchmen were.

'The thing is,' said Wolfe, 'whatever we do the law must not be able to associate us with the Le Feuvre brothers, except as promoters of the fight.'

'Have you got something in mind?' said Frank.

'Not exactly, but I'm open to suggestions,' Wolfe replied. 'Whatever we plan, it has to take place after the fight.'

Well into the night and early morning the six men discussed various scenarios regarding the demise of the Frenchmen without their families knowing what they were about to do. By four in the morning they had their plan, but they needed another person's help.

'Do you think he will go for it?' Wolfe asked.

'There's only one way to find out,' Billy replied, turning to his trusted bodyguard. 'Frank, tell Sergeant O'Brien I have something urgent to discuss with him and would he be so kind as to come immediately.'

'Excuse me, boss, but it's four in the morning.'

'I know that, but we haven't much time.'

While they waited for Frank to return they busied themselves with checking bets on the fight that had been coming in thick and fast.

Wolfe was looking at some betting slips. He let out a low whistle. 'Hey come and have a look at this.'

The men peered over his shoulder.

'Abe the barber has six hundred pounds worth of bets, all at twenty to one in favour of Dubois.'

'So what's odd about that?' Asher asked.

'See who put the bets on?'

'Ah! It was the Frenchmen,' said Billy.

'Hang on, that's not all. See these slips; they're from Jimmy Logie, the newspaper-seller, same bets for the same amount at the same odds.'

'They know these men work for us,' Asher whispered.

'They must have been planning this for a very long time,' Billy commented.

'There's something more to this than meets the eye,' said Wolfe.

'It's a lot of money, that's what it is,' said Asher.

Just then Frank walked in with Sergeant O'Brien who was looking very tired and dishevelled.

'This better be good, Billy,' the policeman said a little grumpily.

'Drink, Jimmy,' Billy replied nonchalantly.

'I'd love to, Billy, but I'm on duty in …' he looked at his watch '… two hours.'

'Frank, can you get the sergeant a cup of tea while I talk to him.'

O'Brien noticed Wolfe and Asher for the first time and smiled. 'I have to thank you for recommending the barber Abe to me.' He ran a hand across his chin. 'He gives the best shave I've ever had, but I have to make him stop telling me jokes while he's doing it.'

'My pleasure,' said Wolfe.

'Sit down Jimmy,' Billy said softly.

The sergeant moved to one of the armchairs and dropped on to the seat.

'What would you say if we could point you in the direction of cop killers?'

O'Brien sat forward in his seat. 'I and my fellow officers will be very grateful.'

Billy told him about the Le Feuvre brothers and their men. When he had finished, there was silence for a few seconds, a shocked expression on O'Brien's face.

The silence was broken by Wolfe. 'Sergeant, we have a plan, but we need your help.'

'You have it.'

For the next hour they outlined their plans to the sergeant, who from time to time added some input.

Finally O'Brien looked at his watch. 'I'd better go.' He got to his feet. 'I'll be in touch.'

'We haven't much time,' Billy pointed out.

'Billy, me lad, don't worry, those Frenchie's are in for a shock.'

22 May 1912

The hall was packed to the rafters and the noise deafening as Wolfe entered the ring. He looked across to the opposite corner at Dubois and frowned. Billy massaged the back of his shoulders as Wolfe looked intently at his opponent and turned to Billy, 'That is not the Dubois we saw sparring.'

'What are you talking about?'

'The man in the opposite corner is a leftie.'

Billy looked intently at Dubois, and then gave a sharp intake of breath. 'Begorrah, you're right.' He swivelled round to look to where the Le Feuvre brothers were sitting. In between the brothers was a clone of the man in the ring. Henri Le Feuvre gave a slight smile and bow of the head. Billy's jaw tightened; it seemed that Henri liked collecting twins. Billy would have loved to wipe the smirk off the Frenchman's face. If their plan went as it should ... He looked in Frank's direction and nodded. The bodyguard smiled and left the hall.

The referee called the boxers and their seconds into the ring. Asher and another of Billy's men guarded the water, making sure no one came near them.

Wolfe looked into Dubois grey eyes, which seemed to be smiling at him.

The mouth twisted in a sneer as he said in a guttural French accent, 'Jew, you go down as Gérard asked you too, otherwise your family will suffer.'

Wolfe didn't reply but turned without touching gloves, mouth set in a determined line as he returned to his corner. Billy placed the gum shield in his mouth as the bell rang and the two fighters moved into the middle of the ring. The Frenchman jabbed out a right which Wolfe easily avoided and counter-punched, but missed as Dubois slid away. It was then he knew he had a fight on his hands.

Suddenly, as the bell went to end round five, he saw it – that one weakness – and returned smiling to his corner. Both men had cuts on their faces and at one time Dubois tried to stick his thumb into Wolfe's eye but he saw it coming.

Wolfe didn't say anything to Billy who was standing in front of him waving the towel to cool him down. 'Stay away from his left, he's caught you a couple of times.'

Wolfe nodded in reply, but was now raring to go. The bell sounded and he leapt to his feet, changing his stance to match his opponents. Dubois was taken completely by surprise as in quick succession Wolfe threw three right jabs, followed by a left to the jaw. Dubois shook his head and moved forward, but Billy's speed training helped Wolfe as the Frenchman swayed from side to side, hatred in his eyes as he threw a couple of jabs but his fist fell on thin air. His head jerked back as Wolfe landed two quick jabs and danced away. Dubois let out a roar of anger and rushed across the ring. Wolfe allowed him to clinch. 'Not so easy when someone isn't drugged.' He moved out of the clinch, landing a right to his opponent's jaw, and was about to follow through when the bell went.

Wolfe glanced at Dubois, a slight smile on his face as he sat on the stall planning the next round.

Asher gave him a drink, swilling the water round his mouth, spitting it out into a bucket as Billy asked with a big smile on his face, 'What was that?' He waved the towel. 'I'm glad I changed my mind about fighting you when we first met. I wish my friend Bull could have seen you.'

'Look over to the next corner,' Wolfe whispered.

Billy turned. Henri Le Feuvre was waving his arms at Dubois, spittle coming from his mouth, yelling at him.

The bell went and Wolfe got quickly to his feet but Dubois was faster and in his face before he had taken two steps, landing a hard right and left to his face. Wolfe wove to the right, away from the next punch, landing a right to the exposed ribs of his opponent. Dubois gasped at the force of the punch, and for a second his arms dropped slightly. Like pistons, Wolfe landed lefts and rights as he would a speedball in the gym.

Dubois back-pedalled, trying to get away from the onslaught, but the speed of Wolfe's punches made that impossible as his back came up against the corner ropes. Wolfe landed another punch to the ribs, the crack audible to both fighters and ringside spectators above the yells of the crowd. The Frenchman's hand went down to protect his injured ribs. Wolfe landed an uppercut that virtually lifted the Frenchman off his feet, who grabbed the ropes to stop himself from falling. Wolfe stepped forward saying, 'This is from the Jew.'

Dubois jaw jerked sideways from the force of the punch, his gum shield flew out of the ring as he slid to the floor, out for the count. Billy rushed across the ring, lifting Wolfe in the air.

Back in the dressing room, Wolfe was getting dressed when there was a knock on the dressing room. Asher opened it to see the Le Feuvre brothers standing there.

'We have come to pay our debt,' Henri said, that slight sneering smile as usual on his face.

Asher allowed them in closing the door once they were inside.

Gérard took an envelope from his pocket, handing it to Billy, 'Your winnings.'

'And our bet?' Asher asked.

'I'll have that later,' Henri replied.

'I hope there are no bad feelings,' Billy said, holding out his hand.

Henri took it. '*No*, it was a brilliant fight by Monsieur Wolfe.'

Billy smiled. 'In that case, we would like to invite you to dinner at the club, eight o'clock sharp.'

Knowing he could not refuse the invitation, Henri smiled, not with the eyes, just the mouth, 'Thank you, we will be honoured.'

*

On the dot of eight, the Le Feuvre brothers arrived, to be welcomed by Mr Shaffer who was catering the dinner, with a glass of champagne.

Billy grabbed Wolfe and they moved across the room towards the Frenchmen. A waiter offered a tray of canapés and the brothers took one.

'I'm so glad you accepted our invitation,' Billy said, close to Henri's ear so he could be heard above the other voices.

'It's our pleasure,' Henri replied, placing a hand into his jacket pocket. 'This is—'

Billy put a hand on his arm. 'Not now, later.'

Henri nodded and took a bite of his canapé. The waiter moved over to him again and he took another, emptying the glass of champagne.

'Would you like another drink of champagne?' Billy asked, adding, 'Or perhaps something more to your liking?'

'What do you have in mind?'

'I have a twenty-year-old cognac in my office.'

Henri smiled. 'Lead the way.'

The Le Feuvre brothers followed Billy into the office, Wolfe bringing up the rear.

Henri handed Billy an envelope, 'Our bet.'

'Thanks.' Billy took the envelope and walked across the room to a drinks cabinet pouring four glasses of cognac, handing one to Henri then Gérard. Wolfe and Billy faced them and raised their glasses.

'Your good health,' Billy toasted.

The brothers clinked glasses and drank.

'How is Dubois?' Wolfe asked.

'Broken ribs and jaw, how do you think he is?' Gérard replied angrily.

Billy poured him another brandy and then moved to stand in front of his desk, gesturing to the armchairs. 'Please sit.'

The Le Feuvres seemed to walk unsteadily towards the seats.

'Here, let me help you.' Wolfe offered a hand, helping Henri into the seat, but his brother Gérard pushed Wolfe away and then fell face down onto the armchair. Wolfe picked him up like a rag doll and turned him around.

'What's going on?' Henri demanded.

'We know all about you and your friends in Paris and drugging your fighter's opponents.' Billy took a couple of paces forward, bending his face close to Henri. 'You would never have left us in peace after Wolfe beat Dubois. There are some people here who are dying to see you.'

'Wwwhat people? What was in the drink?'

Wolfe opened the door and four men entered with Sergeant O'Brien.

Henri's eyes opened wide in fear on recognising one of the men and his voice quivered. *'Non, oh non!'* He tried to get up, but fell back, while Gérard screamed in fear. Two of the men took Gérard's arm and dragged him from the room as Sergeant O'Brien said, 'Billy, Wolfe, May I introduce Monsieur Vernon, Paris Police.'

Vernon shook both men by the hand. 'I and the entire French police force are indebted to you gentlemen. Your men and mine have the rest of the gang in custody. I promise they and their compatriots will never bother you or anyone else again.' He turned, nodding to the other man and they picked up the drugged, semi-conscious Henri and unceremoniously carried him from the room

*

The following morning, Billy, Wolfe and Asher went to the hotel where Megan and her family were staying. Billy explained everything to her. From there the trio travelled to Southend.

The women were pleased to see their men folk, and while a nanny from the hotel looked after the children, Billy explained everything to them. He ended by saying, 'The worst that can happen to the Le Feuvres and their gang is to be transported to Devil's Island, but if they're lucky, the French courts will hang them.'

Wolfe hugged Eva. 'I think you're putting on weight.' She slapped him playfully, and then gently touched his bruised face, the swelling and blackness around his right eye prominent.

She stamped her foot in feigned anger. 'You let him hit you.' She turned to Billy, 'And you promised to look after him.'

With his arm around Esther's waist, he smiled. 'It wasn't my fault; he should have dodged the punch the way I taught him.'

*

After three sunny days with the children, the group returned to London to make preparations for Esther and Billy's wedding. In the meantime, Frank and some of Billy's men went through the Le Feuvres' papers, finding the deeds to the three houses in Brushfield Street and a large amount of cash. After a lengthy discussion with the ten girls, forced to be prostitutes, it was decided that they would keep the three houses. Four of the girls wanted to leave, including the one Frank had befriended. They were given a substantial amount of cash and everyone was happy.

Fifteen days after the shock of the unsinkable *Titanic*'s demise, Esther entered Tower Hamlet's registry office with her friend Hadar who held the hands of Billy's five-year-old daughter April, who was bridesmaid, and Esther's six-year-old son Yaakov as page boy. Esther carried a posy of flowers and was wearing a lace ivory-coloured dress that flowed down to her ankles, with a square collar and puff sleeves, the cuff ending just above the elbow. Entwined in her curly, brown, shoulder-length hair was a small tiara with a fine silk veil.

Billy, for the umpteenth time, looked nervously into the mirror, adjusted his tie and pulled down the cuff-linked sleeve of his white shirt to below the jacket cuff of his dark blue suit.

Frank, his bodyguard and friend for many years and best man, walked into the room. 'She's here.'

Both families waited in the hallway as Billy knocked on the registrar's door, and entered on hearing, 'Come in.'

Billy smiled at the thin, bald headed man in black jacket and striped trousers, starched wing collared shirt and grey cravat standing behind an oak desk.

'She is here,' Billy said; a tremor in his voice.

Esther walked into the room, followed by her entourage. There was shock on the registrar's face at the number of people entering his small office.

Esther moved to stand beside Billy, who whispered, 'You are beautiful,' taking her hand and kissing it.

The registrar wagged a finger, smiling at the couple, 'Not yet, Mr Reid.'

Laughter filled the room as they all squeezed in, the last person closing the door and the ceremony began.

Thirty minutes later, the registrar smiled and said, 'I now pronounce you husband and wife, and Mr Reid, you can now kiss your bride,' as everyone clapped.

Outside the sun shone in a cloudless sky as Billy's brother-in-law Brian took a photo, running to stand beside Megan as the camera clicked.

A marquee had been set up in the garden of the Victoria gambling club which was closed for the day. Once again the Shaffer's excelled with Jewish and Irish cuisine. The band kept the dancers on the floor until the early hours of the morning, even though the bride and groom had left on their honeymoon.

Dancing cheek to cheek, Wolfe moved his head slightly away to look into Eva's brown eyes. 'I promise that was my last fight.'

She laughed. 'Don't say never; you'll get that feeling of wanting to pit yourself against someone and you'll have that forlorn look like a spoilt child not getting its dummy, and I will have to give it to you.'

'You know me so well.' He bent slightly, kissing her on the lips.

December 1912

It was a strange but happy time in the Reid household. The families and friends that usually met on Sunday had got together for a Christmas Eve cum Chanukah party as they learned about each other's religions and customs.

The women had been busy all day preparing the mountain of food while the men bought festive drink and surprise presents for loved ones.

Frank grabbed Wolfe's arm. 'I need your help.'

'What can I do for you?'

'Can you come with me to the jewellery shop in Brick Lane?'

'Why can't you go yourself?'

Frank looked a little sheepishly at Wolfe, cleared his throat and then mumbled, 'I want to buy an engagement ring.'

'What?'

'I want to buy an engagement ring.'

A smile creased Wolfe's face. 'It's the girl that gave you the information about the Frenchman.'

Frank nodded. 'Her name is Elizabeth. We have grown close over the last few months. We laugh a lot and … It's been a long time since I've felt this way about a woman, so I thought …' his voice trailed off.

Wolfe looked at Frank for a moment, a slight bemused look on his face. This is the most Frank had ever said to him. He patted him on the shoulder. 'Come on Frank, I'm sure Mr Kinsky will give you a good deal on such a special ring.'

'Thank you, I won't forget this.'

By five o'clock that afternoon all was ready for the festivities. Tables had been loaned and placed together, stretching the length of the room. A Christmas tree and large menorah sat at one end with presents around them.

Dinner was a great success, with lots of laughter and singing. In front of each person was a sheet of paper containing the words of Christmas carols and Chanukah songs, which everyone sang with great gusto.

After Billy and Esther handed out the presents, Esther held up a hand. 'Today, I am sure, has been for all of us a very happy day.' She turned to her husband. 'I have one more present – well, sort of present – for Billy.' She hesitated and then said, 'I'm pregnant.'

Billy's eyes widened in surprise and a beaming smile lit up his face. He wrapped his arms around Esther and kissed her, while everyone cheered. Once the applause had died down, Billy looked at Frank, 'Your turn.'

All eyes turned to Frank who took Elizabeth's left hand and knelt. 'We haven't known each other long, but in this short time I have come to love you. Will you do me the honour of marrying me?'

With tears of love in her eyes, she said, 'Yes.'

*

Just over a week after the Christmas party, on 7 January 1913, Eva gave birth to another daughter, Frieda. Wolfe entered the room, looked down at his daughter and then at his wife, and knelt beside the bed, said, 'She is very beautiful, like her mama.'

'Have you got it?' she whispered.

He smiled and opened the little box in his hand. As usual, sitting on a bed of cotton wool was a small Star of David, a safety pin and a piece of red ribbon.

'Frieda will like it, I'm sure.' Eva's eyes opened wide when he produced another box, longer and slimmer. 'I have never bought you anything before. I hope you like it.'

She opened the box and gasped, 'My goodness.' Inside was a string of pearls. She looked up at him, 'Can you afford this?'

'Yes and why can't I spoil you if I want?'

'I'll put them on when I have washed. She took his hand. 'Wolfe, I love the children, but three is enough.'

He leaned over and kisses her forehead, gave a big smile and said as usual, 'Thank you.'

11   The Return of a Nemesis

For many superstitious people, the number 13 means bad luck, but for Wolfe all the ill omens forecast about the year 1913 had no significance – until, that was, Friday, 13 June.

Wolfe was getting ready for *shaul*, when he received a phone call from Frank that one of their regular clients, Mr Brooks, was at the casino and had some information that could be important to him. Wolfe looked at his watch: at this time of the year Shabbat came in late: he would have time to go to the casino, see him and get back for the start of the service.

Mr Brooks was waiting for him when he arrived at the Victoria Club and made a beeline for Wolfe.

'Excuse me for inconveniencing you.'

Wolfe smiled. 'No problem, Mr Brooks.'

'I don't know if this means anything to you, but a one-armed man is offering a substantial amount of money to anyone who knows a Jewish boxer...'

Wolfe's face was ashen.

'Do you know this man?' said Brooks.

Wolfe silently nodded.

'He looks a nasty piece of work, and I wouldn't like to meet the men with him on a dark night.' Brooks placed a hand on Wolfe's shoulder. 'I'm sure it won't be long before someone gives him the information he needs and takes his money. If it means anything to you he's staying at the Cumberland Hotel.'

Trying not to show the turmoil inside him, Wolfe said calmly, 'Thank you for the information, Mr Brooks. Tell one of the barmen to give you a double whisky on me.'

'Thank you, that's most generous of you.'

As soon as Brooks had disappeared, Wolfe grabbed Frank. 'Come on, we have to see Billy immediately.'

Wolfe burst into the office with Frank trailing behind. 'Hey, where's the fire?'

'It's worse than a fire,' said Wolfe, taking a cigarette from the box on the desk and lighting it with a slightly shaking hand and blowing out a cloud of smoke.

If it were just about Goran Kroshnev being in London it wouldn't faze him, but he knew what Kroshnev was capable of, and getting to his and Asher's family would be his priority once he found out where they lived.

'Hey, I've never seen you as nervous as this. What's going on?' Billy got up from the chair and walked quickly around the desk to face Wolfe, but it was Frank who replied, 'A one-armed man is looking for Wolfe.'

'Whatever he wants, we can handle it,' said Billy.

'He is much more dangerous than the Le Feuvres,' said Wolfe, taking another puff of the cigarette and stubbing it outs in the ashtray. 'He is capable of killing anyone, women and children, without a thought. He's the man that killed Esther's husband.'

Billy leaned towards his friend. 'You knew this and never said anything?'

'I didn't think he would come looking for us in England, as he knew Asher and I wanted to go to America.'

'What's the story with you and this one-armed man?'

Wolfe didn't reply at first, just walked over to the drinks cabinet and pointed the bottle in their direction.

Frank shook his head.

Billy moved quickly to his friend. 'It's a bit early for me—' he took the bottle from Wolfe '—and you. Now calm down and tell me about you and this one-armed man.'

Wolfe dropped onto the armchair, and Frank sat in the one beside him as he told them about Poland, the pogroms, and the boxing contests organised by Goran Kroshnev, describing how the Cossacks had ridden into the village, raping, looting and killing indiscriminately men, woman and children. Wolfe lit another cigarette, letting the smoke trickle from his nostrils.

Asher came into the office and was about to say something, but Billy held up a hand, shaking his head. Asher quietly closed the door, standing with his back to it as Wolfe leaned forward, elbows on his knees, looking down at the floor.

'Ivan Kroshnev, a Cossack officer, in his arrogance thought he could beat me. So, he offered me a deal, and I accepted.' He looked up at Billy. 'I beat him and he kept his promise. Asher and I buried our family and left, but the Kroshnev's caught us at the border. We had no alternative but to fight. What do they say – kill or be killed. I killed Ivan with a sabre and Asher shot Goran. We thought he had killed him, but we found out later he hadn't. We took the first boat out and the rest, as they say, is history.'

Wolfe stood and paced slowly up and down the room, stopping in front of Billy. 'This is our fight and we have to deal with it by ourselves.'

'How do you intend to do that?' Billy asked.

'We have no alternative, but to kill him and his men. How? Well I'll have to think about that.'

'You'll have to think quickly but, Frank and I will help, because if Esther hears about or sees this Goran—' He left the rest unsaid.

'If Goran finds us,' Asher moved away from the door. 'He will kill every member of our families before killing us.'

'Well then, we'd better get planning,' Billy said.

*

Goran Kroshnev and his bodyguards had just returned to their hotel after another fruitless search for Wolfe when the concierge moved from behind his desk and confronted him.

'Excuse me, sir, but there's someone to see you in regard to the person you've been looking for.'

'Where is he?' Goran asked, digging into his pocket for some change to give the man.

Discreetly taking the offered money, the concierge said, 'Please follow me.'

They followed him into the bar where Billy sat in a corner reading a paper. The concierge gestured, 'That's the gentleman that has been asking for you, Mr Goran.'

'Thank you, I'll take it from here.' Kroshnev sat down in the chair opposite Billy. 'I hear you have the information I'm looking for.'

Billy dropped the paper onto his lap, and in a good imitation of a cockney accent said, 'Well, guv, what's it worth?'

Goran gave a slight smile and a gesture with his hand stopping one of the bodyguards who had taken a couple of steps towards Billy. 'If it is the Jew I'm looking for, I'll give you two hundred pounds. I'll give you another—' he looked down at his empty sleeve '—three hundred pounds if you give me his brother.'

Billy grinned. 'Well then, you better hand over the money now.'

'I'll give you the money as soon as I set eyes on those Jew bastards, and not before.'

'How do I know you have the money, or will not kill me when I show you where they are?'

Goran looked at one of the bodyguards, then at Billy. 'Why would I want to kill you? And as far as the money is concerned—' he made a gesture with his hand '—get the case,' he ordered.

One of the men moved across the foyer to the concierge and said something to him. The concierge handed him a small case which he carried over to Billy, unlocked it with a key from his pocket, and opened it, showing him the money.

Billy nodded and got to his feet. 'Is now a good time, or would you prefer the morning as it's …' he looked at his watch '… eleven o'clock.'

'Now, I will not wait another minute—'

He was interrupted by someone saying, 'I hear you're looking for us.'

Kroshnev got to his feet and turned to face Wolfe and Asher, a sneering smile on his face. 'As a matter of fact I am.' He looked at the bodyguards who took a step forward. 'I owe you Jew bastards for this,' he spat out with venom, looking down at his empty sleeve. 'And revenge for the death of my brother.'

Asher looked at the bodyguard. 'I don't think that is a wise move in this crowded bar,' Asher pointed out, adding, 'You killed our family.'

'We will meet you tomorrow,' said Wolfe, writing something on a napkin. He gestured to a waitress with a tray standing nearby, the pen poised in the air as he spoke to her in a whisper, looked at Kroshnev and then continued writing and speaking. 'I do not intend to go through life looking over my shoulder.' The waitress returned, placing a glass of white liquid in front of Kroshnev, the bodyguards, Wolfe and Asher.

'What's this?' Kroshnev asked, surprise in his voice.

'Well, Goran, you don't mind me using your first name?' Wolfe didn't wait for an answer. 'I think we—' he pointed to them and the bodyguards '– should have a—'

'I don't drink with Jews,' Kroshnev said disdainfully.

'I think as you intend to kill us, you can at least make an exception in this case,' Wolfe stated quietly.

The Russian laughed. 'You were always a cool person, even when you had the crowd yelling for your blood. Okay, just this once.'

Wolfe and Asher smiled as they picked up their glasses and gestured to the three men. 'The first and last,' Wolfe said, downing his drink in one go.

The Russians clinked glasses and drank, slamming their glasses on the table and leaning back into their seats.

Wolfe slid the napkin across the table. 'This is where we will be tomorrow.'

Kroshnev went to take it, but couldn't move his arm; his eyes widened in fear and he opened his mouth to speak, but all that came out was a gargled noise as his tongue swelled.

Wolfe said, 'In a few moments you and your bodyguards will be dead.' The waitress stood beside Wolfe. 'This is Esther. You beat her husband to death. This is her vengeance. Your arrogance made you assume that you were superior to the Jews you killed, but as you have now discovered, it's that very arrogance that has led to your downfall. While you take the last miserable breaths of your life, I hope the ghosts of all those you have murdered come back to torture you.'

He picked up the case as Asher placed the glasses in a bag and Billy put his arm around Esther's waist.

Tearfully she kissed his cheek and said, 'Thank you.'

The last thing Goran Kroshnev saw was the four of them, with Frank the concierge, leaving the bar.

22 September 1913

Eva was angry and had not spoken to her husband for over a week. She stood in front of the mirror, looking at her figure, turning sideways and looking backward, her lush brown hair hanging down to her waist. She pouted angrily, as once again she was pregnant. But slowly a smile returned to her face as she remembered how happy Wolfe was when she had told him.

'How are you?'

The rest of what he was going to say was cut short as she turned and ran to the toilet to be sick. He heard the toilet flush and Eva appeared face white not only from being sick, but angry at him, thinking he would understand when she had said that three was enough. She stood hands on hips, lips drawn tightly together.

'It's okay for you – I'm the one being sick—' she wagged a finger in his direction '—and you're not the one who's going to have a figure like a bloated elephant.'

He moved towards her, engulfing her in his arms and kissing the top of her head. She pulled slightly away, looking up into his eyes. 'This is the *last* one; otherwise you will be sleeping with the children.'

He wanted to laugh as she looked so beautiful when she was angry, but instead kissed her on the lips.

A few days later Eva found out that Sarah was also pregnant again – and of course Asher was ecstatic.

As their wives talked about swollen ankles and ugly maternity dresses, their husbands were talking about the East End, its dirty cobblestone streets, the men hanging around outside their tenements feeling inadequate as they were unable to find work and support their families. Men and women drowned their sorrows in cheap gin, while their children wore hand-me-down clothes, living in dirt and squalor.

'We should open a club for the youngsters,' Billy suggested.

'It's not a bad idea,' Asher agreed.

'The Repton Boxing Club had the right idea, but that's for boys,' Wolfe pointed out. 'We need something for the girls too, or like many women in the area they'll soon turn to walking the streets,'

'The young lads are forming gangs, and I know what that's like,' said Billy.

Wolfe rubbed his chin, points a finger in Billy's direction. 'Do you still own that old gaming house?'

'Yes?'

'We could convert it into a clubhouse. Turn the basement into a boxing gym.' He pointed at Billy. 'You and I can train the youngsters. It will get them off the streets and interested in something other than gangs and stealing.'

'What about the girls?' Asher asked.

'I'm sure, Mrs Burns will help and then there's the seamstress, Mrs Flynn. She could teach the girls about dressmaking.'

'Even though our wives are pregnant I'm sure they will help with cooking skills,' said Asher.

He was right: as soon as they put the idea to the women they want to get involved, as did Billy and Wolfe's men. It took three months to get the house ready. In that time, Wolfe, Asher and Billy approached the boys and girls in the streets about the Club.

On 18 January 1914 the Club opened to the joy of the children and the organisers. In no time at all, Wolfe and Billy had started getting the boys interested in boxing. The flat roof of the building had a railing around it, and a wired roof, Here Asher and Frank set up a small football and netball pitch. The billiard table was still at the Club, and they added a table tennis table and darts board. Eva and Sarah taught the girls how to dance, and it wasn't very long before the girls roped the boys into being their partners.

On 16 May Eva had a baby boy. Wolfe sheepishly entered the bedroom and looked down at his baby son, lying in the crook of his mother's arm.

'How are you?' he asked, kneeling by the bed and taking a small box from his jacket pocket, opening it to reveal once more a small Star of David and a red ribbon through the little gold safety pin.

Eva smiled. 'What shall we name him?'

'Isaac, it's a strong name.'

Eva nodded in agreement.

'He is a handsome baby,' said Wolfe, taking another box from his pocket. Opening it, he removed a ring with four small diamonds in a row and placed it on her finger.

Eva looked astonished: she spreads her hand to look at it. 'It is beautiful,' she whispered. 'Can we afford this?'

He didn't reply, just kissed her on the lips, and then got to his feet. She looked once more at the ring and then at him, saying, 'Wolfe, four is enough.'

He patted her arm, smiled down at her and said, as he had done three times before, 'Thank you.' He turned and left the bedroom.

Two days later Esther had a little girl, naming her Baruch (Blessing), and the very next morning Sarah also had a little girl, naming her Davora. Three weeks later, the three families and their friends held a small party to celebrate the births.

28 June 1914

When Gavrino Prinple, a Serbian, assassinated the heir to the throne of Sarajevo, Arch Duke Ferdinand, an argument ensued between Empires and on Tuesday, 4 August, Britain declared war on Germany. With the fervour of patriotism and thought of adventure, young men eagerly joined the ranks. By the autumn of 1914 a blackout of London had been put into force, and people were being issued with identity cards.

By the end of the year, Eva was pregnant again. She gave a wry smile as she brought out her maternity wear, resigning herself to being pregnant for the rest of her life. In spite of the fact that she had told him she wanted Isaac to be the last, she couldn't be angry with him for long: Wolfe was a wonderful husband and father, helping with the nappies, feeding and keeping the children amused, and there was always someone around to help with their growing family. Now that she was pregnant again, Wolfe was toying with the idea of getting a nanny, but that would mean moving to larger premises.

And in London there was another side to the war. With the sinking of the *Lusitania* in May 1915, anti-German riots had broken out.

Many of the recipients of the riots and beatings were Jews. This angered Wolfe and a defence group was being formed to protect innocent people and their property as rioters did not know – or did not want to know – the difference between Germans and Jews.

Wolfe, Asher and Billy made sure their families were protected wherever they went. The bakery in Brick Lane had a twenty-four-hour guard, as did the brothers' other business interests.

On the last day of May 1915 air-raid sirens pierced the air. Eva picked up Isaac, saying more quietly and calmly than she was feeling to Jacob, 'Take your sister's hands and follow me.'

As she and the children hurried to a large warehouse, they were joined by Sarah and her children. Above them the drone of the Zeppelin engines grew louder and louder. Eva and Sarah sang and played with the children, jumping slightly at the sound of exploding bombs, and when the raid was over, they returned home, Eva breathing a sigh of relief on seeing that her house was still intact.

*

At ten o'clock on 11 July 1915 Eva and Wolfe had another son, naming him Saul. As he had done four times previously, Wolfe pinned the small gold Star of David and red ribbon, to ward off evil spirits on his son's vest, then he placed a bracelet around Eva's wrist.

This time she didn't say, *Five is enough*, but Wolfe as usual, before leaving the bedroom, gave a slight smile, kissed his wife tenderly and said, 'Thank you.'

They didn't know it at the time, but their family was now complete.

12   ...To End All Wars

October 1916

A YEAR HAD GONE BY AND STILL THE WAR in Europe dragged on. It was the last day of October and the roar of transport Lorries and marching feet resounded through the streets of East London, as men, munitions and supplies were brought to the docks to be transported to France.

The War Office had decided on a campaign to attract those men who were still undecided, thinking that soldiers marching through the streets of London would inspire young men to join up and using the motto, *Wake up London.*

Military recruitment brought a shortage of labour. Now, formerly unemployable men and women, including the elderly as well as some children, became employable, and for the first time in many years the war provided full-time jobs. The Suffragette movement called a temporary truce as women went to work in industry, transport and agriculture, taking over the roles usually carried out by men.

Billy and the brothers were worried as their croupiers wanted to enlist. They were discussing how to replace the croupiers when their wives paid them a visit.

Billy was immediately at Esther's side, asking before kissing her, 'What have we done to deserve this pleasure?'

Esther laughed as he kissed her, unaware that the brothers and their wives were doing the same thing. When eventually they parted, Sarah was the first to speak.

'We have managed to find babysitters for our lovely children and thought that we could take you out to lunch so we can show off our handsome husbands.'

'We would love to,' said Wolfe. 'But we have a problem that needs to be sorted out pretty quickly; otherwise we might have to close the Club for a while.'

'Probably for the duration of the war,' Asher added sadly.

'Well, we are here, and six brains are better than three,' Eva smiled.

'You mean three and three-quarter brains,' Esther giggled. 'So what's the problem?'

'Why is it that all women think they are better than men?' said Asher, gesturing to the seats around the room. 'Please ladies, take a seat.'

'Would you like something to drink?' said Billy.

'No, thanks,' the three women replied in unison.

Wolfe sat on the edge of the desk. Taking a cigarette from a box on the table and picking up a box of matches, he said, 'Most of our croupiers are leaving to enlist in the army, and we cannot find replacements.'

There was silence for a moment as the women took in what he had said, and then Esther, sitting between Eva and Sarah, whispered something to them. Both girls nodded, their teeth white against their lipstick smiling at their husbands, then looking at each other as Esther said, 'I'm right, we are brainier than the men. They should have the children while we go to work. The answer is simple, use women.'

The three men stared open-mouthed at their wives. A big smile appeared on Billy's face, and Wolfe let out a roar of laughter as Asher said, 'Why didn't we think of that?'

After talking to the croupiers that wanted to enlist, they agreed to stay on and train the women. Billy and the brothers discussed with their wives the sort of attire the women should wear. Arranging for their husbands to babysit, the three wives met with the women croupiers about appropriate outfits.

The following day the wives and their husbands sat around the table in Eva's kitchen who said, 'We and the croupiers have come up with outfits so the men will not get hot and sweaty ogling them as they gamble. It's a loose blouse with a cravat, waistcoat and three-quarter-length skirt.'

Late February 1917

Billy was at home, playing on the floor with his daughter April, with Devora asleep, when his sister Megan burst into the playroom with tears streaming down her face.

'Billy,' she sobbed, 'you have to stop him.'

Esther followed her into the room as Billy got to his feet, a bewildered expression on his face. Esther didn't say anything, just patted him on the arm, and lowered herself to the floor, stroking April's cheek.

'Auntie Megan needs to talk urgently to Daddy,' she said. 'I'll play with you till he comes back.' Just then the baby began to cry.

Esther took April's hand. 'Would you like to help me feed your sister?'

April smiled happily. 'Yes please, it's better than feeding the dolls.'

Billy placed an arm around Megan's shoulder and turned to look at Esther as they left the room mouthing, 'Thank you.' He led his sister into the front room. 'Can I get you something to drink?'

She shook her head, dabbing her eyes with a handkerchief. He ignored this and poured a small whisky, holding out the glass for her to take. 'Megan, drink this.'

She looked at him, eyes red from crying, and took it from him, whispering, 'Thanks.'

'Okay, who do I have to stop?'

'Brian.' Tears once more streamed down her face.

'You have to tell me more than to stop Brian – stop him from what?' But he knew what she was going to say.

'He wants to go to the Front and take photos of the war for one of the newspapers. He leaves next week.'

Billy moved across the room to sit beside his sister, placing an arm around her shoulders. 'Megan, he's a grown man. It isn't my place to tell him what to do.'

'But he could get killed.'

Billy kissed her wet cheek. 'That's a chance he seems to be willing to take. For any photographer it's an opportunity not to be missed. Surely you understand that.'

'What about the business?'

'Find someone to take his place, or, I'm sure you know how to take photos and Brian has been teaching John about developing.' He pointed to a photo on the wall of April holding Devora and Alice behind them, taken by Megan and Brian's son. 'John took that photo with a camera Brian bought him.'

Megan had stopped crying and a slight smile appeared on her face. 'He is good, isn't he? Brian says that John's a natural.'

'Megan, you have to let Brian go, and you don't have to worry about the business.'

'I want John to go to school. It's important for his future.'

Billy laughed. 'Stop putting obstacles in the way.'

Megan placed the glass on the table, without drinking the whisky, and got to her feet. 'I knew I could rely on you to see the practical side of this. What would I do without you?'

She kissed him on the cheek and left, but not before going to the nursery to see her nieces and say goodbye to Esther and Alice. As soon as Megan closed the front door, Alice entered the front room. Billy was reading the paper as she moved across the room to stand in front of him. He looked up, studying her face for a second, and then asked, 'Okay, what can I do for you?'

'Dad, I have ...' she hesitated '... I've volunteered to be an army nurse.' It came out like an express train. 'I want to nurse the soldiers wounded in France.'

Billy was dumbstruck by the news.

Alice, thinking he was angry with her, moved forward, kneeling at his feet. 'I am alive and owe you more than you realise. You and Nancy took me in and treated me as your own child. I want to help and this is the only way I know how. Please don't be angry with me.'

There were tears in Billy's eyes as he got to his feet, placing a hand under her elbows helping her up. 'Angry, I'm not angry. I'm proud, does Esther—'

'Yes, Esther knows, but I haven't said anything to Mrs Burns or April.'

'When do you leave?'

'I have to report on Monday morning.'

He wiped his eyes with a handkerchief, smiled, hugging her to him, kissing the top of her head saying, 'It gives us a couple of days to do a bit of shopping.'

April 1917

Brian armed with the latest camera that money could buy, a present from Billy, who as he hugged his brother-in-law, whispered, 'Keep your head down.'

All his family and friends were there to wave him goodbye as he boarded the boat to France. Standing beside him at the rail of the ship was Frank, the corporal stripes prominent on his sleeve, along with six of the croupiers.

Elizabeth, Frank's wife, had an arm around Eva trying not to cry, but as the boat left the dock, tears streamed down her face as she stood on tiptoe waving goodbye.

Megan, with her son John stood proudly by her side and daughter Nancy in her right arm, trying to hold back the tears, hugging her daughter to her. A hand grasped hers. 'Don't cry Mum, Dad promised me that he'll be okay and while he's away I must be the man of the family and look after you and Nancy.'

Megan lowered Nancy to the ground and knelt beside her thirteen-year-old son, already so grown up. Hugging him fiercely, she kissed his cheek. 'I'm sure you'll do a good job,' she said, wiping the tears from her cheeks.

Walking side by side, Billy said to Wolfe, 'If truth be known, I wish I was going with them.'

'I know what you mean, but the businesses and our families come first.' He stopped, holding Billy back. 'If you really want to go, I would make sure that everything and everyone will be looked after.'

Unexpectedly Billy reached up and kissed Wolfe on the cheek, his voice shaking with emotion. 'Wolfe Brown, I love you like a brother.'

Wolfe was silent for a second, looking into Billy's eyes. 'I feel the same way. If I didn't have so many children, I would volunteer myself.'

Billy smiled. 'I think if you did that, the Germans would be less scary than Eva.'

Wolfe laughed. 'Come on, let's catch them up, otherwise I will get an earful from Eva as her mother's looking after the children.' Arm in arm, they walked quickly to join the others.

Billy and Megan received letters from Brian, which were naturally censored, but his photos in the national newspapers spoke for themselves. He was gradually becoming very famous as an outstanding photographer and because of that, Megan and her son John was busy with families wanting photographs of their loved ones in uniform before they were shipped overseas.

Meanwhile Billy received a long-awaited letter from Alice. She was happy, but could not tell him where she was. She had also taken time to write to Mrs Burns and April.

22 December 1917

Smoke drifted across no man's land, the ground between the adversaries pockmarked with craters; the trees still standing bare and blackened; there was no grass, just mud and the many indented boot-marks of unsuccessful assaults on each other's positions. Here and there, a sentry or sniper stood on fire steps looking over sandbagged emplacements, or loopholes in the sandbags through a trench telescope towards the German lines some fifty yards away with its barbed wire defences. Now and again there was the crack of a rifle-shot as a sniper spotted a target. Machine guns opened up from emplacements strategically placed along the zigzag line of trenches.

Some of the men sat at the back of the trench smoking, others making silly jokes, but apprehension – fear of the known and unknown – was etched on their faces; thoughts of loved ones were embedded in the faraway look in their eyes as they awaited the order to leave the safety of the trench, leap over the top and charge the enemy.

It was the coldest winter in living memory, many soldiers suffering frostbite and trench foot from the damp, freezing conditions, or various diseases from living in such a harsh environment. Many had an assortment of scarves and coverings around their feet to keep them warm, wearing boots one or two sizes larger so they could wear two or three pairs of socks to keep their feet dry.

Frank, now a sergeant, moved along the trench, giving his men a word of encouragement. He placed a hand inside the breast pocket of the tunic under the heavy coat and pulled out a fob watch, a wedding present from his wife. In ten minutes they would go over the top. His platoon commander, Lieutenant Higgins, approached. Frank didn't bother to salute as Higgins didn't like it when they were in the trenches as the lieutenant liked to live with his men, only meeting his fellow officers when he had to. The men respected this easy-going man deeply and would follow him anywhere.

Higgins pulled a cigarette case from his coat pocket and opened it. 'The men ready, Frank?' He offered the case to Frank, who took one.

'Yes sir.' He lit the cigarette, letting the smoke out through his nostrils. 'Any news about our leave?'

The lieutenant took a drag of the cigarette, looking along the trench at the men, many with one foot on the fire step, bayonets fixed. He looked down as he dropped the half-smoked stub on to the muddy ground and stepped on it. 'We're going back to the rear in the morning; the third battalion will be relieving us.' He looked away, knowing that many of the men, including perhaps himself and Frank, might be dead in an hour or so.

Suddenly, without warning, shells began to rain down on and around the British positions. As one, the men dropped to ground, being showered with earth and mud; shrapnel whizzed through the air, maiming and killing. Frank and Higgins quickly got to their feet, moving to a lookout post and picking up a trench periscope to see lines of German soldiers advancing.

'Man your positions,' Frank yelled at the men as he ran along the trench, ignoring the lethal shrapnel raining down like stones.

The machine gunners opened up on the German troops as the enemy's artillery continue its bombardment, the men yelling obscenities at the advancing Germans and their artillery, wanting to bury themselves into the ground and get away from the continuous noise of exploding shells and the screams of wounded and frightened men, but they stood their ground, firing at the advancing enemy, who were met by withering fire from machine guns and mortars. Falling like rag dolls to the ground, or wounded, trying to crawl away, some sliding into a crater for protection, but by now the British artillery had opened up in reply and German casualties mounted until they retreated back to their lines, to the cheers and relief of the British soldiers.

That evening Frank and the men were told by Higgins that they were going back to the rear in the morning and a two-week leave back to England.

Frank went in search of Brian who was about to take a photo of some gunners manning a machine gun. Frank waited until the photo had been taken, then grabbed Brian by the arm, pulling him to one side. 'I'm going on leave for Christmas and New Year. You're coming with me.' It was an order rather than a request.

'But I—'

Frank placed a hand on Brian's shoulder and looked straight into his eyes, saying angrily, 'If I have to drag you away from here, I will.'

Brian looked at the men, some brewing hot potato soup or tea, others writing to loved ones, relief on their faces that for today they were alive. Brian turned his head slowly, a tear in his eyes. 'My photos are all that there is to show the people back home what their loved ones are going through to win this G-d forsaken war. I have to stay.'

There was a determined look on Frank's face, lips drawn in a tight line. 'If I don't take you with me I will not be able to face Billy, and you need a rest from all the shelling and noise.'

Suddenly he grabbed Brian, throwing him to the floor, instinct telling him to do so as a shell landed in the trench a few yards away. Men were thrown into the air, their arms and legs like those of puppets on a string, and then suddenly there was silence, broken by the yells and screams of wounded men. Frank and Brian got to their feet, running towards the wounded to help as best they could.

Later, as they sat inside a dugout smoking, Brian said, 'Thanks.'

Frank picked up the mug of hot tea, 'For what?'

'I know Billy told you to keep an eye on me, but he didn't mean kill yourself doing it.'

'I wouldn't—'

Brian smiled, holding up a hand. 'When that shell landed, you were lying on top of me. I know you are not that way inclined.'

Frank laughed at the joke and moved to squat in front of Brian, his face serious. 'You owe it to Megan and the children to come with me. We will be home for Christmas and New Year. Please, Brian don't make this hard on me.'

Brian took a last drag of the cigarette, dropped it onto the floor and stamped on it. 'You're right. I promise you won't have to drag me.'

*

Brian and Frank walked side by side down the gangplank. There was no one there to meet them at the crowded dock as they wanted to surprise everyone. They arrived at Billy's house and knocked on the door.

There was a pause and the sound of footsteps, then the door opened. For a second Billy didn't recognise them. Then with a yell he grabbed each one, ignoring the grime and smell of unwashed bodies, hugging them to him, sobbing with happiness, tears streaming unashamedly down his face.

Frank and Brian had decided on the boat that as much as they wanted to see their wives, they didn't want to go home smelling like a sewer, and would therefore call on Billy first, knowing he would understand.

After a cup of tea laced with a little whisky, and while Frank and Brian had a bath, Billy went to the Victoria Club. Elizabeth was busy helping the lady croupiers with their make-up, so without her noticing, he packed some of Frank's clothes. He knew it would be hard trying to do the same at his sister's place, but when he got there he needn't have worried as she was at the photography studio with the children. He let himself in, packed some of Brian's clothes and returned home.

Shaved, bathed and cleanly attired, Brian knew it was late and the shop would be closed. Arriving outside the front door, taking a key from his pocket and was about to unlock the door, but changed his mind, returning the key to the pocket and knocked on the door. He heard Megan say, 'I'll go,' and a second later the door opened. Her shock and surprise turned into a huge smile that lit up her face and she leapt into his arms, showering him with kisses. The children came to see what the commotion was all about. Megan moved slightly away to allow the children access to their father who had tears in his eyes. He stroked the top of John's head, whispering, 'You have grown so tall.' John hugged him, tears streaming down his face. Brian knelt and picked up Nancy. 'You are so beautiful, just like your mum.' With that the three of them entered the house, quietly closing the door behind them.

Frank entered the Victoria Club unseen and climbed the stairs to his flat. He could hear Elizabeth singing and silently let himself in. She was in the kitchen, making a sandwich. He stood by the door, looking at her, a smile on his face.

'Would you like to make me one of those?'

Elizabeth turned slowly to face him, her pregnancy prominent. Tears of happiness filled her eyes as he moved quickly to embrace her. They kissed a long, lingering, loving kiss.

*

Wolfe was at home, reading an article in the *Jewish Chronicle* about the newly formed Jewish Regiment of volunteers from Britain, America and Canada. He looked up as Asher entered the room, but immediately returned to the article. He was sorely tempted to enlist, as the report stated the Regiment would in all certainty be sent to Palestine. To him, as a religious Jew, this was significant, especially since the Balfour Declaration in November when the British Foreign Secretary James Balfour made a formal statement that the policy of the British Government would favour the establishment in Palestine of a national home for the Jewish people, with the understanding that nothing would be done which might prejudice the cultural and religious rights of the existing non-Jewish communities in Palestine. This letter was sent by Mr Balfour to Lord Rothschild a leader of the British Jewish Community.

Asher poured himself a cup of tea from the pot on the table; taking a sip, he looked over the rim of the cup at his brother. 'You have that look again.'

'What look?'

He pointed at his face, 'That one where you are desperate to do something and can't, but are looking for a way around it so you get what you want.'

'You know me so well. But this time it isn't going to happen.'

'Want to tell me about it?'

'It will make no difference if I do; the outcome will still be the same.'

'Try me.'

Wolfe leaned forward, elbows on the table. 'Have you read the article about the Jewish Regiment?'

'Yes – oh – I see. You want to join up.'

Wolfe pointed a finger at his brother, 'Got it in one.'

'I know it's the sort of thing you would like to do, as you haven't had any excitement for some time.' He took a swig of tea, placed the cup onto the saucer, leaned back in the chair and undid the button of his blue serge suit, showing the palm of his hand to his brother. 'Be sensible, you have five children, what will happen to them if you are killed?'

'Don't you think I know that?' Wolfe played with the spoon in his saucer, a disconsolate look on his face. 'It would not be fair on Eva.' He smiled. 'She's fantastic with the children. How she manages everything I do not know.' He took a sip of tea. 'She cooks, cleans, although the elder children do help her with that. She goes to the bakery three days a week to help her parents, and helps in the youth club.' He stood and paced the room. 'I know Billy would go at the drop of a hat. I told him if he wanted to go, you and I would look after the business and his family.'

Asher gazed at his brother, an amused look on his face. 'What makes you think that it's only you and Billy that want to go?'

Wolfe stopped in his tracks, amazement on his face and in his voice. 'You want to go too?'

'What's so strange about that? You don't hold the monopoly on who wants to go. I would have enlisted in August when it was first announced, but, like I said, we have to be sensible, and we owe it to our wives and children to stay. So as much as it leaves a bad taste in my mouth that others are fighting and I'm not ...' He left the rest unsaid, stood and gave his brother a wry smile. 'I would be more scared of Eva than I would a German or a Turk. And to tell you the truth, Sarah is just as scary when she's angry.'

'We are like mice.' He shook his head. 'We, two big men are scared of no man, but our wives, they are frightening.' They both laughed.

'Come on,' Asher said, 'we'd better get down to the Club and help with the decorations.'

It was the afternoon of Christmas Eve, and the youth club was full to bursting with children having a Christmas dinner. At the far end of the room stood a Christmas tree and a Chanukah menorah, both with mountains of presents at their base.

The youth club had gone from success to success. Keeping the children amused with table tennis, netball, football, and round robin games on the roof; holding competitions amongst themselves with the formation of four teams, Red, Green, Blue and Yellow. Every third Saturday was dance night.

Wolfe and Billy had to their amazement found some wonderful boxing talent, and managed from time to time to hold competition bouts with other clubs. With the help of Eva, Sarah, Megan when she wasn't busy, and Mrs Flynn, they had taught the girls to sew and cook. The mixture of religions had not caused any problems, especially with the singing of songs and dances from Ireland, Poland and Russia. Many of the non-Jewish children had a smattering of Yiddish, and the Jewish children were using Irish sayings like, *begeebers* and *begorrah.*

They had just finished distributing presents, and what was left of the food and home-made cakes, and cleared away, when Elizabeth went into labour. It happened so quickly that there wasn't time to call the midwife, but with experienced childbearing women around, everything went smoothly, and they delivered a baby boy, the proud parents naming him Aiden.

*

The sound of people talking, laughter and gaiety filled the air in the marquee set up in the grounds of the Victoria Club. Waiters moved amongst the tables serving the dessert, while others replaced empty bottles of wine. Once again, even with rationing still in force, the Shaffer's had put on an excellent meal. A stage had been set up where a five-piece band was playing.

Wolfe and Billy, each with a glass of champagne in their hands, mounted the stage. The band stopped playing, and everyone turned to face them.

'Ladies and gentlemen,' Billy began, but Wolfe with a smile gently and playfully shouldered him aside saying with his slight accent, 'Sorry for that, Billy's been having elocution lessons.'

The guests burst into laughter as Wolfe added, 'Family and friends,' he looked at Billy who gestured his glass towards him, and they moved together, placing an arm around each other's shoulders.

Billy smiled, saying in a posh accent, 'Sorry about that chaps.' After another round of laughter, which he waited to die down, he continued in a more serious tone, 'I'm sure, that like us,' he pointed to Wolfe and himself, 'we are happy to see my famous photographer brother-in-law, Brian, and, our friend Frank safely home, plus congratulations to Elizabeth and Frank on their new arrival.'

There were cheers, clapping and banging on tables. 'But before we carry on with tonight's revelry, we would like to make a toast.'

Wolfe stepped forward, 'Family and friends, please be upstanding and charge your glasses. The toast is: absent family and friends.' The guests repeated the toast and then Wolfe looked at the drummer, who nodded and did a drum roll.

'One last toast,' said Billy, raising his glass. 'The King,' The band played the National Anthem and everyone joined in enthusiastically.

It was now two minutes to midnight and Wolfe, Asher and Billy got everyone in a circle as the band's singer stood with a gong in his hand, counting down the time, banging the gong on the stroke of midnight, to yells of 'Happy New Year' which echoed throughout the country along with a universal wish for the war to end.

1918

Frank and Brian returned to France in early January, but in late February both were wounded, Frank losing his left leg below the knee, and although Brian's wounds were superficial, he decided to return with Frank.

On their usual Sunday gatherings, Brian told Billy and the others about the day he was wounded.

'For some unknown reason, the Germans managed to get right up to our trench before being discovered. For over an hour there was hand-to-hand combat, but gradually Frank and his men got the upper hand. I, a non-combatant, had to defend myself, using my camera to fend off a German soldier. As I retreated from his onslaught I tripped and fell back into the mud. Just as the German was about to thrust his bayonet into me, Frank appeared and killed him.

'As the enemy retreated, one of them threw a grenade into the trench. Frank threw himself on top of me, the blast shattering his ankle. A quick-thinking medic placed a tourniquet around Frank's leg and he was stretched back to the aid station where the surgeon had no hesitation in amputating the leg. He saved my life.'

Elizabeth was naturally relieved that Frank would not have to go back to the fighting and so that he wouldn't have to climb the many stairs to his flat at the Victoria, and for saving Brian's life, Billy bought Frank and Elizabeth a house, and replaced Brian's camera.

With a growing family, Wolfe decided they needed a bigger place to live. He found a house in Berners Street, with five bedrooms, a toilet with washbasin and bathroom on the second floor and toilet on the ground floor, a dining room and lounge, and a kitchen large enough for their table and chairs.

Wolfe, Eva and the children moved to their new home, and the brothers rented out the old property. But Sarah was missing Eva and the children, so Asher and Wolfe went in search of another property. As with many things in life, luck played a big part and by chance they learned that a widow living two doors from Eva and Wolfe wanted to sell her house. It was a tragic story. Her husband and two sons had volunteered for the Jewish Regiment and all three were killed in Palestine.

Three weeks later, Sarah and Asher moved into their new home.

'As long as our wives are happy,' Asher said to his brother, 'that's all that matters.'

Billy was at the Club. He was worried about Alice – by now they hadn't received a reply to his letters for three months and when the door opened and Esther entered, he could see by the look on her face and the redness round her eyes that something was terribly wrong.

'What's the matter?' He half stood.

There was no way for her to soften the blow so she said, 'Alice is dead.'

'What, how, when?' He slumped back in the chair, tears streaming down his face.

She strode quickly behind the desk, cuddling him to her until he was cried out. He looked at Esther's face streaked from his tears.

'She was a nurse – why would they want to kill her?'

That night the house was full of people who had come to pay their respects. Two weeks later, on 11 November 1918, the Armistice was signed. Londoners went crazy with delight. There was not a family throughout the country that had not lost a father, son or brother, or that knew someone who had. With forty million casualties, it was called a human tragedy and the War to End All Wars.

*

As the troops came home, peace parades and street parties were organised. Like many streets throughout London, Berners Street was festooned with Union Jacks, streamers and balloons. Tables full of sandwiches, cakes, biscuits and sweets stretched from one end of the street to the other.

But, the country was now fighting another war, a germ war, as the Spanish 'flu epidemic broke out. In May, Eva's mother and father succumbed to the dreaded disease. Solomon tried to get up and work but was too weak and it was left to Eva, her sister Rachel and Sarah to keep the shop open. Wolfe decided that because of Eva's commitment to the shop, they needed a reliable housekeeper to look after the children.

Billy asked his old housekeeper, Mrs Burns, who still lived with them if she was interested in the job. Being bored with very little to do now that Esther had taken over the reins of running the household, she jumped at the chance.

For some time, Wolfe had had the idea of opening another gambling house – they were now called casinos – in the West End of London.

'Why do we need another club?' Billy asked.

'People need food, clothes, and a roof over their heads, and something exciting other than the boredom of everyday living,' Wolfe replied. He pointed an unlit cigarette at Billy. 'With the war over, people have a different outlook on life, especially ex-military. The shift in the poor and rich is changing, gambling is big business, and as you know, the house always wins.'

'I agree with Wolfe,' Asher joined in. He leaned forward in his chair. 'Tell me, Billy, what trade were you in before—' Billy was about to reply but Asher added, 'Probably, like Wolfe and I, nothing that will earn you the money you have now.'

Billy smiled. 'You're both right, so let's get on with it.'

They found the property they were looking for in Hanover Square. The location was exactly what Wolfe has envisaged and the property ideal. They agreed to buy it.

In June 1919 Eva's beloved father Solomon Goldberg died. The brothers and Billy put the refurbishment of their new project on hold as Wolfe tries to help Eva, her sister Rachel and his mother-in-law cope with their grief.

The children made teas and sandwiches and sat in front of those in mourning talking about their beloved grandfather sitting by the fire, lighting his pipe with its sweet-smelling tobacco and telling them stories. They made the mourners and visitors laugh by playing the characters in those stories.

Wolfe kept an eye on the bakery and, to his surprise, enjoyed being there. He didn't want to stand around all day doing nothing, so he asked Sam Zaman, one of the Goldberg's employees, to teach him how to roll the dough and make bagels. He loved the feeling of the dough in his hands as he kneaded it into the right texture and rolled it, making sure that every bagel was the same size. As the week passed, Wolfe learned more about baking bread. Sam said he was a natural, and had never seen anyone learn so quickly. Wolfe wondered if this was his destiny now that his father-in-law had gone, or was it is his duty to take over from him, but then there were the casinos and the properties he owned with Asher. He knew that no matter what, Eva would never give up the bakery: her father's reputation for fairness and his good name in the community means a lot to her.

The week of mourning was over, but a few days later Yaakov, Esther's son, died. Wolfe had never seen Billy so sad – he loved the boy like his own son.

Billy wondered how he would ever get over the loss of his two adopted children, but logic told him that, as with Nancy, time was a healer.

The epidemic had finally passed. In one year, the Spanish 'flu had killed 280,000 people and millions throughout the world. How the Brown family were able to survive this horrific time they didn't know, as many families around them were decimated, leaving children orphaned and parents childless.

*

Eva was humming a lullaby to Saul, a big smile on her face. She stopped singing as Wolfe came in.

'Why are you smiling?' he asked, bending to kiss his son, then Eva.

'If you read the paper this morning you would know why. We have a woman MP, Lady Astor.'

'She isn't British – she's American.'

'Like all men, you don't like an independent woman with brains who might be your equal.'

Wolfe burst into laughter. 'Where is all this coming from? Where is my bubbly wife?'

She smiled. 'I'm here silly. You're not a woman so you don't understand. Not everything for a woman is having babies, cooking, cleaning, and washing. We do have brains and are capable of using them, as I would like to point out, you know only too well.'

He kissed the top of her head. 'Okay, I'm going now as I remember what your father said to me before we were married.'

'And what was that?'

'Never argue with your wife and always agree that she is right.' As he opened the door to leave, she threw the baby's bib at him.

13   The Twenties

1920

IT HAD TAKEN BILLY NEARLY A YEAR to find out how Alice had been killed. She was in a convoy taking wounded to the main hospital when two German aeroplanes attacked them even though the red crosses on the roof were clearly visible. Billy fumed for many months because he could not avenge Alice's murder – and that's what it was, murder. He hoped those German pilots burned to death.

The war changed many people's outlook on life, especially the young who had seen the horrors of war, and it had also given birth to the twentieth-century woman. They were educated, entered politics, and showed off their sexuality. Women's skirts were shorter, just below the knee. Dress styles loosened, sleeves disappeared, giving women the freedom to dance to the latest music crazes from America, especially the music they called jazz.

The cinema offered a double bill of silent movies, westerns, epics and tragedies. The biggest screen heartthrob, Rudolph Valentino, had young girls and even older women swooning with desire as he portrayed a sexy Arab sheik. Comedies with Buster Keaton, Charlie Chaplin, Harold Lloyd and Laurel & Hardy had people rolling with laughter in the aisles, for a moment forgetting their troubles.

The world was moving quickly as if time was of the essence. There were new developments in science and technology, the automobile and electrical industries. Women professors in Oxford were being given equal status with their male counterparts. Motor buses made journeys faster and longer and the first night service started.

*

January 1920 began with two pleasant surprises. Billy and Esther announced that she was pregnant, but that wasn't the only surprise. On the families' usual Sunday get together, Billy pulled Wolfe to one side and said quietly, 'I want to become a Jew.'

'What?' Wolfe stepped back, surprise in his voice and on his face.

'I love Esther with all my being. I have spoken to April and Megan about it, and they said that if that's what I want, I should go for it. I have spoken to the Rabbi of your synagogue. In fact he refused me twice, but on the third occasion said yes, but I need—'

'Do you know what it entails?' Wolfe interrupted.

'Yes, the Rabbi told me what I will have to do, but I need someone to sponsor, and help me. Please Wolfe; will you do this for me?'

'Does Esther know?'

'No, and I don't want her to know, not until I have become Jewish.'

Wolfe smiled. 'You speak Yiddish, with an Irish accent, that's a start. Yes, Billy, I will help you, but it isn't going to be easy. It isn't like going to church and being baptised.'

'It will be worth it, I know it will make my Esther very happy.'

Wolfe frowned, saying seriously, 'Esther hasn't put any pressure on you into doing this, has she?'

'No, she knows nothing about it, and I want it to stay that way.' Billy smiled, 'For the time being anyway.'

'You'll have to grow a beard and be circumcised.'

'What?' Billy's face dropped for a second, and then he smiled. 'If that's what I have to do, so be it.'

'I'm only joking about the beard. We will go and see the Rabbi tomorrow and begin your transformation into one of God's chosen people.'

*

In February 1920, Eva's mother went to live with them. The children adored her because of the wonderful and funny stories she told them about the people in her village when she was growing up.

In May, Sam Zaman said to Wolfe, 'I'm thinking of leaving and—'

Shock showed on Wolfe's face as he interrupted, saying softly, 'You can't leave. I thought you were happy working here?'

'I am, but ...' he hesitated, looking down at the ground.

Wolfe spread his hands, leaning slightly forward, 'But?'

'My landlord asked us to leave as his son is getting married and wants the flat for him.'

'Is that all? You can have the flat upstairs.'

'Are you sure?'

Wolfe smiled. 'Eva and I have been wondering what to do about it now her mother is living with us. Come, I'll take you upstairs. If you like it we can come to some arrangement.'

He stopped in mid-stride as Sam said, 'That's not all.'

Wolfe looked silently at him, waiting for him to continue, a puzzled look on his face.

'My wife and I have been talking about opening our own bakery,' Sam went on, 'and—' He was unable to continue, seeing the dumbfounded look on Wolfe's face that changed as his brow furrowed in thought.

After a couple of seconds Wolfe responded, 'Can you wait a couple of days before making any decisions?'

Sam hadn't expected this. He thought the man in front of him would be angry, knowing how much the bakery meant to him and his family. He gave a sigh of relief. 'Yes, I can.'

'Thanks, I'll be in touch.' Wolfe left the shop and quickly made his way home.

The house was as usual full of singing and laughter. He found his mother-in-law in the kitchen, teaching Sally (Chandel's name had now been anglicised) and Frieda how to make meatballs. Moving out of the kitchen he was nearly bowled over by Eva as she ran from the dining room, her eyes twinkling mischievously as Jacob, who for some reason everyone called Jack, yelled, 'Ready or not, I'm coming.'

Eva grabbed her husband and turned him about. 'Quickly put your back to the wall, I'll hide behind you.'

Jack came out of the room. 'Hallo Dad, have you seen Mum?'

Wolfe wanted to burst out laughing and move away from the wall, but didn't, instead saying in a matter-of-fact tone, 'No, I've just come in.'

With that, Jack ran off, looked under the stairs, but no one was there, so he ran two at a time up to the bedrooms.

Wolfe turned to face Eva. She tried to move away but he leaned gently against her, bent and kissed her softly on the lips, running his hand down her body, knowing she liked it, but that she would be angry in case one of the children saw them. She moved her lips from his, saying a little breathlessly, 'You know I don't—' He landed his lips on hers, stopping anything else she was about to say. Just then they heard footsteps running down the stairs and the children laughing and he moved away from her.

'I need to speak to you, and your mother,' he said to Eva. 'We have a slight problem, nothing serious.'

'What is it?'

'Let's go into the kitchen and I'll tell you.'

Over a cup of tea he revealed his conversation with Sam. 'Is there anything we can do to stop him from leaving?' Eva asked.

'I've been thinking about it on the way home, and I think there is a way, but you both have to agree to it.' He took a sip of tea.

Eva impatiently stamped her foot. 'Well, what is it?'

'Make him a partner.'

'What? No, I heard it,' said Eva.

'It's a well-established bakery,' said Hadar, adding, 'He cannot just walk in as a partner.' She gestured to her daughter, 'We are partners – Papa stated that in his will.'

Eva placed a hand on her mother's arm seeing how upset she was, while looking at Wolfe. 'If I know you, you have something in mind, so, tell us.'

'I know what the turnover is every week, and what the business is worth, including the property, which we own. Sam needs accommodation. He has been given a week to vacate his flat. If he accepts the partnership, Sam will pay a third of the value to be a partner. If he hasn't the money, then I will work out a loan plan.' He looked at his wife, seeing her eyes narrow in thought. Taking a cigarette from the pack on the table and lighting it, exhaling, waving the smoke away pointing a finger. 'You must also take into account the probability that his wife will help in the shop.' He leaned back in the chair waiting for a decision.

Eva stood and walked across the kitchen, lips pursed in thought. She knew that lately they hadn't spent much time together, or as much as they would like with the children as they had been busy with the bakery, youth club, casino and helping Billy. She and Sarah knew about Billy converting as they were helping him with the kosher side of things and had been able, although with some difficulty, to keep it from Eva's mother and Esther.

Sam had twin daughters a year older than Jack. She turned quickly, her mind racing with her thoughts. *What about our son?* She sighed. *Jacob insisted they call him Jack as everyone at school called him that. He's been helping in the shop the last year.* Jack told her he loved the smell of baking bread, and had been nagging her to teach him how to make pastries and cakes. He had a natural flare for baking. She sat back on the chair.

'What about Jack? He loves being in the bakery, and that's what he wants to be, a baker. The Zamans have twin daughters – will they work in the shop too?'

Wolfe spread his hands. 'I don't know; we will have to ask them. Eva, it's just an idea. If you want to carry on the way we are and wait for Jacob – Jack – to leave school, then we'll have to find someone to fill Sam's shoes. But before we go off wondering this and that, we have to talk with the man himself, and probably his wife.'

The two women nodded their heads. 'You are right,' his mother-in-law agreed.

*

The following morning Eva invited the Zamans over for a meal to discuss options to stop him leaving the bakery.

Once the meal and small talk were over, Wolfe explained their proposition.

Sam rubbed his chin and looked at his wife, Channah. 'It's a very generous offer.'

'Naturally there are a few things that need to be ironed out,' Wolfe looked at Eva. 'A few questions that need answering before we … all make that final decision.'

'Noo, such as?' Mrs Zaman asked.

'Will your daughters be working in the bakery – sorry, do they want to work in the bakery?'

'Why do you ask that?' Mrs Zaman looked suspiciously at Eva and Wolfe, ignoring Hadar.

Eva gave a light smiled. 'A question with a question, which means you don't trust us?'

Hadar had kept quiet the entire evening, except for a polite greeting when the Zamans arrived, but now, because of the last remark, she was angry, and it showed in her voice and demeanour. 'I think Mrs Channah Zaman, you are a very rude person, and I think we can manage without your husband.'

There was a shocked expression on Channah's face; her husband looked awkward and was about to say something but his wife spoke first, her neck and cheeks red with embarrassment, 'I am sorry if you think I offended you, it wasn't meant that way. And yes, I do trust you. My husband has nothing but kind words to say about you all, and from what he told me, I believe the question has been asked because of your son, Jack.'

Eva's estimation of the woman changed in that instant as she replied, 'Yes, that's correct.'

Mrs Zaman smiled. 'As for my daughters, I don't think they are interested, but, if it is deemed necessary for them to help, then yes, they will be in the shop serving. As far as Jack is concerned, he can work there full time, if that's what he wants. It's his grandfather's bakery, and he has every right to be there.' She looked at her husband.

'We will accept your generous offer.' She held up a hand stopping Eva, who was about to say something. 'I know what you are going to say, and in answer to it, no, you don't change a winning formula.'

Eva was smiling from ear to ear, thinking, *this is a strong-minded lady,* but asked, 'Do you agree to carry on with distributing unsold bread to the poor at the end of the day?'

'Certainly,' Sam had at last spoken.

'I will get the lawyer to draw up the papers, and deliver it to you. The accountant will show you the books and what the bakery and flat are worth.' He handed Sam a set of keys. 'You can move in right away if you like.'

Before Sam could take the keys, his wife took them from Wolfe. 'Thank you, Mr Brown.'

They were getting ready for bed when Eva started giggling, which soon turned into laughter.

'What are you laughing about?'

'Poor, Sam Zaman, can you imagine what his life is going to be like now they're going to live above the shop.'

Wolfe got into bed, a smile on his face. 'He likes it.'

'Being domineered?'

'You weren't looking at him because, well, I wouldn't say that, but he's madly in love with her, and doesn't mind his wife being the boss.'

Eva slid beside him, nestling her head in the crook of his arm. 'I'm not like that, am I?'

He kissed the top of her head. 'No, of course not,' Looking up to the ceiling, silently asking forgiveness for the lie.

August 1920

The synagogue was full, and there was an air of excitement, for today Billy was going to be called by the Rabbi to read a portion of the law as a Barmitzvah boy would do, as a week ago Billy had been converted into the Jewish faith after having a ritual bath at Schevzik's Jewish baths, in Brick Lane. Up until that day, everyone had devised various ways of keeping it from Esther, especially after Billy's circumcision, which would be a very funny talking point for years to come; especially at the lengths he went to keep it from his wife.

The different expressions of surprise, joy and pride at what Billy had done for her and their unborn child showed on Esther's face.

Tears rolled down her cheeks when the Rabbi gave Billy his Jewish name, Binyamin.

As soon as the Sabbath was over, the party in Esther and Billy's house began. Billy and Esther danced by candlelight, their friends forming a circle around them. Billy whispered, 'Esther, my love, I have spoken to the Rabbi and he can marry us next Sunday.'

Her eyes opened in surprise, gradually to be replaced by a smile that lit up the room. 'Oh, Billy, what did I ever do to deserve someone as wonderful as you? Sunday will be perfect.'

Everyone was staring at them as they had stopped dancing, even though the music was still playing, wondering what was going on, but they were about to find out as Esther and Billy turned slowly to look at the people around them. 'You are all invited to a wedding next Sunday at the Stepney Synagogue, followed by a scrumptious meal at Shaffer's.'

Suddenly they were mobbed and lifted high on shoulders as the crowd danced around the room, singing, 'We're going to a wedding.'

That Sunday the synagogue was a buzz of excitement as they waited for the bride to appear. Wolfe stood beside a very nervous Billy, looking splendid in his black serge morning suit, white waistcoat, bow tie and shirt, a heather horseshoe in his left buttonhole, and white yarmulke on his head. Billy bit his bottom lip, turning to look towards the entrance. The doors opened and a lump caught in his throat at the beauty of his bride, as it had a few minutes ago when in a small side room, as tradition stated, the groom lifted the bride's veil to study her face. This custom recalled the biblical story of Jacob, who married the wrong woman when she covered her face with a veil.

Esther held a bouquet of lilies, the ivory satin wedding dress with cuffed sleeves, pleated at the front hiding her pregnancy. The long train flowing out behind her was held by, Eva's two daughters, Sally and Frieda, and Sarah's daughter, Davora. The girls were attired in lilac dresses, with small flowers in their hair matching those of the brides. Ahead of Esther was Billy's daughter April throwing rose petals on the floor ahead of the bride.

Billy took Esther's hand as they stood side by side, whispering, 'You are beautiful.'

After exchanging wedding vows, the marriage blessings were read, and then the groom stepped on a glass to symbolise the fragility of human happiness. Everyone shouted, 'Mazeltov,' and the Rabbi said, 'You may kiss your bride.'

To the cheers of family and friends, Esther and Billy kissed. After signing the register, the couple were whisked off to Shaffer's to a sumptuous meal, singing and dancing, that continued until well after midnight.

On 10 October 1920, Esther gave birth to a beautiful baby boy with flaming red hair like his father. At the Bris (circumcision ceremony) he was named, Ariel, which had been Esther's father's name and meant 'Lion of God'.

1921

It was raining outside and Wolfe was playing dominoes with Jack, Sally, Frieda and Isaac, who was trying to cheat by looking at his father's slates as he glanced across the room at Saul playing with bricks.

'Dad, Isaac's cheating again,' Frieda said, smiling at him.

'No, I wasn't,' he lied, poking his tongue out at his sister.

'I can't go,' said Wolfe.

'Yes, you can,' Isaac said quickly, and then bowed his head sheepishly, knowing he'd been caught out, while everyone laughed. Just then Eva burst into the room, waving the *Jewish Chronicle* and saying excitedly, 'You have to get tickets – go now.'

'Go where? Tickets what tickets, for what?'

'To the Ravioli,' Grabbing his arm trying to pull him up from the chair. 'Sophie Tucker is going to be there on the 1st of August.'

As much as Wolfe, like everyone, loved Sophie Tucker, he was engrossed in the game. 'Can't this wait till tomorrow? In case you haven't noticed, it's raining outside, and I'm playing dominoes—' he pointed at Isaac '—and we have a cheating son.'

'You must go before all the tickets are sold—' tugging at his arm '—get your coat on, I'll play in your place.'

'How many tickets do you want?'

'Oh! I never thought of that.'

He pushed back the chair and got to his feet. 'Asher and Sarah will want to go, Mum, and I'm sure Esther would want to, and Billy as well.'

'What about my sister?'

'Okay, I'll get nine tickets – I'd better take my cheque book, I don't think I have enough cash.'

Three hours later a soaked Wolfe returned home waving the tickets. 'Front stalls for the 5th.'

Eva leapt out of the chair, taking the tablecloth and dominoes with her, as the children yelled 'Mum.'

*

The women walked arm in arm, chatting excitedly about Sophie Tucker.

'She's wonderful,' Sarah said.

'The jokes; I nearly wet myself,' laughed Esther.

'I couldn't help crying when she sang "My Yiddisher Momma",' Hadar swayed as she hummed the tune. Eva was silent for a moment, eyes shining happily, and then whispered, 'Fantastic, what a woman.'

The men walked behind the women, trying to remember some of the jokes Sophia Tucker told.

'I wonder if she's as happy as she makes out,' Wolfe said.

'She's one of those women that look sexy from afar, up there on the stage,' said Billy.

'I know what you mean,' Asher said. 'But would you feel the same if you met her on the street, not knowing who she was?'

'If I'm truthful, probably not,' Billy replied.

Eva has tried to give her children a happy environment at home, remembering that she and Sarah had to be very careful where they played. There was so much for the children to do safely in London. On sunny days, they played in the garden, re-enacting films they had seen with gangsters, or cowboys and Indians. The girls captured by the Indians tied to a tree, while their captors danced, whooping around them. Eva and Sarah were like children themselves joining in a game of tag. Wolfe, Asher and the other fathers played cricket or football. When the weather was particularly sunny they went to the park in Cable Street with its slide and swings, or Victoria Park to paddle in the pool or play rounders – the parents against the children – which was always exciting and extremely funny. On rainy days the whole family sang and danced to music from the radio or gramophone.

By the mid-1920s many people had radios and were listening to the British Broadcasting Company (BBC). In 1924 King George V made his historic broadcast from the British Empire Exhibition at Wembley. In the early hours of the morning of March 1925 the family huddled around the radio listening to the first broadcast relayed to the USA.

Like a whirlwind the Charleston hit Britain. Billy was toying with the idea of opening a nightclub with the brothers. Their two casinos, horse and dog betting businesses were all doing very well, as were the brothers' properties in Lucas Street.

With the building of the King George V docks, the volume of imports rose and there was work to be had. Many Jews, not wanting to stand out, quickly learned to speak English and dress like everyone else.

The most important items in Eva and Wolfe's household were the piano in the front room and the gramophone with a green horn in the corner of the kitchen. Sally was learning to play the piano, but Isaac only had to listen to a piece of music once and he could play it, much to the annoyance of his sister.

One morning in late August 1926 Sally burst into the kitchen, tears streaming down her face, waving a newspaper, 'Mama, Mama, Rudolph Valentino is dead.'

Eva turned from her hot stove and pushed a lock of hair from her forehead with the back of her hand. 'No, it's a joke he is so young, and handsome. Not as good looking as your father,' she added quickly.

'Mama, it says here that women are fainting on hearing the news – some have tried to commit suicide, another has shot herself.'

'How ridiculous,' Eva remarked, turning back to her cooking. 'No man is worth killing yourself for.'

1927 began badly as another 'flu epidemic hit the country, with hundreds dying every week.

'There is nothing like chicken soup with *lokshen* and *knaidlach* to keep the 'flu away,' said Eva ladling the hot soup into bowls. Wolfe smiled reciting the prayer for bread, feeling that it could also be the power of prayer.

The family were glued to the radio as the BBC commentator excitedly related the American Charles Lindberg landing his aircraft, *The Spirit of St Louis,* in Paris, becoming the first man to fly the Atlantic.

'I wouldn't mind learning to fly,' said Wolfe, but no one was taking him seriously.

A newspaper report about the forthcoming Total Eclipse of the Sun, which had not been seen in Britain for two hundred years, had everyone in frenzy. Billy and the brothers decide to hire a bus to take the family to the highest point in London, Hampstead Heath. On 29th June, armed with a mountain of food and drink, with not an empty seat on the bus, they headed for Hampstead Heath.

Wolfe, his arms around Eva's waist as she leant back against him watched with oohs and aahs from everyone at the awe-inspiring sight of the Total Eclipse.

On Christmas Day, sweeping blizzards hit the country and London. January 1928 didn't get off to a good start as the snow melted and the country had its worst flooding for seven hundred years. Wapping was knee-deep in water as the River Thames burst its banks. The Houses of Parliament was like an island surrounded by water. Billy, the brothers, their families and friends helped their neighbours in Wapping as best they could. The youth club was dry, and they set up mattresses and bedding for those families unable to return to their homes. Eva and the other wives with their children set up a food kitchen, supplying hot soup and drinks, running a continuous supply of bread from the bakery as Sam and Channah Zaman with Jack and Wolfe worked night and day to keep the supply going.

Gradually as the waters receded and the mop-up began, old animosities disappeared. Irishmen, Jews, Catholics and Christians helped each other. Those that could afford it gave bedding, blankets and clothes. Gradually, Wapping and the rest of London got back to some form of normality. Now in East London there was a different atmosphere from before the flood. People smiled and greeted each other, knowing that as a community they had survived and won. A seed had been sown, that no matter whatever happened to them, they would always pull through as a community.

In October, Billy, the brothers and their wives waited excitedly outside the Regal, Marble Arch, to see the first talking film. *The Jazz Singer*, starring Al Jolson. Although they had been queuing for two hours, they weren't bored as they were being entertained by street buskers, acrobats, singers, dancers and magicians, time passed quickly. At last the doors opened and they moved slowly forward, stopping for a moment on entering the cinema to stare at the lavish surroundings; a million miles away from the stark austere decor of the Cable Street and Majestic Cinema's in East London. In the foyer they were met by a man dressed in a tuxedo who directed them to the ticket window and sweet counter. On receiving the tickets they walked down a plush carpeted aisle and were shown to velvet-covered seats by an usherette. During the performance, girls walked up and down the aisle, selling sweets, ice cream and cigarettes. Afterwards the six of them strolled the short distance to Lyons Corner House for tea and cakes. On their way home, arm in arm, smiling, eyes shining happily they sang 'Blue Skies'.

Wolfe and Eva encouraged their children to bring their friends home, and there were many social evenings at the Browns, dancing to the music from the radio or gramophone, which Eva especially enjoyed as it gave her a chance to catch up with the latest dances with her sons. Sally and Frieda encouraged their father to join in, which he did from time to time, but in reality he was happy to watch everyone enjoying themselves, now and again wondering what his life would have been like if he had stayed in Poland, though he knew they would probably be dead.

Wolfe was sitting on the top deck of one of the new red buses. He dropped the newspaper he was reading onto his lap – the headlines glaring big and bold: **WALL STREET STOCK MARKET CRASHES**

He looked out of the bus window as it stopped opposite Kings Cross Station. Luckily for him and his partners, they had never invested in the stock market. He shrugged his shoulders; there were other things to think about. Wolfe pursed his lips. Jack and Sam were opening another bakery in Clapton, which was slowly becoming a Jewish area as families moved out of East London to the newly built and cleaner areas around Clapton and Stamford Hill. Sally was off to Paris for a few months to study fashion.

Wolfe sighed: yesterday they were children, and today they were men and women.

14 Entente Uncordial, 1933

IMMIGRATION TO BRITAIN AND AMERICA, which for the last twenty years had been a trickle, had now became a stampede as Adolph Hitler was appointed Chancellor of Germany. Immediately Germans were ordered to boycott all Jewish shops and businesses, and Jewish bank accounts were seized.

Wolfe was in the office of the Victoria Club, reading a report about the Nazis opening a concentration camp at Dachau. He was angry at world as they stood by, allowing Hitler and his thugs to do whatever they wanted to innocent people, especially if they were Jewish. Just then there was a knock at the door and without waiting for him to say 'enter', it opened. Frank strode over to the desk.

'We have a problem in the casino and I need to know how you want me to handle it.'

Wolfe stared at Frank for a second, knowing by the look on his face that this was more than the usual gambling argument. He slid the chair away from the desk and got to his feet. 'What's this all about?'

'There are four men in the casino who insist on seeing the owner. I told them that I am the manager, but they insist on seeing you, and—'

'Okay, let's go and sort this out,' Wolfe interrupted, walking from behind the desk, heading for the door, following Frank who came to a stop just inside the casino, and gestured towards the four men standing by a roulette table having bets about the length of the nose of one of the gamblers. One of the men had a tape measure and was about to move towards the victim of their banter, but Wolfe walked quickly across to intercept him saying, 'You want to see me?'

The man turned to face him. The thin moustache above his lip widened with the false smile, grey eyes staring coldly at him.

'Yes, my friends and I—' he gestured to the three men who stood in a line behind him '—have a proposition for you.'

Wolfe glanced at the men their hair slicked back with a right-hand parting; wearing dark grey double-breasted suits with a lapel badge of Sir Oswald Mosley the maverick politician's newly formed Fascist Party. Most of its members were young unemployed men from poor backgrounds.

'And that is?'

The man looked around the casino. 'Can we discuss this in private?'

Wolfe nodded. 'Just you; your friends can wait here. Any more nonsense and my men will throw them out.'

The man, who had not given his name – not that Wolfe was interested – followed him to the office. On entering, Wolfe stepped aside, gesturing towards a chair, closed the door and walked across the room to sit on the edge of the desk arms crossed facing the fascist.

'Your proposition is?'

The man sneered as he said, 'You pay us a hundred pound a week.'

Wolfe took two steps forward. 'What?' he waved his hand. 'Never mind, I heard what you said. Why should I pay you a hundred pound a week?'

The man's mouth widened in what one might call a smile, 'Protection.'

'I have security.'

'Yes you do, here, but what about your families?'

Wolfe wanted to leap at the man, grab him by the throat and strangle him, but picked up a pack of cigarettes, shook one free, and didn't offer them as he lit up, exhaling smoke into the air.

'I have partners; I'll have to run it by them. It's too late to contact them now. Why don't you come back tomorrow evening when we've closed and discuss this some more?'

The fascist stood and Wolfe noticed the butt of a pistol in a shoulder holster. 'Okay, you talk to Mr Reid and your brother, I'll be back tomorrow.' He walked to the door and opened it.

Wondering how he knew their names, Wolfe moved away from the desk. 'I'll see you out.'

Once in the casino, the fascist gestured to his friends, just before exiting the casino. He turned to Wolfe. 'See you, Jew.'

Wolfe stared at the trio as they left, eyes slit, and mouth set in an angry straight line. He beckoned to Frank who was immediately by his side.

'Get two men to follow them.'

Frank didn't say a word, just nodded. Wolfe angrily put out the cigarette into an ashtray, returned to the office reaching for the telephone when there was a knock at the door.

'Come in,' he said.

Frank entered. 'What did they want?'

'They wanted protection money.'

'We have—'

Wolfe spat out the words, 'For our families.'

'How do they know about our families?'

'They know Billy, Asher and I are partners.' He picked up the telephone. An hour later Billy and Asher arrived at the casino.

'What I want to know is – how do they know us?' Billy asked.

Wolfe shrugged his shoulders, 'No idea. I have never seen them before.'

'Did they have an accent?' Asher asked.

'English,' Wolfe stared at the wall, moving his head slowly from side to side in thought. 'They had guns – well, their spokesman did.'

Billy pinched his bottom lip, saying grimly, 'They threatened our families. Is this a Mosley thing, or are they independent?'

'You think the badges are a trick to throw us?'

I never thought of that,' said Wolfe.

'Let's get Frank in here. He might have noticed something and the men might have returned.'

Asher opened the door to find Jimmy O'Brien standing there. Now an inspector, his hand was raised to knock on the door; hat in the other hand. Asher stepped back, knowing by the look on the policeman's face that something was terribly wrong; his first thought was their families.

'Wwwhat's happened,' he stammered as O'Brien entered the office, moving across the room to face Billy.

'We received a phone call that there were two dead bodies on the bank of the Thames by London Bridge.'

Billy leapt to his feet, like Asher fearing the worst. 'Who are they?' he whispered.

'Doyle and Brennan,' was the reply.

'How did they die?' Billy asked.

'Hands tied and shot in the back of the head, like an execution.' O'Brien faced Billy making eye contact. 'Do you know who could have done this?'

Billy glanced quickly at Wolfe who shook his head. 'No.'

There was silence for a moment. O'Brien headed for the open door. 'If you hear anything, let me know.'

'What about the bodies?' Billy asked.

'Have to be an autopsy first, and then we'll release the bodies.'

'They have family in Ireland,' said Billy.

O'Brien nodded. 'We'll notify them.'

'Thanks. We'll let you know if we hear anything.'

O'Brien nodded, put on his hat and left. Billy, a grim look on his face, said menacingly, 'Who are these bastards?'

'They aren't Mosley's man that's for sure,' replied Wolfe.

'We have to get our families away,' said Asher.

'I'm sure they have someone observing our houses,' Wolfe pointed out, 'and as soon as our families leave, they'll follow. If they can kill the way they already have, these are ruthless men.'

'This is not about protection, or a hundred pounds,' said Billy. 'It's more than that.'

'Wolfe, try and remember what their voices were like.' Asher looked at his brother. 'Close your eyes and concentrate.'

'I'll get Frank,' Billy said, walking quickly out of the room.

Closing his eyes, Wolfe slowly detached himself from everything around him, seeing the man in front of him, hearing his voice – 'See you Jew.' There it was: a slight change in tone. He opened his eyes and paced up and down the room, turning to face the door as Billy and Frank entered. He walked over to Frank. 'Where's Elizabeth?'

'At home, why?'

'Come on, I'll tell you who that man is as we go, but we must get to Elizabeth. I think she might be in danger.'

*

The taxi sped along the street, the driver seeing the ten shilling note still in Wolfe's hand. Before the taxi had come to a full stop, Frank leapt from it and in an instant had the front door open, calling his wife's name. Elizabeth rushed into the hallway, alarm on her face wiping her hands on an apron. 'What's the matter?'

Wolfe, Asher and Billy entered the house. 'Wolfe wants to ask you something,' Frank said.

'Did the Le Feuvre twins have a younger brother?'

'Yes.'

'Leave what you are doing, go with Frank and pick up the children from school. Billy, Asher and I will pick up the rest of our families and some men.'

Two hours later, having closed the Victoria casino for the rest of the day, the families gathered in the dining room. Wolfe clapped his hands to get their attention.

'We,' he gestured with his hand towards them, 'are in danger from a man named Christian Le Feuvre.' He then told them about the twins who, on their return to France, were executed for their crimes. 'It seems their younger brother is on a road of revenge. I am hoping he keeps his appointment with us tonight, and one way or another we can solve the situation. All we ask –' he pointed to Billy and Asher '– is to leave it to us.' He turned away and headed for the office with Billy, Asher and Frank trailing behind.

In the office, Wolfe asked Billy, 'Are the men in place and armed?'

'Yes. How did you come to the conclusion that he was a Le Feuvre?'

'His English accent was perfect, except for the letter, R. It was the way he said 'brother'. I didn't notice it at first as I was angry. If he hadn't killed, Doyle and Brennan, I would not have thought about it. His brothers were sadistic killers. It seems it runs in the family.'

'We found Le Feuvre's observer,' said Frank, adding, 'We haven't done anything about him, but when the Frenchman enter the casino we'll take care of him.'

'Don't kill him,' Billy said. 'Take him down to the wine cellar and hold him there.'

Frank nodded and moved across the casino to one of his men and whispered instructions. The man nodded gestured to another and they left.

Just before two o'clock, the four Frenchmen entered the casino, coming to a stop in front of Billy, who was standing between the brothers.

Frank stepped in front of Le Feuvre, the Frenchman smiling coldly as Frank patted him down for weapons, removing the pistol and a wicked stiletto hidden in a sheath around his ankle. Frank then checked the other men, removing a variety of weapons.

Wolfe took a step forward, studying the Frenchman's face. 'I can now see the family resemblance, Monsieur Le Feuvre.'

The fixed sinister smile was still on his face, but now the French accent was unmistakable. 'What gave me away? I thought my English accent was very good.'

Wolfe was about to reply, but Billy stepped forward and slapped Le Feuvre once, very hard. The Frenchman reeled backward, hand going to his face, as in a voice of steel Billy said, 'You killed two of my men and you'll pay dearly for that.'

The shock of the slap quickly melted away. Le Feuvre straightened his jacket and tie, the imprint of Billy's hand seen clearly on his cheek; the eyes flashed angrily and there was menace in his voice.

'You think you have me, by—' he snapped his fingers, looking for the word '—aha, by the balls.' He looked at Wolfe. 'Your daughter Sally is a very beautiful woman. No, she isn't in Paris. It took a little persuasion, but she eventually agreed to accompany us to London.'

Wolfe moved towards the Frenchman fists clenched. 'Now, now Monsieur Brown, it isn't that easy.'

'What do you want?' Wolfe asked harshly.

'I want you and your partners—' he pointed to Billy and Asher '—to suffer as my brothers did the last week of their lives. Living in filth and dirt, and then hung like dogs.' He took a step towards them and looked directly at Billy. 'Have you seen your daughter April today?' Not waiting for an answer he turned his attention on Asher. 'Your son Abraham put up a good fight. In fact he broke the nose of one of my men.'

Asher's fist slammed into the Frenchman's face. He staggered backwards from the blow; Asher's face an angry mask pointing a finger at Le Feuvre. 'If you've harmed my son in any way ...'

Le Feuvre's face was white with anger, eyes staring insanely, as he screamed, 'Your children will pay for this, and what you did to my—' As quickly as his anger appeared, it disappeared. He shook himself, pulled back his shoulders and smiled, taking control of his feelings saying contemptuously. 'I know you want to kill me, but then you will never see your children again. If I do not return to my men within the hour—' he ran a hand across his throat to emphasise '—they will kill your children.'

'Let them go,' Wolfe said. 'It's us you want, they mean nothing to you.'

'Ah, but Monsieur Brown, they mean a lot to you.' Le Feuvre and his men picked up their weapons and walked towards the door which one of his men opened. Le Feuvre came to a halt just before it turned to look at them for a moment, a smug smile on his face. 'Don't try and follow us unless you want to lose more men. I shall be in touch within the next twenty-four hours.'

As he turned away to leave, Wolfe said vehemently, 'If anything happens to our children you'll wish you had never been born.'

The Frenchman turned to look back. 'Is that a threat?'

'No, it's a promise.'

As the four Frenchman disappeared, Billy said, 'Come on; let's find out where they have our children.'

'I think we should let our families return home,' Asher suggested. 'Le Feuvre has what he wants for the moment.'

'I agree,' Wolfe stated.

*

The car with Le Feuvre and his men inside moved away from the casino. The Frenchman closed his eyes. It had taken six months to put into motion the plan to avenge his brother's deaths. He rubbed his chin with the fingers of his right hand. It still hurt, but not as much as he was going to hurt the Brown brothers and their friend Reid.

Opening his eyes, he pulled a cigarette case from the pocket of his coat pocket, extracting a cigarette and lit it, letting the smoke trickle through his nostrils, remembering how it all started.

Christian was a very good dancer, going to a variety of venues. It was at the Côte d'Azur in Paris that he met Lily and her four aunts. All good dancers, but Lily was far the best. He loved dancing with her and they became friends – nothing romantic, mind you – with her aunts keeping an eagle eye on her it would have been impossible. On hearing his name, the aunts told him that Lily's father and his were friends, but didn't go into any details.

Lily asked him if he would go with her to Madeleine Vionet's fashion show at the La Bohme dress shop. He didn't want to go, but something made him change his mind at the last minute, and that's where he met Sally Brown.

Lily and Sally sat next to each other in a design and dressmaking class. Although Sally was a little older than Lily, they became friends, going to the cinema, dancing and sometimes Sally stayed at one of Lily's aunts' homes. The aunts spoiled their only niece.

Over the next few weeks Sally and Christian met from time to time for lunch or an evening meal. She told him at their first meeting that at the moment she wasn't interested in a relationship. All she wanted to do was design and make ladies clothes. He didn't realise who she was, until she told him about her family and that her father was once a boxer and a partner in a casino. That's when he put two and two together and the seed of revenge took hold.

It was through carefully asked questions that he knew about Asher's son Abraham and Billy Reid's daughter April. He hand-picked nine men from his drug and gun running businesses; all had worked for and known his brothers; all would kill just for the pleasure of it.

A couple of weeks before putting the final phase of his plan into action, he and three of the men arrived in London, spending three days memorising various routes to and from the Victoria Casino. On his return to Paris, Christian arranged to meet Sally for dinner.

Sally didn't know anything about his business. Her friend Lily said that he was in importing and exporting. At first they made small talk but then Christian asked, 'Sally, there's an American fashion show next weekend at the Ritz Hotel in London, would you like to—'

'I told you,' she said a little angrily, 'I thought you understood, I don't want a relationship now, and to tell you the truth Christian, I don't feel that way towards you.' She touched his hand, her voice softer, and a smile on her face. 'I look on you as a good friend, like a cousin.'

Inside he was seething, but he smiled and kissed her hand. 'I didn't mean it like that. I thought that it would be a good opportunity for you to see a different type of fashion and at the same time visit your family.'

'That is so kind and thoughtful of you, but Lily and I have been invited to Monsieur Galliard's party. You know, I think he likes Lily. Would you like to come with us?'

'I'm sorry, but I have to be in Marseille this weekend, but I'll be back on Monday. How about meeting up for dinner on Wednesday, and you can tell me all about it.'

On the Wednesday they went to Louise Restaurant for dinner. After the meal he offered to drive her home. She thought nothing of it as he had done this before. She suddenly noticed the driver was going in the wrong direction.

'Where are you taking me?' Panic in her voice.

Christian was silent, just smiled, not his usual smile but one that sent a shiver up her spine. Her lip curled in defiance. 'Christian, please take me home, this isn't funny.'

He slapped her around the face. 'Shut up, and be quiet.'

Her hand went to her cheek in surprise, dark brown eyes glared at him as she went to return the slap, but he grabbed her wrist and laughed.

'Where are you taking me?' she demanded.

'You'll see, now be a good girl and keep quiet otherwise I'll have to—'

She tried to open the door, but it was locked. Suddenly a hand went around her neck and something over her face; she struggled for a while and then everything went black. Sally awoke with a splitting headache and slowly sat up to look around the room which was dimly lit by a naked light bulb. The room was bare except for the mattress she was on. There was no window, just wooden stairs leading up to a door. She got to her feet, climbed the stairs and tried to open the door, but it was locked. She banged on it, yelling, 'Open this door.' Hearing footsteps she moved back down the stairs as the door was flung open and a man she had never seen before shouted in French, 'Shut up.'

'I need to go to the toilet and wash, and I'm hungry, where am I?'

'London, come out, don't try anything silly.'

He was a big man whose bald head sat on his shoulders like a bowling ball. She walked through the open door into a hall. He pointed to a door on the opposite side and to the right. 'Toilet, I'll be waiting, and leave the door open.'

She didn't say anything as it was not unusual in France for men and women to use the same toilet facilities.

Feeling better after the wash she walked back into the hall. He grabbed her arm steering her roughly along the hall, turning into the kitchen where Christian and two other men sat smoking and drinking coffee.

He smiled up at her. 'Good morning,' gesturing to a seat opposite him. 'Join us for coffee. Would you like something to eat?'

'What am I doing here?' she demanded.

He ignored the question. 'Have something to eat – you're going to need your strength.'

'How long do I have to be here?' She looked around the kitchen. It wasn't very clean and the windows looking out onto an overgrown garden were grimy.

Christian walked around the table, looking at her for a moment, and then stroked a tress of hair away from her eyes. She smacked his hand away.

He laughed. 'I never realised that you were that fiery.' He grabbed her chin between his fingers and kissed her. As he pulled away she spat in his face. His lips widened in a smile, wiping the spittle from his face, and then slapped her. 'That is a turn on, and when this is over, my dear, I shall have my way with you. How long am I going to keep you here? Well, that depends on your father and his partners.'

'What's my father got to do with it?' She was still looking at Christian as a cup of coffee and buttered bread was placed in front of her by the bald-headed man. 'Thanks. Are you going to tell me how you know my father?'

'No, not yet, but I promise you'll know everything in the next couple of days. Eat – it may be a long time before your next meal.' With that he gestured to the two men sitting at the table and they left the kitchen.

Realising that there was nothing she could do at the moment, Sally made short work of her breakfast and then was roughly half carried and dragged back to the cellar. Bored, she found a piece of stone and, using it as chalk, passing the time by drawing dress designs. Suddenly the door opened and Bald Head carried an unconscious girl down the stairs, dumping her unceremoniously on to the mattress, and without a word turned and left.

Sally walked over to the bed, and was shocked to see that it was April. There was a bruise on her right cheek and the top of her dress was torn as if someone had grabbed it. She ran up the stairs, banging on the door yelling, 'We need something to drink.'

She heard footsteps on the bare floorboards and stepped down two stairs as the door was flung open to see an angry Christian standing there.

He stepped down one stair. 'If you don't shut up, I'll shut you up.' He slapped her hard across the face.

She grabbed the handrail, stopping herself from tumbling down the stairs. Her eyes watered and bottom lip curled, but she was determined not to cry. She was angry and wanted to attack, but was also frightened of him as she said calmly, which she didn't feel, 'Can we please have some water to drink and wash? It's very stuffy down here.'

He grabbed the door handle to close the door, saying, 'I'll think about it.' He slammed the door and locked it. She heard him walk away. Fifteen minutes later, Bald Head, who seemed to be their jailer, placed a bottle of water inside the door then quickly closed it. Sally climbed the few stairs and picked up the bottle, taking it over to April. Tearing a strip of her dress wet it and gently wiped April's mouth; April began to stir, blinking her eyes to clear her vision and recognised Sally; she went to sit up, but fell back holding her head.

'I feel like I've been hit over the head with a hammer. Where are we? What are we doing here?'

Sally placed an arm under April's head, lifting it slightly placing the bottle of water against her lips. 'Drink slowly.'

A few seconds later, feeling a little better, April sat up. 'I thought you were in Paris.'

'I was, but this man Christian, who I thought was a friend, brought me here against my will. It's something to do with our fathers, but I don't know anything else. What about you?'

'I was walking along Commercial Road when a car pulled up; two men jumped out, one of them grabbed me while the other placed a cloth over my face. The next thing I knew, I'm here. Who are they and what do they want with us?' She began to cry.

Sally placed an arm around April's shoulder to comfort her. 'I really don't—' She was interrupted by the door bursting open. Both women looked up to see two men, one swearing at the man they were dragging down the stairs dumping on the floor. One of them kicked the prone body, saying, 'That's for breaking my nose.' The two men quickly climbed the stairs, slamming the door behind them.

Sally and April moved across the room, turning him on to his back. They gasped, both saying, 'Abraham.' His nose and mouth were bloody and there was a cut under the right eye.

He moaned and began to stir, slowly opening his eyes to see the girls looking anxiously down at him. 'Am I in heaven?'

April slapped him playfully on the arm as Sally asked, 'What happened to you?' She handed him the bottle of water.

He took a sip before answering. 'I was walking across the road in Lincolns Inn Fields after one of my lectures.' He was studying law. 'A car pulled up beside me, and two men tried to grab me. I fought them.' He grinned, holding his face as it hurt. 'I know I broke the nose of one of the attackers', and then suddenly someone came up behind me, and the next thing I know I'm here. What's happening? Who are these men?'

Just then the door opened and three men descended the stairs, one being Christian. 'I have my three little chicks, and now the fun begins.'

'Who are you? What do you want with us?' Abraham asked.

'My name is Christian Le Feuvre.' He looked at the three prisoners who stared at him, the name seemingly to mean nothing to them. 'It seems that you have never heard the name Le Feuvre, but your fathers have.'

'What has that got to do with us?' Sally asked.

'Your fathers killed my brothers.'

'How?' the trio asked in unison.

Le Feuvre waved an arm. 'That doesn't matter.' He slammed his right fist into the palm of his left hand. 'I want revenge; and *Mon dieu*, I'm going to get it.'

Abraham the trainee lawyer asked, 'What sort of revenge do you have in mind? And where do we come into.' He got to his feet pointing a finger at the Frenchman. 'Ransom, you are holding us to ransom. How much do you want?'

'How much are you worth?' Christian sneered.

'It's not money,' April remarked. 'No it's more than that.'

'I always knew there was something shady about you, somehow I couldn't trust you,' said Sally. 'What do you do for a living? I'm sure it's not importing and exporting.'

There was an amused look on Christian face. 'It doesn't matter if you know; I import and export drugs and anything else that makes money.'

'Anything illegal you mean,' Abraham said.

'Enough of this, I'm bored. Anyway, I'm leaving now to meet your fathers.' He turned to the bald man. 'Make sure they don't escape – and Julius, no touching, otherwise you'll have me to deal with.'

The three men left the cellar and April began to cry. Abraham took her in his arms cuddling her to him. After a minute he leaned slightly away, stroking red hair away from her eyes.

'April, we must be strong. I'm sure our fathers will find us.'

Sally placed her arms around them saying, 'Abraham's right.

*

Once their families had left the casino, Billy and the brothers descended the stairs to the wine cellar. The Frenchman, left behind to see if Le Feuvre was being followed, was tied to a chair, hands bound onto the armrests.

'Strip him,' Billy ordered. Once the man was naked Billy stepped close to him, saying softly, 'Do you speak English?'

The man looked at him, but didn't reply. Billy slapped him hard across the face shouting, 'Do you speak English?'

The prisoner's mouth drew into a straight determined line, the eyes staring unwaveringly back.

Billy walked across the cellar to a box in the corner, bent and picked up something, returning to the Frenchman, whose eyes widened on seeing the hammer in Billy's hand.

Billy looked at Wolfe, and then at the man in the chair as he said, 'Hold his right arm, don't let it move.' There was a cold certainty in his voice as he said in barely a whisper, 'Do you speak English? If you don't reply, I'm going to break every bone in your right hand.'

He lifted the hammer and was about to bring it down when the man screamed in heavy accented English, 'Yes, I speak your language.'

Billy gave a tight smile. 'That's better. Now, I want to know where Le Feuvre has our children.'

'I don't know.'

Billy slammed the hammer down on to the prisoner's hand. The man screamed in pain as his interrogator said menacingly into his ear, 'I'm going to break your other hand if you don't tell me what I want to know, and then I'll move to your testicles.'

There was fear on the prisoner's face and voice as he uttered shakily, 'Cold Harbour, off Manchester Road.'

'What number?' Wolfe squeezed the damaged hand. The scream filled the air as the prisoner said between gasping for air. 'Four.'

'How many men does he have?' Asher asked his face close to the prisoner's.

'Eight and Le Feuvre make nine.'

Billy held a piece of paper in front of the Frenchman. 'Can you draw an outline of the house, and where the guards are situated?'

The man stared at Billy, shaking his head. Billy grabbed the hammer and was about to bring it down on the prisoner's left hand when the Frenchman said, 'Then I won't be able to draw at all.'

Billy stepped back, his face an angry mask. Turning quickly he strode over to the toolbox, picked something out of it, returning to face the prisoner holding up a nail, and in a sinister whisper asked, 'Which testicle?'

The prisoner's face drained of blood, shaking with fear as Billy stretched the skin of the right testicle placing the point on the nail on it and lifted the hammer saying, 'First the right, then the left, then—'

'Okay, okay, I'll do it, screamed the man, spittle of fright sliding down his chin.'

Billy gently slapped his face. 'There, why didn't you say that in the first place?' Billy released his left hand, placing the paper on a piece of wood, handing the man a pencil.

Five minutes later they had a plan of the house and where the guards were situated.

Billy turned to one of the men. 'Keep him here till I get back, put his clothes on and hand in a sling.' He turned to the prisoner. 'If you are telling the truth and we get our children back, I'll let you go, but the pain you have received so far is nothing to what you will go through if you're lying.' Without another word, he turned and left the cellar, with Wolfe, Asher and Frank following.

After arming themselves and filling their pockets with extra ammunition, Billy gathered everyone into the casino. 'It seemed from what Le Feuvre said he is giving us twenty-four hours before telling us what his demands are going to be. What he doesn't know is that we know where he is keeping our children, and how many men he has, and more important the layout of the house.' He looked at his watch. 'We have about two hours, maybe a little more before daybreak, so let's start planning.'

The moon played hide and seek with the clouds as a car coasted silently to a stop and the rear door facing away from the house opened. Billy and Wolfe crawled from the car, and crouching low, moved silently towards a shoulder-high wall. At the same time two men, holding on to each other for support, tottered drunkenly along the street, stopping outside number four to urinate against the wall.

Two armed men suddenly appeared in front of them on the other side of the wall.

'Get away from here,' one of the men hissed.

While they were occupied with the drunks, Billy and Wolfe climbed the wall and crept behind the two guards.

'Sorry, mate,' said one of the drunks, 'but when—' Suddenly the guards were jerked backward as Billy and Wolfe slid their right arms around the guards' throats, left hand pressing the nape of the neck. They struggled for a minute and then were still. Tying and gagging the two men, they rolled their bodies into the undergrowth while the two drunks taking the guards place.

While the guards were being taken care of at the front of the house, a boat, its engine muffled, approached the small jetty at the rear of number four. Asher and three men rolled off the slow-moving boat onto the jetty crawling behind some wooden crates. Asher looked back to see the boat disappearing into the night, and then peered around the crates. As expected he saw only one guard, who had his back to them, head on his chest asleep. Asher crept slowly towards the unsuspecting man, rising like a ghost from the ground, clamped a hand over his mouth and hit him over the head with a truncheon, lowering the unconscious body to the ground. With the help of one of his men, they tied and gagged the unconscious man, hiding him behind the crates. The man with Asher took the guard's place.

At the front of the house, Billy glanced at his watch, then quickly up at the sky, estimating they had about thirty minutes before daylight. Billy drew his pistol from its shoulder holster and whispered, 'Let's go,' and strode up to the front door.

*

Sally, Abraham and April, sat huddled together, trying to come up with a plan of escape.

'With Le Feuvre out somewhere, our biggest problem,' said Abraham, 'is we don't know how many men, apart from baldy, are left in the house.'

'We have to cross that bridge when we come to it,' said Sally.

'I have a plan, well a sort of plan,' said Abraham moving closer to the girls.

Sally banged on the door, shouting, 'Let us out.' April was at the bottom of the stairs and to one side, adding to the noise yelling, 'Help.'

Sally heard footsteps moving quickly along the hall and stepped back from the door just as it was flung open and Baldy took a step inside, face red with anger.

'What the fuck is—' Whatever he was going to say was lost in the look of surprise as Abraham, clinging to the handrail, with his right hand, feet on the edge of the step, leaned across, grabbed the front of Baldies shirt with his left hand and pulled. Their jailer overbalanced and tumbled down the stairs.

As he reached the bottom, April leaped on to his back, hitting him with the heel of her shoe. Sally joined in, punching and scratching his head and face. Baldy tried to fight them off, while at the same time rose to his feet. Abraham jumped from the stair, reaching the jailer just as he got to his feet.

Abraham was tall, broad-shouldered and muscular like his father and uncle, who had encouraged him, his brother and cousins to box. He landed a left to the Frenchman's jaw, followed by a right to the flabby stomach, as he doubled over; Abraham uppercut him. Baldy shook his head, trying to clear it when it was jerked back by the force of a sledgehammer blow and he dropped to the ground like a sack of potatoes.

'Let's get out of here,' Abraham said, shaking his hand from the pain of the punch he had just landed. With Sally in the lead they ran up the stairs and out into the hallway. Seeing the front door, Sally headed in that direction. They had nearly reached the door when it opened and Christian walked in. For a split second, surprise showed on his face, and then he stepped to one side while at the same time drawing his pistol from its holster. The man behind him grabbed Sally as she reached the door. She clawed at his hands, struggling to free herself from his clutches. April ran past her, but was grabbed by another of Le Feuvre's men. Abraham was about to leap on Christian, but was stopped in his tracks by the pistol pointing steadily at him.

'Stop,' Christian yelled, looking at the girls, 'otherwise I'll kill him.'

Sally stopped her struggles, as did April, both turning to face Le Feuvre, who unexpectedly slashed Abraham across the face with the barrel of his pistol, opening the skin. Abraham staggered backward a couple of paces from the blow, but would not go down; staring defiantly at Le Feuvre, who, like a flash, was beside Sally; slapping her hard with the palm of his hand, followed by a backhand, knocking her to the ground.

Men ran down the stairs, guns drawn, wondering what the commotion was all about. Le Feuvre, breathing heavily, not from his exertions but anger, uttered between clenched teeth, 'Where's Julius?'

They didn't answer.

He punched Abraham in the stomach and he doubled over from the blow. 'I asked you where's Julius?'

Abraham looked at him with a slight smile, trying to hide the pain. 'Oh, you mean baldy. He's in the cellar.'

Christian turned on the men he had left to guard the house when he went to the casino. 'You allow two women and a young man left in your charge to get the better of you.' He walked along the hall to the men standing shamefaced in front of him, spitting out a tirade of swearwords at them in French.

'I thought you were men.' He leaned forward, screaming. 'You're women. What were you doing to allow them to escape, playing with yourself?' He stopped in front of one of the men and unexpectedly kicked him in the groin. 'You won't be able to play with it for a while. Take them down to the cellar and tie them up.'

Dragging the trio unceremoniously along the hall and down the cellar steps, they propped them up against the wall, binding their hands and feet.

Le Feuvre threw a bucket of water over Julius, who leapt to his feet, crouching in a fighter's stance.

Christian smacked him around the head. 'Idiot, imbecile, they nearly got away. I ought to kill you for jeopardising months of planning.' He waved an arm. 'Get out of my sight, and clean yourself up.'

He saw Julius looking with hatred at April. 'When this is over, you can have her.'

'I'm sorry, boss; they caught me completely by surprise.' He walked over to Abraham and dropped a knee on to his ribs. The crack echoed around the cellar. 'I owe you that, and more.' He looked at April. 'You and I have a date.' He bent and licked her face, fondling her breasts. She spat in his face. He laughed and slapped her.

'That's enough,' ordered Christian, turning to leave. Halfway up the stairs he looked back at Sally. 'I'll see you later.' He turned off the light, leaving their prisoners in darkness.

April was crying, despair showing on her face, moaning, 'They're going to kill us.'

Abraham, doubled over with pain from his broken ribs, tried to placate her, saying softly, 'I won't let anything happen to you.'

'How you going to do that, bite his bum,' Sally scoffed.

'Please don't make me laugh,' Abraham grimaced.

April had stopped crying and continued the banter. 'If Abraham did that, he would need to wash his mouth with disinfectant.'

The mood of despair was broken, and as with people facing adversity they clung to hope by making fun of their situation.

'Do you think the two of you can move back to back?' Abraham asked.

'Why would we want to do that?' April questioned.

'Perhaps one of you can untie the others' hands,' Abraham suggested, adding, 'I'd try it, but the slightest movement is painful.'

'It's a good idea,' the girls said in unison, moving sideways, using their shoulders against the wall to lever themselves around. Sally was the first to try.

As day turned into night the temperature in the cellar dropped dramatically, but Sally was perspiring from the effort of trying to untie April's bonds.

'Wait,' said April, 'I think I can wriggle my hands free.'

A second later she was helping to untie Sally. They helped Abraham to stand moving slowly towards the stairs when the door opened.

*

Billy slowly opened the front door, gun ready, stepping to one side to allow Wolfe to enter. At the other end of the hall, Asher and Joseph entered via the overgrown back garden. They could hear someone moving around in the kitchen. Asher turned to Joseph, pointing to the kitchen. Joseph nodded and they moved quietly towards the door which was slightly open.

A man was sitting at the kitchen table, his back to them, eating a sandwich and reading a magazine, a rifle leaning against his leg. Joseph moved slowly and silently towards him while Asher kept watch by the door. The Frenchman stopped eating, the sandwich held in mid-air, and cocked his head to one side, listening, then began to turn; Joseph clamped a hand over his mouth while at the same time landing a heavy blow with a truncheon to his head, knocking the Frenchman senseless.

They tied the man up and gagged him and then met up with Wolfe and Billy. Leaving Joseph and Asher to guard the door to the dining room, the duo climbed the stairs to the second floor hallway where there were three bedrooms, two on either side of the hall and another at the far end. Facing them at the top of the stairs were a bathroom and toilet. The door on the right began to open and light streamed out from the bedroom. Whoever was at the door said something to someone in the room, laughed and walked through the doorway to find Wolfe pointing a gun at his head, saying quietly, 'Don't speak, or shout, as it will be the last thing you'll ever do. Now move slowly towards the stairs.'

Wolfe shoved the Frenchman in the back and he tumbled down the stairs with Wolfe and Billy close behind.

The Frenchman came to stop at the bottom of the stairs. He was knocked unconscious. The dining room door opened and a man walked out into the hall to see what the noise was, coming to an abrupt halt on seeing his compatriot in a heap on the floor and the barrel of Asher's pistol pointing at him. Quickly disarming the man, Asher and Joseph tied and gagged him, while Billy and Wolfe did the same with the unconscious Frenchman. After checking there was no one else in the dining room they left them there.

'It's time to get our children,' Wolfe said. They opened the cellar door.

Sally, April and Abraham held their breath, fearing the worst as the door opened. The girls stifled a scream and began to cry with relief on seeing their fathers who ran down the stairs cuddling their daughters to them. Asher went to hug his son, but Abraham said, 'I would love to, Dad, but my ribs are broken.'

When Wolfe saw the bruises on Sally's face, he turned to Billy. 'We have some unfinished business to attend to.'

'O'Brien will be here very soon, let him sort it out.'

'Billy, take a good look at April.'

Billy frowned, not understanding what his friend was saying, pulling slightly away from his daughter to see the bruises on her face and torn dress. He looked at Wolfe and nodded.

'You three stay here for a little longer,' Wolfe said. 'I'll send someone down to help you, but we have some unfinished business to deal with.'

In barely a whisper, Billy asked April, 'Who did this to you?'

'A bald-headed man, his name is Julius,' she said.

Wolfe had done a quick count. 'There are four Frenchmen left, including Le Feuvre, and they're holed up in—' Two shots interrupted what he was about to say. They could hear men moving around upstairs. 'It's coming from the rear of the house,' Billy said, moving quickly to the back door, opening it and yelling, 'Shaun, you okay?'

'Yes,' was the reply. 'There are a couple of men who are trying to climb out of the bedroom—' A fusillade of shots stopped him from saying anything else.

'Joseph, go help Shaun,' Billy ordered. He didn't wait for a reply, just said, 'Come on,' to Wolfe and Asher. At the bottom of the stairs he told Wolfe, 'Wait here, we won't be a moment,' and ran to the front door, opened it, turning to Asher and pointing upward. 'You and the two men out here make sure they don't get out through those windows.'

'What are you going to do?' Asher asked.

Billy didn't reply, just patted him on the shoulder, turned and walked quickly to join Wolfe at the bottom of the stairs.

Meanwhile, Le Feuvre, having heard the commotion on the stairs, realised that somehow they had been discovered. He was very angry trying to figure a way out of his predicament. Julius, who was with him, opened the window leading to the back garden and was about to climb out when shots were fired at him, Julius dived back into the room and returned fire.

Le Feuvre moved to the door, turned the knob and slowly opened it a fraction. The hall was empty. Closing the door he sat on the bed, head down, thinking.

Julius let off another shot, and then turned to Christian. 'How are we going to get out of this one, boss – any ideas?'

Christian didn't reply, his mind racing. He got up from the bed and strode quickly over to the door again and opened it. The hall was still empty, but it wouldn't be for long. He glanced up and snapped his fingers, *the loft*. Leaving the door open he grabbed a chair and looked over his shoulder at Julius. 'Come on, we might be able to get out of here. Le Feuvre moved out into the hall, placing the chair under the loft hatch.

'What are you doing?'

Christian stood on the chair, whispering, 'If we can get into the loft and remove some roof slates we can escape along the roof.' He pushed the hatch inward, sliding it to one side hoisting himself into the attic moving across to the far wall, removing the slates. Julius was on the chair about to follow his boss.

Meanwhile, Billy and Wolfe crawled up the stairs to the hallway. Billy peeked round the corner, just in time to see the bald man April had told him about. Anger took over from caution and he leapt to his feet. In three strides he was by the chair kicking it from under Julius, who fell onto the floor, swearing.

Billy grabbed the lapels of the Frenchman's jacket, hauling him to his feet, and slammed him against the wall. Through tight angry lips he said, 'You hit my daughter, now try and hit me.' He let go the lapels and stepped back.

The big Frenchman smiled, accent strong. 'When I have finished with you, I'm going to fuck your daughter.'

Wolfe was stunned by Billy's actions, knowing that at any moment one of the other two men, or Le Feuvre could appear and shoot his friend. Just then the toilet door opened and a thin bony man holding a pistol appeared. Wolfe fired two shots and the man fell back into the toilet. Wolfe was upset as they agreed to try and not kill anyone, but knew that if it came to the crunch they might have to. There was someone in the bedroom on the right. He wondered if it was Le Feuvre.

Billy gave a slight smile, dancing on the balls of his feet as Julius, a sneering grin on his face, moved towards him. Billy threw a left jab to the face; the Frenchman blocked it but was not quick enough to stop a right hand to the stomach. He gasped with the power of the punch, moving quickly forward, trying to wrap his arms around his opponent, but Billy was too quick, and for his efforts Julius received a right and left to the face in quick succession. He shook his head and rushed at the Irishman, but once again Billy danced away and to one side, landing a flurry of punches on the Frenchman's face and body. Julius was puffing heavily and slowing down.

Billy taunted him. 'No wonder you have to hit women, you fight like one.'

With a roar, Julius ran at Billy throwing left and rights, all missing their target, but he was not so lucky as his opponent landed a left to the jaw, followed by a right to the ribs, then a left to the nose, the bone shattering under the power of the blow. Blood spurted from the Frenchman's nose and his hands dropped.

'This is for my daughter,' Billy said. The punch to the jaw was so ferocious that it cracked, a slither of bone entering Julius larynx and cutting off his air supply. Within seconds he was dead.

Hearing the crash of Julius falling and Billy's voice, Le Feuvre decided to go back. Pistol in his hand, he crawled to the hatch, looked down to see Julius lying in a heap on the ground and Billy looking down at him. Christian gave a sinister smile, took aim and was about to pull the trigger when someone shouted his name, spoiling his aim, the bullet hitting the wall.

Something made Wolfe look up, Christian about to shoot Billy. He yelled, 'Le Feuvre,' and tackled Billy to the ground, feeling the bullet pass, embedding itself in the wall.

Wolfe untangled himself from Billy and fired through the hatch. There was a cry of pain and Le Feuvre tumbled from the opening onto the hall floor, blood flowing from his shoulder. Just then, the sound of police bells ringing grew louder. Cars and police vans screeched to a halt and policemen ran from them into the house.

Wolfe stood over Le Feuvre pistol aimed at the Frenchman's temple. Billy rose to his feet and moved over to his friend. 'Don't do it. I want to kill this scum as much as you do, but we agreed to do as we did with his brothers. Let the law deal with them.'

A grim-faced Wolfe nodded, taking a step backwards and then kicking Le Feuvre in his wounded shoulder. Christian screamed in pain. Wolfe bent, taking his chin between thumb and forefinger forcing the Frenchman to look at him. 'You're lucky that's all I did to you. What you failed to consider is that we have the death penalty for murder in this country.' He let go of Le Feuvre's chin and got to his feet just as O'Brien ran into the hall.

Billy pointed to Le Feuvre. 'This is the man that murdered Doyle and Brennan.'

Wolfe said, 'One of his men is holed up in that bedroom, and two others are tied up in the dining room.'

Billy took O'Brien's elbow and steered him to the end of the hall, gesturing at the dead Julius. 'I'm sorry, Jimmy, but that man over there and I had a fight. His death was an accident. There's another in the toilet, he was about to shoot me, and Wolfe had to shoot him.'

'Don't worry, Billy, I'll take care of everything, but you need to tell me the full story of what's been going on here.'

'All I can tell you for now is that he is the Le Feuvre twins brother and he kidnapped, April, Sarah and Abraham. Come to the house tomorrow afternoon, bring Mrs O'Brien, Esther would love to see her, and I'll tell you the whole story.'

'That's a date,' O'Brien said, turning away to give orders to the policemen now entering the hall.

Wolfe and Billy walked slowly down the stairs to be met by their men and children.

Two weeks later, Le Feuvre was sentenced to be hung for murder. His men turned against him, giving evidence that Le Feuvre killed Doyle and Brennan. They were sent to prison for twenty years for aiding and abetting.

Wolfe and the others were in the office of their Hanover Square casino. 'I'm glad we did not kill him, but I wish we could have roughed him up a little.'

'I know what you mean,' Billy said. 'The only satisfaction I have is killing that Julius, although it was an accident.'

'Abraham broke that man's nose,' Asher pointed out.

'We taught him well,' Wolfe laughed. 'How are his ribs?'

'Mending slowly, but he is getting a lot of nursing from his cousin Sally and Billy's April.'

15 'Dancing in the Dark'

August 1933

THE FIRST THING WOLFE DID after the business with Le Feuvre was to buy a car. He walked round the Humber 12 saloon, stroking it and polishing the burgundy and ivory paintwork with the sleeve of his jacket, saying to Billy and Asher as they inspected the vehicle, 'I bought this as I am fed up with having to find a cab if we have to go anywhere in an emergency.'

'You know, when you're right, you're right,' Billy said thoughtfully. 'Start her up. Let's hear what she sounds like.'

Wolfe slid onto the leather upholstered seat, turned on the ignition and stroked the steering wheel lovingly. 'Quiet isn't she? Do you want to see the engine?' He asked eagerly, moving from the driving seat to the front of the car opening the bonnet but not before wiping an imaginary speck of dust from it.

'It's a big car – where did you buy it?' Asher asked.

'John Gray, he has a garage in Bethnal Green Road.'

'Who taught you to drive?' Billy asked.

'Mr Gray's son, it's not that hard.' Wolfe didn't realise he was bragging. 'If I can do it, anyone can.'

Two weeks later, Billy and Asher were driving their own Humber 12 cars.

It had taken a couple of months for Sally, April and Abraham to get over their ordeal and things, as they say, began to happen. Most Sundays mornings, Sally and her sister Frieda met other Jewish boys and girls at London Bridge Station and went on rambles to Bexhill and Dorking. At the top of Leith Hill they could see St Paul's Cathedral and ships in the channel. If it was raining they would go to a museum or the library.

Frieda and Sally were running for the entrance to the library just as the clouds opened up and the drizzle of rain became a torrential downpour. Sally tripped on the step and a man standing nearby grabbed her. If he hadn't, she would have had a nasty fall. He held her close for a moment, a slight smile on his handsome face. 'You okay?' he asked.

For a second she was speechless, eyes wandering over his face, noticing the blue eyes and dimpled grin. A tuft of red hair protruded through his grey flat cap. 'Yes, I'm fine. Thank you, I—' both took no notice of the rain as Frieda ran back.

'Sally, you okay, what happened?' Frieda looked concerned. 'I reached the entrance, looked round and you weren't there. Hey, it's raining and you're getting soaked.'

Sally blinked the rain from her eyes, not looking at her sister. 'If this man, what's your name?'

He held out his hand, 'Phillip, Phil Hyams.'

'If he hadn't caught me I would have had a bad fall.'

Sally took the offered hand, 'Sally Brown and this is my sister Frieda.'

'It's very nice to meet you both.'

'You too, but don't you think we should get out of this rain?' Frieda suggested.

They walked towards the library door Sally explaining to Frieda what happened, 'I tripped and Phillip stopped me from falling.' She looked at Phillip. 'You going into the library?'

'Yes, I'm in the furniture trade and interested in Regency and Georgian furniture, they have some very good reference books here.'

He hadn't released her hand, but Sally didn't mind. 'Do you live in East London?'

'Yes,' he smiled.

Sally's heart skipped a beat. They reached the entrance to the library. 'We are having a party on Saturday night,' she stopped, unable to think becoming flustered – his eyes were smiling at her, his hand comfortable in hers. 'Would you like to come?'

'I'd love to.'

Reluctantly, she let go his hand, took a piece of paper from her bag, saying as she wrote down the address, 'Any time after eight o'clock.'

He took the piece of paper. 'Do I have to wait till Saturday to see you?'

'Well, no, not really.'

He looked down at the address. 'Are you free Wednesday night?'

'Yes.'

'Is seven o'clock okay?'

Her heart was racing, 'That will be fine.'

Someone called his name. He looked round, 'Okay, Harry, I'm coming. Sorry, Sally, I have to go. I'll see you on Wednesday.' He joined his friend, turned and waved.

Sally lifted a hand to wave back.

That evening, in the kitchen, Eva, with an amused smile on her face watched Sally washing up the dinner plates. Every now and again her daughter would stop; head tilted to one side, staring out of the window to the garden, hands in soapy water, give a fleeting smile and then carry on. Halfway to placing a plate on the drying rack, she stopped, sighed, and then absent-mindedly put it back into the water.

It dawned on Eva that her daughter was in love. She pushed back the chair and got to her feet, moving across the kitchen to help Frieda with the wiping up. Picking up a tea towel and a plate from the drying rack, she said casually to Frieda, 'What happened at the library?'

Frieda glanced at her sister and then back to her mother. 'She met this boy. She slipped on the step of the library, he stopped her from falling. He's taking her out on Wednesday, and she invited him on Saturday night.'

Eva didn't say anything to Sally, but knew love at first sight when she saw it. She took a deep breath, remembering how she felt the first time she set eyes on Wolfe. Even now, he made her heart beat faster.

*

'I'm wondering if I'm ready to open my own dress shop.' Sally said on Tuesday at breakfast. 'What do you think, Papa?'

Wolfe didn't reply immediately. Folding his newspaper, he lay it down on the table, and looked at Sally. 'I think this is not the right time for you. To be honest you have no experience in running your own business.' He gave a wry smile. 'You don't just open a shop and watch the money coming in. You have to find the right place in the right street. Then there's decor, electricity, stock, advertising, and many other things before you even open. My advice is to look in a fashion magazine to see if there's a job vacancy in a shop where you can gain experience. See how you feel after a year, and if you think you're ready to go on your own, I'll help you.'

It wasn't what Sally wanted to hear, but she knew in her heart of hearts that he was right. She smiled. 'As always, Papa, you are right.'

That afternoon there was a knock on the door. Isaac opened it and for a moment was speechless, immediately smitten with the young woman standing in front of him. The blue dress with long sleeves and white cuff that matched the collar that swept round her neck ending in a small bow that showed off the contours of her perfectly rounded breasts and waist. The skirt flowed down to just below her knees with inverted pleats at the side. On her head she wore a matching cloche cap, a curl of brown hair protruding from the sides.

She smiled. 'Is Sally in?'

He didn't reply – not because he didn't want to, but because he was unable to speak. Just then Sally came to the door, surprised to see Lily Levine. 'I hope you don't mind me calling. I arrived in London yesterday. I'm staying with my mother in Arbour Square.'

'Of course I don't mind.' Sally nudged Isaac, who didn't respond, his eyes fixed on Lily. Sally couldn't help laughing on seeing her brother's face. 'Lily, this rude person is my brother, Isaac.'

Lily held out her hand. 'Sally has told me so much about you and the rest of the family.'

Isaac took the offered hand.

'Isaac, meet Lily Levine.'

He bent at the waist and kissed the back of Lily's hand. 'It is a pleasure to meet you,' wishing he had thought of something better to say.

'Come in,' Sally said, moving beside Lily, sliding a hand through her arm. 'Isaac, you can let go of Lily's hand now.'

'Oh-umm-sorry.' Reluctantly he let go her hand stepping aside to allow his sister and Lily to enter the house.

'You never told me you had such a handsome brother,' Lily said in the dining room.

Sally laughed. 'He is handsome, isn't he?'

'Like a film star.'

'We are having a get together on Saturday night – would you like to come?'

'I wouldn't miss it for the world.'

'What about Paris?' Sally asked. 'Your aunts love you and ...' she didn't want to be rude '... well, you have a better life there than here.'

Lily laughed. 'What you mean to say is I'm spoilt.'

Sally giggled. 'Okay, yes, you're spoilt. You have everything in Paris that you could ever wish for, why—'

'Not everything,' Lily interrupted. 'I don't have any friends.'

'Oh! I see ... Do you know about Christian?'

'What about him?'

'Let's have a cup of tea, and I'll tell you all about it.'

As Sally poured the tea she asked, 'How is it that you know Christian?'

'From what I've been told, our fathers were friends.'

She handed Lily a cup of tea, 'In what way?'

'Thanks,' Lily frowned. 'From what my aunts have told me, and snippets picked up here and there, it went back to before I was born. My father worked for René Le Feuvre. To tell you the truth, it's a mystery to me. My parents and aunts won't talk about it. All I know is that we came to London at the end of 1914. When we arrived here my father destroyed all our documents, including my birth certificate, changed our name from Gilbert to Levine. The story is that he tried to get out of being conscripted into the army in France, but within three months of coming to London he enlisted and was sent back to France.'

'What about Christian's father?'

'He was a bit of a villain—'

'Like father like son,' Sally interrupted again.

'What?' Lily looked confused, her cup in mid-air.

Sally waved a hand. 'Forget it for the moment, please, carry on.'

'It seems Christian's father was into, well, shady deals. From what I could gather, he double-crossed someone and ended up in the River Seine.' Lily sat bolt upright nearly spilling her tea. 'Do you think my father—' There was shock in her face and voice. 'No he wouldn't.' She gulped down the rest of her tea. 'What did you mean, like father like son?'

'Did you know that Christian had twin brothers?'

'Had? I don't understand ...'

'In France the twins were wanted for importing and exporting drugs, extortion and murder.' Sally then told Lily about the twins being taken back to France and executed. 'Christian imprisoned me, my cousin, Abraham and my father's partner Billy Reid's daughter, April, to avenge his brothers.'

'My goodness – poor you; how did you escape?'

'My father, Uncle Asher and Billy, who you will meet on Saturday, found out where we were being kept prisoner and rescued us, naturally with the help of the police. Christian killed two men. He was hanged for murder.'

Lily's hand went to her throat, an expression of disbelief and shock on her face. 'I never knew he was like that. He was always the charming gentleman with my aunts and me, and a fantastic dancer.'

An hour later, Lily left, her thoughts on what to wear on Saturday, and excited about meeting Isaac again.

*

Eva pulled the curtain to one side, just enough to peek out as Sally and Phillip walked arm in arm along the street. She placed a hand to her cheek whispering, 'Oy! He is so handsome.'

Just then Isaac came into the room humming. Eva glanced curiously at him then back to the window, looking up at the sky to see if it was a full moon. She shrugged her shoulders, looked once more in the direction of Sally and Phillip as they turned the corner and disappeared. She let the curtain fall back into place, turned to speak to Isaac, but he had already left the room.

Sally arrived home and closed the front door to find Frieda sitting on the stairs waiting for her. 'Well?'

'Well, what?'

'What's he like? Did he kiss you? Is he coming on Saturday night?' she asked quickly.

'Whoa, slow down, one question at a time.'

'Where are you going?' Frieda asked, getting to her feet.

'I'm going into the kitchen to make a cuppa.'

'What about your date?'

'If you want to know about my date, you had better come into the kitchen and then I might tell you about the evening.'

Sally walked towards the kitchen, her sister not noticing the mischievous grin on her face. As Sally entered the kitchen she came to a full stop to unexpectedly see her mother sitting at the table. 'Have a nice time?'

Sally smiled to herself as she put on the kettle. She had had boyfriends before, but they had never come to the house and never ever been invited to a Saturday night at the Browns. 'Would you like a cup, Mama?'

Eva smiled. 'That will be nice, thank you.'

'I'll have one too,' Frieda said as she entered the kitchen, sitting cross-legged on a chair.

Sally poured the tea. 'I'm surprised Papa and the others aren't here for the interrogation.' She placed the cups in front of her mother and sister, picked up her own and moved to the door.

'Where are you going?' mother and daughter asked in unison.

'Bed, I'm tired and I have to get up early as I have an interview for the job at the dress shop in Oxford Street.'

In a flash, Frieda stood in the doorway, blocking her way. 'You are not going anywhere until you tell us all about it.'

Sally laughed. 'I was only kidding.' She walked back to the table to sit opposite her mother, takes a sip of tea, the two women leaning forward expectantly. 'He is a proper gentleman, quietly spoken, funny.' She looked dreamily at them.

'Is he a good kisser?' Frieda asked.

'That's for me to know.'

'That means he is,' their mother said, looking at Frieda.

'Well?' was the first word Eva heard on entering the bedroom and taking off her dressing gown.

'I think we are about to meet our first son-in-law.'

'How do you know that?'

Eva got into bed and snuggled up to Wolfe. 'Mmm, call it women's intuition.'

*

Since Wednesday, Sally had been nagging her brother Jack to make some special cakes for Saturday night.

'What's so important about this weekend – it's just another party.' He knew about Phillip from Frieda.

'My friend Lily from Paris is coming and I want to impress her.'

'You sure it's only her you want to impress? Okay, I'll make something special.'

For Sally, the three days seemed to have dragged by. Even now, the minutes seemed like hours. Sally's shoulder-length auburn hair shone in the light; the silk floral dress she had made herself had short loose sleeves, the plain V-neck ending just above her breasts; the skirt, flaring out from the hips, ended at the calf, fitting her slim figure perfectly. For the umpteenth time she went to the window, peeping through the side of the curtain, wondering when and if he would arrive.

Isaac, wearing grey slacks, white short-sleeved shirt under a light blue V-necked sleeveless jumper, looked at his watch wondering if Lily would come. There was a knock at the door. Like a flash he was beside it, took a deep breath to compose himself and opened it. To his disappointment it was a man, someone he had never seen before, with a bunch of roses in his left hand. Before he could say anything Sally was there.

'You're here,' she said a little breathlessly. 'Come in.' Holding out her hand for him to take, she pointed at her brother. 'Phillip, this is my brother Isaac; he's waiting for my friend Lily to arrive.'

Before either could shake hands or say anything, she pulled Phillip into the hall towards the dining room, as Fred Astaire sang 'Night and Day'. The carpet, that usually covered three-quarters of the room, had been rolled back. Jack was tonight's barman and record player. Wolfe and Eva were dancing as Sally and Phillip, still clutching the roses, entered the room. She introduced him to everyone, frowning at her sister as she silently mouthed her swooning admiration.

The record ended as Eva and Wolfe walked back to their seat. Sally, still holding on to Phillip's hand, moved in front of them.
'Mama, Papa, this is Phillip Hyams.'
Wolfe held out his right hand, 'Nice to meet you, young man.' They shook hands.
Eva smiled sweetly at Phillip, jokingly pointed at the roses saying, 'Are they for me? Thank you, they are my favourites.'
'Uh, hum.' Looking embarrassed and not able to say no, Phillip handed her the flowers. 'Sally told me you liked roses.'
Thinking the young man would see she was joking, Eva was taken aback by his gesture, saying a little uncomfortably, 'That is very kind of you.' She took the offered flowers. 'Thank you very much, I'll go and put them in a vase.'
'Would you like a drink?' Sally asked.
'Yes please.'
'You know my mother was only joking.'
He laughed. 'Yes, I know, but for a moment I was a little tongue-tied, and giving her the flowers was the easiest thing to do.'
She kissed his cheek. 'It was a nice thing to do.'
Eva returned to the dining room, moving to one side of the door to look at Sally and her boyfriend dancing. She sighed – they made a lovely couple.
There was a knock at the door, and as had been the case all evening, Isaac opened it. For two days he had rehearsed what he would say when he saw her, but now was lost for words, taking in every inch as he looked her up and down.
Lily's royal-blue silk dress was scalloped at the neck down to the top of her chest, with thin straps on the shoulders, hanging loose over her breasts to the waist which was gathered in, then fell from the hips in folds down to just below her knees. Her short brown hair had waves at the sides and a curl down the right side of her forehead.
'Good evening, Isaac.' She smiled at the expression on his face.
'You are absolutely ...' He hesitated, moving to one side. 'I'm sorry, please come in.' He closed the door turning to face her. She slid an arm through his. 'Why don't you introduce me to everyone?'
As Isaac introduced her, Lily had a strange sense of déjà vu, as though she had known everyone her entire life. The Brown men were handsome, and as for the women, they felt almost like sisters to her. Eva danced throughout the evening, mostly with the girls. Isaac introduced Lily to his grandmother. It was apparent that the grandchildren adored her.

'Hi everyone,' Abraham and April walked arm in arm into the room. She said something to him, he nodded and she left his side to join the girls.

'Sorry I'm late, Doris Spivak came round, said it was an emergency. She knows I don't open on Saturday, but could I do her a big favour as she had a last minute date, and can I do her hair? I couldn't refuse – the matchmaker hooked her up with a recent immigrant from Germany. Poor girl, I hope this one likes her.'

April owned a hairdressing shop in New Road. Because her father Billy and stepmother Esther were practising Jews, she didn't open on Saturdays. Since their ordeal, April and Abraham had become very close and in love, but April herself was not Jewish. They had tried to tell their parents but had chickened out at the last minute. In truth they were old enough to get married, but they respected their parents and each other's families. Abraham was now a practising lawyer, and with April running her own business, they felt that the time was right. Tomorrow, Sunday, as usual, everyone would be together and that's when they were going to tell their parents they loved each other and wanted to get married. Little did they know that everyone, family and friends, knew. Asher and Billy, with their wives, had discussed the situation and all were willing to help April if she wanted to, like her father, become a Jew. The idea of Abraham becoming a Christian never entered their heads.

Sarah and Phillip danced cheek to cheek, as did Abraham and April, to Bob Lawrence singing 'Smoke Gets in Your Eyes'. Isaac stepped in front of Lily and was about to ask her to dance when she moved forward and just slipped into his arms. Eva said to her friend, Sarah, 'It won't be very long before we are grandparents.'

'They have grown up so quickly,' Sarah replied.

The following day Abraham and April at last confronted their parents.

'It's about time,' Wolfe said.

The weekend after the party, Sally was invited for tea by Phillip's parents. She was immediately at ease with them, especially Phillip's father, who told her funny stories about his son as a young man.

Phillip worked with his father running their furniture business. They had a factory in Hoxton and a small shop in Commercial Street.

'Phillip has a good eye for fabrics and design,' Mr Hyams told Sally. 'He prefers working in the factory than working in the store. Have you seen any of his designs?'

'No,' Sally replied.

'Dad, not now,' said Phillip, embarrassed by all this praise.

'Phillip tells me that you are also into designing,' Mrs Hyams said as she poured the tea.

'Yes, in dressmaking.'

'Are you working?' she asked.

'Yes, in Oxford Street. I want to open my own shop. My father advised me to work for someone else to get experience first, so I'm taking his advice.'

The Hyams exchanged a quiet look of approval.

*

That following Sunday, Sally and Phillip planned to go for a hike, but it was raining so they visited the Victoria and Albert Museum instead, fascinated by the treasure trove of textile designs, costumes, jewellery, and furniture from around the world.

After a couple of hours of wandering around, they were in the medieval art gallery when Phillip took Sally's arm leading her to the corner. Before she could ask what was going on, he dropped to one knee, taking a small velvet box from his pocket and opened it to reveal a solitaire diamond ring. He looked up at Sally saying softly, a tremor in his voice, 'I know we haven't known each other long, but I fell in love with you the moment we met. Will you please do me the honour of becoming my wife?'

For a moment Sally was speechless with surprise. She leaned over to kiss him saying, 'Yes, of course I will marry you.' Overbalancing she fell on top of him and they kissed, only to be interrupted by people cheering and clapping. He placed the ring on her finger and red-faced but smiling they quickly got to their feet as people thronged around, congratulating them, and naturally the women wanted to see the ring.

At last they were alone. 'I'm afraid I cannot concentrate any more,' said Sally.

'Me neither. Anyway I have to ask your father if I can marry you.'

Sally held her hand out to admire the ring. 'What about your parents?'

'They know. My mother helped me choose the ring. Do you like it?'

'I absolutely adore it – your mother has good taste.'

That evening, Sally, with Phillip in tow, arrived home. He immediately asked if he could have a private word with her father.

Wolfe smiled, 'Let's go into the lounge.'

As they left the room, Sally scratched her nose and straightened her hair to show off the ring. Frieda was the first to notice it, and with a screech leapt from her chair, grabbing Sally's hand. 'That must have cost a fortune, it's beautiful.'

Eva had tears in her eyes as she took her daughter's hand and gazed at the ring. 'I wish you *mazel* – he is a lovely man.'

Meanwhile in the lounge Wolfe seated himself in his favourite armchair and gestured to Phillip to sit next to him, but Phillip declined, licking his lips nervously.

Wolfe gave an inward smile, remembering the time he and Asher stood in front of Eva's father.

At last Phillip said, 'Mr Brown, I love Sally very much, I would like your permission to marry her.'

Wolfe got to his feet. 'Yes, you have my permission.' He looked towards the door on the other side of which Sally, Eva and Frieda were listening and let out a scream as they heard him say, 'Yes.'

'I think a drink is in order and maybe a cigar,' Wolfe said to Phillip, 'and you'd better open the door for your fiancée.'

Screams rent the air in the cinema as Lily clung to Isaac and the audience gasped in terror; some had hands in their mouths to stop them from screaming, while others like Sally hid their faces but looked through spread fingers at the terror of *King Kong.*

Lily said as they left the cinema, 'I'm going to sleep with my mother tonight. That was terrifying.'

'If you like,' Isaac placed a protective arm around her shoulders. 'I'll stand guard outside your door to make sure you come to no harm.'

Lily giggled. 'There's no need for that, but I appreciate the gesture.'

1934

Isaac decided he wanted to work in the casino and learn as much as he could about running it. Now that Lily was in his life it was even harder to juggle everything, especially as Lily liked going out and enjoying herself. He knew he could give her a good life, but she had to be patient, especially if she loved him.

Between Brady Street and Valance Road in Whitechapel the pavement was very wide. It was called Shiduch (Marriage) Avenue. On holidays and Sabbaths, boys and girls eyed each other up as they pass. Frieda was with an old school friend, Hannah, when a young man, also with a friend, pointed at the costume jacket she was wearing, 'What that needs around the neck is a fox fur.'

Frieda looked at him and smiled. Within seconds he was walking beside her and introduced himself, holding out his hand, 'Max Rothstein.' Still with a smile on her face she looked at his hand for a moment and then took it. 'Frieda Brown.' They continued walking.

'May I be so bold, Frieda, to ask if I can take you out one evening?'

She turned to look at him thinking, *He's pretty good looking and those brown eyes,* 'That would be nice.'

He took her hand, moving to one side of the pavement. 'I have to work this week, but I have Saturday off. Can we meet then?'

'Where?'

'Do you like dancing?'

'Yes, I do.'

'I'll meet you outside the Continental at eight o'clock.' He frowned. 'You will be there, won't you?'

She smiled. 'Yes, I promise.'

His face lit up. 'Got to go, I'll see you on Saturday.' He ran across the road to join his friend. As they walked away he looked back and said, 'I'm going to marry her.'

On the Wednesday, Jack had two tickets to a dance. He asked Frieda if she would like to go with him and she jumped at the chance.

The band was playing as they entered and to their surprise Isaac and Lily were there too.

'You didn't tell me you had tickets,' Jack said to his brother.

'I didn't. Lily did. I have some studying to do but she is so persuasive, I couldn't say no.'

Jack made a motion with his little finger. 'She has you tied to hers.'

Isaac didn't reply as they found a table and ordered a round of drinks. The band was playing a rumba and Jack took his sister's hand, leading her on to the dance floor. Jack was a great dancer, especially when it came to Latin American. Frieda glanced at the band as they passed, humming to the tune. She faltered, treading on Jack's foot.

'Ouch.' She didn't take any notice of her brother, but just stood staring at the drummer.

Jack followed her gaze. 'Do you know him?'

'Yes,' she whispered. 'I have a date with him on Saturday.'

Just then the music stopped and Max moved away from the drums, said something to the band-leader and leapt from the stage to stand in front of Frieda. 'You look amazing.'

'Thanks, Max, this is my brother, Jack.'

The two men shook hands. 'I have to get back – can I see you later?' he said.

She nodded. He kissed her on the cheek; turned and leapt on to the stage as the band-leader said into the microphone, 'Ladies and Gentlemen, tonight we are having a singing competition, which will begin at 9.30.' He gestured to the right of the stage. 'If you would like to sing with the band – and please, I mean sing – give your names to the lady over there.'

As Jack and Frieda joined the others, Isaac said, 'Go on, Frieda, have a go, you can sing.'

'No, I'm shy, I'll dry up.'

'You can do it,' Jack encouraged her.

'No, I can't.'

At 9.30 the singers were called up one at a time. Suddenly the announcer said, 'Please give a warm welcome to the last contestant of the evening, Frieda Brown.'

Frieda looked at Jack, who spread his hands and shook his head, pointing at Isaac, who, in turn, smiled and clapped his hands. Now unable to say no, she walked to the stage, said something to the band-leader who nodded, instructing the band, 'Page Ten.'

The band started up and Frieda sang Noel Coward's 'Mad about the Boy'. The dancers had all moved to the front of the stage to listen to her. As she finished the song the applause was deafening. Frieda smiled and bowed as the band-leader announced, 'I think we have our winner,' and handed her five pounds.

Frieda was about to leave the stage when the band-leader asked, 'Can you sing something else?'

'What, well yes.'

'Please tell me which ones?'

'"Dancing in the Dark", "A Song in My Heart", almost anything,' she replied.

'Will you please sing "Dancing in the Dark"?'

She shrugged her shoulders. 'Okay.'

Frieda never left the stage for the rest of the evening as dancers clapped and cheered, asking for more. She was worried about Jack not having a dancing partner, but needn't have. He had seen a young lady sitting on the next table and asked her to dance. After a couple of dances, Jack, holding his new partner's hand, walked back to the table to introduce her to everyone.

'Sophie, this is my brother Isaac and the pretty young lady next to him is his girlfriend, Lily. I hope you two don't mind, but Sophie is joining us.'

'What about the people on your table?' Isaac asked.

Sophie smiled, 'That's okay, they're friends from work.'

Just before taking the floor for the last dance, Jack asked Isaac, 'Can you take Frieda home?'

Isaac grinned, 'Of course.'

But it didn't end up that way, as Max the drummer said he would make sure Frieda got home safely.

The next morning at breakfast there was friendly banter among the children, except Saul, who stared at his brothers and sisters as if they were mad. Eva was smiling as she looked across the table at Wolfe with a look of amazement on his face; breakfast had never been like this. He looked at Eva and gave a little nod towards the children, his eyes asking a question. She touched her heart, puckered her lips and moved her eyes towards the children.

He didn't understand at first, thinking she was telling him she loved him, but then it hit him like a hammer. His head snapped round to look at each of them in turn, and suddenly realised they were men and women, no longer children. He turned to look at Eva, a big grin on his face, wondering why he hadn't seen it.

But the course of true love never did run smooth, as Isaac was soon to find out. By the end of the year his relationship with Lily was proving tempestuous. Half the time he didn't know where he stood. Now she wanted to get engaged, like Sally. He said it was too early – he needed to earn a decent living before he could even contemplate marriage.

'If you loved me it wouldn't be a problem,' she said.

'If you loved me, then you would understand that I want to give you the best life can offer, while at this moment I can't.'

Without saying goodbye, she went off to stay with her aunts in Paris.

16 'I'll Be Loving You Always'

1 March 1936

SALLY WAS A PICTURE OF HAPPINESS, holding a bouquet of Lilies as she walked slowly down the stairs wearing a knee-length, round-necked white satin wedding dress with open work down the sleeves the white satin shoes matching her dress, Nestled on her short auburn hair that flicked up at the bottom was an orange blossom headdress with a long veil.

Wolfe had tears in his eyes as in a choked voice he whispered, 'You are so beautiful it takes my breath away.'

Sally smiled as he moved towards her, kissing her cheek and then stepped back, bestowing a traditional blessing on her.

'The cars are here,' Lily said.

She returned from France in October the previous year, still as spoilt as ever, but this time Isaac put his foot down by telling her bluntly that if she truly loved him she would have to wait at least two years before they could marry. If not, then it was better they end their relationship.

Lily checked the three bridesmaids before they left the house to follow Sally out to the car. Lily had made and designed their pale pink taffeta dresses, with frills at the hem and plain top. The headdress was a small saucer-shaped hat of frills with a ribbon tied into a bow under the chin. Neighbours had come out to see Sally, waving and calling good luck as she got into the Rolls Royce wedding car with her father.

In the synagogue, she walked slowly up the aisle on her father's arm towards the canopy where Phillip, looking handsome in his dinner suit, stood waiting. At last she was by his side and the wedding ceremony began.

After the dinner and speeches, the bride and groom stepped on to the dance floor to begin the dancing. The band played 'I'll Be Loving You Always', guests cheering and clapping as they danced around the floor. Sally looked towards the stage as Frieda sang, turning sideways at the microphone to glance towards Max, standing not far away. She ended the song, but the band kept playing and she left the stage. Max lifted her from the last step, lowering her gently onto the floor and holding her close. They kissed and began to sway to the music, moving on to the dance floor.

'Will you marry me?' Max whispered in her ear.

Frieda nestled closer to him. 'Yes please.'

An hour later, while Frieda had gone with Lily to powder her nose, Max approached Wolfe. 'May I speak to you for a moment, Mr Brown?'

Wolfe patted the empty chair next to him, 'Sit.'

As Max slid onto the seat he asked, 'Well, Max, what is it you want to talk to me about?'

'I would like your permission to marry Frieda.'

Just then Frieda entered the hall. Since meeting Max, she had virtually bounced around the house and was now singing regularly on weekends with the band, and on weekdays worked in a sweet shop.

Wolfe turned to Max, 'Can you support a family by being a drummer?'

'Yes, sir, I can.'

'It means leaving my Frieda alone at night. Do you think it will work? It will be very lonely for her.'

Max watched Frieda walking towards them, then back to Wolfe. 'I love her with all my heart, I have from the moment I saw her. I promise she won't be lonely and I will look after her.'

'You have my blessing.'

Max shook Wolfe's hand. 'Thank you, thank you very much.' He ran over to Frieda, lifted her off her feet and twirled her around.

Sally, wondering what all the commotion was all about, ran over to her sister. 'What's happening?'

Laughing, Frieda said, 'Max asked Papa if he can marry me, and Papa said yes.'

Sally grabbed her sister's hands and they jumped up and down with happiness. Through all the excitement, Max had slipped over to the band and asked if he could play with them. Suddenly the drums began to beat, a slow tom-tom rumba, becoming faster and faster. The dancers crowded around the stage, moving to the rhythm, Max's ebony drumsticks a blur, moving from one drum to another, gradually slowing the beat to a sexy deep bass tom-tom, then stopped, going back to the beat for the rest of the band to join in as the guests clapped loudly and cheer.

17 'Let's Face the Music and Dance'

'Hitler is ignoring the Versailles Treaty and calling up young men into National Service,' said Jack.
'The Prime Minister won't gamble on peace, not this time,' Isaac pointed out.
'What makes you so sure?' their father asked.
Isaac showed him an article in the *Daily Mirror*. 'It said here the British Government has instigated a major increase in military spending, including air defences and the expansion of the Royal Air Force. I wouldn't mind having a go at flying.'
'I said that years ago and was ignored,' Wolfe said indignantly.
'What's happening with your on–off relationship with Lily?' Jack asks.
'All she wants to do is get married. I told her that I am not in a financial position to get married yet; I'm just getting to know about being a croupier and the running of the casino. I'm not going to change my mind, so off to Paris she went. But I must admit I can't help wondering who she is dancing with tonight. I mean Paris is the city of love and fun.'
'There is a saying: what will be, will be, if it's going to happen, it will,' Wolfe said philosophically.
In August, Wolfe and his three sons were glued to the radio as the announcer related the exploits of the Black American athlete, Jesse Owens, winning four gold medals at the Olympic Games held in Berlin, to the anger and discomfort of Hitler and his Aryan race. But the joy was short lived as Germany passed a law to legalise anti-Semitism and making the Swastika its national flag. This gave Oswald Mosley, leader of the British Fascist Party, the idea of sending his black-shirted goose-stepping men through East London with its large Jewish population.
Billy Reid, the brothers and male members of their families headed for Tower Gardens where Mosley was inciting his followers with a venomous speech against Jews. As one, the fascist black-shirts began their march towards Commercial and Whitechapel Roads with Mosley surrounded by an army of policemen and personal bodyguards.
Isaac was amazed at the solidarity of the people of the East End, young and old, bearded Jews, Irish Catholic, Dockers, communists, trade unionists all stood shoulder to shoulder, chanting in unison,

'They shall not pass' and 'One two three four five, we want Mosley dead or alive' while the communists shouted in Spanish '*No pasaran*'. The noise was deafening as mounted police baton charged, trying to disperse the protesters to allow Mosley and his followers through.

Suddenly, from a loud speaker someone said, 'They are going to Cable Street.' Within seconds, a barricade of old mattresses and carts were erected. A lorry straddled the middle of Cable Street with thousands of voices chanting, 'They shall not pass.'

Seeing there was no way through, Mosley was persuaded by the authorities to call off the march. As his men dispersed they were attacked. Isaac and his young brother Saul became separated from the rest of the family when suddenly two black-shirts appeared. They both came to a halt on seeing them. One, a big bruiser of a man, his black shirt tight across his chest, grinned at Isaac. 'This is a pleasure I never expected, two Jew-boys all on their lonesome.'

His companion, tall and slim with a Hitler moustache, placed a hand inside his jacket, pulling out a cosh which he began to smack into the palm of his left hand. 'I'm going to enjoy this.'

Isaac and Saul looked at each other, nodded and moved apart. Isaac laughed as he faced the big man saying, 'You're *not* going to enjoy this.' As he moved to the right the fascist charged, and at the last minute Isaac sidestepped; as his attacker passed he landed a right to his kidneys. Roaring like a bull, the black-shirt turned, going into a wrestler's crouch.

Isaac egged him on, knowing that an angry man made mistakes, beckoning with his hand. 'Come on, pussy cat.'

The man moved forward, slower this time, beady eyes angry, face red. Isaac danced on the balls of his feet, weaving his body left and right, then suddenly darted forward, landing a left jab to the unprotected face. The man shook his head and moved forward, throwing a right at Isaac's head and missed.

'You're slow,' Isaac goaded, 'you need to be faster, like this.' He landed two quick jabs to the face and danced away. He knew the big man would get lucky some time and land a heavy punch on him. He had to find a way to end this quickly.

Meanwhile Saul was moving around the tall man, weaving and ducking, landing quick lefts and rights. He blocked the arm holding the cosh and landed a right to the stomach. The brothers had been taught well by Billy and their father. Like his brother, Saul realised his opponent might get lucky and land a telling blow with the cosh, which he had already felt, the arm still stinging from the blow.

Isaac circled the big man who was breathing heavily. The fascist threw a right at Isaac and once again missed, but only just, the knuckles grazing his forehead. He gave a tight smile, as his opponent stopped to take a deep breath.

Meanwhile Saul had found a way to end the fight. His eyes narrowed slightly, allowing his opponent to attack him. As the cosh came down he blocked it with his left arm and kicked the fascist in the groin; with his forward momentum Saul's right hand slammed into the black-shirt's ribs with such force that the sound of breaking bones could be heard above the scream as his opponent fell to the ground.

Isaac danced to the right, moving in slightly to entice his opponent to move forward. The big man grinned, thinking he had got Isaac, threw a left and dropped his right hand to his waist. Like a streak of lightning Isaac landed a left and right to the jaw and the man wobbled. Using the full force of his weight, Isaac stepped in with a right hand to the stomach; the black-shirt bent slightly forward, his head jerking backward from the force of the uppercut to the chin. For a second he stood swaying and then gradually crumpled onto the ground to the sound of clapping. Isaac and Saul turned to see their father, Uncle Asher, Billy, Jack and the others.

'Well—' Wolfe never got any further as about twenty policemen appeared with batons in their hands.

'Run,' yelled Saul, but they were too late to help Isaac who was surrounded and fought back, knocking off a policeman's helmet but was soon overwhelmed. That evening the Battle of Cable Street was front page news, with some photos taken by Brian. The following morning, Wolfe with his nephew Abraham the lawyer, went to the police station to obtain Isaac's release.

On 6 December Abraham and April married at the Stepney Green Synagogue with a reception at Billy's home where a marquee had been erected in the garden. It was a night to remember with a mixture of Irish whisky and Jewish food. The bride and groom managed to stay sober before leaving on a honeymoon to Paris.

A few days later, on 10 December, King Edward VIII told the country he was abdicating for love: he wanted to marry the twice-divorced Mrs Simpson. The marriage was opposed by the government in Great Britain and in the Dominions on religious, legal, political and moral grounds.

'It's a shame,' Wolfe said to Eva. 'I liked him, as did the rest of the country.' Wolfe would change his mind about the ex-King in a few months.

Five days after the King's abdication, Isaac and Wolfe were on their way to a meeting.

'What are you smiling at?'

'Nothing, Papa, just feel happy.'

'You shouldn't be smiling, we should be worried. It's unusual for Billy to phone and say something needs my attention. It sounds serious. Have you any idea what it might be?'

'No, Papa, your guess is as good as mine.'

Wolfe looked at his watch. 'Well, whatever it is, it better not take long. It's getting late and I have a special date with Mama tonight.'

Isaac tried not to smile as he turned into Bouverie Street, Stoke Newington, stopping outside the newly opened Bouverie Rooms.

A doorman was quickly by the car door, opening it and doffing a finger to his cap. 'Good afternoon, sir.'

'Can you park the car please,' said Isaac.

'Yes sir.'

'Why does he need to park the car? I'm hoping we won't be long.'

'Force of habit, Papa.'

'It's quiet in here.'

Isaac didn't reply but moved in front of his father opening the door.

The place was in darkness, 'What's going—'

The lights suddenly went on and there was a shout from the throng of people in front of him, 'Happy Birthday.'

For a second Wolfe was taken by surprise, then a big smile lit up his face as Eva handed him a glass of champagne, eyes shining happily, 'Happy birthday my love.'

The hall was decked out in balloons and bunting with banners saying, '*Happy Fiftieth Birthday, Wolfe*'.

Isaac was talking to his cousin Davora when a voice he knew well said, 'How about getting a girl a drink.'

He turned in surprise. 'When did you arrive?'

'Five minutes ago.'

'I mean from Paris, who told you about—'

'Please, get me a drink of champagne and I'll answer your questions,' said Lily.

He picked up the drinks and returned to Lily who was sitting at a table with Frieda, Max, Sally and Phillip. He handed Lily the fluted glass, taking the seat next to her.

'Do you know—' she looked around the table '—that you can board a train at Gare-du-Nord and wake up for breakfast in Victoria Station, it's fantastic.'

'I didn't know that, but I do now,' Isaac said sarcastically. 'Who told you about—?'

'I did,' Sally interrupted. 'Mama asked me to.'

He was about to say something when his mother rushed over. 'Lily, I'm so happy you are here.' Lily stood and hugged Eva. 'I wouldn't have missed it for the world, thank you for inviting me. My mother sends her regards, but she isn't feeling too well, her arthritis.'

'I'll pop in and see her later this week.'

'That's very kind of you. I'll tell her when I get home.'

Eva placed a hand on Isaac's shoulder and whispered, 'Make up, be nice.'

'But Mama, it's not—'

'Yes I know that, but you cannot carry on the way you have. I cannot stand you moping around. Like Papa said, what will be, will be.'

After the dinner and speeches, Frieda stepped up to the microphone to sing one of the latest tunes, 'Let's Face the Music and Dance'. Wolfe took Eva in his arms and moved on to the dance floor which was soon filled with dancers smiling, and wishing him happy birthday as they passed.

'Well, are you going to ask me to dance, or shall I sit here posing until someone else does?' said Lily.

'This must be a little tame after the bright lights of Paris,' Isaac said, adding, 'Why are you here?'

'I was invited.'

'Don't play games with me, Lily.'

She took a cigarette from a pack in front of him, opened her bag, taking from it a slim holder and fitted the cigarette into it, leaning across for him to light it.

'When did you start smoking?'

She crossed her legs and said as she exhaled, 'A month or so ago. Yes, Paris is a fun city, you must go there some time, but to tell you the truth, I didn't enjoy it that much. My aunts tried to match me up with some of their friend's sons, but all I could think about was you.' He was about to say something, but she held up a hand. 'Please let me finish. When Sally and your mother sent me the invitation, my aunts told me to tear it up, but I couldn't, and here I am.'

'Would you like to dance?'

'I thought you'd never ask.'

They joined the other dancers as Frieda sang, 'I've got you under my skin'. Isaac wanted to laugh at the irony of the song as Lily slid into his arms.

'I know I love you,' he whispered in her ear, the smell of her perfume filling his nostrils, 'But do you love me?'

'You know I do.'

'Okay then, how about September, can you wait that long.'

'What did you say?'

They came to a stop in the middle of the dance floor. He dropped to one knee and said, 'Lily Levine, I love you with all my heart, will you marry me?'

She looked across at the band, 'What did you say?'

'I said,' he repeated loudly, 'I love you with all my heart.' He hadn't noticed that the band had stopped playing. 'Will you marry me?' It was then he became aware of the silence as Lily said loud and clear, 'I love you, yes, I'll marry you.'

They were instantly surrounded while everyone clapped and cheered.

*

1937 began sadly with the death of Eva's mother, Hadar. Her grandchildren would miss her, as she was dearly loved by all who knew her.

In May pictures of *Hindenburg* filled the evening papers. The largest airship in the world and pride of Nazi Germany was about to land at Lakenhurst, New Jersey, after its maiden transatlantic voyage, when, two hundred feet from the ground, it suddenly burst into flames. Thirty-six passengers and crew died, but miraculously sixty-two survived. Six days after the disaster George VI was crowned King of England and its Dominions.

Wolfe slapped the paper he was reading, 'I take back what I said about Edward. Thank goodness he never became King.'

'Papa, he is now the Duke of Windsor, what are you talking about?' said Saul.

'That no good—'

'Papa, you're getting worked up for nothing,' Isaac joined in.

'Every week, Jews are arriving here from Germany and Austria, fleeing Nazi persecution, and Edward and his *curava* (prostitute) are being entertained by Hitler and other Nazi leaders.'

'I wish I had been a fly on the wall at that banquet,' Saul said.

On 15 May, after a whirlwind romance, Jack and Sophie married at Vine Court Synagogue in Whitechapel, where Wolfe and the family were now members. On 20 June, Frieda walked arm in arm with her husband Max out of the synagogue, and finally on 12 September, Lily at last had her wish: today was her wedding day. She approached Isaac standing under the canopy, thinking he looked like the film star Clark Gable, while Isaac gasped at her beauty, his love for her showing on his face.

For the first time the family met all of Lily's aunts and gazed with awe at the diamonds they were wearing.

Eva burst out laughing when she saw Lily's aunt Sarah hike up the back of her dress when she sat down. 'Why does your aunt do that?'

'She will tell you,' Lily replied, 'that it's okay for her knickers to get dirty, but not her dress.'

Eva nearly fell off her seat with laughter. 'I like Aunt Jennie, she is so beautiful and the French accent is charming.'

Lily looks in Aunt Jennie's direction. She was staring at Saul, apparently intent on raping him with her eyes. Meanwhile Aunt Julie was in deep conversation with Jack about patisserie, of which she was an expert. Aunt Kitty, the American with her husband Willie, was talking to Sally about fashion in America.

As they got into bed, Eva burst into laughter.

'What are you laughing about?'

Do you realise that we may soon be hearing children's laughter again?'

'More like hungry crying, messy nappies; I'm not looking forward to the teething stage.'

She punched him playfully on the arm. 'Why do you have to spoil everything?'

*

In Germany, Hitler was on the move, creating the High Command of the armed forces, giving him direct control of Germany's military. At the same time he had sacked politicians and military leaders unsympathetic to his philosophy and policies. In May 1938 Germany annexed Austria which immediately sets off attacks on Jewish property throughout the country, forcing Jews out of jobs and passing draconian laws against them.

Isaac was reading the paper as Lily entered the dining room. She and Isaac were living with Eva and Wolfe while they looked for an appropriate property, which as far as Eva was concerned, would be many months from now as she enjoyed having Lily and Isaac around.

'Things are getting serious,' she said, lowering herself on to the chair. 'This is not the world I want to bring my children into.'

Isaac didn't reply, lowering his newspaper to look at his wife who was genuinely frightened.

'Germany has mobilised its army,' she said loudly. 'You know—'

Isaac leapt from the chair and was quickly by her side, cuddling her to him. 'Shhh, I'm sure this is just Hitler preening his feathers and shaking his tail.'

The tears streamed down her cheeks. 'Can you honestly tell me that there will be no war?'

He was silent for a second. 'Lily, everyone is scared of war, but we have to trust the politicians in doing what is best for the country. I personally believe that Hitler wants to show the world he is a powerful man. The Prime Minister is at this moment in talks with the German Chancellor and we have mobilised our navy just to show this ogre that we are ready.'

He wiped the tears from her cheeks with a finger and then kissed her.

On 9 September 1938, the day that Sophie gave birth to a son, Samuel, the Prime Minister Neville Chamberlain returned from Germany waving a piece of paper that said, 'We are guaranteed peace in our time.'

'You see,' said Isaac triumphantly. 'Now the world will realise that all our fears about Hitler were groundless. There will be no war.'

Wolfe wished he could go back to a point in his life when he still had his son's optimism. But time and experience had taught him to expect the worst, to question and to be sceptical. In his mind's eye he could see once again the Cossacks storming into his village, the sneering Goran Kroshnev, the duplicity of the Le Feuvre brothers, and the sinister smile of Christian Le Feuvre; he thought of the fanaticism in the eyes of the black-shirt fascists and finally, the bitterness and rage in the face of Adolf Hitler.

It was always there, that violence, that rage, that duplicity, below the surface, behind the eyes of some human beings, and when you encountered it, all you could do was to find a way round it, or protect yourself from it and not let it destroy you; to pray that in confronting it, you didn't let it fester and grow, in yourself and others; and to dare to dream that there could be.

'I do hope you're right,' he said simply.